Return to Me

Julie K. Matthews

Summary: Laura Di Angelo is a successful concert pianist living a perfectly happy and peaceful life until her husband goes missing on a business trip to Mexico. She and her three children fall victim to her husband's corrupt business partner, bent on covering up his own fraudulent insurance practices and claiming Laura for himself.

Armed with a trust in God and believing in Anthony's love for his family, Laura and the children begin an exhaustive search and never give up hope that he will return.

Bloodied and bruised, Anthony Di Angelo regains consciousness in the Cabo San Lucas desert with no memory of his identity or his past. He is nursed back to health by a kind Mexican family but struggles between love for his new home and fleeting glimpses into his past.

Acknowledgements

To Ann Singleton, Rosalie Payne, and Emily Di Girolamo
for your time spent reading, editing, and encouraging.

To Jamie Robyn Wood, Editor, dandelionediting@gmail.com,
for invaluable suggestions and excellent final editing,

To Laura Parkinson, meemossis@hotmail.com,
for the perfect cover truly capturing the
heroine waiting hopefully for the miracle
of her husband's return.

To my daughter, Debra Di Girolamo, whose beauty and talent
were the vision for the lovely Laura Di Angelo, heroine of
"Return to Me".

To my granddaughter, Emily Di Girolamo, for taking over
many of my responsibilities
so that I could dream and write.

JULIE K. MATTHEWS
RETURN
TO
ME

Chapter 1

Anthony Di Angelo stopped mid-brushstroke. Capturing the beauty of the morning haze on the lake was suddenly arrested by the arrival of something more lovely than any sunrise Anthony could ever paint. In a snowy white robe flowing over silky, white pajamas, Laura moved to lean against the deck railing, her back to Anthony. She drew a deep breath of morning air and turned toward her husband of nearly twenty years. Reaching across the back of her head, she swirled thick, dark hair around to her shoulder and slid her hand suggestively down her throat.

Anthony sucked in his breath and let out a low whistle. *Had she no idea what that simple motion did to him?*

"At what time must you catch your plane, my love?" She spoke in that fake British accent she always used just before she turned his gut to jelly with a "come hither" look that told him the kids were safely off to school and the parents were alone.

Even so, he asked, "Kids all off to school?" He raised his eyebrows hopefully. "My flight doesn't leave until 1:00."

"Last one just boarded the bus." She swayed toward him, closing the space between them, leaning in to brush a feathery kiss across his lips. She took the paint brush from his hand and dropped it into a jar of water. "You won't be needing that, my dear," she said huskily and, grasping his lapels, pulled him willingly to his feet.

Anthony's arms encircled her, his mouth raining tender kisses up and down her neck until she giggled and ran through the open French doors, a private entrance from the patio to their bedroom. She was ticklish and she was a tease, a passionate woman one moment, a playful sprite the next.

They'd sometimes wondered when their joy and delight in each other would come to an end, the fire of their passion becoming only dying embers as it seemed was the case in most couples their age. Anthony, for one, couldn't imagine the day would ever come when he wouldn't be anxious to return home to Laura. She was his lover, his best friend, and the person with whom he knew his deepest feelings would be treasured as though they were her own.

A few moments later, she wore only the silky robe as she watched him shave his face and comb his wiry black hair. "What time do you get into Cabo?" she asked.

"Would you believe I have a twelve-hour layover in LA? I swear, Marty chooses the most inconvenient flights. I won't get into Cabo until 1:45 tomorrow afternoon!"

"Call me before you check into your hotel, okay? I have a concert tomorrow night and I won't be able to concentrate unless I know you're safely there."

"I will, my darling. And maybe we can talk for a while tonight while I'm trying to sleep in the airport."

"With a twelve-hour layover, don't you think you should get a hotel?"

"I can't sleep without you, my love. Why should I pay good money just to crawl between some unfamiliar sheets, freeze under a flimsy blanket, and stare at the ceiling all night?"

"Honestly, Anthony. You can be so stubborn. You could at least shower, you know."

"Why would I need a shower if I'm not going to be with you?" he asked as he dropped the comb and pulled her to his chest. Walking her backwards into the bedroom, he pushed her gently down on the bed. They drew apart just in time for Anthony to dress and throw clothes for a couple of days into a bag. "I swear, woman," he said, "one of these days I'm going to miss a flight because of you."

"Me!" she protested before winding her arms back around his neck. "Take care, my love."

He kissed her deeply, like he couldn't get enough of her and then, pulling himself away, strode down the hall and swung open the door. She followed, reluctant to end the moments together. He turned back toward her. "I love you, Laura."

His eyes were serious. Something in them frightened Laura. Anthony's eyes either smoldered with desire or crinkled with happiness, and rarely displayed the anxious look she'd just glimpsed. He was worried about something. But wasn't this just a run-of-the-mill hotel fire to be investigated? Wouldn't it only require a simple report?

Putting two fingers to her lips she blew him a kiss. "I love you, Anthony. Hurry back to me."

Laura held the door open and watched until Anthony's car disappeared down Lakeside Road. She closed the door reluctantly and stepped silently across the hardwood floor. She entered Anthony's office and sat down at the rolltop desk once belonging to his father. Anthony's father had built their home when he was just a young newlywed. Over the years a deck and gazebo had been added, but other than that, the home remained just as Anthony's parents had designed it.

Anthony always left Laura a copy of his itinerary on his desk. Her fingers lifted the sheet of paper for a closer look. Flight from Stewart International to Detroit and then to Los Angeles for the long layover. Los Angeles to Los Cabos International, and then a shuttle bus to the hotel. The hotel name, Cabo San Lucas Resort, seemed familiar. Didn't Anthony mention another fire there just a few months ago?

Marty Longston, Anthony's partner in their independent insurance adjustor firm, usually investigated the fires in Mexico. Although Anthony spoke fluent Spanish, Marty was single and enjoyed the out-of-country contracts; whereas Anthony preferred to handle the stateside jobs so he could spend more time being a family man. Unfortunately, Marty's emergency gallbladder surgery left Anthony to cover this new Cabo fire.

Laura knew Anthony considered the twelve hours in Los Angeles a waste of time, which was what he considered any time not spent with his family or in service for their church. He'd often mentioned how he longed for the day when he could sell his half of the company and find a job where he could work from home and never leave his wife and three children.

The children were growing up fast, and Anthony was missing ball games and recitals due to his hectic travel schedule. It was amazing how many suspicious fires cropped up in hotels and businesses, forcing Anthony to crisscross the country nearly every week to adjudicate the value of each loss and report back to the insurer.

Pictures of the children were scattered on the top shelf of his desk in a motley assortment of frames. At seventeen years old, Luca was already a star baseball and football player. Sixteen-year-old Emma was a quiet child, a reader, and a serious musician like her mother, although she played the cello rather than the piano. Isabella had just celebrated her thirteenth birthday. The exact opposite of her sister, she was full of spice and mischief. Her nickname, Izzie, fit her perfectly. Getting her to spend a half hour a day at the piano was pure misery for both mother and daughter, though she would play her acoustic guitar for hours and hours, softly crooning made-up ballads about the events in her own young life.

Laura's attention returned to the desk. There was a worn manila envelope under the itinerary, placed as though Anthony might have meant for her to see it. Undoing the clasp, she peeked inside. After a long, curious look, she reached in and pulled out several insurance reports.

Her eyes searched for something recognizable in the checklists and columns of numbers. *All hotels and businesses in Mexico, and all owned by Salazar, Inc. Marty had been the investigator on every one of the fires.* It seemed odd that the same independent investigation firm would have been called for each of these fires. She looked for the insurer and found that Medina Independent Hazard Insurers was the insurance company listed on each report.

Laura carefully slid the reports back in the envelope. It was plausible that Salazar Inc. could have contracted with the same insurance company for each of its properties. But seven fires in the last three years at Salazar-owned companies seemed excessive. Obviously, Anthony must have felt the same or he wouldn't have brought the reports home to study.

She felt a little guilty for looking through Anthony's business papers if he had not indeed intentionally left them for her to see. It was not a guilt she could hide. Anthony would be able to read it in her eyes, discern it in her face. Theirs had been a relationship of openness and honesty. There were no secrets. But he typically protected her from sensitive issues that arose in many of his investigations as she protected him from critical reviews of her performances. She'd tell him how worried she'd been about him and ask him about the reports when he called that night from the airport. He'd laugh at her for being a worrywart and he'd understand.

Laura spent the rest of the morning straightening the house and preparing an extra dinner for the kids for the next evening. Her schedule as a concert pianist was set a year in advance. Typically, Anthony would arrange to be home when she was on tour. He usually accompanied her when she had a one-night performance in New York City, with Luca or Emma watching over Izzie. But tomorrow night was an exception, due to Marty's untimely gallbladder surgery.

Laura settled on the padded bench of the ebony concert grand that had displaced the dining room furniture soon after Anthony and Laura took over his parents' home. First major and minor scales and little ditties, as her mother called them, on each of the scales. Up and down the keyboard her hands flew until she lost her connection to the outside world and responded only to the voice of the piano. Nearly two hours passed. Laura noted the passage in time by the subtle change in lighting in the room, from high-noon brightness to the dimmer light of mid-afternoon. *The children will soon be home,* she told herself as she began the Bach Inventions, magically weaving whimsical but intricate patterns that left her feeling like she had run and won the first leg of a triathlon.

Hopefully tomorrow evening's performance would leave her feeling just as victorious. There were those who had discouraged Laura from attempting to blend her career as a concert pianist with motherhood. But nothing made Laura more determined to succeed than the suggestion that she might not. Her children were well-loved and well-adjusted, and Laura never struggled to find performance opportunities. Then there was her Anthony. Nothing gave her more joy than to be enfolded in the arms of her husband who, at local concerts, always managed to make it backstage and be waiting in the wings before the applause died.

Chapter 2

Anthony called Laura at 10:30 p.m. East Coast time from Los Angeles Airport. A perturbing "beep, beep" signaled the soon-to-be loss of phone power and an interruption to their conversation about the happenings of their day. Scrambling to open the zipper in the front of his carry-on, where he usually kept his phone charger, Anthony heard Laura say, "Anthony, sweetheart. There's something I need to ask you about—" just before the phone went silent. He dug through the compartment like a wild man and realized the charger was not to be found. It was probably still connected to the outlet in their bedroom. His mind had been focused on other things when he packed. More than once his obsession with his beautiful wife had caused him to forget something on his way out the door.

Anthony loped from store to store, unable to find a charger that matched his phone in the entire airport. The shops were either closed or didn't have what he needed. His eyes darted around the terminal, searching for an internet kiosk. It looked like the airport offered free Wi-Fi for T-Mobile subscribers. As the luck of the day would have it, he had Verizon cell service. He would have to pay.

Anthony's hands trembled as he fumbled for a credit card to start the internet service in the kiosk. Laura would probably already be in bed. She was careful to get a good night's sleep before a performance, but maybe she'd check her e-mail first thing in the morning before his flight left LAX for Los Cabos.

"Sweetheart," he began the e-mail. "You were going to ask me something?"

And then he related his desperate search for a phone charger. She'd be shaking her head, he knew. She always cautioned him to make a list of the things he needed for a trip and to check them off as he put them in his bag. He traveled nearly every week. You'd think, by now, packing would be automatic.

"I'm a bit nervous about this trip."

He backspaced through the words, not wanting to do anything to make Laura anxious or nervous before a performance. She'd already be working on that anxiety with no outside influence.

"Have a wonderful performance, sweetheart. Put your heart into it and your fingers will follow. I have complete faith in you. And I love you so much. Remember, when you're performing, even though I won't be waiting in the wings, I'll be under the same moon. My thoughts, my heart, and all my hopes will be with you. Yours forever and always, Anthony."

After a sleepless night in Los Angeles Airport, Anthony hefted his carry-on baggage into the overhead compartment on his flight bound for Los Cabos. This trip was destined to be full of trouble. He looked at his seat assignment. Window seat. At least Marty had good taste in seat choices even if his flight choices were inconvenient. Luckily the occupants of the aisle and middle seats hadn't yet boarded, and he slipped easily into his seat immediately putting on his seatbelt. He leaned against the window and called up the memories of Laura. Laura looking out over the lake, Laura in his arms, Laura blowing him a kiss goodbye.

The force of the speed as the plane accelerated down the runway brought Anthony's thoughts back to the present. He was pushed back into his seat until the big bird lifted its belly aloft as though it were as light as a pigeon. Anthony turned his head toward the window, not even seeing the city below.

Something was wrong with this fire. Yesterday morning, from the moment Anthony had taken the call from Salazar's vice-president, he'd felt apprehensive. The Cabo San Lucas Resort? Again? Marty had just investigated a fire there not too long ago.

Anthony reflected on the conversation he'd had with Marty after he jotted down the information about yet another fire in a Salazar hotel. The phone rang over and over before Marty finally answered with a gravelly, groggy, "Hallo?"

"What's up, man? Thought you'd be in the office by now." Anthony tried to hide his frustration. He was used to Marty dragging into the office late after indulging in a night of partying, but it was nearly noon.

"It's my darn gallbladder again. You wouldn't believe the pain." Marty moaned, loud enough to make his point.

"You gonna make it buddy?" Anthony made an attempt at sympathy. "What can I do for you?"

"I've got someone coming to take me to the hospital. Doctor's orders. Says the thing's got to come out today," Marty answered, just above a whisper.

"That bad, huh? Well, I'll hold down the fort here," Anthony reassured. "By the way, there was another fire at that resort hotel in Cabo. What's up with those people down there?" Anthony tried to sound lighthearted, but he was getting the feeling that these fires were no accident.

"Don't worry about them." Marty sounded suddenly more alert. "I'll only be out for a few days and then I can fly down there and see what's goin' on."

"It's no problem, really," Anthony responded.

"Seriously, man. It's my account. I'll take care of it," Marty insisted.

"You're not thinking clearly," Anthony answered, already regretting that he'd have to go to Cabo. "You know we can't wait on an investigation like this. There could be tampering with the scene, evidence could be covered up. No, as much as I hate leaving the family that long, I've got to go."

"Really, Anthony. Just give me a couple of days." Marty's breathing quickened almost to gasping.

"I'm going, Marty. Get well soon, and I'll keep you updated."

Anthony had tapped his phone to end the conversation, and now here he was, traveling to Mexico.

Marty had been Anthony's college roommate, and their dream of joining forces to start a company that would provide both with a decent income came true shortly after Anthony received his MBA, and just after Luca was born. Those early years had been happy but lean years for Anthony's family, with Anthony working and studying, while Laura mothered their two young babies as she began her career as a concert pianist. But most of all, beyond the late nights and the often-empty bank account, he remembered the love of the most amazing woman any man could ever imagine keeping him sane through it all.

Marty was the consummate bachelor and man about town dating one beautiful woman after another and never settling for the married life that Anthony so enjoyed. Work was ancillary to his social life, but Anthony didn't mind being the responsible partner in the business. Marty's ideas were often out in left field and sometimes leaned toward the shady side of business deals. Anthony listened, disregarded Marty's suggestions, and did his best to make sure all business transactions were above board. Marty seemed happy with international investigations as his contribution to the business.

The pilot announced that the plane was now at cruising altitude. In the cocoon-like cabin of the plane, surrounded by thick white clouds, Anthony couldn't stop thinking about his conversation with Marty. *Why was Marty so insistent on going to Cabo?* Thoughts came to the forefront of his mind that had been bothering him for months about the Medina Insurance account and particularly the Salazar fires. Anthony was beginning to think he had been unwise to rely on Marty to be trustworthy in those dealings.

He recalled that the receptionist had been on the phone when he crossed the room into Marty's office area. His area was a mess. Marty never filed anything! Just piles of paper everywhere.

Anthony spent the next half hour digging for the reports on the Salazar fires—seven of them in the last three years. He shoved the reports into a wrinkled envelope he found in one of Marty's drawers. When he glanced up from the drawer, his eye caught the corner of an airline ticket. He slipped the ticket out from under a pile of newspapers and discarded notes. United Airlines to Los Cabos leaving the next day at 1:00 p.m. Marty had already scheduled his flight to Los Cabos before the fire report even came in!

Anthony gazed at the clouds out of the plane window. He leaned his head back against the plane seat as the plane cut though the dense white shroud. He closed his eyes and continued to go over every moment of when he was last at the office. He remembered dropping into Marty's chair and swiveling back and forth once he found the ticket, turning the piece of paper over and over in his hands as if trying to determine if it was real.

Anthony had grabbed the crinkled envelope and the ticket and left Marty's desk and crossed the few steps to the receptionist's desk. There was no privacy in the office with all of their desks in one big room without dividers. He remembered the startled look on the receptionist's face as he appeared at her desk. Marissa hung up the phone quickly. She had been hired at Marty's request. Someone he'd met on one of his trips to Mexico. The daughter of a friend, Marty said. The girl was a United States citizen, born in Los Angeles but raised in Mexico. Marty said her father wanted her to come to America, get an education, and then return to help him in his business.

"Marissa," he'd held out the ticket. "Would you mind calling the airport and changing this ticket from Marty's name to mine? It's going to cost us a bundle, but don't worry about it."

"But Anthony," she began to protest, but he waved off her words and retreated to his own desk. She brought him the ticket later slapping it down on his desk exhibiting her irritation at having to make the change.

Anthony went over the morning two more times in his head before he remembered something and shot bolt upright in the plane seat. The receptionist's name plate—Marissa Salazar. Why had he never put it together before? Salazar Hotels, Marissa . . . and Marty. He hoped there was no connection, at least none other than bad luck with fire.

Anthony's stomach met his throat as the plane took a sudden dip. A ripple of "yikes," "holy cow," and a few more colorful exclamations, punctuated by a couple of shrieks, spread through the cabin.

"We've run into a bit of turbulence. Please keep your seat belts fastened until the light turns off. We'll be out of this rough spot before you know it," the pilot reassured his passengers.

Anthony had flown frequently and while dips and bumps were to be expected, he still said a silent prayer that he'd return safely to his family. He let his mind wander again to the comfort of the previous morning, picturing Laura sitting beside him on the couch with sleepy, pajama-clad children gathered at their feet.

"Weary the Lord until he blesses you," Luca had read from Doctrine & Covenants 104:82.

"Is that a good thing . . . to weary Heavenly Father?" Emma asked. "We're not supposed to be pests, are we?"

Anthony remembered his wife's sweet reply, "I suppose that all hinges on how you ask Heavenly Father for what you need. If you tell him how much you love him and that you are willing to accept his will no matter what, then letting him know often of a blessing you need is probably welcomed by him."

"And always remember to thank him for the blessings you've already received," Anthony added.

"And remember to only ask for good things," Izzie chimed in. Both parents turned toward their youngest daughter. Izzie always seemed to begrudgingly participate in scripture study, but she must have been listening somewhere, sometime to answer so wisely.

"Thank you, Izzie," Anthony responded. "You are very right about that. We must only ask the Lord for things that are right."

"Hey," Luca cut in. "Don't suppose that works with earthly parents?" He grinned hopefully.

They knelt in prayer, holding hands, and then Anthony called for a group hug. He tickled Izzie, smoothed Emma's hair, traded some manly shoves with Luca, and asked his son to "take care of my girls." He knew Luca would watch over his sisters and mother more carefully and responsibly than a typical seventeen-year-old boy.

Anthony crossed his arms over his chest, remembering the feel of his wife and children in his arms. Even with the sweet comfort of the morning's remembrance, he still felt a forewarning tightness between his shoulder blades. This was no run-of-the-mill hotel fire.

Chapter 3

The big metal bird bounced down on the runway and then up again, finally landing hard enough that Anthony felt like his hip bones were drilled into his kidneys. Moans and groans due to the rough landing rolled through the cabin.

"Sorry about that, ladies and gentlemen. We often encounter a pretty hefty downdraft at this airport, but that was a doozy. Again, we apologize for a less than desirable arrival in Cabo, San Lucas."

Anthony unbuckled his seat belt and rose to half-height, ducking his head until he was able to move from the window seat to the aisle. He helped an elderly lady retrieve her carry-on bag from the overhead compartment. Then, slinging the strap of his laptop case over his shoulder, he reached for his bag. He always packed light. He saw no need to check his luggage and wait for it at the end of the flight or, worse, run the chance of having his luggage miss his flight. He couldn't count the times he'd had to wash the same shirt and underwear for several nights, and then his luggage would arrive just in time for him to pick it up for the flight home.

The shuttle to the Cabo San Lucas Resort was already waiting at the curb. Only Anthony and two men boarded the shuttle. They spoke Spanish, which Anthony clearly understood, though it had been some time since he served his Spanish-speaking church mission. The big, burly man boarded first, empty-handed, while a smaller man hauled two duffle bags up the steps.

"Drop 'em there," the larger man commanded in Spanish, jerking a clenched paw toward the floor beside the front row of seats.

The small man, *kind of wimpy,* Anthony thought, scurried to carry out orders. He seemed afraid of the bigger guy, whose biceps bulged like a body builder's, a grimy black leather vest stretching taut around his shoulders. Anthony sat about three quarters of the way back in the shuttle, while each of the other two men took the two front seats behind the driver.

The driver waited a few moments at the curb, perhaps hoping for more passengers. Anthony felt sorry for the Mexican people who were paid so little to do so much, sometimes transporting travelers to sleep in comfortable beds and eat lavish meals while they earned a pittance and went home to sleep in mod-podged huts of discarded, mis-matched materials.

With obvious exhaustion, the driver swiveled up and off his seat and made his way down the aisle with a pen and clipboard. He stopped by the little guy, whose eyes darted back and forth before mumbling, "José Juarez."

The driver jotted down his name and turned to the big guy.

"Oh, um," the big guy hesitated, which Anthony thought was odd since he was only being asked for his own name. "Um, Manuel, Manuel Juarez."

"Brothers?" the driver asked.

"Um, si," replied Manuel.

Yeah, right, Anthony thought. *They're no more brothers than I'm their brother.*

Anthony tilted his head toward the window, avoiding the furtive glances in his direction from the two men in the front seats. The shuttle, with its typical navy blue streaked with confetti upholstery, lumbered out of the airport. Within a mile the lush, imported vegetation surrounding the airport gave way to bushy desert plants with tiny leaves. Large clumps of creosote bushes bunched together provided desert villas for the many rodents claiming the desert floor as home. Aging cacti stood guard over huts constructed of corrugated tin and cardboard. Small brown children ran barefoot between spiny cacti of various species. Though they were living in poverty in the humblest of homes, they looked happy as they chased each other with sticks and tried futilely to catch the jackrabbits bounding between bushes.

They'd traveled for several more miles when the big man, Manuel, suddenly growled at the driver to turn off on a dirt road. The driver balked at the gruff command, but Manuel brandished a gun from inside his vest and slammed it into the driver's head. The driver slumped over the steering wheel, and without the driver's steady hands the shuttle careened from one side of the road to the other. With the unconscious driver's foot heavy on the accelerator, the bus surged ahead on its own, finally slamming into a tree and throwing the burly man into the windshield. Screaming like a raging bear, the man lumbered to his feet and let out a mighty roar as he thundered down the aisle toward Anthony.

The impact had flung Anthony from his seat into the aisle. As he attempted to scramble to his feet, his head was slammed to the floor by the giant's dirty, worn boot. Pain shot through his head. His stomach regurgitated into his throat as he tried to focus. The floor and seats of the shuttle seemed to be twisting and rolling before his blurred vision. No sooner had Anthony's head been slammed onto the filthy floor than he felt his collar jerk against his windpipe as the burly guy grabbed him by his shirt and dragged him up the aisle. Anthony tried to get his feet underneath him to no avail. He flailed his arms, trying to grab the man's boot, which stopped its lumbering march long enough to slam into Anthony's shoulder.

"Still got some fight in ya, huh?" The ogre yanked him to his feet. As one fist smashed into Anthony's stomach the other meaty paw clutched the hair on the back of Anthony's head and nearly snapped his neck as he yanked it back. "That'll teach ya," he sneered and spat into Anthony's face.

Like an echo in a tunnel, Anthony heard the voice of José, the smaller guy. "Take it easy. You're just supposed to scare him and rough him up a bit, not kill him."

"Shut up or you'll be next," Manuel growled. He yanked on the handle to open the door, but the crash had damaged the mechanism. Anthony's face and the guy's boot met the door at the same time. The door gave way and Anthony hit the hard desert floor face down with the big guy crashing on top of him.

"Hurry," the wimpy guy hollered. "Someone's coming."

Somehow Anthony was on his feet, dragged over needle sharp cactus and rocks as his attackers ran for cover from the road with his helpless body in tow. They ducked behind a big pile of rocks. Anthony tasted the blood running from the scrapes and cuts on his face mixed with the salty grime of the man's hand over his mouth. A car careened past, whoops and hollers flying from its open windows.

"Crazy drunks," José whispered.

"Look who's talkin'," Manuel sneered.

As soon as the dust from the car settled, Manuel grabbed José's arm, yanking him roughly to his feet. "Come on, loser, we gotta get outta here." He took a second to smash Anthony's head into the rock, seeming to enjoy continuing the violence.

With his head lodged against a large, jagged rock, Anthony squinted against the sun at the outline of Manuel above him pointing the barrel of a gun at Anthony's head as he turned to run. Anthony closed his eyes and weakly turned his head away as if to somehow ward off the inevitable. This was it. He was going to die. *Please God. Take care of my wife and children.* Then the shot rang out and Anthony felt a sharp pain just above his eye before his world dissolved into blackness.

Chapter 4

Laura clutched the phone to her chest. What had Anthony wanted to tell her when his phone went dead? She glanced at the dressing table. Just as she suspected, Anthony's phone charger remained attached to the outlet. Sweet, lovable Anthony. She'd never figured out how anyone could be such a meticulous investigator and accountant yet overlook some of the simple but important things that kept life running smoothly—like a charged cell phone, a tank of gas, or a few extra dollars in his wallet.

She smiled briefly until the apprehension that had hung over the day shoved aside the warm feeling of just having connected with her loved one.

Laura padded down the hardwood hallway and into Luca's room. She tousled his thick, black hair and turned out the light on the young man sleeping with one hand on closed scriptures and the other clutching a baseball. Laura set the scriptures on the nightstand and tucked the ball into the glove lying on the floor by Luca's bed. Baseball season never ended for that boy. There was the season of games and the season of reliving every moment of the season past.

The brass knob wobbled as Laura pulled Luca's door shut as quietly as possible. The home, built in 1975 by Anthony's parents, had its share of creaks and groans, but Laura was adept at tiptoeing around the squeaky spots in the upstairs hallway. Luca had the largest room on the street side of the home. He had chosen it not because it was bigger than the other two rooms across the hall, but because it didn't face the lake. Even when he was a little tyke Luca wouldn't go near the lake. While the girls spent their summer months diving off the dock or floating in tubes along the shore, Luca never joined them, preferring instead to toss his baseball against the old garage or playing basketball with invisible opponents in the driveway.

Laura tapped lightly before entering Emma's room. As usual, Emma was still awake, still reading. "Lights out, sweetheart," Laura said as she sat down on the edge of the bed.

"Ah, Mom. I've just gotta finish this one chapter," Emma pleaded.

"And then one more and one more." Laura kissed her daughter on her forehead, slipped the book from her hands, and put a piece of paper between the open pages to mark Emma's place in the book. Book still in hand, she hugged her middle child and stood to leave. "I'll just keep this safe for you tonight."

"Mom!" Emma drew the word out in two syllables. "I'll just finish the chapter I'm reading. Really!"

"No way, my love," Laura shook her head lovingly. "I know you and your books. You can't part with one until you've read it from beginning to end."

Emma smiled. "But you're glad I'm a reader, aren't you Mom?"

"Sure am, sweetheart. Good readers make good students. Night, honey," Laura hugged the sixteen-year-old and blew a kiss on her way out the door.

As usual, Izzie had fallen asleep upside down in her bed, one arm dangling off the side, covers askew. Laura set Emma's book on the end of the bed and pulled the slight thirteen-year-old up on to her lap. Sitting on the edge of the bed with the sleeping child cuddled against her, she brushed tendrils of damp hair from the olive skin on her forehead. *My goodness,* she thought, *Izzie is looking more and more like Anthony every day.*

Izzie nestled closer. "Daddy," she whispered.

"It's Mama, sweetheart," Laura replied, knowing that Izzie always preferred her daddy to tuck her in at night.

"Did Daddy call?" Izzie murmured sleepily.

"Yes, but his phone wasn't charged, so we didn't get to talk much."

"Can I talk to him when he calls again?"

"Of course, honey," Laura replied to the little daddy's girl. "I'm sure he'll call as soon as he gets a phone charger, but that probably won't be until he gets to the hotel in Mexico."

"Okay, Mama, night," Izzie spoke groggily and drifted back to sleep as her mother settled her right side up in the bed and tucked her covers around her from shoulders to ankles just like she'd seen Anthony do. Something solid poked out from under Izzie's pillow. Slightly lifting the pillow, so as not to disturb the sleeping child, Laura retrieved a picture frame. Turning it over, tears came to her eyes as she saw a picture she had taken of Anthony and Izzie all dressed in white five years ago on Izzie's baptism day.

"Oh, Anthony," her heart cried out. "Be careful, my love, and return safely to me."

When sleep finally came to Laura, she slept deeply for what seemed like only minutes before she awoke, her heart thudding, then, after drifting off again only to awaken to the brush of a tree branch on the side of the house. By morning, she wondered how she'd ever pull off the concert that evening on so little sleep. She was tired and felt feverish. Patting cold water on her face, she glanced in the mirror at her dark-circled eyes. Dorothy, her makeup artist at Lincoln Center, would have her work cut out for her tonight.

She was greeted in the kitchen by eager faces. "Do you think Dad will call before we go to school?"

"I wouldn't count on it," Laura replied. "But we'll see. How about we just have cold cereal this morning?" She could avoid cleaning up the kitchen from a hearty breakfast and get a few hours' sleep while the kids were at school.

The kids were unusually quiet as they munched down the sugared cereal. Luca and Emma put their bowls in the dishwasher and hurried up the stairs to get ready for school. Only Izzie lagged behind.

"I miss my daddy," she sobbed and put her head on her arms on the counter.

"I know you do, sweetheart. You're his special girl, but he'll be back in a few days."

Izzie turned teary eyes toward her mother. "Something feels wrong right here," she rubbed her chest, "like when we lost our kitty, and she never came back."

Laura pulled the child into her arms. "Let's get your brother and sister and we'll say a prayer that Daddy will be safe and come home to us soon, okay."

"Okay, Mama."

Laura called Luca and Emma to the family room and sat in Anthony's recliner with Izzie tucked close by her side. "Luca, would you like to be responsible for calling on someone to pray until Dad returns?

"Will you, Mom?"

"Sure, son," Laura said. She reached for Emma's hand to start their circle of prayer to ask a special blessing for Anthony, whose love and presence was so vital to their family.

Chapter 5

The bus dropped the Di Angelo children at the corner by the lake, and Izzie raced down the street and up the driveway ahead of her sister and brother. She twisted the knob and shoved the wooden door open with her knee. "Did Daddy call yet?" she hollered as soon as she was in the kitchen.

Laura turned from the stove. "Not yet, honey, but it would have taken him an hour or so to get from the airport to the hotel, and then he had to find a charger for his phone."

Izzie dropped her lunch box and folder on the counter, climbed onto a bar stool, and slumped with her chin on her arms. "Well, when he does call, I get to be the first to talk. Okay?"

Laura went around the corner of the bar and put her arms around the little girl. "I'll probably be gone by the time he calls, so you make sure you remember every little thing so you can tell me when I get home . . . now clean out your lunch box and show me your school folder before I have to leave for the concert."

"Luca," Laura motioned to the pile he left inside the front door, "put those things in your room, young man, and then hustle out here so we can go over what needs to happen this evening."

"Sure, Mom." Luca good-naturedly bent to pick up his backpack, baseball glove, and cleats.

Laura's eyes grew misty. Luca was such an agreeable child, so much like his father—anxious to please, eager to help. When he returned to the kitchen, Laura showed him how to serve the stir fry she'd left simmering on the stove and then reminded him to help Izzie with her homework. Responsible Emma would get right to her homework after dinner, but Izzie would put hers off as long as possible, even sometimes denying she even had any homework.

"Uh, Mom," Luca paused. "Uh . . . did you hear from Dad?"

"No, dear, but I'm sure he'll call while I'm at the concert. He's probably been busy all day with the investigation. I'm just hoping he found a charger to fit his phone."

"Okay if I check the family e-mail? Maybe he sent something if he couldn't call."

"Sure, honey, that would be great." Laura didn't want to discourage Luca, although she herself had checked the e-mail hourly throughout the day.

Laura turned toward the master bedroom to gather up the clothes bag containing her formal black gown, black patent leather heels, and jewelry. It was nearly an hour's drive into the city, but at this time of the day most people would be headed for home, so perhaps the traffic wouldn't be too bad.

Laura knew by the dejected look on Luca's face that there had been no e-mail from Anthony. She pulled him to her. Even big boys needed a hug now and then. "Don't worry, son. I'm sure we'll hear from him soon."

Even the children were more concerned than usual!

She kissed each of the children goodbye and rushed out to the black Toyota Camry parked in the driveway. The day had been busy, and when she was finally on the road in the solitude of the car, worries about Anthony finally found room in the turmoil of her mind. *Why hadn't he called or even e-mailed? I'll get this concert over with and then get to the bottom of this non-communication,* she assured herself. It was just so out of the ordinary for Anthony not to call. Surely, he could have borrowed a phone just to let her know he was safely there.

The young man in valet parking at the Lincoln Center gave her a broad smile. "Good evening, Ms. Di Angelo," he said as he opened the driver's side door.

Laura flipped the button to unlock the back door and took the gallant hand the valet extended. "Skyler, you are one in a million," she smiled as he retrieved her clothes bag from the back seat.

"All the best, Ms. Di Angelo," he called after her as he stepped into her car to park it until her return.

"Thank you and have a good evening," she called back and turned to walk the few steps to the entrance.

Laura hung her bag in her dressing room and walked down the hall to one of the soundproof warm-up rooms. Normally she was a bit nervous yet excited about performing, but tonight a blanket of doom hung over her like a sheet of fog over the Hudson River. She slid onto the thickly padded bench of the well-worn practice grand. With her elbow on the piano case just above the keyboard, she cradled her head in her left hand while her right hand stroked out a random melody on the keys. Closing her eyes, she prayed for peace of mind and focus. She was beginning to worry about Anthony to the point that her heart was almost quivering. *Just get through the concert,* she encouraged herself.

She began her warm-up routine, playing scales up and down the keyboard like an ice skater tracing compulsory figures over and over until only one single-lined pattern carved the ice. By the time Dorothy, the makeup artist, tapped on the door, she had completely lost herself in the music, almost as if her consciousness floated somewhere above, guiding her hands through thought waves rather than nerve impulses.

"Ms. Di Angelo?"

"Yes, Dorothy. Thank you. I'll be right there," Laura replied kindly. So many of the performers treated the crew with impatience, even though the crew members were the ones who actually made them look and sound good on stage. To Laura, their talents were every bit as important and valuable as hers. She just happened to be out front.

In the makeup chair, Laura could hear the orchestra warming up as Dorothy stroked on a creamy foundation. The doors would not open for admission for several minutes and the musicians were taking every last moment to get their instruments in tune and their fingers loosened up. She heard the piercing, nasal tone of the oboe and then the brass followed. Laura's cell phone rang, just as bows were drawn across violin strings to tune to the oboe.

"Excuse me, Dorothy. Just a minute," she said as she grabbed her bag and dug for the phone that always sunk straight to the bottom of her purse. She hadn't retrieved it once she got to her dressing room knowing Anthony would call home first since he knew she had a concert.

"Hello, Luca? Is everything okay?"

"It's me, Mom," a tearful Izzie replied. "Dad hasn't called yet. I'm scared."

"Don't worry, darling. I'll be home as soon as I can after the concert, and we'll call Marty and see if he's heard from Daddy."

"But it will be late, and Marty will be asleep."

"Well, he'll just have to wake up for a minute then."

"Okay, Mom."

"I love you, sweetheart. Say a special prayer for Daddy, okay?"

"Okay, Mom, but wake me up after you talk to Marty."

"We'll see, sweetheart. You have school in the morning." She soothed her youngest child even though she herself was fraught with worry. "I've got to go now and let Dorothy smear some more war paint on me, as Daddy calls it," she said, with a wink in Dorothy's direction.

Dorothy skillfully transformed Laura's face into a porcelain finish that would defy even the most precise camera lens. "You look beautiful, Ms. Di Angelo," Dorothy said as she put the finishing touches on Laura's makeup and stood back for a look at her work.

"Please call me, Laura. What's it been now, ten or so years you've been making me presentable?" She paused. "I do appreciate you, Dorothy, and your ability to transform me. My goodness, if I didn't know better, I'd think you studied the history of every piece I played and then worked your magic to make me look like I'm right out of that period of time.

Dorothy glowed at Laura's appreciation. "It doesn't take much, with your beautiful features. All the best to you tonight, Ms. Di Angelo," Dorothy curtseyed and scurried out of the dressing room,

Laura slipped out of the makeup smock and into the shimmery black gown. She slid on her heels over what she considered some rather expensive hose and then slipped the posts of the dangly faux diamond earrings into her pierced ears. She fluffed the ends of her hair that she always preferred to style herself. She hated the hair-sprayed helmet-head feel the hair designers usually achieved, and instead tucked her hair behind her ear on the audience side and allowed her long dark hair to swirl down on her other shoulder, using only a light spritz of hair spray to keep stray frizzies in place.

Laura waited in the wings for the cue from the stage manager. Although it would not be the case tonight, she still imagined Anthony waiting in the wings after the performance with the single flower he usually purchased from a street vender—almost always a rose, though the colors varied. She always walked off the stage straight into his arms.

"Bravo, my love," he'd whisper in her ear and then turn her back toward the stage to accept the continued applause. Then he'd watch her change, admiration gleaming in his eyes, and they'd stroll arm and arm out of the performance venue. She'd be famished, and he'd obligingly stop wherever she wanted and patiently allow her to relive the performance.

"Three minutes, Ms. Di Angelo," the stage manager whispered. And then, a moment later, "Oh…," he uttered an expletive. "What do you mean she has an urgent phone call?"

Laura spun around to see Dorothy's outstretched hand with her phone. "It's Luca," she said. "I heard it ringing in your dressing room. He says it's urgent."

The stage manager swore again. "You've got two minutes, Ms. Di Angelo."

"What is it, honey?" Laura cupped her hand around the mouthpiece of the phone.

"It's an e-mail from Dad . . . he sent it this morning, but we just got it."

"What did he say?"

"Oh, a bunch of mushy stuff about how much he loves you and that you'll both be looking at the same moon tonight."

"Thirty seconds, Ms. Di Angelo," the stage manager hissed.

"Thanks, Luca. I've got to go. I'm on in a few seconds. I love you."

"Love you, too, Mom. Break a leg."

"You're on Ms. Di Angelo," came the raspy voice of the stage manager. Laura wiped a single tear from her cheek with her index finger and stepped onto the stage. Anthony wouldn't be waiting tonight. She already felt cold and lonely, but reminded herself that they would be beneath the same moon.

The first movement of Rachmaninoff's Second Piano Concerto began, bell-like tolling gradually climaxing. Laura was at first the soloist and then the accompanist to the orchestra. Many theme songs had been inspired by this work that Rachmaninoff composed after recovering from a long depression. But as the allegro scherzando began in the third movement, the violas poured out the melody. The passion of the words to "Full Moon and Empty Arms"—made popular by Frank Sinatra, its melody derived from this last movement, flowed from Laura's heart to her fingers.

"The moon is there for us to share, but where are you?"

Tears rolled down Laura's cheeks. Worrying about Anthony distracted her and caused her to feel like she was fighting for every note. Yet as the concerto ended, the crowd roared to their feet, the applause thunderous. And yet, Laura's heart was elsewhere. She bowed. She smiled. She acknowledged the orchestra and the conductor, all the while thinking, *"Oh, Anthony. Where are you?"*

Chapter 6

Lying prone on the desert floor, a sharp pain in his torso startled Anthony into consciousness. And then another jabbing pain in his arm, accompanied by giggling. "Is he dead?" a young voice asked.

"I don't know," another child nearby answered. "We'd better get Mama."

Anthony struggled to open his eyes, but only managed a tiny slit that let in a piercing light from the desert sun. He ran his tongue over his parched lips, felt a jagged split in the skin, and tasted dried blood. The left side of his head was pounding. He tried to raise his hand to his face but was too weak. His hand dropped onto the desert floor. He groaned and sank again into darkness.

At the sound of Anthony's distress, the two little boys scurried back to their hut, which was built on a slight rise above the gully where Anthony had been dumped and left for dead by his attackers. "Mama, Mama! Come quick!" they said, once they'd got inside. "We found a dead man."

"He's not dead, Oscar! He made that awful sound, remember?" The younger of the two argued with his brother.

"Yeah, he gurgled or something," Oscar agreed.

Graciela wiped her hands on her apron. Probably another one of their tricks. "Come boys. Take me to this dead man." Graciela had been helping the boys' grandmother grind some cornmeal for dinner before she needed to leave for her shift as a maid in the Cabo San Lucas Resort Hotel. There had been another fire the previous day, with smoke sifting into some of the rooms closest to the utility closet. The closet had somehow caught on fire and destroyed the entire workout room next to it. Graciela would have her work cut out for her that afternoon—airing out the rooms, washing windows and walls—all on top of her regular duties.

The boys each grabbed one of her hands and dragged her frantically down the sandy slope to the gully. She gasped when she saw the man lying there, his head and face swollen and covered with blood. She bent over him. "Senor, senor? Are you okay?" She brushed away an insect making its way over Anthony's cheek.

Anthony used all his strength to open his eyes. Again, just a tiny slit of light appeared and then the face of a lovely woman with long dark hair. "Laura," he whispered and then lapsed into unconsciousness again.

"Quickly, get your uncles!" Graciela ordered the boys back to the hut. She patted Anthony's hand and gently patted his bruised cheek. "Come back. Please come back."

Ramon and Alvaro were soon at her side. "My gosh, Graciela. What happened?"

"I don't know. Just pick him up carefully and get him to the house."

Ramon supported Anthony's shoulders while Alvaro held his legs.

Deep inside Anthony's consciousness, he heard someone yelling, someone in pain. His lip split wider and fresh blood poured into his mouth and down his chin. *Was he screaming? Were those his own cries of anguish?*

Adelita met them at the door. "What have you boys done now?" She punched Ramon in the shoulder as she witnessed him carrying the injured man.

"Nothing, Mama. The little guys found him in the desert."

"We just dragged him in here because Graciela made us. We'd just as soon have left him for the vultures."

"Hush. You boys put him over there on the bed and then get back to work." Adelita was tiny, but there was no question that she was in charge. Her sons lumbered out the door before she could take another swat at them.

"I have to get to work, Mama," Graciela said. "Will you be okay with the man?"

"Just leave me to him. We'll have him back on his feet in no time." Adelita replied confidently, but she wasn't so sure. While she was used to cleaning up the wounds of Ramon, Alvaro, and their friends after a night of drinking, the man's head had an unusual wound, like a bullet had grazed his skull. Rock chips were embedded in his face on the same side as the wound. His face was bloody, his eyes swollen shut. She gasped when she lifted his shirt. His whole belly was discolored. "Who did this to you"? she whispered, knowing he wouldn't answer. She slid her hand along his ribs. From the way he jerked and winced when she touched his ribs, she was pretty sure they were broken, at least some of them.

He would be a handsome man, she thought, when the swelling went down. He was dressed well, although his clothes were filthy and torn. She'd been praying for just such a man for her Graciela whose no-good husband ran off and left her when the little boys were just babies.

A glint of gold on the man's left hand caught her eye. His hand had somehow survived the attack. She guessed he didn't have a chance to fight back. The ring was snug, so she smeared a little lard on his finger and slipped the band off, telling herself she didn't want to take a chance on the hand swelling. But she knew that if it hadn't swollen by now, it wasn't likely to happen. She dropped the ring into her apron pocket and went about attending to his wounds.

Eventually, he awakened, and she offered him a few sips of water from an earthen mug. He was too weak to hold the cup in his hands, so she gently raised his head and allowed him to taste the coolness of the liquid.

"Gracias," he mumbled.

She spoke to him in Spanish. He seemed to understand and nodded slightly yes or no.

"What is your name?" she asked. He looked puzzled. No answer.

No matter what she asked, he had no answer and finally looked away, a tear rolling down his cheek.

I feel lost. Nothing seems familiar, he thought. *And when I try to figure out how I got here, a black void separates me from remembering.*

*****

When Anthony awakened again, the sun was streaming through an opening he supposed was a makeshift window. He turned his head to the right. The pain was agonizing. *This is the worst stiff neck I've ever had,* he thought, though he couldn't think of a time when he remembered having a stiff neck.

He glanced across the room, looking for something, anything familiar. He could see the tracings of a broom on the dirt floor. A beaten-up wood table was pushed against one wall, while a stack of woven mats rested against the opposite wall. In between was a countertop, in reality just a rough plank supported by scrap wood. But what he noticed was how neat and clean the room was in spite of what must be the extreme poverty of its owners.

The door creaked open. A woman stepped inside and set a ceramic jug on the table. "Good morning, Senor," she spoke in halting English.

Anthony responded in Spanish. How did he know this woman? He found it odd that he thought in English yet spoke in Spanish.

She came closer and Anthony noticed the way her dark brown hair swirled over one olive shoulder. The memory of a dark-haired woman looking out over a body of water flashed before his eyes but was gone before he could attach it to anything that would help him figure out his past. *Heck,* he thought. *I can't figure out yesterday let alone a woman in my past.*

"My name is Graciela," the woman said as she came closer. "What is your name?"

My name. My gosh. I don't even know my name. Anthony turned his head away. Once again, a tear slipped from under his eyelashes.

"It's okay, Senor." She was gentle, her voice soothing. "We will call you Ramirez."

"Ramirez?"

"Yes, Ramirez—one who is powerful in battle."

Anthony chuckled, then grunted in pain as the smile stretched his split lip. "It seems I lost the battle," he replied.

"You are alive. To have done that, you must be very strong."

Anthony tried to raise his hand to his aching head, but only managed to lift it a few inches off the blanket. "Not so very strong," he replied dejectedly.

"Madre will restore your strength. You wait and see." She smiled and turned as her mother, a diminutive, bent women stepped through the door. "Wait and see," Graciela shook her finger and went through the open door.

"My Graciela, she is a beautiful woman, is she not?" the grandmother of Graciela's children asked hopefully, as she fingered the ring in her pocket. If he didn't remember his past, she would not return the ring.

"Yes, she is . . . uh thank you for taking me into your home," Anthony replied. "What . . . what happened to me"?

"Don't you worry, Senor. We will have you on your feet in no time," she soothed, skillfully ignoring his question. She poured water from the jug into an earthen bowl and pulled out a rag tucked into the waistband of her long, faded blue skirt. She pulled a stool up to the cot and began gently sponging Anthony's face.

"Arghh," he shuddered. The pain was awful, especially at the side of his forehead.

"You are very lucky, Senor," Adelita whispered. "Someone tried to shoot you here," she stopped where the pain throbbed. Anthony could feel the cloth dipping into an indentation in his skull. "'But they missed, Senor. El imbecile brutos!"

Stupid thugs, Anthony translated silently, and just the effort of considering his past became too much. He shut his eyes to escape.

Adelita felt the smooth ring in her pocket and crossed to the window. Taking it out, she looked closely. There was something scratched into the inside of the band. It wasn't in Spanish, not that she could read it, even it was in Spanish. She slipped the ring back in her pocket vowing to find a good hiding place. This man was surely sent from God for her Graciela, and she aimed to see that they were a match.

Chapter 7

It was nearly midnight when Laura turned into the driveway. The house was ablaze with lights. *Those children. They should be in bed. They have school tomorrow.*

Leaving her gown behind in the car, she marched up the steps to the house and turned her key in the door. As usual it stuck, and the lock wouldn't turn. *Darn old door.* She was worried about Anthony, and now the children were still awake and would have trouble getting up for school in the morning. The sticky lock was the last straw.

She gulped back a sob, then took a deep breath and gave the key a hard turn and pushed on the door at the same time. Ready to chide the children for not being in bed, she strode into the room. Luca was sitting by the phone, leaning forward, his elbows on his knees. Izzie was curled up next to Emma, the older sister encircling the little girl protectively with her arm. Three pairs of worried eyes turned in her direction. Emma, as usual, remained silent as Izzie cried out, "Daddy didn't call."

"I've been sitting by the phone all night, Mom. I didn't want to miss his call. We couldn't go to bed, but we promise to get right up in the morning."

Laura dropped her purse and went to her son's side. "You did the right thing, son. No call, huh?"

Laura turned to Izzie and Emma on the couch. Izzie flung herself sobbing into her mother's arms. "It's okay little one. He probably just couldn't find a charger for his phone," she comforted, although she knew that was not the case.

Something was wrong. Dreadfully wrong.

"You kids get ready for bed. It is probably too late to call Marty. I'll call him first thing in the morning and see if he's heard from your dad."

"Can we have a prayer, Mom," Luca, the ever-faithful child asked.

"Yes, son. Would you lead us." They knelt in a circle holding hands as Luca offered a simple prayer asking for his dad's safety and return to the family.

After sending the children off to bed, Laura tried in vain to sleep, but no slumber would come. She finally left her bed in the early morning hours and went out to the deck overlooking the lake. "Where are you, my love? Oh God, please let him be okay."

*****

The tiny incisions in Marty's abdomen hurt like he'd been stabbed over and over with an ice pick, not that he'd ever experienced a stabbing of any sort. In spite of the anesthetic lingering after his gallbladder surgery the previous day, he didn't sleep a wink. Perhaps it was the continual beeping of the monitors in other patient rooms or the nurses who came to check on him just as he was about to drift off. More likely it was the panic growing moment by moment about what would happen if old man Salazar didn't intercept Anthony before he got to the resort. There was no way he could let Anthony investigate this fire. Thorough, but naïve Anthony. When it came to a fire that he suspected was arson, he went after it like a bloodhound and trusted absolutely no one involved.

But Anthony trusted Marty, and Marty knew it. For several years Marty had been the sole investigator for the Medina account and had been the only one to investigate the Salazar fires. Anthony had never so much as mentioned a

40

concern that the fires were questionable. Their shared past as high school buddies, then college roommates, and now business partners had cemented their friendship. *Anthony had it all*, Marty often mused jealously. A beautiful home, the loveliest of wives, pretty good kids . . . and Marty was still alone. Laura was the only woman Marty had ever loved, and always from afar, since even in college she'd never had eyes for anyone but Anthony.

The ring of his cell phone jolted him back to reality. "Hullo," he answered, his voice still raspy from the tube stuck down his throat during the surgery.

"Marty?" It was Laura sounding frightened.

"What is it, Laura?" he responded, wishing she were actually in the room with him. Well, maybe not. He hadn't shaved or bathed since the day before and smelled bad even to himself.

"Have you heard from Anthony? He hasn't called since he got to Mexico. He always calls us, Marty."

"I'm sure he's fine, Laura. I'll make some calls." Marty felt a horrible sense of panic and doom. He'd just asked old man Salazar to delay Anthony. Something must have gone wrong. He hoped that Anthony's streak of "goody two-shoes-ness" hadn't gotten him into some trouble.

"Please, Marty, and get back to me soon."

"I will, my dear." Oh, how he loved that woman.

For a moment Marty felt guilty for thinking about Laura, which was something he did almost continuously. He was obsessed and was the first to admit it, but he just couldn't get her off his mind. He groaned out loud as he tried to roll over and sit up on the edge of the bed. Gingerly, he lowered himself back down on the pillow. He felt sorry for himself because he was on his own, in pain with no one to care. Laura didn't even ask how his surgery had gone.

Marty reached for his cell phone on the bedside tray. He punched in the country code, and then the area code, and then the phone number of his Salazar contact. Renaldo Salazar answered.

Marty didn't even bother with pleasantries. He just got right to business. "Did you intercept Anthony?"

"Si," Renaldo replied. "He won't be a problem."

"What do you mean he won't be a problem. Is he on a plane back here?"

"Uh, well I sent the boys out to rough him up a bit . . ."

"Rough him up! You were just supposed to delay him and convince him to head back without an investigation."

"Well, things went a little wrong."

"What do you mean a little wrong?"

Far away from Marty, Salazar looked across his desk at the guys he'd hired to accost Anthony. Marty was so stupid. Anthony had to be put out of the way completely, not just bundled back on an airplane.

"Look, Marty. You are in this as deep as I am. Let's just say Anthony won't be coming back."

Marty's heart pounded. He was torn between the loss of his friend and the enormity of the hole he'd dug for himself thinking he could make a bundle from insurance payments for the hotel fires. After all, Salazar had agreed to split the insurance payments 50-50 with him.

"Who knows about this besides you and your thugs?" Marty asked the Salazar hotel owner. He heard two pops like gunshots. "Renaldo? Renaldo? What's going on?

Anthony's attackers slumped, dead in their chairs opposite Salazar's desk. "You know, Marty. And I know. And that's all anyone's gonna know. You understand?"

Marty swore. "We're done Renaldo. No more."

"You're in this with me, Marty. And don't you forget it, or you'll end up worse off than your friend. Anybody who crosses me will be watching the vultures circle their broken body in the desert. Don't you be telling anyone about this. As far as you know, your buddy just disappeared in Mexico. Happens all the time, anyway. Why not him?"

"You don't know his wife. She'll never believe that."

"You'd better make sure she does." Marty heard a click, and the phone went dead.

How could he explain this to Laura? She was no dummy. Not that woman. She'd grill him to death. Maybe he'd be better off left for dead in the desert. Marty's mind spun frantically, unable to focus on any concrete thought. Anthony . . . dead. He felt a rush of sadness quickly overcome by a sense of panic. He should have known better than to trust Salazar. Lives obviously meant nothing to him. Marty had shaken hands with thieves, had become one of them, and the consequences were frightening.

Marty stroked his thumb on the cell phone, stopping at the last call received, and pressed send. Laura answered immediately. "Marty?" Her distress was almost palpable, and he longed to be with her, comfort her.

"It's not good, Laura."

"What do you mean, Marty? Not good?"

"Anthony never showed up at the hotel. I haven't wanted to tell you this, but there have been several suspicious fires . . . fires at hotels owned by some pretty corrupt characters. I've been worried about Anthony. Uh," he hesitated. He had to get this straight or Laura would see right through it. "I'm sorry, Laura, but some of those fires really smacked of arson, but Anthony processed them as accidental. I think . . . my dear, I don't know how to tell you this . . . but I think the crooks were paying him off."

"You just stop right there, Marty." He was lying, she could tell. She'd seen the envelope Anthony brought home and Marty had investigated every one of those fires. "You and I both know Anthony was as honest as they come. He'd never choose the wrong path."

"Maybe he felt in over his head, you know. The big home, all the trips you've taken with the whole family."

"That's it, Marty. I won't hear any more. You need to call the police and tell them everything you know about what happened to Anthony . . . and don't be trying to pin any sort of fraud on my husband!" She slammed the phone to its base. *My darling, where are you?*

She wanted to scream and cry with frustration. Anthony was lost in Mexico. But she hurriedly composed herself. Something terrible had happened to Anthony, but she knew with every beat of her heart that he was alive, and she'd find him. Blast Marty and his accusations. He was no friend, no friend at all.

Chapter 8

Every morning, Adelita spoon-fed Anthony some sort of thick broth until he was finally able to raise his hand to his mouth by himself. Supported by one of Adelita's muscular sons on either side, Anthony plodded around the inside of the small home once a day.

"Let me see you stand on your own, just for a moment," Adelita all but commanded when it had been two weeks since he was carried from the desert to her home and still could not walk on his own.

Ramon and Alvaro released their grip on Anthony's upper arms, and he stood, wavering, but nevertheless on his own. He smiled for the first time in weeks, or however long it had been. He couldn't remember much further back than the previous day.

"Good job!" The tiny grandmother cheered him on. "Now take a step or two."

"Anything you say, Senora," Anthony replied as he slid one foot forward and then the other. It was only two steps, but he felt a rush of joy, a sense of freedom. Though he couldn't remember ever being anywhere but on the cot in Adelita's home, he felt he must have had a life somewhere before.

Anthony wobbled and the boys latched onto his arms again and helped him to the cot. He slunk to his back totally zapped of strength.

Adelita was smiling and her happiness was infectious. "Gracias, Adelita, for everything. Muchas Gracias," he said with gratitude and sincerity. This humble Mexican woman had almost nothing, but what she had she shared with him and her family. She was the force that kept the older boys out of trouble, but she was a tender abuelita to her fatherless grandchildren.

"One day soon you will walk outside with my Graciela," Adelita remarked with a coy expression and sat on a stool by Anthony's cot.

"Adelita?" Anthony suddenly felt able to stretch his mind beyond the confines of his very limited thinking and reasoning power. "Who usually sleeps on this cot?"

"Never you mind," she turned her face to look somewhere off in the distance.

"This is where you usually rest, isn't it?" Unusual feelings overcame Anthony. He felt grateful and guilty. So many emotions flooding the black void of his mind.

"It is your place of healing, my son," she replied.

Tears ran from Anthony's eyes. He felt so grateful for the kind woman's sacrifice, and he felt an overwhelming sense of loss although he didn't know what he may have lost.

"Tell me again, Adelita, how the young ones found me, how I came to be in your home."

And Adelita rehearsed the story of his rescue once again as she had done every day since he'd first regained consciousness. Maybe this time he would remember. But she was caught between wanting him to remember his past life and wanting him to start anew, making all new memories with her Graciela. She turned the gold band over and over in her pocket, momentarily wondering about the woman Anthony had now forgotten.

Several days later Adelita declared Anthony strong enough to walk outside. "Come Graciela, Anthony needs a bit of sun. That's it, put your arm around his waist, and Anthony,

46

you put your arm around her shoulders. It will keep you steady."

Adelita hoped that a walk together would bond them in friendship leading to love. She so wanted her Graciela to have a good man. Although she should have done so, she had not sent a message with Graciela to contact the police. They may take this man away and then there would be no chance for their love to blossom. Besides, the police were corrupt and may have been the ones to have inflicted these wounds on Anthony.

Anthony squinted in the bright sunlight. It felt good to be outside, to feel the slight breeze, to feel Graciela so close to him. He smiled down at her. "You are every bit as lovely as your mother tries to tell me every day."

Graciela's long lashes swept low on her cheeks. "I'm afraid my mother has not been very subtle in her matchmaking."

Anthony laughed. "No, she has not, but she is right about you."

"Ramirez." She called him by the name that had been bestowed upon him when he couldn't come up with a name for himself. "I want to tell you something, but you must not tell my mother. Two things I want to tell you."

"Okay." Anthony answered haltingly and felt her pull slightly away so that their sides were no longer touching.

"There is someone who is my true love," she said softly, and Anthony's heart sank. He was just feeling close to someone and now she was telling him that she didn't want him. "My mother does not approve of him, although he is a good man. Mostly, she does not approve of his church. She calls it a silly church."

"And you, do you approve of his church?" Anthony asked.

"I am learning about his church for a few minutes after work each day. Two young men tell me about his church and then I have to run home very fast so that Mama doesn't worry."

"Must be some church for you to go to all that trouble."

"It is a wonderful church. So much love of Christ and so much promise of love from Christ."

"Well, then I'm glad that you have found this church," Anthony replied realizing that he knew Christ. He knew Him in his heart, and he felt comforted.

"And the other thing you had to tell me?"

"There is someone you left behind, Ramirez. I think her name is Laura."

"And how do you know this when I can't even remember much of yesterday, let alone be able to tell you of a woman in my past named Laura."

"When I bent over you in the desert, you opened your eyes for a moment, looked into my eyes and whispered 'Laura.' And you said it with so much love and so much relief that she was there with you. Only it wasn't her, it was me."

"Laura? I don't think I know anyone by the name of Laura."

Graciela laughed. "Oh, Ramirez. You don't know any names, not even your own. I just want you to think. Think of Laura and maybe your memory will return, and you'll be whole again."

Laura. He'd think about 'Laura,' this mystery woman whom he must have loved.

Feeling like he had to salvage the moment to keep Graciela from seeing just how sad he had been at her confession, he changed the subject and tried to be interested and cheerful. "So, when will I meet this young man of yours, Graciela?"

"Maybe you could help convince Mama to let me bring him here, and keep my brothers from beating him up, she smiled. I know when Mama sees him and the peace that he brings with him, she will forget about his church and just learn to love him . . . as I love him."

"I'll tell you what, you help me get strong enough to actually help with a little work around here, earn my keep, and I'll work on Adelita. She's a woman with a big heart, just a little tough to break inside to the kindest heart I've ever known."

"Since you've known, or should I say remember, so many hearts," Graciela teased.

"Sometimes I think I know a lot more than I remember and other times, I think I must have always had this empty head of mine."

Graciela grew suddenly quiet, looking off in the distance, perhaps envisioning her true love, Anthony thought.

"Tell me about this man you love."

"He's a wonderful man. A good man like you, Ramirez. Several years ago, when my Felix and Oscar were very young, he was here as a missionary like the two young men who teach me about Christ."

Something seemed vaguely familiar to Anthony about young men being missionaries. "And does this man have a name," Anthony winked, "Or shall he remain nameless like me?"

Graciela laughed, "His name is Lane, Lane Peterson. Mama calls him the gringo from the North Country."

"North Country?"

"America," Graciela replied.

"Oh, I see." Anthony grew thoughtful and brought his hand to his chin, deep in thought. He hoped this man was not just playing with Graciela, a beautiful Latina girl to keep him company while he was in Mexico, quickly forgotten once he went back to the States. "I'd like to meet him, Graciela."

"Mama doesn't want him to come here, but perhaps you could talk her into letting you come into town one day to walk me home from work."

"Oh, she'll go for that alright," Anthony chuckled, thinking of how Adelita was always trying to bring him and Graciela together. "I'll be there soon, I promise. I will just have to learn to walk a lot better on my own! You'll have to draw me a map or something. I've never been past the dirt road in front of your home."

*****

Within a week, and with much determination to make use of his newfound strength, Anthony set off for the town with Graciela's map in hand. She said it was only a couple of miles, but considering he hadn't done more than walk around the perimeter of Adelita's property and a short distance into the desert with Felix and Oscar, he was tired long before he reached his destination. It didn't help that the old sandals on loan from the much bigger Ramon, Adelita's deceased husband, slid around on his feet, exhausting him even further as he tried to keep an even gait. As he entered the small town, Graciela was coming toward him, her hand locked in the hand of a tall, blond fellow who Anthony guessed to be in his late twenties.

"Ramirez," Graciela said shyly, while looking up with adoration into the blue eyes of the gringo. "This is Lane."

Anthony's hand was grasped and locked into a powerful handshake. A flash of memory slipped through his mind of a little boy vigorously shaking the hand of a man in a dark suit greeting people at the door of a church house. *Now how did he remember that and how did he know the building was a church?*

"I'm very pleased to meet you, Ramirez," the young man said, looking Anthony straight in the eye.

"And you likewise, Lane." Anthony liked the guy, but he wanted to remain objective. He had to make sure this guy was for real and not just out to take advantage of Graciela.

"Come, sit over here," Lane gestured toward a round table with bench seating and an umbrella overhead. "I'll get you something to quench your thirst."

"You do look tired, Ramirez. Your face is all red. Are you sure you are okay?" Graciela touched his arm lightly, distinct worry gathering her smooth features.

"Yeah, I'm fine. Just not used to doing anything but sitting around. I've got to get Adelita to let me do more around the house, maybe in the garden, too."

"Good luck with that," she smiled. "She's always shooing Ramon and Alvaro away from the garden. Says they eat more than they harvest."

Lane returned with three ice-cold fruit drinks, and they spent the next half hour talking about the reason Lane returned to Mexico after he finished college.

"I'm just a farm boy at heart," he said humbly. "Raised on a sheep ranch in Idaho. Studied agriculture at Utah State University. I've always been interested in organic farming and there's a lot of that going on down here. I've been working with one of the large farm owners on the outskirts of town." He gestured toward the other side of the town. "He raises a beautiful crop without the use of pesticides. But they have no way of tracking their profit or losses or the success of crops in general. I am trying to set up a program to help them with those necessary tasks to help them succeed."

Anthony nodded. For the life of him, he couldn't remember the meaning of pesticide. Oh well, he was getting used to half-understood conversations. He changed the subject.

"So, how did you and Graciela meet?" Anthony liked this man. There was something solid yet peaceful about him.

Lane slid his arm around Graciela's waist. "When I was here as a young missionary, we met, and I briefly shared my message with her. I was transferred to another area and never saw her again until last year. There's a farmers' market in town, and I was bringing in some produce to sell. Graciela," he paused momentarily to pull her closer to him, "was selling some of her grandmother's handiwork. She was the most beautiful woman I had ever set eyes on. Wouldn't have anything to do with me, at first, but I was persistent, and each time I met her at the market, I bought her flowers. Finally, she started speaking to me, and the rest," he paused as his eyes moistened. "I have a temporary work Visa but I can work here for a few years."

Graciela was sobbing now. "I will find a way to bring you to my home, my love," Lane cradled her in his arms, one hand stroking her dark, satiny hair.

"My love." *Those words sounded so familiar. Where had he heard them before?* A brief picture flashed through his mind of a woman in a flowing white robe. But her face was turned away from him. Who was that?

He was coaxed back to the present with Graciela's palm resting lightly on his arm.

"Do you see, Ramirez, why I must convince Mama of Lane's goodness, so I can take my boys and make a life with him in his country someday?"

"Yes, Graciela, I do understand, but I don't know how you will ever convince Adelita."

Graciela buried her face in her hands and sobbed, and Lane looked as though he might break down as well. "We'll pray, my love."

Those words again! "We will fast and pray harder than we've ever prayed before that the Lord will soften her heart toward me . . . and my church."

"Just what church is this?" Anthony asked.

"The Church of Jesus Christ of Latter-day Saints," Lane replied with pride in his voice, and then when Anthony looked puzzled, "The Mormons. You've heard of the Mormons haven't you, when you were in the States?"

"What makes you think I'm from the States?"

"The way you talk. The way you act. Most everything about you," Lane said in a lighter tone.

"Gosh, I don't know," Anthony rubbed his head. "I don't know where I'm from, why I'm here, or where I'm going."

"You know, Ramirez, if you'd let me tell you more about my church sometime, I think I can help you with the answers to those questions."

"Really?" Anthony got excited for a moment.

"Really," Lane replied, "though maybe not what city or town you came from, and maybe not why you are here in Mexico, and maybe not where you are going in your future. But you will learn that before you came here you were a child living with a Heavenly Father who loved you then and still loves you and cares about you now. When you were hurt, He placed you with a family to love you and bring you back to health. And where you are going is your choice. Will you follow the example of Christ, or will you become like so many others, a worshipper of the things of the world?"

For once, Anthony felt a little bit of direction in his life. "A child of a loving Heavenly Father." Those words sounded true, even a little bit familiar.

Chapter 9

Marty's accusations tore through Laura again and again, bringing a sickening taste of bile to her throat. Her heart struggled to keep a steady beat; her lungs fought for air. Marty was dead wrong. She knew Anthony to his very honest core. He would never be involved in such subterfuge. She couldn't wait any longer for Marty to report the police findings. The children couldn't wait a moment longer to find their father. Each of them dealt with their anxiety and worry in their own way, but she knew that all of them were in agony. She'd called Marty nearly every day for the past two weeks, and the answer was that he was still waiting. She would go to the police herself in the morning.

The front door rattled. A solid knock was not possible on the old door. It had kept out mighty winds and turned away many a salesperson, but the wood, though solid mahogany, was tired. Hung from its original frame when the house was built in 1975, it shook a bit with the slightest rap.

Laura took a deep breath and walked to the door. Her hand grasped the knob. It was original to the home, an ornate glass and brass design, and a bit wobbly.

"Good afternoon, Mrs. Di Angelo," greeted the man in the suit, white shirt and tie.

"Hello," Laura replied hesitantly. He didn't look like a solicitor. Something told her to hear him out, although she longed to slam the door, run to her room, throw herself on her bed, and sob out all her fears and frustrations with Marty's accusations.

He produced an FBI badge. By this time, Luca had come up behind her, ever the protector in his father's absence. "May I come in for a moment? I'd like to ask a few questions about Mr. Di Angelo's disappearance." He looked past her to Luca. "May we speak privately?"

"Luca, could you give me a moment."

"Sure, Mom." Luca turned to leave. Laura knew he would stay within earshot, but she didn't want his presence to hamper the man from telling her everything he came to say.

Laura opened the door for the gentleman to enter and led the way to the armchairs near the piano. The listening chairs, she called them, in which Anthony or the children sat to listen to her rehearse from time-to-time. The listening chairs would be put to good use today.

"Mrs. Di Angelo," the man began. "I know this must be a very difficult time for you, but I need to get right to the point. We have reports that your husband may have been involved with some insurance fraud related to the Salazar hotels insured by the Medina Independent Hazard Insurers."

Dang that Marty. He'd spread his lies to the police, and now the FBI was involved. "Sir, you are completely wrong about my husband being involved in anything illegal. He was the most honest person I've ever known."

"Ma'am, even honest people make mistakes." Laura could tell this conversation was difficult for this man. Should she show him the envelope she found with Anthony's suspicions about the fire? Her mind wrestled with the decision. The agent was about her father's age as she last remembered him. Not overweight, not thin, just a bit portly, with a shock of beautiful white hair accompanied by an equally white mustache.

Laura blinked back tears. Her decision was made. She couldn't let Anthony be accused of something that he didn't do. Maybe the FBI would help find him, wherever he was. One thing she knew was that he was alive, not dead and disparaged as Marty presumed.

"Give me a moment," she rose. "I'll be back." As she turned to leave, she noticed the man's hand go to his right side under his suit jacket. *My goodness, he thinks I'm going to get a gun to shoot him.*

Laura lifted the envelope from the center drawer in Anthony's office where she had secured it. Holding it to her chest, she went back into the hallway where she'd left her guest as he followed her. She held the envelope away from herself, and her other hand in the air as she approached. "No weapon," she smiled, although a bit begrudgingly considering this man had leveled such a dastardly allegation at Anthony. How many times had she heard Anthony arguing on the phone with Marty about being upfront and truthful with their clients?

"Anthony left this with his itinerary the morning he left for Mexico. He doesn't usually investigate these cases." She was hesitant to admit that Marty always investigated the fires in Mexico.

"Who does?"

Now she had to answer. "His partner, Marty."

"Mmh." The agent was intent on the information in the envelope. "May I take these?"

"I'd be happy to make you a copy," Laura replied, hesitant to let go of any evidence that might clear Anthony of the horrible things Marty was trying to pin on him.

"Mind if I accompany you?" the agent asked.

Laura supposed in his career, which must have been a long one considering his age, he'd had people try to pull the wool over his eyes more than once. "Certainly, but could I see your badge again, I've forgotten your name." She'd glimpsed Luca with his cell phone around the corner, where the hallway turned to the master bedroom. He was peeking out and recording the whole encounter.

The agent held out his badge. "Do you want your son to take a picture of it, too?"

"That won't be necessary." She half smiled. Not much got by the guy. She made a mental note of his name, Sam Brady.

Sam accompanied her to the printer/copier in the kitchen, where the family computer resided so she could keep an eye on the children's computer use. She picked out the staple, forgoing the staple remover she would normally use to protect her fingers. She placed the papers face up in the sheet feeder and pressed the copy button.

When the machine was done, Laura stapled each group of papers together, handing the copies to Sam.

"Thank you, ma'am," he responded.

"Now, may we talk about how to find my husband?" Laura gestured to the armchairs again in the sitting room.

"Certainly," Sam responded. "Tell me everything from the time Anthony learned of the fire until today."

Laura relaxed a bit in her chair. While initially leery of Sam, the feeling that he might be the avenue to finding Anthony filled her with hope. She recognized the guidance of the Holy Ghost telling her Sam could be trusted. It was a peaceful feeling, unlike the utter turmoil she felt in Marty's company. She took a breath and began.

Chapter 10

Anthony swept the dirt floor of the place he'd come to know as home. He was meticulous. Every time one of the little boys ran in the house, Anthony smoothed the surface of the hard, packed dirt. But still, he felt useless. He paused in front of the kitchen window. It was hard to see through the scratched glass Adelita must have scavenged from somewhere to allow light into her cooking area.

Outside, Adelita bent over a hoe, furrowing the soil around the shoots of green that would soon grow into corn, a staple of their diet. When she drew herself to her full height, usually when shaking her finger back and forth at one of her sons or grandsons, she wasn't even five feet tall. Her figure had thickened around the middle, but her legs and arms were stick thin. Yet, the boys did whatever she asked, however reluctantly. She was in command of the house and the yard, and everyone knew it.

Anthony leaned the broom against the wall. The door was comprised of weathered two by eight planks that creaked in protest as he opened the door into the room and stepped over the threshold which was a mere two by four that kept the rivulets of rain from running into the home. He stepped outside and sauntered over to the garden like he was just out for a stroll. Adelita had leaned the hoe against a cactus while she bent to pull a few stubborn weeds by hand.

Looking over his shoulder, Anthony took the hoe from the cactus like a young boy stealing a penny candy from the drug store. He paused as a memory of a store with many bins of small candies flashed through his senses. Clinging to a moment of his past, he replayed it over and over in his mind as he walked to the end of the long row and began gently churning the dirt around the infant plants.

"Ramirez!" Adelita frowned, her hand on her hip. "Get yourself out of my garden."

Anthony straightened and smiled as she walked with quick steps toward him, her hand outstretched, ready to wrest the hoe from his grasp. He pointed down to soil meticulously spaded around the infant plants. "But how did I do?"

Adelita stopped short. "Mmhh. You've had some teaching in this, chico," she replied and turned on her heel and headed toward a tin bucket by the cistern. The cistern was a big tank that was supplied with water from a truck with a large plastic tank that periodically serviced their area. The water deliveries were unpredictable and sometimes the water was so dirty, she didn't even want to put it on her plants. She was always careful not to spill a drop of this water as she worked.

She would have liked to use the clear water from the well on the hill above her home, but it was unreliable during the hotter weather, so she saved as much money as she could to be able to afford deliveries to the cistern when needed.

A tin cup hung on a nail in a wooden post. Lifting the cup from the nail, Adelita bent over the first tomato plant growing about eight inches out of a mound of dirt. She ladled just enough water to fill the bowl-like indentation around the base of the plant.

Anthony smiled to himself, his heart swelling within his chest. He'd pleased her, and he'd find a way to be useful. As he worked, carefully loosening the dirt around each of the plants in the twelve rows of corn, the sweat ran down his forehead and stung his eyes. He wiped his face and eyes with the edge of his shirt. He gazed at the cactus dotting the surrounding landscape. Adelita's place was an oasis in the middle of a rocky desert, and to Anthony it was home.

Finished with the tomatoes, Adelita attacked the task of purifying drinking water for the next day. Filling the bucket again with water from the cistern, she poured small amounts of water over a T-shirt stretched like a strainer over an aluminum pan. The pan was elevated about eighteen inches off the ground by three bricks stacked at each corner. Adelita took a clamp off a plastic tube dangling from the lowest corner of the pan and drained the water into several plastic bottles. The bottles were then placed in the grooves of the corrugated tin roof where the water baked in the sun the rest of the day, becoming sanitized enough to drink.

Anthony finished the last row and splashed his face with the water remaining in the bucket. Stomping his feet on the woven mat outside the door, he slipped inside, somehow without a creak, and over to the cot where he'd practically lived for how long he didn't know. He rolled up the mattress—made of straw covered with a course, linen-like fabric—and carried it outside to the opposite side of the house from the garden to the clothesline held upright by two poles, one leaning in one direction and one in the other. Each somehow remained upright but dipped low enough for the petite grandmother to hang the clothes to dry that she'd washed by hand with a scrub board in a steel tub. Every week she threatened to make the older boys, Alvaro and Ramon, wash their own clothes, but they were empty threats she only hollered at them when they came home each night—grubby and dirty from working at a large farm on the other side of town.

Anthony hefted the straw mattress over the clothesline and went back inside for the broom. He wacked the mattress with the broom as he'd seen Adelita beat the dust out of the hand-woven rugs. He went back for the handmade quilt that he'd pulled around him during many long, lonely sleepless nights when he tried in vain to remember anything about his life before he'd awakened in the desert.

He replaced the mattress and quilt on the cot before Adelita came through the door with some beans from the garden and motioned for him to join her by the wooden slab where she prepared the food.

"Snap them in half like this, Ramirez," she demanded, but a smile twitched at the corner of her mouth, and despite her gruff tone, her dark eyes said it all. He'd made a place for himself in the heart of this hard-working, compassionate woman, and he'd proven, by the care he took not to disturb the young plants, that he respected her garden for its importance to her family.

By the time Adelita made corn cakes to go with the beans now simmering on the stove. Ramon and Alvaro returned from work. The older boys slid the table out from where it was pushed up against the wall and sat at the bench that had been tucked beneath it. Sensing that their supper was soon to be served, Graciela's little boys stopped their play in the dirt. They had been trained early to wash their hands in the bucket of water by the door before even attempting to enter their grandmother's home and certainly before eating. Bursting through the door, they ran to Adelita by the stove where she was arranging corn cakes on a clay platter.

"See Abuelita," they said in union raising little hands to show their grandmother they had washed up for dinner.

Adelita smiled and gave each boy a pat on his chubby cheek and turned back to scoop the beans from the boiling water and add them to the platter. Ramirez hurried to her side to take the platter to the table.

Ramon reached for a corn cake before Adelita had offered a humble prayer on the food and received a slap on the wrist. They all bowed their heads as Adelita thanked the God she loved for the food and as soon as the prayer finished the boys dug in like they hadn't eaten in days. When the last bits of corn cakes and green beans disappeared from the platter, Adelita sent the boys off to feed and water the chickens. Dipping a cloth in a bowl of water, she washed the little boys' faces and helped them lay their mats on the floor. "Your Mama will soon be home to sing you to sleep," she reassured, and tucked a woolen blanket around each boy. She reached for the mat that had been her bed ever since they'd rescued Ramirez from the desert. She was surprised when he took the mat from her hands and led her over to the cot.

"Thank you, Adelita, for making me so comfortable," he said, "but I'm healed now, and I want you to have your bed back." She began to protest, but he persuaded her with a hurt look, and replied, "But see, I've beat the dust out of the mattress and aired out the blankets for you."

Weary from a hard day's work in the garden, Adelita sat on the edge of the cot. She'd forgotten how soft the straw mattress was compared to the hard-packed earthen floor. "Gracias, mi hijo," she said as she lay back on the cot, and Anthony put a blanket over her. She reached up and touched his face but pulled her hand back down to her side, wondering if he had a mother somewhere who was worrying about him. He had a wife, she knew that, but it was her secret and tomorrow she would convince him to marry her Graciela.

The next morning, Anthony was on his knees plucking prickly little weeds from around the tomato plants when Adelita crouched down beside him.

"Ramirez," she touched his arm, which was unusual. Tenderness didn't come easily to Adelita, and he looked up in surprise.

"What is it, Adelita? Did I pull up a plant instead of a weed again?"

There were tears in her eyes. "Ramirez, my Graciela, she is a beautiful woman, is she not?"

"She is indeed beautiful, Adelita. She looks just like you."

"Don't be foolish," she replied. "She needs a good man, Ramirez, and I will just ask you this once. Can you find it in your heart to marry her? She will make a good wife and I know you will be kind to her."

"Adelita. Adelita." How could he find the words to tell Adelita about Graciela's true love without sending her into a rage? "Graciela," he paused. "Graciela loves another man. He's a good man. He works hard. He's kind to her and he loves her very much."

Adelita pulled herself to her full height. "Who is this man? He's from that silly religion, isn't he!" she demanded, not really asking a question.

"His name is Lane. He was a missionary from his church here several years ago. He is an expert in organic farming and is here to help the farmers be more productive. He and Graciela reconnected when they met at the market."

"He's a good man, Adelita. He wants to care for Graciela, to give her a good life."

"She has a good life right here," she replied and stomped her foot and pointed to the ground. And then she grew very quiet. "No, she does not have a good life here does she, Ramirez?" She didn't wait for an answer. "She works too hard and so late at night. I am afraid for her." Adelita wrapped her hands in her apron.

"She loves you very much, Adelita. And you have given her a wonderful life, the very best you could give."

"But it wasn't enough, was it? She will leave me now for this gringo. I know this." She turned her back to him, her shoulders shaking.

"One day you'll remember where you came from, and you will leave me, too," she said.

"I don't know where life will take me, Adelita," Anthony replied, wishing he could take away her sorrow, "but I will always come back to you. Let's just hope that maybe I'm a filthy rich gringo and I'll take you to the United States," he added.

"My home is here," she replied, gesturing toward her home with the garden and the desert. He knew she couldn't be swayed.

"Then I'll buy you a wonderful home with running water and indoor plumbing and a nice tile floor with a bedroom just for you." *How do I know about such things,* he asked himself. But then he was getting used to spouting off mysteries while wondering how he even knew the things he was saying.

Chapter 11

Upon Laura's graduation from Julliard with a master's degree in Piano Performance, the Piano Performance Department Chair had continually e-mailed her about joining the faculty. First, he offered her a position in the collaborative piano department, which didn't excite her in the least. The collaborative students spent little time as soloists and a lot of time as accompanists to vocal and other instrumental students. Her forages into the world of collaborative piano as a freshman at Julliard convinced her that becoming a solo concert pianist was her passion.

Still, there were some rewards to her short time accompanying student violinist, Marco Russo, which had led to a continued friendship and an introduction to his fellow Italian New Yorker, Anthony Di Angelo. Laura smiled, a warm feeling rushing over her as she recalled the first moment in her first year at Julliard, she set eyes on her handsome future husband.

A student trio comprised of Marco on the violin, Dade Carlisle on the cello with Laura on the piano rehearsed Arensky's Piano Trio No. 1, Opus 32 in D Minor for hours and hours before the Julliard Chamber Fest. It was hardly a 'piano' trio. Even the program listing put the piano dead last. But she had to admit the collaboration was beautiful and exciting. Sometimes the piano was the accompaniment, and other times a contender in the race. She loved the parts where the piano spelled out a challenge, and violin or cello answered. She enjoyed the runs from one end of the piano to the other.

But she didn't love the arguments during the rehearsal, or the eye rolling Dade gave her if she made a mistake or asked to rehearse a passage more than once. Marco and Dade had grown up in the world of renowned music teachers. Laura's path had been more haphazard. But Laura had a heart full of desire, a willingness to learn, and it was a great blessing when she became one of the Gina Bachauer Competition Semifinalists during her freshman year at Arizona State University. After a year in piano performance at ASU, through the Bachauer Competition, she'd earned a scholarship to Julliard and had the opportunity for so much more.

In the end, solo performances invigorated her from the top of her head to her toes. Her heart soared and the absolute thrill of performing with the Julliard orchestra transported her to a near out-of-body experience. That was what she wanted later in life, not more collaborations.

Until she met Anthony at a church dance, the piano was her life and love. While most of the Julliard students had begun piano lessons before the age of five, she'd started at eight. Her best friend, Gladell, was taking lessons, and Laura begged her parents for lessons, too. Looking back, it must have been so hard for them to come up with the twenty dollars a month for lessons. They found an old upright piano that cost fifty dollars and weighed fifty tons. The board that held the lid when it was closed was loose and fell into Laura's lap whenever she dropped her wrists. As a result, she had exemplary hand position on the keys. A mirror above the keys reflected her every movement, and sometimes the family's sky-blue parakeet would sit on her hand as she played and watch its reflection in the mirror.

Laura's work ethic and motto came from writing on a gold pencil she earned from her hometown piano teacher,

"Perfect makes practice. Perfect practice, perfect lesson. Mrs. Hulme is my teacher."

Unlike most children, Laura had to be stopped from practicing. She woke her parents up at 6:30 a.m. with her "pounding" as they called it. The church building was nearby. It was before church members volunteered to clean the church buildings, and a janitor was hired to take care of the building. She'd watch for the janitor's car to show up. Then she'd sneak in while the door was unlocked and play the grand piano in the chapel.

No words were adequate to explain the joy she felt as her fingers first glided and then crashed down on the keys, that is until the janitor forgot she was there and locked her in. This was in the days before crash bars were required in public buildings for safety, so she went to one of the classrooms and turned the crank to open the window, pushed out the screen, and hauled her much smaller teenage body out of the little opening. She fell onto the prickly pine bush under the window, rolled to the ground, and ran home, never daring to tell anyone what happened until she was much older, well after the five-year moratorium she imposed on herself before confessing something out of the ordinary she had done.

The thrill and warmth of falling in love day-by-day with Anthony spilled into her music, lacing it with passion and a new maturity. Their separation during his two-year church mission to Mexico brought a loneliness and sometimes sadness the naïve eighteen-year-old had never before experienced.

On his preparation days, or P-Days as he called them, Anthony sometimes captured the beauty of his new surroundings in miniature water colorings and enclosed them in his weekly letters. Laura mailed cassette tapes of her latest musical conquest, imagining as she played that Anthony was in the practice room, listening, waiting until she finished to wrap her in his arms and rain kisses on her face until he reached her lips.

The two years of Anthony's mission seemed an eternity, but by the time she waited with his family at LaGuardia Airport for him to exit the plane, she had nearly finished with her Junior year at Julliard and had made a name for herself as an outstanding solo pianist and chamber musician.

Anthony and Laura became as inseparable as two people could be for the next two months. Anthony enrolled for the fall semester to continue his business program studies at New York University and spent the summer working in his father's insurance office in White Plains, an hour's train ride repeated often to be with Laura after her classes and practice time at Julliard.

Laura flew back to Arizona to teach at Northern Arizona University's Summer Music Camp for high school students, but by mid-summer, Anthony was at her parents' home asking for her hand in marriage. Their wedding date hinged on how soon they could find a New York City apartment that was both affordable and not too far from either Julliard or NYU.

They were married shortly thereafter, the enchantment of the Christmas lights on the palm trees at the Mesa Arizona Temple provided a beautiful backdrop. They began their lives together forever in a tiny studio apartment overlooking Central Park.

Moments together were precious, after school, studies, work, rehearsals. Semester after semester Anthony often completed assignments on a chair outside her practice room. Laura finished her senior year and two years later performed her master's recital between bouts of morning sickness. Anthony completed his bachelor's degree while rocking Luca's baby carrier with one foot as he worked feverishly to finish his senior paper.

While for others their lack of many of life's comforts and their intensely busy schedules could have led to dissatisfaction or contention, the two of them with little Luca were happy. Their lives were filled with gratitude for a home, however small, plenty to eat, and cherished snippets of time together as Anthony completed his Master of Business of Administration and Laura began a performance career. Somehow, they also squeezed in time for church service. Recognizing that putting God first made each day go better, they made daily scripture study a habit, even if it was just a page or two of the Book of Mormon read over breakfast before they attacked the day ahead.

Their years together had been happy and successful, and they had grown to a family of five. After several years in his father's insurance business, Anthony and his college buddy, Marty, had opened their own independent insurance adjustment business. The business had thrived. While Anthony and Laura still managed their finances carefully, having enough was no longer a worry.

But now, since Anthony had been gone, Laura sorted through the mail, marveling at how much companies must spend to send out elaborative marketing flyers that were usually tossed unopened into the trash. As she tore piece after piece in half and stored the remains in the round file next to Anthony's desk, a Wells Fargo official-looking envelope caught her eye. She opened it.

The words in bold, "Insufficient Funds," popped out at her. What! Her bank account had retained a positive balance since she learned early in her college days to manage her own finances. Even when Anthony and she were poor students, they had never bounced a check or had a negative balance.

Laura looked over the bank statement. Their expenses had been minimal. She ran her finger down the deposit column. The only deposit was from the New York Philharmonic. There were no deposits from Anthony's business. She grabbed her cell phone and dialed Marty.

"Laura, my love" he answered, his voice deep and annoyingly amorous.

Laura ignored his flirty salutation. "We seem to be missing Anthony's bi-weekly deposits into our personal account."

"Well, Laura," he paused. "Anthony isn't working. Not contributing. Why should you expect him to be receiving his salary?"

"Honestly, Marty. Really? Anthony owns half the company. He's put his life into it. He's not here because he went to Mexico for you."

"But he's not here, Laura. Therefore, he's not bringing in any clients."

"Marty, we can't financially survive without Anthony's income. I'm not asking you to give me anything that is not deserved."

"What do you want me to do? Sell his half of the company?"

"I doubt that he'd appreciate that very much when he gets back."

"Laura, I wish you would get with reality. Anthony must have tucked away a pretty penny, and he's gone. Left you and the kids. Gone."

"Bite your tongue, Marty. I'm sick of your accusations. You know Anthony, and he'd never do anything like that. He's honest and loyal. You know that!"

"Do I, Laura? Anthony knew I loved you. You were meant for me, not him, just because he met you first. He should have stepped aside when he knew I wanted you. I wouldn't have disappeared and left you penniless."

"I wasn't meant for you, Marty. Never was. Never will be." Laura punched the button to disconnect the call.

Chapter 12

Anthony paced a dusty path as he wove around the mesquite trees and cacti in the desert surrounding Adelita's home. He paused under the umbrella of an acacia, gazing up at the wide stretch of its branches shading the desert floor. "Heavenly Father," he began and stopped.

Wait! Where did that come from? Adelita only spoke of God. God's goodness, God's care, God's help, God's love. How did he know to begin a prayer with "Heavenly Father?"

He began again. It felt comfortable. It felt right. He would have to ask Lane. Maybe he knew what religion used that terminology for deity.

Anthony poured out his heart asking his Heavenly Father to help him find who he was, where he should be, to protect anyone who he had left behind. Then he asked for the right words to open Adelita's heart to the gringo that Graciela loved.

He opened his eyes to see a tiny figure marching toward him. "Ramirez," Adelita called out. "Ramirez, why are you pacing about in the desert."

He strode toward Adelita and, taking her arm, helped her toward a flat boulder under the acacia that seemed it had been placed there for some weary traveler to gain respite from the summer's smoldering heat and humidity. Holding Adelita's hand, he lowered her to the rock and then leaned against the trunk of the tree.

"Go on," she urged. "Tell me. Are you leaving me? Did you remember who you are?"

"No, no," Anthony responded. "Nothing like that. I want to talk to you about Graciela and her gringo."

She sighed and turned her head, brushing back her hair that had escaped her scarf. "That again? Okay. If you must."

"I have met him. I used my best male intuition and judgment of character." He made an attempt at humor. "Yes, me, the one who can't even figure out who I am!"

"Humph."

"My gut feeling is that he is a good man, one who truly loves Graciela with all his heart, and one who truly loves and worships God."

"Which God would that be?" Adelita turned a skeptical eye in his direction.

"Your God. My God. The same God."

"So you remember your God?"

"Yes, I believe I do. I think I felt His presence this morning. Anyway, it felt like what Lane described when I met with him and his missionary friends."

"So Lane is the name of the gringo who was here years ago knocking on my door wanting to tell me about his church, and now he's hooked you, Ramirez? I'm Catholic. That is all the religion I need, but I suppose if you need or want more, then that is up to you."

"I respect your beliefs, Adelita. I admire your strength and conviction. But something about Lane's religion seems so familiar to me. I feel like I've heard it all before."

"Perhaps you have. Perhaps it will awaken you to who you are. Perhaps I am just wanting you to stay here with me, make a home for Graciela."

"I know you do. I know you do. But she loves Lane and home is with the one you love. I wouldn't want to take that from her. Perhaps there is someone I once loved."

Adelita fumbled in her apron pocket and brought out a golden band. She reached for his hand and pressed it into his palm. "Yes, I do believe there was someone you loved. Your hand was swelling, so I took off the ring. Perhaps I was selfish, but I wanted a good man for my Graciela, and my heart told me you were a good man."

Anthony turned the ring over and over. There was an inscription inside. "Always yours forever, Laura."

Laura. The name Graciela said he mumbled when she found him. The name flowed through his mind and heart. Laura. Was she out there somewhere, wondering where he was, waiting for his return? The vision of the woman in the flowing gown flashed as if seen through the back of his eyes rather than right in front of him, but this time she was looking at a body of water and thick, dark hair was flung over her shoulder. He grabbed a stick and began scratching the scene in the dirt at Adelita's feet.

"Are you angry with me, Ramirez?"

"Not at all. How could I be? I wouldn't even be alive to have these memories if you had not cared for me. This ring is not going to get me home, but it does fill my heart to know that I was once loved before I was lost." His heart couldn't hold any anger toward this woman who had sacrificed so much for him and just wanted a good man for her daughter.

"You are not lost. You were found . . . by our family. Perhaps this Lane can help you find where you belong. Perhaps you were an artist." She stood and grasped Anthony's hand. "Come with me."

"Seems like a lot of 'perhaps' we need to resolve," he smiled down at her.

Adelita only smiled and led him to a shed behind her home. She heaved open the sagging door. The light was dim, but she seemed to know exactly where to go. Reaching up to a shelf, she brought down a half-inch paint brush and then plopped it into a small pail. "Put some water in this pail and mix in some different colors of soil. I am sure it will all come back to you if you start painting what you see in your mind on the walls of this shed. It could use fixing up."

Anthony gave Adelita a quick hug and a heartfelt, "Muchas gracias," and got started right away. He used the cup to dip water from the cistern and into the pail. He scooped red dirt into the pail and mixed it thoroughly with the brush before returning to the shed and beginning to paint the body of a woman on its smoothest side. The woman was voluptuous, not model thin, but curvy. Perfect. She stood by the side of a lake and appeared to be looking off in the distance with the tilt of her head. The fabric of her flowing gown, crafted by a textured application of red paint, looked real, like it was billowing in the wind. The way the brush felt in his hand, the way he managed each stroke, seemed so familiar. He was an artist. One more snippet of his past life to hang on to.

He outlined the lake with a rust red shore. He set the pail in the sun to dry, hoping to conserve water used in the cleanup from the red dirt for the gray he would find to use for the lake. And then he would find some deep brown to mix in for the woman's hair. Long, thick deep brown hair. Laura. Was the woman who flitted in and out of his mind Laura?

Chapter 13

Several months had trudged by since Anthony's disappearance. Despite Marty's continual pleading for Laura to have Anthony declared dead and collect the life insurance, or divorce him for abandonment, she knew in her heart that he was neither dead nor had he abandoned them.

Sam Brady checked in frequently. "No news is good news," he encouraged. "Don't worry. I am digging deep, and a few things have come to light that exonerate Anthony."

When she pressed him further, he asked for her patience and his commitment not to reveal details of his investigation and findings until they were confirmed.

Money had become tight without Anthony's income and her inability to continue concert tours. Marty was refusing to provide any support for the family out of Anthony's equity in the business until Laura "got her head out of the clouds," and accepted that Anthony wouldn't be coming back.

On Saturday morning, Laura made an extra special breakfast for the family with waffles drizzled with warm chokecherry syrup, link sausage, scrambled eggs, and orange juice. It was a traditional breakfast they always had on the Saturday before Fast Sunday when Anthony was home. She had bottled enough chokecherry syrup to last a few years and their freezer was still quite full of sausage and cans of frozen orange juice.

It was time to bring their lives back to something resembling normal. After breakfast on Saturday morning, she announced to the children that they would be having a family meeting on Sunday. She asked each of them to fast for inspiration and guidance and Heavenly Father's help in the decisions they would need to make.

Saturday morning, they knelt in prayer as a family to begin the weekend, with Luca leading the prayer, pleading with the Lord for his father's safe return and asking Heavenly Father's help to go on as a family. After the prayer, Laura asked the kids to be sure to look at the chore list on the fridge. Once their chores were finished, they were free for the rest of the day. Emma, of course, would read. Izzie would play her guitar, and Luca would call some of the boys from the Church and the neighborhood to meet at the club at the end of the lake to play basketball. Laura would take a trip to the LDS Temple in Manhattan to serve the Lord and receive peace, comfort, and hopefully some much needed inspiration in return.

While the children knew that the FBI was involved in finding their father and that Marty's lack of effort had caused considerable delays, what she didn't tell the children was that big changes would have to be made in their lifestyle if they were to still be here in their home when their father returned. Anthony had no siblings and his parents had been gone for several years. Laura's brother was a career military photographer traveling the world. Her mother lived in Arizona on the limited income of a single retiree. Even if financial help was available, she wouldn't ask.

The Manhattan Temple with the Angel Moroni standing atop was backed by a lofty skyscraper. The Temple blended in yet somehow stood apart from the surrounding apartment buildings and offices. When Laura entered the Temple doors it was as if her burdens were lifted, and she was carried by the tender, loving spirit that dwelt there. She left a few hours later with a renewed strength to guide and care for the needs of her family until Anthony returned. She knew he would return. She had prayed that she would know the truth and that her mind would be clear and filled with accurate thoughts. Though she knew not when or how, she was absolutely certain Anthony would return to her, to their family. And although she didn't like to ask for help, she knew she needed to respond to her mother's pleas to let her come and help until Anthony returned, allowing Laura more time to financially support the family.

Emma stared silently out the car window on the drive to church the next morning. "A penny for your thoughts, Emma," Laura said.

"Oh nothing, Mom. I just hope no one asks if we've heard from Dad."

"Yeah," Luca agreed. "It's getting old."

"Just say what I say," Izzie replied.

"What's that?" Laura asked.

"When I know something, I'll tell you. Until then, don't ask!"

Sounds like Sam Brady, Laura thought.

They all chuckled. That was their Izzie. Tell it like it is, and this time, Laura didn't even chide her for being blunt. If Izzie was finding a way to cope, then so be it. Laura had enough concerns about her as it was.

Izzie had taken to dressing in black with nary a spot of color. When asked, she said she'd be wearing black until her dad came home. Since she didn't previously have enough black clothes for a weeks' worth of outfits, Laura would hear the washer running nearly every night and find a tiny load of black clothes inside. If the girl was determined to wear black, then they'd better buy more black clothes before the washer gave out. It would be worth the expense in the long run. As she looked in the rearview mirror, she noticed Izzie's fingernails painted black and a black haze on her lips.

"Izzie, my love," she said.

"Yes, Mama?"

"You are too young for black lipstick. Luca toss her a tissue." Better to pick just one battle at a time and let the black nail polish slide for a time. She just hoped the whole Goth look wouldn't come to pass with the ratty fishnet hose, black combat boots, and thick black eyeliner.

Each child was dealing with the uncertainty about their father in their own way. Emma usually kept her thoughts to herself and became obsessed with her homework and helping Laura at home. Luca spent hours voicing his concerns to his mother and exploring possible scenarios and resolutions to finding his father. And Izzie definitely was exhibiting her way of coping although at times she cried real tears as Laura stroked her forehead and tucked her in for the night.

Laura found it interesting that none of the children grumbled about being hungry after missing Saturday lunch and dinner and Sunday morning breakfast. They were a solemn little group sitting on their usual third bench on the right from the front in church. Luca sat with the Priests at the sacrament table, ready to offer the sacramental prayer. Laura contemplated Christ's suffering for God's children and the enormity of his pain. He had felt the sorrows of every person. She could barely hold up under her own sorrows.

Luca came back to sit with the family after the sacrament, putting his arm around his mom just as Anthony used to do. The young man was truly doing his best to be strong for his mother and sisters.

The bishop had asked Laura several times how she was doing and even sent the Relief Society President to their door. But Laura was determined to manage on her own.

Laura was careful not to share all of the feelings she had in the Temple with the children. Her own faith wasn't perfect and from moment to moment she hovered from the certainty of Anthony's return to the "what if he did nots." Izzie was already struggling with her prayers not being answered right away, wondering if Heavenly Father really heard her prayers as she begged Him to send her daddy back to her.

They knelt in prayer before their family meeting on Sunday night with Laura asking that each person be open-minded and not afraid to say what was in their heart. Financial concerns and Laura's need to be away more to bring in money were on top of her list of items to talk over with her children. She found that her children had the same worries. How would they manage without their dad, not just as a father figure but in the day-to-day contributions he made to the family?

Laura explained that Julliard had been asking her for several years to teach at their campus in New York City. The commute would add two hours to the time she would need to be away each day, in addition to the time spent teaching locally, but the salary would enable them to keep their home waiting for Anthony's return. Since Laura would be teaching three days a week, Emma suggested that each of the kids be responsible for dinner one of the three nights. Izzie looked concerned, but Emma encouraged her.

"Izzie, you are an expert at hot dogs, and we'd love them once a week." Izzie smiled.

Luca rolled his eyes and then agreed that he could definitely eat hot dogs once a week.

"You kids are the best kids a mother could ever want," Laura said as she pulled the children together for a group hug.

"We know," they said in unison.

"In the Temple, I felt like I should take Grandma up on her offers to come and stay with us until Daddy returns. What do you think of that?"

The woots and cheers—and of course Izzie jumping up and down—cemented Laura's feeling that asking for help from her mother was a good idea, truly inspired, as stubborn as she always had been about managing by herself.

"We will be asking a lot of the Lord to be with us and help us to find Dad," Laura said. "What can we do on our part to show our gratitude?"

"I know," Izzie was the first to shout out. "We can be kind to everyone. If we are kind and help others not to be sad, Heavenly Father will have more time to help us find Dad."

"You are so right!" Laura responded.

"I want to try to do a service every day for someone," Emma said.

"That is a great idea but remember not to run faster than you have strength. I once learned when I was in college that even a small thing can be of service to others. I made sure the copy machine was filled with paper every morning at work so no one would get caught with an empty paper tray and have to fill the machine when they were in a rush," Laura said.

Luca was unusually thoughtful and then he replied, "I will try in everything I do to live the gospel and do my best at things."

"Like baseball and basketball," Emma teased and nudged him in the side.

"Yes. I'll be a good sport and pass the ball to others." He put on a sideways grin. "I'll study hard. I'll read my scriptures, and I'll even listen at church."

"I'm trying to be like Jesus," they all sang a line from a Primary song.

Laura pulled them all close to her. "You kiddos are the very best"!

Laura acknowledged the Lord's hand in the cooperation and willingness of her children to band together and make the best of the worst.

They talked about worries, concerns, hopes, plans, and solutions until it was time for popcorn and a Sunday night movie.

Chapter 14

Sam had been both pleased and relieved when Laura told him her mother was coming to stay. He had to admire Laura's strength and resolve, but he doubted she could keep up her teaching and performance career, take care of the children, and worry about finding her husband. But those things couldn't be his problem however much he wanted to resolve Laura's troubles for her. His problem was the investigation to prove Marty a fraud and to find Anthony. Although the latter seemed to be saddled with a grim outcome.

When Laura called to tell him her mother, Estelle, would be arriving on the 11:30 a.m. flight from Phoenix and reassure him that she wouldn't try to do everything herself, he realized that she was still in that mode. He knew she had classes at Julliard to teach all day at least three days a week, and that she would have to leave a class for the airport, so he volunteered to pick up Estelle and take her to White Plains. He used the excuse that he needed to check out things at her home anyway. Laura reluctantly agreed and Sam left for the airport with a description of a petite woman with curly dark hair who may have a semi-frantic, but typical for her look on her face. He was reassured that Estelle would be one of the kindest, friendliest women he would ever meet. She just worried a lot.

Sam used his FBI credentials to avoid the Park n' Ride lot and waited at the curb until Estelle arrived. He noticed her immediately, just as Laura described her. He exited the car quicker than usual as she hauled her mismatched red and blue luggage to the sidewalk. She had to be in her sixties, but he gawked like a sixteen-year-old. She did have a worried look on her face, but she was gorgeous. Within moments he recovered and called out, "Estelle?"

"Sam?" she responded. The worry immediately left her face and was replaced with the prettiest smile he had ever seen. He stepped toward her and offered his hand. Her hands were small, but her grip was confident. "Thank you so much for fetching me. Laura has told me so many nice things about you."

"I know they are overjoyed to have you stay with them."

Pleasantries aside, he opened the passenger door for her, and then with a click of the fob he had secured safely in his hand, he opened the trunk and hefted her luggage inside, wanting to make it look light even though his back groaned at the weight.

As they drove, she insisted that he fill her in on her family, on how they were handling Anthony's disappearance, and on what he was doing to resolve the issue.

He appreciated the love she expressed for her daughter's family and for Anthony as well. He had never met anyone who could be so forthright in their questioning and still appear kind and patient with his answers.

The conversation somehow turned to his life. She seemed genuinely interested in getting to know him as a person and not just the FBI agent watching over her family. They chatted non-stop until they reached White Plains. Sam felt reluctant to end their conversation and asked Estelle if she would like to stop for lunch.

"Oh my, yes," she responded. "I am starving."

Sam turned into Prima Deli and Catering, an amazing sandwich shop he had frequented on his way to Laura's several times. She or the kids always invited him for dinner, and he wanted to make sure he could honestly say he had already eaten so he wouldn't be taking any of the food he knew Laura struggled to provide.

"This looks delightful," Estelle said, as he took her hand to help her out of the car.

"I can vouch for it. It is very good."

Estelle ordered a Reuben with corned beef and Swiss cheese, which she declared her favorite, sauerkraut, and Russian dressing. Sam breathed a sigh of relief. *Thank goodness. She eats meat.* He had been out a few times with women who were all vegetarians and insisted on vegetarian restaurants. He needed a big hunk of meat to fill him up. He ordered the T-Bone Malone with steak, peppers, and American cheese.

They were so lost in conversation that they barely noticed the food being placed before them. Finally, they decided to eat before the sandwiches were cold. It was nearly 3:00 pm when Estelle looked at her phone. "My goodness. The girls will be home soon. This was lovely, Sam. Thanks so much. I owe you a meal. Perhaps you will join us for dinner sometime."

"I'd like that very much." *Did he really just say that?* But he would like that very much. In a few short hours he had come to really enjoy Estelle's company.

Over the next few weeks, Sam found numerous excuses to make sure the Di Angelo's were safe, and at Estelle's insistence he began confiding in Laura as to his findings in Anthony's case. The trouble was, he kept hitting a wall. The police department was evasive at times, depending on whom he talked with, and the Federal Ministerial Police, Mexico's equivalent to the FBI, were more interested in organized crime than finding a missing American man of little importance to anyone but his family.

More and more, Sam wondered if organized crime was involved in Anthony's disappearance. His business partner, Marty, was cagy and antagonistic every time Sam talked to him. He would get one of his best agents on the search as well. Perhaps a trip to Cabo would reveal some clues. But he had to be careful not to step on the Federales's toes. He didn't want any doors to slam shut before he could open them.

Sam usually hung around after Estelle's delicious dinners to visit while the children cleaned up the kitchen. That was the deal Laura had made with her mother. She said she didn't want her to work herself to death taking care of them, so if she would cook, or help the girls prepare meals, the kids would do the cleanup.

The two of them sat on the back deck overlooking the lake and watched the moon's silvery pathway across the water. Sometimes they would look up to see Emma and Izzie looking at them through the patio doors and then run away giggling.

Just the brush of Estelle's hand against his made his heart actually ping. *Was this good for an old guy?* He declared that whether or not it was good for his health to have a heart pinging away with electricity, it was the best he had felt in a long time.

Eventually he got up the courage to reach for her hand across the patio table, and adored the way she smiled at him and squeezed his fingers. She was a special, wonderful lady and while professionally he told himself he was too involved, personally he wanted time with Estelle to never end.

Chapter 15

"Bring the gringo home with you," Adelita requested as Anthony brushed his hair in front of the tin mirror hanging on the wall by a string slung over a nail.

He was adept at washtub bathing and had even cleaned out part of the shed for privacy. Although Adelita had a curtain she drew across the area in which the others bathed, he still felt vulnerable there and preferred his own space. He wondered how bathing took place wherever he used to live. Adelita was tiny but her snoring could be like the roar of a lion, so he'd eventually made his bedroom in the shed as well. Adelita didn't seem to mind. One less person when her sons ventured home to stay for the night.

"Thank you, Adelita. I will. You will like him."

"Don't be so sure, but I will try."

Anthony walked with Graciela and the boys toward the meetinghouse at the edge of town. They had only covered a short distance when Lane stopped to pick them up in his Jeep.

"Hop in," he called out to them.

The little boys scurried into the back seats and Anthony slipped in beside them after opening the front passenger door for Graciela. Once settled and heading down the road again, Lane reached across the gearshift to hold Graciela's hand. Anthony noticed the look of pure adoration exchanged between them. Did the Laura of the inscription in his ring ever look at him like that? He slipped the ring from his pocket and onto the fourth finger of his left hand. Adelita had a ring on the same hand and finger. He supposed that was where it should go. Then he took it off again and put it securely in the bottom of his pocket.

Two young men in white shirts and dark pants with black name plates engraved with white lettering on their left pockets met them at the door to the church. The Latino missionary, Elder Suarez, was the same young man as the last week when they had met at the cafe, but there was a new missionary by his side from the United States. They were led to a room with several chairs arranged in a semi-circle. The missionaries sat on two chairs at the front of the group.

They opened with prayer and the new missionary began with "Heavenly Father." Anthony's eyes shot open. That was the name for God that came into his mind under the acacia tree. He closed his eyes as the missionary continued in somewhat halting and actually pretty horrible Spanish, although at least understandable. When he said, "Amen," they echoed his closure softly except for the little boys who shouted it at the top of their lungs to their mother's dismay.

Graciela apologized for the boys, but Elder Jameson was already blushing beet red after his struggle with Spanish during the opening prayer.

The last time Anthony had sat down with the missionaries, they had just talked to him and then left with a prayer. Those had both been Latino missionaries, and very fluent, praying fervently to their Padre Celestial. He remembered the prayer as being quite beautiful.

This night they said they were going to talk about the restoration of the gospel. They asked about Anthony's belief in God. He didn't know much, but he did believe in God, though he didn't know how he came to that belief. Elder Suarez narrated a quite fantastic story about a young boy named Joseph Smith who went into a grove of trees and prayed to know what church to join. They talked about some gold plates that Joseph had to wait to receive and how he eventually received them and translated a new book that testified of Christ from those plates.

The new missionary, Elder Jameson, looking straight into Anthony's eyes, handed him a book with a deep-blue softcover indicating it was "The Book of Mormon." The words "Another Testament of Christ" were printed beneath. The missionary asked in his clumsy Spanish if Anthony would read this book and pray to know if it was true. Anthony nodded in the affirmative. He supposed if a fourteen-year-old boy could ask God what church he should join, he could ask if a book was true.

The talk turned personal, and Anthony was asked about his family. He had to tell the whole story again about his lost memories. He fumbled with the ring in his pocket. He showed it to the group. "I may have been married to someone named Laura." He pointed to the inscription and each asked to see for themselves.

"You called me Laura when you first opened your eyes," Graciela said. "Where did you get the ring?"

"Adelita had put it away when she had to take it off my injured hand. She gave it to me," Anthony hesitated. "She gave it to me when I explained how much you love Lane and what a good man he is. In fact, she would like us to bring him home tonight."

"Oh, Mama," Graciela smiled and pulled herself closer to Lane.

"That's a start," Elder Suarez said. "Do you know anything else about your past?"

"I think I was an artist," Anthony replied. "Adelita figured it out somehow. I have been painting what my mind has envisioned of this Laura on the shed."

"We will have to come see your masterpiece," Elder Suarez replied.

Anthony smiled and thanked them, knowing it would take some doing to get Adelita to let two Mormon missionaries on her property.

Chapter 16

Luca leaped off his bike, leaving it lying in the front yard, fully intending to hop right back on and head for baseball practice as soon as he had his forgotten cleats in hand. His mom's car was not in the driveway and his grandmother had flown back to Arizona for a couple of days to "tie up a few loose ends" as she put it, so he pulled his key from the front pocket of his jeans and inserted it into the keyhole just below the door handle. He turned the key and twisted the handle. It didn't budge. He must have locked rather than unlocked the door. His mom never left the house unlocked, but she had a lot on her mind, and she must have been in a hurry.

He turned the key again and hurried through the door and down the hall to his room. He heard a rustling in his dad's office just one door past his room. Stopping short, he left the cleats where they sat by his bed and backed out of his room and into the hall.

Luca gasped when he saw his dad's partner, Marty, rifling through his dad's desk. All the drawers were hanging open, as were the file cabinet drawers.

"What are you doing?" he demanded of the man, unperturbed that Marty was much older and bigger.

"Trying to find something to clear your dad's name," said Marty.

"Yeah, right. Then why are you making such a mess, and why isn't my mom here?"

"She won't believe that your dad could possibly do anything wrong," Marty sneered.

"Well, she is right. My dad was the most honest man I know," Luca defended.

"Your dad was in so much hot water with his illegal dealings that he probably jumped right of a cliff to escape facing the music when the authorities found out what he'd been up to. You know, taking bribes to turn his back on arson that wasn't arson at all." Marty tried to sound convincing.

"My dad would never do anything like that!"

"Then why isn't he here? Why is the FBI investigating him?"

Luca was near tears, but he'd never let Marty see how his accusations were affecting him. "You're wrong about my dad. Dead wrong!"

"You sure about that, boy? You and your family had better watch out. Your dad was taking chances with some real bad people."

"Couldn't be any worse than you," Luca shot back.

"Better be careful, young man. You have no idea who you are dealing with here."

With that, Marty spun on his heel and stormed out the door.

Luca was still gathering his senses when he heard Marty's car door slam and the tires squeal as he backed out of the driveway. His sisters!! They would be at the bus stop within a few minutes. Dropping his baseball gear on the floor, he yanked open and quickly shut the door, ran to his bike, and pushed it into motion as he was still swinging his leg over the seat. He had to warn them. Stop them. Protect them. So anxious was he to get to the bus stop that he didn't notice Marty's car hidden by some bushes several yards down the road.

The bus stop was a good three-quarters of a mile down Lake Road as it curved along the lake. Luca rounded a secluded bend where the willows from the lake came right up to the road. He heard a car coming up close behind him and moved over as far as he dared onto the gravel. Suddenly there was a bump on the back of his bike, and he was flying over the handlebars and tumbling down toward the lake. He landed hard, his leg slung over a boulder, his head on the damp ground, his hand in the water. He tried to move and cried out in pain. His leg! What happened? Ball practice. His sisters. He had to get there, and then his world went black.

*****

Laura walked out of the Piano Performance Department Chair's office both relieved and fearful. Relieved because the position she was offered to teach the Keyboard Skills course would alleviate her financial worries. Fearful since Marty's refusing to give Laura Anthony's monthly share of the profit from the agency meant keeping up with monthly expenses—that in the past her performance schedule just supplemented—was now at crisis level. She refused to dip into their savings, feeling more and more each day that she would need those funds to find Anthony and clear his name from Marty's dastardly allegations. Not that they had a considerable amount of money set aside. They had agreed to put a good portion of Anthony's earnings back into the agency. And now Marty was the sole keeper of those funds.

The girls would be home from school by now and Luca would be at baseball practice. He usually rode his bike to and from practice. He liked the freedom of coming and going. Anthony and Luca had been having serious conversations about finding a small car for Luca to drive himself and Emma to and from after school activities. But a car would have to wait, and Luca said he understood. What a good young man he was.

She was nearly an hour from home when she dialed Emma's cell number. "Hi, honey. Is everyone home safe and sound?"

"Izzie and I are home, but Luca's baseball cleats are on the floor in the hallway. Dad's
office is a mess, too. Drawers opened and papers everywhere."

"I'll be there just as soon as I can, honey." A million thoughts vied for attention in Laura's mind as she fought with the traffic, wanting to get home as soon as possible. Sam, the FBI agent, had stopped by at least once a week, eventually confiding in Laura that Marty had become a person of interest in Anthony's disappearance. He couldn't divulge any details, but he told her to be at rest, that there had been no wrongdoing on Anthony's part. He also said that in discussions with the police departments, both locally and in Mexico, that no one, including Marty, had notified the Mexican authorities of Anthony's disappearance.

Sam had asked Laura for all of the original business documents in Anthony's desk. He had watched and waited while she made copies and then advised her to put them in another location, perhaps a safe deposit box. "Are you expecting someone to want these documents besides the FBI?" she had asked. His reply worried her.

"I can't really speak to that at this time," he said, "but promise me you will either destroy or secure these documents.

Laura had taken his advice and had rented a safe deposit box at their bank the following day and then put it to the back of her mind where it lay buried under her concerns for Anthony's welfare.

After an hour's travel, Laura finally put the car in park in her driveway and turned off the key. Snatching it from the ignition, she grabbed her purse, jerked the handle, and burst out of the car door. She rushed up the steps, her heart pounding. Emma opened the door and flew into her arms as Izzie clutched her waist.

"We're scared, Mom."

"I can see why." Laura looked at the discarded glove and cleats. She tried to remain calm and refrain from uttering a scream when she saw Anthony's office. She knew without a doubt that Luca wouldn't have made this mess. He would have been a complete, undiscoverable sleuth if he were looking for something to help find and clear Anthony.

Laura pulled her cell phone from her purse and scrolled to the Ss in the contacts. Sam Brady answered on the second ring. "Laura?" His deep voice brought immediate assurance.

"Sam, someone has been in our home. Anthony's office has been tossed and Luca is missing. His bike is gone but his cleats and glove are here on the floor. He would never go to ball practice without them."

"I'll be right there, but in the meantime, check with Luca's coach and see if he is at ball practice. Will you do that for me?"

"Yes," Laura replied, her voice and hands shaking uncontrollably.

Chapter 17

Anthony stretched and sat up on his mat. He awakened refreshed, just as the sun was beginning to peek through the cracks in the shed walls. Pulling on his trousers and a cotton shirt, he bent over a ceramic bowl containing a little water and sloshed it up on his face. He dried with a rag made from some worn-out clothes that had belonged to Adelita's sons.

Since meeting Adelita and seemingly accepted by her, Lane came regularly to bring receipts to Anthony from the previous day's work on the farms. Lane would greet her with a friendly "Hola, Senora" and Adelita would respond with a quick nod and a mumbled "Hola". Anthony considered this a great stride for a woman who had expressed her disgust with gringos and especially Mormons.

Anthony's job had begun with keeping the books for one farmer, and now eight farmers entrusted Anthony with recording their expenditures and earnings. Meanwhile, Lane was able to continue helping them run their farms more productively. Anthony had no idea why he was so good at managing the finances of a business, but he just did what came naturally to him when Lane presented him with light-green ledger paper and asked him to keep track of a few things. It had gradually become nearly a full day of work every day. Lane paid him for his services, which enabled him to help Adelita with her expenses and also to perform some repairs to the home.

Anthony pulled open the door expecting to see Adelita bent over the plants in her garden, but it was empty except for a few birds chastising each other as they vied for insects. The birds particularly sought after the leaves of the pepper plants but were thwarted by cages Adelita had instructed him to make out of sticks and strips of cloth that waved in the breeze and frightened the birds away from the precious plants.

Anthony went around the house to the front door and knocked lightly, waiting for Adelita's answer before entering. No answer. He rapped again, this time a little louder, but no answer. He went to the window on the side of the house and peered in through a little space in the handmade curtains. He gasped as he saw Adelita still lying on her side in her bed, facing away from him.

Rushing back to the front of the house, he pushed open the door quickly but quietly. It was possible she was still sleeping, tired from long days in the garden preparing vegetables for the market. But even as this possible reason flitted through his mind, he brushed it aside. The Adelita he knew would never sleep late.

Standing by her bed, he noted the slight rise and fall of her side beneath the covers and breathed a sigh of relief. "Adelita?" He shook her arm gently. "Adelita, are you okay?"

She didn't respond. He felt her forehead and jerked his hand back. It was hot to the touch. Her lips were parched. He reached for the cup of water on the rickety wooden table beside her bed. Slipping his arm under her shoulders, he rolled her toward him and raised her to a slight incline. "Adelita, have a sip of water," he begged.

She only moaned and her head rolled over on his arm. He had to get help, get a doctor, but he didn't want to leave her, and there was no way to summon someone for help.

Anthony poured some water from the clay pitcher into a ceramic bowl. Using a clean cloth, he dipped it into the water, wrung it out almost dry, and then wiped Adelita's face, neck, and arms, patting them dry with a larger piece of cloth. Lane wouldn't be by for another hour with receipts from the farmers. Even so, Anthony listened intently, hoping to hear the crunch of tires turning down the dirt road to the house.

After what seemed like hours, but was probably only a short time, Lane's car stopped in front of the house. Anthony was on his feet and out the door within seconds.

"Adelita is sick. I can't wake her up. Can you go for the doctor?"

"Yes," came the quick reply. "I'll be right back," and Lane got back in the car and shut the door as the vehicle began to move.

It wasn't long before Lane and the doctor were lightly knocking and entering the home. Anthony jerked upright. He'd been talking intently, his head bowed on Adelita's frail hand, to this person he now knew as his Heavenly Father, someone who cared about him and about Adelita.

The doctor went immediately to Adelita's side and turned her gently onto her back. He withdrew a stethoscope from his bag. Slipping it gently under her nightgown, he listened to her heart. He lifted and moved it up, down and then from side to side. Frowning. Frowning. What did that mean?

"Help support her while I listen to her back." It was a command, not a request and Anthony immediately slid his arm beneath her shoulders, noting how her frame protruded through her honey-brown skin. He sat behind her, holding her steady as the doctor placed the stethoscope in various areas, and then paused and concentrated.

"It is as I expected. Adelita has been suffering from a heart condition for years, always refusing treatment. Her lungs are filling with fluid and her heart is really struggling. We should take her to the hospital and try to give her some relief."

"No hospital!" Adelita lifted a weary head and struggled to open her eyes and focus on the doctor. "No hospital," she said again.

"They can help you, Adelita," Anthony began and was cut off as she grabbed his hand and squeezed. "No hospital. Promise me. I want to die here, where I was born, where my husband loved me and gave me babies, where he died. Promise me."

"It's not my place to make that promise," Anthony tried to protest. Graciela or her brothers should make that decision. And Graciela was still at work and the brothers couldn't be trusted to make a wise decision.

Anthony gently eased Adelita back on her pillow.

"I go now," she said and closed her eyes. She drew one long, halting breath and then the woman who had brought him back to life was gone.

The doctor took out his stethoscope again and placed it over Adelita's heart. "She is no more," he said, as a single tear ran down his cheek. The doctor was one of many, for miles around, who had been touched by Adelita's kindness and wisdom.

"I'll go get Graciela and the boys," Lane said. Anthony could only nod in agreement. He felt like his heart was rising out of his chest to choke him. Was it even beating, or had it just broken in half? The doctor patted him on his shoulder and rose to leave.

Anthony remained by Adelita's side. It wasn't long before Graciela burst through the door.

"Mama," she cried out and Anthony quickly moved from his place by Adelita. Graciela flung herself over her mother and sobbed. Adelita's sons stood stoically in the doorway and the little boys rushed to their mother and grandmother. Lane's hand rested gently on Graciela's back. After a few minutes she lifted herself to a sitting position by her mother's side as Lane stood by, his arm on her shoulders. The little boys began to sniffle. Graciela wagged her finger back and forth.

"You must be strong," she urged. "Latino men do not cry."

"Si, Mama," they replied with chocked voices. "Abuela?" the younger one asked.

"She is happy. She is with God. Your Abuelo holds her in his arms now."

For hours the family watched silently over their beloved Mama and Abuela. Just before the sun set, the older boys left and the sound of shovels hitting the dirt in the area where Adelita's parents and husband were buried scraped holes into Anthony's heart. What could he do? How could he show his love and appreciation for this dear friend. He called Lane aside.

He motioned for Lane to follow him to the shed where Anthony pulled a pewter jar from behind several boxes on a low shelf. Reaching inside, he brought out several large denomination pesos. Handing the money to Lane, he instructed him on some purchases and asked him to make it back as early in the morning as possible.

"I may still be able to get these things tonight." Lane turned and hurried toward his car. "Let Graciela know I'll be right back."

Lane returned in just under an hour. Anthony met him at his car and surveyed the lengths of pine pushed through the trunk into an opening in the back seat of the car. He slid the pine carefully from the car and carried it back to the shed. Lane followed with a hand saw, a hammer, some nails, sandpaper, miscellaneous hardware, paint, and brushes.

"Thanks, Lane. I appreciate this so much. Did you have enough to cover all this?" Anthony gestured over the recent purchase.

"You bet," Lane reached into his pocket.

Anthony made a motion to refuse the pesos that were left. "You keep it for your trouble." The two men argued good naturedly back and forth with Anthony finally turning away to start his work of love for Adelita.

All night as the family kept vigil in the house, he sawed, fitted, and hammered until at last he attached hinges on the lid. The natural pine was beautiful in its original state, but as the sun rose, Anthony began adding something special along the edge of the lid to honor Adelita. First, with a small brush he painted greenery similar to the different vegetable plants Adelita grew in her precious garden. Then, he added tiny flowers and fruits. While the paint dried, he went back into the house for the first time since Adelita had gone on to her new life.

Graciela was puttering about the woodstove, scrambling some eggs for her sons for breakfast. Her brothers were asleep on their mats at the back of the one-room home. Adelita had been dressed in her light-blue cotton dress and covered with the handmade shawl she wore to Mass each Saturday and Sunday. Lately, Anthony had begun walking to and from with her although he usually sat outside under a tree. He would miss those times.

Anthony went to the cupboard where Adelita stored her linens, not fine linens, but simple white cotton with hand embroidered edges. Catching Graciela's eye, he got her okay for taking the cloth with him.

The paint had dried on the lid and Anthony laid the cloth on the top. He grabbed his saw and walked a short distance down into an arroyo where the blue palms flourished. He cut several palm fronds, ignoring the thorning prongs that could rip a tear in one's skin. He trudged back out of the arroyo, took the palms to the shed, and performed some careful trimming. The fronds were arranged in the bottom of the pine coffin, providing a soft resting place for this woman who had provided such unselfish love and care to a beaten and broken stranger.

Anthony carried the coffin into the house and placed it on the floor by Adelita's bed. He placed one of the cotton linens over the palm fronds.

Adelita's sons were awake now and attentively placed their dear Madre inside. Graciela lovingly placed another linen over her mother, this time covering her face, and the boys lifted the casket onto Adelita's bed.

"The priest will be here soon," she said. "Mama will not want a huge velorio, just the members of the parish and a few friends."

"Velorio?" Anthony asked, raising an eyebrow.

"Wake, gringo," Graciela responded, smiling for the first time since the previous day.

For two days, friends and people from Adelita's Catholic parish passed through the tiny home, some crying, some moaning with grief or clutching rosaries. Father Garcia stood by, quietly comforting his parishioners as well as Adelita's sons, who long ago set religion by the wayside.

The day of Adelita's Velario and burial dawned with the chirp of birds and a light sprinkling of dew on the ground and plants. Adelita's homemade casket was closed, and Anthony nailed it shut. Adelita's sons, Lane, and Anthony lifted the pine box with ropes attached on both sides at either end. They carried the much-loved woman up the slight rise to the family resting place. The little boys and Graciela, with a black scarf over her thick hair, followed behind with over thirty mourners.

Father Garcia presented the Rosary. Anthony shifted uncomfortably. The words were unfamiliar, and he felt like God and Christ and Adelita should be recognized, but the Mother Mary seemed to be the focus of the priest's words. When the priest finished, he said, "Let us pray," and he recited a long prayer like the ones Anthony remembered from attending Mass with Adelita. Several men from the parish stepped forward, grasped the ropes, and lowered the casket into the grave, ultimately kneeling to gently settle the casket at the bottom of the grave.

Father Garcia sprinkled something over the grave and said a few more words to the mourners who expressed their appreciation as they passed by him to express condolences to Graciela. He loved and knew his parishioners and knew the familiar words they needed to hear at the loss of their dear friend. Anthony felt overwhelmed with respect for Father Garcia's devotion to have given his life to serve these people.

The people surrounded Graciela, hugging, sobbing, and kissing her cheeks until backing away one by one. Soon only Graciela, the little boys, Lane, and Anthony were left. Adelita's sons had gone back down the hill to retrieve shovels to cover the grave.

Anthony stared down into Adelita's resting place. After a few moments, he turned to Lane. "Shouldn't we dedicate the grave?"

"Yes," Lane replied and looked quizzically at Graciela and then back to Lane. "Would you like to offer the prayer?"

"I'd be honored," Anthony replied, and words spoken humbly from his lips were somehow familiar. "In the name of Jesus Christ and by the power of the Holy Melchizedek Priesthood…" A vision flashed into his mind of a family at a cemetery with many headstones surrounding an ornate metal casket.

"Anthony," Lane put his arm around the man next to him he finished the prayer. "Anthony, I think you are a member of my church and most likely your church. I think at some point the Priesthood was bestowed on you. You knew Adelita's grave should be dedicated. Those words came naturally to you."

"I don't know. I wish I knew. But everything I feel at your church feels comfortable. It feels right. I am at peace. Perhaps it was wrong to use those words to dedicate her grave when I'm uncertain."

"Your Heavenly Father knows the intent of your heart. And though you don't remember, He knows exactly who you are. One day He may provide a way for you to find your family."

Chapter 18

Laura scrolled through her phone contacts until she came to "Coach Aimes (Baseball)." She had to designate the sport to keep Luca's coaches and various sports straight. He was such an active boy with rarely any downtime. Sleeping in or just hanging out was something he never did. Every day was planned with things "I just gotta do" from early morning until he finally ran out of steam around ten at night.

The phone rang six times and went to voicemail. How she hated voicemail, especially now that no one listened to their messages. She didn't have the patience to text or wait for an answer. But her phone vibrated immediately after hanging up, and Coach Aimes' name flashed on the screen.

Laura answered, barely able to breathe. She knew something was wrong. She felt it through and through.

"Mrs. Di Angelo? Coach Aimes here. We missed Luca at ball practice. Some of the guys said he went home to get his cleats. But it seems he didn't make it back."

Laura sunk down in the chair by Anthony's desk. "He's not here, Coach." Her mind was spinning between answering the coach and what she needed to do next. Luckily the doorbell rang, signaling Sam's arrival. "I've got to let you go. I'm sorry. I need to find him." She pressed the red telephone icon and slipped her phone into her pocket.

Sam was surveying the disaster in Anthony's office when she looked up. "Luca is missing," were the only words she could eke from her trembling lips.

"We'll find him," Sam assured. "Now tell me everything."

"All I know is what I can guess. Luca must have come home for his gear before practice. He would have been on his bike. His bike is gone. He is gone. He never made it to ball practice. Emma and Izzie rode the bus home and found this." Her hand made a sweeping motion across the room.

Sam turned to Emma and Izzie. "Did either of you see him?" Izzie stood wide-eyed. "I saw a bike down at the edge of the lake when the bus went around the corner." She turned to her sister. "Emma, did you see it?"

Emma shook her head from side to side as Izzie ran from the room. "No. I didn't."

Emma looked from her mom to Sam. "You don't think . . . ?"

"Let's not jump to conclusions." Sam tried to comfort the teenager, but his gut told him the worst had happened.

"I'm going to go find Izzie," Emma said. "She's probably hunting for some chocolate to calm herself."

"Come here first, dear." Laura embraced her daughter and then released her to check on Izzie.

"Sam?" She held back the tears, but her panic rose to a debilitating point. Before she could continue, Emma ran into the office. "The deck door is open. Izzie's gone and the boat is gone!"

Laura and Sam ran out onto the deck and looked toward the dock. The Jon boat was indeed missing, and Izzie was nowhere to be found.

Laura ran to the side of the deck with the gate and stairs. She flung the gate open and leaped down the stairs, not caring if she slipped or fell. She had to find Izzie. She had to find Luca. Her neighbor, George, an older gentleman who liked to advise her on everything from lawn care to child rearing was just tying up the small motorboat he used to fish on the man-made lake nestled along Lakeside Road and the backyards of all the homes surrounding it.

"Give me the boat key, George," she shouted as she ran down the grass-covered hill toward the docks.

"What on earth, Laura?" He held up the key. "Surely you don't think I'll let you take my boat. Take your own."

"Just give me the key. Izzie is out there on the lake and a storm is coming." She snatched the key from his hand and reached one foot into the boat as she unwrapped the line from the cleat and pushed away from the dock. Laura was no stranger to boating on the small lake. She inserted the key, pumped the choke a couple of times, lowered the engine into the water, and pulled on the cord. The motor roared to life. Of course, it did. George was also an expert on boat maintenance. She opened the throttle and grasped the tiller, pushing it hard to swing in a wide circle away from the dock and sped toward the shoreline along Lakeside Road where Izzie thought she saw a bike.

Winds on the lake increased dramatically in the late afternoon and this day was no exception. The wind howled around her and whipped up white caps on the gray-blue water. *Izzie. Too young, too small to be out here alone.* The wind was blowing away from the shoreline, scattering debris from the edge out into the lake. Panic rose to near nausea as Laura imagined her little daughter wrestling the oars and fighting the turbulence.

The bow of the boat flew up and smacked down hard as it plowed through the waves, but as it drew closer to the wide curve Laura could see a figure in black near a small boat tied to a tree. That had to be Izzie bending over something, or was it someone, on the shore.

Laura eased back on the throttle, slowing the boat to prevent any wake from slapping up on the shore. She pulled as close as she could to some sturdy bushes, cut the engine, and tied the bow to the thickest branch.

"Mama!" Izzie cried out. "It's Luca. He's hurt."

Laura kicked off her shoes and leapt from the boat, not caring that the water was nearly up to her knees. She waded several feet to where Izzie leaned over Luca on the rocky beach. His eyes were closed and one of his legs was up on a rock. It was bleeding and twisted at a terrible angle. For some reason, Laura felt calm. Sometimes in the worst of circumstances she could remain calm, but then would fall apart later.

She felt his neck and noted a strong pulse, although his normally tan face was a pasty shade of cream. She pulled her phone from her pocket and dialed 911. Putting the phone on the speaker setting, she related the emergency to the dispatcher and then handed Izzie the phone, instructing her to climb up to the road and direct the EMT's to Luca. She determined the amount of blood oozing through Luca's baseball pants was not life threatening and decided not to put any pressure on the wound. A compound fracture was surely causing the white pants to turn a dull shade of scarlet.

Laura spoke softly to Luca, reassuring him, although she had no idea if he could even hear her. His head had landed on the soft mossy dirt so she hoped there would be no lasting injury. The only thing she could do now for her boy was pray and as she did, she felt a sense of peace come over her, followed by sirens. Help was almost there.

Three EMTs scrambled down the bank. The road was perhaps thirty feet higher than beach level and the incline was quite steep. The lead EMT quickly assessed Luca's condition and then began shouting instructions to the other two.

The ground surrounding Luca was minimal so Laura hunched back into the bushes as far as she could, watching over the surreal happenings, almost bereft of feeling. The lead EMT glanced her way and shouted to a female EMT to take Laura up to the road and bring down a stretcher. The EMT jumped to her feet and, holding Laura by one arm, pulled her up the bank to where Sam stood with Emma. Although she was shoeless, the prick of rocks and brush barely caused any discomfort.

Emma had directed Sam to the curve in the road where Izzie said she saw the wrecked bike. Sam was there to open his arms and enfold Laura as she scrambled up the bank. Then she realized how badly she was trembling. The feeling of peace that had sustained her until help arrived disappeared as quickly as it had come. All the emotions she had kept at bay burst out in one choking sob. Izzie and Emma rushed to her side, and they were all enveloped in Sam's comforting presence. Suddenly Laura realized how frightened Izzie must have been. She turned to the young girl and pulled her close.

"You did a wonderful thing, finding your brother. Thank you so much for trusting your instincts."

"It was the Holy Ghost, Mama. I know it. Something just told me that bike I saw was Luca's."

"You are a very brave girl." Now was not the time to chastise her for taking a boat out on the lake when the wind was stirring up its anger.

Within a few minutes the EMTs were bringing Luca up the bank on a stretcher. He was conscious and reached his hand toward her as they stepped onto the asphalt. "Mom. I need to get to baseball practice."

"Okay, honey. But let's get you cleaned up first."

"Mmhuh," he responded and closed his eyes.

Laura rode with Luca in the ambulance and Sam followed with Izzie and Emma. Once at the hospital, Luca was whisked away, and Laura was left to wait and to wonder. Would there be any more baseball for her boy? Would he be crippled? How had this happened?

Laura was directed to the surgical waiting room. Sam and the girls were there shortly. Izzie and Emma curled up beside her on a couch, one daughter under each arm. Laura was still trembling and shivering. Sam put his jacket over her and went to find some blankets. It would be a long night.

He came back with three heated blankets that settled the shivers and brought a measure of comfort. A doctor had come out of the emergency room to let them know they would need to take Luca immediately to surgery. It seemed the surgery was taking an inordinate amount of time. But the wait was eventually punctuated by the appearance of two police officers.

"Good evening, Mrs. Di Angelo." One of the officers greeted Laura and then nodded at Sam. "Agent Brady."

"We are sorry about your son's accident. We understand he was on a bike at the time. We'd like to have a look at the bike."

"Thank you, officers, but we are not sure where it is. My daughter thought she saw it by the edge of the lake, but it wasn't there when we found Luca. It was pretty windy. It probably either sunk or is on the other side of the lake."

"Hopefully it will wash up somewhere," the officer replied.

Sam restrained himself. This wasn't his jurisdiction, and these small-town police didn't have the resources he was used to, nor it seemed, the desire to turn the lake upside down to find the bike. Just let it wash up somewhere they said. Humph.

Sam turned to Laura, "I'll be right back." He had a pretty good idea of how Luca ended up injured and as close to drowning in the lake as he could come. Marty was the only one with a reason to search Anthony's office, and Luca probably caught him in the act. Marty was covering something up and Sam knew it.

From all the interviews he'd done with people who knew Anthony, there was no way Anthony could have been taking kickbacks. He just didn't have it in him to be that kind of person. They spoke of him fondly as a kind, fair man who was always honest in his dealings. And even if his gut told him that Anthony wasn't the guilty party, the documents Laura gave him proved it. He tapped on the phone number for his lead agent. Time to change the direction of the investigation.

But with a snake like Marty, he'd have to have a rock-solid case to keep Marty from slithering through a loophole.

The surgeon was consulting with Laura when Sam returned to the waiting room. It seemed there would be a long road to recovery for the young man. The compound spiral fractures in both his femur and fibula, combined with other injuries, would require at least a week in the hospital and then confinement to bed for several weeks after his release from the hospital.

Sam knew what was causing both the overwhelmed and devasted expressions on Laura's face. Laura had to work to support her family. There was no way she could stay at home with Luca, and a full-time home health aid would be entirely outside of her ability to pay. He had to take a breath and pull himself back a moment. He was getting entirely too involved personally with this family. He knew Laura would not want to ask her mother to take on the responsibility for Luca's recovery. She would try to do it all herself. Thank goodness Estelle would return soon from Arizona, and her quiet and persuasive personality would be there to bring Laura to her senses.

Chapter 19

It was two a.m. when Sam dropped Laura and her family at home. Luca was still in recovery and wouldn't be in a room where Laura could see him for another couple of hours. Laura was finally feeling pain both in her heart and in her feet after being shoeless since the day before. She opened the front door, left unlocked during their hasty flight to find first Luca and then Izzie. A note slipped out onto the floor and landed by the heels she had hastily kicked to the floor of George's boat.

"Got our boats back," it read. "Sorry to hear about your son. Your neighbor, George."

Bless George. She'd forgotten about the boats. As gruff and critical as he seemed at times, there was a soft heart in there somewhere.

Laura asked the girls to wash up and get ready for bed. Meanwhile, she soaked her feet, filthy from walking on the road and down hospital hallways, although only scraped slightly from her trek up the rough bank.

Laura went to Izzie's room first and smoothed her dark hair away from her freshly washed face as her eyes drooped closed. Then to Emma. Emma would have to bear some pretty hefty responsibilities for a while since she could drive. She had no doubt Emma was capable. But was it right?

"Mama," Emma broached the subject first. "How are we going to manage all this? School, working, taking care of Luca."

"Let me worry about that, my darling. If you can just help get us through tomorrow, that would be great."

"Sure, Mama," the teenager replied. "What should I do?"

"I am going to call in to work and get subs for the week so I can stay with Luca during the day and into the evening. I will get you and Izzie excused for today, but if you could make sure you both get to school the rest of the week and watch out for Izzie in the evening, that would really help."

"What about your concerts?"

"I have to perform with the New York Philharmonic on Saturday night at the Lincoln Center, but hopefully I will have something figured out after that."

"You could ask Grandma to help."

"Grandma already does so much for us. I hate to ask her to help with Luca, too."

"But Grandma loves us, and she wants to help."

"I am sure she will want to stay at the hospital with Luca when I can't be there. So, I will think about it, but you and Izzie need to plan on coming with me Saturday night. Grandma will just be getting back that day, and I am sure she will want to visit Luca. I don't want you two here alone."

Emma agreed readily. She'd done a lot of thinking while they waited for Luca's surgery to be over. There had to be a reason why Marty was trying to frame her dad for these fires. There had to be a reason Marty had searched their dad's office. She'd watched enough NCIS, her favorite show about the Naval Criminal Investigative Service, to know that the bad guy would try to make himself appear absolutely good and innocent, all while absolutely blaming someone else for his crimes. And in this case, Marty was blaming his best friend and more importantly Emma's dad.

It would work out perfectly to go to her mom's concert. While her mom was involved in the performance, she could take Izzie and slip out of the concert hall, walk to their dad's office, and have a look around, maybe find some evidence of

Marty's lies. Izzie used to go to the office with their dad quite often. She would know the security code, and with any luck, it had not been changed. They could be back before their mom took her last bow.

Laura spent the following days at the hospital with Luca. The boy was wracked with pain but refused to be what he called "over-medicated." He had heard of athletes who were injured and then became addicted to pain pills. The two of them practiced meditation and relaxation techniques, listened to peaceful music on Pandora, and heard the doctor and nurses tell Luca over and over not to let the pain get ahead of him. In between medications, sometimes all they could do was pray. And miraculously, the Lord sent peace and Luca slept until time for the next dose.

"Mom," he said one day. "I think someone hit me on my bike."

"Why do you say that son," Laura asked.

"Because I remember hearing an engine rev just before something hit my back tire. I remember starting to fly over my handlebars, but that's it."

"We should tell Sam," Laura said as she immediately retrieved her phone to dial him. It was terrible to think someone would have purposely hit Luca and just left him injured and alone. But the medical bills were going to be astounding, and if the police could find the bike and find who hit Luca, perhaps there would be some insurance to help. The police in their area were notoriously lackadaisical, but perhaps Sam could get them more interested in finding out what happened. Luca couldn't have just flown off his bike without an outside influence propelling him over his handlebars, down that bank, and almost into the lake.

"Laura." Sam answered on the first ring. "What's up?"

She related what Luca had told her and was asked to hand the phone to the injured boy. At Sam's insistence, Luca related word for word what he had told his mother and then for several minutes after answered Sam's questions before handing the phone back to Laura.

"I have already assigned an agent to find the bike. I was beginning to suspect Marty had something to do with it." It was the first time he had divulged his suspicions. "You and the girls stay safe. Be aware."

Emma and Izzie were doing an outstanding job of caring for themselves and each other while her mother was away. On time for the bus to school every day. Homework completed. Even the house was neatly kept. How was she blessed with such amazing children?

Laura managed to find an hour or two in the early morning or late evening to rehearse for Saturday's concert. It was a piece she had performed many times with various symphony orchestras. It wasn't the most difficult of concertos, but this A Minor Piano Concerto was certainly one of the more beautiful pieces written by Schumann.

It was about an hour's drive to the concert hall, and Laura liked to be at least an hour early. Some key performers would show up at the last minute and have everyone involved in a dither, wondering and waiting. But Laura liked to be early and allow plenty of time to visit with Dorothy as she applied her makeup. It wasn't really a two-way conversation, as Dorothy insisted Laura remain completely still, but Dorothy entertained her with lively stories of performers and movie stars she had assisted in the past. Typically, the drive was a time to relax and mentally prepare for the performance. But tonight, all she could think of was her wounded son in pain both physical and emotionally. His long-awaited senior baseball season had been brought to an abrupt and painful end.

This time, with her children there, Laura caught Emma's reflection in the mirror as the girl sat on a stool with a pensive expression. She wondered what Emma was thinking. Emma had always been mature and responsible, but now she had a beauty beyond her years.

Izzie, on the other hand, sat totally enrapt with Dorothy's abundant supply of makeup and application techniques. One day Laura would ask Dorothy to give Izzie some lessons in subtle makeup. Her current black lipstick, that always had to be removed before Izzie left home, and black eyeliner, that also had to be removed, would not do in the long term. For now, just the black nail polish was all Laura allowed. And maybe one day, when Anthony returned, Izzie's penchant for black would go away altogether.

Laura was given a ten-minute warning until she had to be on stage, so she asked the girls to go find their seats. Emma grabbed Izzie by the hand. Blowing their mother good luck kisses, they scurried out the door, down the hallway, behind the main curtain, and through the double doors leading to the hallway. Since their attending the concert was somewhat last minute, they were seated back far enough that the spotlight would prevent their mother from seeing them from the stage if she happened to look for them. They were also slightly behind her.

Perfect seating, Emma thought.

Dressed in appropriate concert attire, the girls blended in with the concertgoers. Emma had worn her high school symphony, full-length, black satin dress with black ballet slippers. Izzie, who shunned dresses whenever possible, wore the flowing pantsuit Emma had worn to play the cello in junior high. Some of the female high school symphony members chose to wear tuxedos versus dresses for various reasons. Emma genuinely accepted her classmates for whoever they wanted to be, as did Izzie. Their parents had taught them to be open minded and remember that each child was one of Heavenly Father's precious children, no matter their gender, ethnicity, or beliefs. As a result, the Di Angelo children were well liked and respected among their peers.

Laura came on stage, bowed slightly to the audience, and looked their way. They knew she would do that before the performance began, but never during. It was like she was in another world once the conductor raised his baton, and the orchestra began.

"Ready?" Emma squeezed her sister's hand. "You remember the plan?"

"Of course, I do," Izzie whispered back.

The music began, and Emma clutched her sister's hand. "Let's go."

The exit doors were directly to their left and they slipped from their seats quietly, catching them so they didn't make a sound when they snapped back into their folded position.

Outside, the girls walked at a near run around the curve of Columbus Circle and exited onto Broadway. It was a bold and bright area with all the sparkling lights, but seemed to dim as they neared Central Park. Izzie shivered. "I'm a bit scared, Emma. Mom will be so upset if she knows how close we came to the park."

"We'll be fine," Emma reassured, although apprehension was creeping up her spine as the glow from the Lincoln Center lights grew farther away. The inside of the little bakery, the deli, and the vegetables, fruits, and snacks in the corner bodega were illuminated only by the green glow of security lights. A guitarist was crooning ballads on the patio of the Starbucks as people working late and students studying and sipping coffees were taking advantage of the free internet. Skyscrapers loomed overhead. A hodgepodge of night goers wearing everything from designer clothes to black, drab, or dirty homeless rags mingled on filthy sidewalks, ignoring each other's presence as they passed.

Not wishing to be seen both for safety and for their plan to break into the office, Emma and Izzie rounded the corner at 57th Street and slipped furtively down the alley to the back of their dad's office building located on the bottom floor of a ten-story brick building. A black dumpster blocked all but one parking space behind the office, illuminated by a single light above the steel door. Emma pulled down on the door handle, knowing it would be locked, but automatically giving it a try. "Do you remember the combination, Izzie?"

"Of course, I do," her sister responded, "unless the creep changed it."

"Izzie," Emma chastised and then smiled as the door clicked open. "You're the best, little sis."

They pulled the door open halfway and peeked in cautiously. "No one home," Izzie assured.

They slipped through the partially open door, pulled it shut behind them, and turned the bolt lock. Emma headed for Marty's desk, while Izzie checked out the secretary's desk. "Look at this." Izzie pointed at the name plate on the secretary's desk. "Marissa Salazar. Isn't that the name of the hotels that keep catching on fire?"

"Yes! And look at this." Emma held up an envelope. "It's a check stub from Salazar. The check was made out to Marty for the Salazar fire. A kickback!"

"Huh?" Izzie looked puzzled.

"Salazar Hotels have planned fires, not accidental fires. Medina hires Marty as the adjustor to determine how the fire started and the cost of the fire. Salazar pays Marty to say the fire was accidental and probably reports the loss bigger than it really was. It's called a kickback and it's completely illegal. Dad must have been caught in the mess when he went to Mexico for Marty."

"Sounds complicated. How do you know all that?"

"I worked for Dad last summer in the office. I listen."

Emma stood with the check in her hand as the lock on the back door screeched. She slipped the check into the front of her dress, tucking it into her bra as she'd seen her mom secure various items from time to time. The girls ducked behind Marty's desk, hands clutched, staring wide-eyed at each other. Determined footsteps strode toward their hiding place.

Marty stood over them with a handgun pointed in their direction. "Think you're pretty smart, sneaking in here. Times have changed. You triggered a silent alarm. Cameras caught you in the act." He waved the gun toward cameras mounted above the doors and in the corners of the office. He grabbed Izzie by the hair and dragged her out from behind the desk.

"Don't you touch my sister," Emma screamed at him.

"What's that you are trying to hide in your inadequate cleavage?" Again, he waved the gun toward her.

"You're drunk." Emma stood her ground, the aroma of alcohol spewing from Marty's distorted face.

Dropping his hold on Izzie's hair, he took a step toward Emma, grabbed her arm, and twisted her around until her back was pressed against his chest. His hand holding the gun was jammed so tightly into her neck she could barely breath. She struggled and the gun released the pressure on her throat. "Maybe I'll just shoot your little sister and save you for last." He waved the gun toward Izzie. "Cameras are off now. No one will know."

At Izzie's screams, Emma stomped hard on Marty's foot, whirled, and caught him in the neck with her forearm. Her knee came up and hit him hard where a boy never wants to be hit, and then the heel of her hand met his nose. He grabbed his groin and then his nose, the gun flying out of his hand. He staggered backwards, fell, and hit his head on the corner of his desk and fell silent.

Emma gasped. *Had she killed him?* He moved and groaned. *Apparently, he was still a threat.* She grabbed Izzie by the hand. "Come on."

They burst through the back door and were met by NYPD, guns drawn. Both girls threw their hands in the air. "We can explain," they said in unison.

"Better be good," one officer commented, jerking his head toward the door. "Check inside."

Marty's dark blue sedan was parked next to the dumpster. "Look," Izzie pointed to the car.

"Hands up," the officer commanded. "No talking."

Emma looked toward the car, its right front bumper scraped and dented, the turn signal light cracked from top to bottom. She nodded to let her sister know she understood.

The second officer returned holding Marty by the arm. "Guy's out of it. It's his office, but he has no idea what's going on."

"Awright. You take him to the hospital, and I'll take these two hooligans downtown."

The officer led Emma and Izzie to his patrol car and opened the back door. Izzie slid in first followed by Emma, who suppressed a giggle as her sister whispered, "at least we're not cuffed." The station was less than five minutes from the scene of their crime and soon they were sitting in banged-up wooden chairs against a wall, assuming they would soon be interrogated.

"Excuse me, Officer." Emma motioned to the arresting officer who stood across from them, arms crossed, a glare scrunching his brow.

"What is it now?"

"We do get one phone call, don't we?"

"You've been watching too much TV," came the terse reply, although his lips quivered, keeping a smile at bay.

"Could we make that phone call?"

"Awright. Who do you want to call? Your mommy?"

"She's performing at the Lincoln Center. We'd like to call Sam Brady. He's from the FBI, working on our father's case."

The officer smirked. "FBI?"

An officer manning a busy desk looked up in their direction. "Sam Brady? FBI? Fat chance he'll help you little troublemakers. I'll put in the call myself." He picked up the phone and punched in some numbers from memory.

Chapter 20

Only the dancing flames from the fireplace and a mini handheld flashlight illuminated the room. Mahogany paneling surrounded the slate-gray, floor to ceiling, stone fireplace. It boasted a mahogany mantel dotted with family pictures, seemingly floating in place. Mavis had detested this room that Sam loved, but it had always been his haven away from the daily tragedies that demanded his attention to find lost loved ones, stop the ever-flowing influx of drugs into New York City, or out-maneuver masterminds of theft and fraud. Even though Mavis and her complaints were gone now, Sam was still racked with guilt for reverencing his sanctuary, or man-cave, as men called such a place nowadays.

Mavis had been so unhappy that she used more and more prescription pills of every kind, shape, and color to temporarily chase away the gloom. But the dissatisfaction of their life committed to the FBI always lurked beneath the surface, ready to bring her into the depths of despair again and again. And then one day, the pills were followed by Vodka, and the toxic result took her life while Sam was away trying to save other peoples' lives.

Sam closed the softcover blue book he had been reading, switched off the flashlight, and placed his glasses on his knee, leaning his head back against the high-back leather chair. He liked the darkness of the room. Maybe he was accustomed to dim light from years of stakeouts, reading with just a tiny flashlight so as not to give away his presence.

He leaned toward the lamp table and pulled open the tiny drawer in front. He took out the black velvet case and held it in his palm. He hoped he had chosen well, that Estelle would like the ring. With two fingers he rocked the lid back on its tiny hinges revealing a large ruby set in rose gold with smaller square-shaped rubies branching out on either side. He didn't know the actual gemstone terms, but whatever the square cut stone was called, it looked very nice on the ring surrounded by tiny diamonds. More little diamonds, but not too little, cascaded along the band on either side.

One of these days he would get the courage to ask Estelle to spend the rest of their days together.

Earlier in the evening he had picked up Estelle from the airport while Laura was preparing for her concert and dropped her at the hospital to be with Luca. Just having her next to him in the car was such a delightful, calming feeling. He never wanted time with her to end.

He didn't belong to her religion. He didn't know if ever would. But he would be good to her, just as the meaning of a ruby suggested: passion, protection, wealth. Passion would be no problem. Even as two youngsters over sixty they could ignite a passion that took all of Sam's strength to conquer. He knew the direction Estelle's moral compass pointed, and he respected her immensely for her convictions.

Protection. He would protect her and her family with his life if necessary. He had the knowledge and tools to keep evil at bay.

Wealth. Estelle would never struggle again, as she had nearly her entire adult life. She could pull up Amazon and click on anything she wanted and not just needed, but actually just wanted.

Sam sighed. His grandson had given him the book resting on his lap just before he left on a mission to Mexico for his family's church and asked Sam to read it, even pray about what he read. He was finally giving the book a chance. "Book of Mormon." A book from the church his daughter joined after she met a man at college who Sam had to admit was a truly good person. Honest, kind, hard-working. Even at twenty-one, his head had been on straight and his priorities in order.

Estelle's church, his daughter's church, and the Di Angelo's church. Good people.

Mavis had not taken kindly to this "Mormon," nor to Meghan's choice to join her fiancé's church. She refused to help her daughter at all with the wedding preparations. But Meg had always craved simplicity, and a society wedding was not something she wanted anyway. Sam had stood alone waiting for Meghan and Stuart to come, literally glowing, through the doors of the Washington D.C. Temple now over twenty years ago. He had never seen anyone so angelic, so completely beautiful as his Meghan. They were raising their children in this church that they loved, and his oldest grandchild was in Mexico where drug lords reigned. He was teaching others about the Lord he worshipped as he said so often in weekly e-mails to Sam.

Lost in his thoughts, Sam jumped when his phone vibrated. He pulled it out of the space between the seat cushion and the chair where it had slipped.

"Hello?" His voice was gravelly after hours of silence.

"Sam!" It was a frantic Laura.

"Sam! I'm at Lincoln Center. The girls were with me at my concert and now I can't find them, and they aren't answering their phones."

His phone beeped. He turned the screen toward him. NYPD. "Just a second, Laura. I'll be right with you."

"Brady?" said the voice on the other line.

"Yes."

"This is Sergeant Templeton, NYPD."

"Of course. 20th Precinct if I remember right. How are you?"

"Well, I have a couple of kids here, girls, who said they know you and have requested to talk to you for their one phone call. Ha ha. Probably little crime show junkies. Anyway, do you want to talk to them before we lock 'em up?"

"Hang on a minute. I'll be right back."

He tapped the phone to switch back to Laura. "I think I've found them, Laura. They are at the NYPD precinct close to the Lincoln Center. I'm going to run down there right now and see what's going on."

"Oh, thank goodness. I'll meet you at the Precinct. I can't imagine what they've been up to."

"Wait for me. I'll pick you up in front of Lincoln Center. I can double-park at the station if I have to. You won't be able to find a place, and it's not safe to be wandering around out there. I'll be there in less than five minutes."

"Okay. Okay." Laura sighed. It was nearly impossible to focus her thoughts. She had been so frightened, then relieved, then totally confused about why her daughters had left the concert and caused enough trouble to be held at the police station. She kept her cell phone and high heels in hand and ran down two interior flights of stairs in the concert hall and out the main doors. Crossing the drive circling a central fountain, she sat on the black marble surrounding the fountain. Once there, she slipped on her shoes and sent a text to Sam with her location.

Sam tucked his phone in his front pants pocket, grabbed his keys and wallet from the hall table, and lifted his FBI jacket from the coat tree by the door. Another thing Mavis had hated. Coat trees. All coats belonged in the coat closet, according to her. But sometimes he had to leave so quickly in the dark of night that having his jacket at the ready saved precious seconds he might have spent searching in the coat closet. Still, no matter where he hung his jacket, it was always moved to be color-coded with other coats in the closet, organized neatly side by side.

Slipping the jacket on, Sam took long, quick strides to the garage where his car was housed. He clicked the button on the key fob to unlock the driver's door and slid into the driver's seat of the black Lexus. He closed and locked the door before clicking the remote clipped to his visor to open the garage door. He had his methods and his protocols for safety to limit the amount of time he could be vulnerable to someone wishing to exact vengeance for past convictions or to try to inflict intimidation into current case procedures.

Sam and Mavis had purchased their home in the Lincoln Square area nearly forty years ago for pennies compared to the cost of homes now, even townhomes and apartments. He felt fortunate and that is why he never left, choosing to serve the FBI in this crazy city nearly his entire career. Passing up promotions to Mavis' angst, he stayed. Stayed where he had a home, where he knew the streets and those who ran the crime scene from back alleys and opulent high rises. He backed out of the garage, instinctively pressing the remote to bring the door down and secure his home. Turning on to 70th, he headed for Broadway and within minutes was turning into the Lincoln Center Plaza and to where Laura was pacing back and forth by the fountain.

Sam reached across the seat with his long arm and opened the passenger door. It was safer to offer his gentlemanly assistance in this way rather than hop out, circle the car, leave it running, or turn it off and lock it and then unlock it when he got to the passenger side. He was constantly analyzing and weighing risks. Would he still be this cautious when he retired? Would the risks then disappear?

Laura automatically reached for the seatbelt as Sam turned toward Columbus Avenue. "How far, how long?" she asked.

After a long drawn out "Well," Sam answered. "Columbus to 82nd, about twenty blocks. Hopefully not twenty slow blocks. Traffic is lighter at this time of night after the shows and concerts end."

"I do appreciate you, Sam. Rescuing us again. I am sorry to be impatient. It's just…"

"I know. We'll get to the bottom of this soon."

Laura closed her eyes in silent prayer, not sure what to ask for, just knowing that she and the girls needed help. It was as if the traffic lights were blessed in their favor and Sam soon turned the black, unmarked vehicle onto tree-lined 82nd Street in front of the three-story precinct building. Laura's heart began its anxious pounding again. All of the parking spaces were filled with apartment resident vehicles parallel parked on one side and police vehicles backed straight in against the curb on the other. The street was so narrow. It was all Laura could do to remain seated and not jump from the car and run into the police station by herself.

"Ah, ha," Sam said as a police car pulled away from its coveted spot and Sam pulled forward quickly and then backed in to replace it.

Laura reached for her door.

"Wait." Sam reached out to instruct her to stay in the car. In this case, he would come around and open her door. He didn't want her standing out there alone while he hauled himself out of his seat. He used to bound from the vehicles. Not any more though. It was more of a slow roll, laboriously unfolding his large frame that used to put every agent in the area to shame in the physical fitness tests. Mounds of paperwork had kept him at his desk more often and slowed him down.

Sam flashed his badge at the glass doorways and a buzz indicated the doors were unlocked. The public had to wait for someone to buzz them in. He held the door for Laura and then went into the lobby area lined with display cases containing pictures of New York's finest heroes.

He guided Laura to the left where Sergeant Templeton rose smiling and came out from behind a large wooden desk with two large computer monitors, a desk phone, a smattering of coffee cups, and half-eaten fast food. The corkboard behind his desk was covered with children's drawings and pictures of school children gathered around the officer. This glimpse into the officer's life brought a sense of ease to Laura's trembling emotions.

The Sergeant guided Sam and Laura to a glass-walled conference room where Emma and Izzie sat at a large table, hands folded in front of them and resting on the table.

"We need to talk," Izzie spoke up at once.

"Hang on a minute, young lady," Sam held up his hand.

"Good luck," the Sergeant chuckled as he walked out and shut the door.

Meanwhile, Laura circled the table and threw her arms around the girls, pulling them close. "I was so worried." She moved Izzie to the right and pulled up a chair between them.

"Sorry, Mom," they replied in unison, "but…"

"No buts," Sam responded. "Let's have it from the beginning."

"You go, Emma," Izzie said. "I am too excited. Tell him about the dent!"

"Dent?" Sam responded. "Wait, from the beginning.

Emma related the events of the evening, giving Sam the check she had saved, and ending with Izzie noticing the dent on Marty's front right bumper.

Sam pulled out his cell phone and tapped in a number. "Curtis." He rattled off the address of the insurance agency. "I think we have some leads on the Di Angelo hit and run case, but I need you to follow up right now. There should be a car parked behind the building with some right front damage. Take a picture of the damage, and then have the car hauled into our shop. Get a search warrant from the office."

"Probable cause?" the agent shot back.

"Attempted murder, insurance fraud, arson. This guy's crimes may run the gamut. Marty Longston, part-owner of the agency, was involved in an altercation there tonight. NYPD took him to the hospital. I am assuming NYC since it is the closest to his office but check on that. Put an agent on him. Watch him. We can't let him back in his office. I'll have NYPD watch him until you can get an agent there."

"Right boss," Curtis responded. "I'm on it."

Sam turned to Emma and Izzie. "Good job, girls," he said and then more sternly, "but don't ever do anything like that again! If you have concerns, call me, text me."

"Yes, sir!" they replied in unison.

"Now can we go tell Luca we know who ran him over?" Izzie asked excitedly.

Sam let out a deep sigh and slapped his forehead. "How do you manage, Laura? I'll be right back. I need to get the police to help us out for a bit. Sit tight." He pointed at Izzie and then Emma.

Sam left the room to talk to Sergeant Templeton. When he came back, there was a concerned look on his face. He pulled out a chair, maintaining eye contact with Laura, and let out a long breath.

"A bit of an issue," he said. "For some reason Longston has been released from the hospital. Not a good thing. Not good at all." Laura's audible gasp broke through the tension in the room.

"Could I get your car keys, Laura?" Sam reached across the desk, palm up.

"My keys?" she questioned, as she reached into her purse for her keys and placed them in Sam's palm.

"I'll drive you and the girls home. I have agents on the way here to get your keys, take your car home, and watch your house until I get there. Longston has proven that he's not to be trusted.

"Oh my." Laura looked down at her hands. "It's a Toyota Camry, black, parked in the reserved parking by the elevators under Lincoln Center. Thank you, Sam. Oh, my goodness. I'm shaking." She held her quivering hands before her on the table.

"Don't worry, Mom," the girls spoke in unison. "We gotcha. We can handle old Marty," Emma said.

"To think what could have happened to you," Laura shuddered. She put an arm around each daughter and pulled them to her. "Do not try that again!"

*****

Sam had been in contact with Estelle several times during the evening after he left her at the hospital with Luca. He couldn't go long without connecting with this woman he had grown to love so much. He dialed the agent again. "Send a couple of agents over to White Plains Hospital. Longston may know that is where Luca is recovering. His grandmother is there with him. Don't let her leave. We'll be by to pick her up."

"Got it boss. Will do."

Sam stood and slapped his meaty hands on the table. "Well then, let's be off."

With everyone secure in their seatbelts, Sam pulled forward into the street. He circled the block and went in the opposite direction of home.

"Uh, Sam," Izzie spoke up. "Home is the other way. You aren't taking us down some dark alley or to a junkyard to kill us, are you?"

"Too many crime shows, my dear. Too many crime shows. I'm just trying to make sure we aren't being followed."

Traffic hampered their drive to White Plains. Not knowing if Marty had already made his way to their home, or even if he would, was nerve wracking. Seated in the front passenger seat Laura tried to ease her mind, giving way to realism and faith instead of total panic. Marty had already broken into their home once. He had tried to silence her son by running over him with his car. He had threatened Emma and Izzie. All appearances pointed to his desperation, and she wondered what he would do next.

Sam's radio crackled. "We are outside boss. No sign of Longston yet."

"Make yourselves invisible, although in his state, he will probably focus on the house and not notice your vehicle. We are just pulling up to the hospital to pick up the grandmother now."

"Will do. We will await your signal and then take the guy down."

"Good work. Thank you."

With Luca safely in the care of two agents, Estelle waited in the lobby and hurried out, opening the back passenger door, and squeezing in with the girls. Sam immediately let his foot off the brake, and they completed the turn along the semi-circular patient drop-off drive.

"Oh, Mom, you should sit up here," Laura, protested.

"I am just fine back here, honey. Got to keep an eye on these two," she joked, motioning to Emma and Izzie.

Sam reached over and gave Laura's tightly gripped hands a squeeze as they turned down the road where Luca had been hit on his bike. He said nothing, but she felt his strength. He was an expert in this sort of thing. She closed her eyes and prayed for faith and for strength to allow Sam to lead them through this crisis safely.

Sam noticed the agents' vehicle right away, even though it was well-obscured and down the street several yards among the willow trees lining the road. Laura's car was parked in the driveway where the agents had left it. He would leave it there, too, as a trap to lure Marty to take some action so they could apprehend him. What a guy. What a totally rotten, deceitful business partner. Sam had never met Anthony but given the caliber and character of Anthony's wife and children, and based on interviews with people who knew him, he knew he was an upstanding guy caught in a terrible scheme by the partner he trusted. Or did Anthony trust Marty? It was apparent from the documents he left for Laura that he had some inkling that all was not well with Marty.

Sam turned to the girls in the back seat. "Now girls, when I say go, I want you out of the car and in the house as fast as you can scamper. Do either of you have a key to the house? I am assuming, Laura, that your key was with your car keys."

"I do," Izzie responded. "Well sort of. I kept misplacing mine, so I have one hidden."

Laura and Emma rolled their eyes. Izzie's irresponsible but resourceful plan broke the tension momentarily, and they all smiled and chuckled.

"Go get 'em, Izzie," Sam encouraged. "You two follow closely and I'll bring up the rear."

Marty could be anywhere. He was a criminal in his business dealings and had become stupidly bold, and from all appearances he was frantic to cover something up. He had to know the police would be after him. But Sam was sure Marty didn't count on FBI involvement.

Izzie hopped out of the car, scurried up the sidewalk, untangled a ceramic frog from the center of a flower container by the door, and lifted the key from where it was taped to the bottom of the frog.

"Ribbit, ribbit," Emma croaked. "Good job, Sis."

Izzie slipped the key in the lock and swung open the door. Sam brushed the girls and Laura aside and began going from room to room looking behind the furniture and going through rooms one by one. After surveying the lower level and making sure all the doors and windows were locked, he holstered his gun.

Estelle put her handbag and jacket on a chair and began preparing a plate of chocolate chip cookies, baked and wrapped tightly in plastic wrap before she left for Arizona a few days previously. She shivered, not so much from the cold—but from nerves and relief that Sam was there now, and her family was safe. A teapot was filled and shortly began whistling. As Estelle reached for the can of hot chocolate powder, a loud rapping on the door jolted them from silence. No one was ready to discuss the evening's events other than Izzie, who probably did not realize the gravity of the situation.

"Sit still, ladies," Sam motioned with one hand, the other opening his jacket to where his firearm was at the ready. He crossed to the door and, standing slightly to the side, he turned the bolt lock to the open position. He knew his agents would be heading for the house to back him up. Yanking open the door, he confronted Marty who immediately tried to push his way past. Within seconds, there was a loud crash as Marty hit the floor flat on his face. He had been holding a weapon, which flew along the hardwood floor and out of his hand.

"Round Two," Izzie remarked, and poked Emma in the ribs.

Sam grabbed Marty's arms and pulled them up behind the perpetrator's back and secured them with a pair of cuffs he drew from his jacket pocket. With a big foot in the middle of Marty's back, he jerked up on the bound arms until Marty cried out. "This should teach you not to ever mess with my family again."

"Your family?" Marty moaned. "I knew Laura couldn't be loyal to Anthony for very long, but aren't you a little old for her?

"I am marrying Estelle, you idiot." Sam spat out.

"You are?" Estelle responded in surprise. She loved Sam with all her heart, more than any man she had ever known, but somehow, she didn't expect someone to love her back enough to want to marry her in return. Her dating years after her divorce had been stellar examples of continual, unrequited love.

Just then the two agents waiting outside came through the door, still wide open with Marty lying on the floor, half in and half out. The lead agent whistled. "What we got here?"

"Marty Longston? All yours?"

"Are you getting married, Boss?" the other agent asked, a smile twisting on his rugged face.

"Guess I'd better ask Estelle if she'll have me?" Sam responded.

"Of course, I will," Estelle put down the teapot and came toward Sam. He put his arms around her and pulled her close. "I had meant to make this romantic. I have a ring," he pled. "But this jerk," he pointed his boot in Longston's direction. "Can I blame him for messing it up?"

"Oh, I think we can blame Marty for a whole lot of things, but not this," Laura said. She hugged her mom and Sam, and the girls joined them. "We are so happy to be your family, Sam."

Chapter 21

Laura's heart fluctuated between happy and heavy. Happy over her mother finally finding love after over twenty years alone, Sam had given Estelle a stunning ring, and his adoration for the sweet woman was hardly concealed. But a heaviness enveloped Laura, body and soul. Could Anthony not just be missing but dead? Did Marty try to hide the arson and insurance fraud by eliminating his friend and business partner? Was money so much more important to him than Anthony?

Sam felt that Marty's desperation and the knowledge that Salazar had murdered the thugs he hired to keep Anthony away from the hotel fire indicated that Anthony was alive. The thugs probably wouldn't have been killed if they had provided proof of Anthony's death. Anthony, wherever he was, remained a witness to the arson, the fraud, and Salazar's ordered assault to hide his criminal deeds.

Laura made her way down the sloping aisle to the stage of the auditorium where one of her students was performing. A gentleman in a suit stood by watching the student perform, a broad smile on his face.

The girl immediately stood and came to the edge of the stage. "Mrs. Di Angelo, this is my father, Clay Holden, the sociology professor I told you about."

"Oh yes," Laura stretched forth her hand. "I am so pleased to meet you. Tara is an outstanding student. We are so fortunate to have her here at Julliard."

"We are the fortunate ones," Clay replied. "Tara speaks very highly of you. I was sorry to hear about your husband and am hoping he soon returns home to you."

"Thank you. Tara has told me much about your work in sociology and I was hoping it would not be presumptuous of me to ask you a few questions."

"Of course not," Clay replied. "I don't know how much help I can be, but I would certainly be willing to help in any way I can."

"Thank you so very much. Um, do you have dinner plans tonight? Perhaps you and Tara would like to come to dinner at my home. My son was in an accident a few weeks ago, and I am sure that Tara's company would surely brighten his day."

"Of course," Clay replied. "We'd like that very much."

"Would you like to ride home with me after classes, and then I can take you to the train station after dinner?"

Both Tara and Clay replied positively. With a wave, Laura turned back up the aisle.

Once Laura left the auditorium, Clay turned to Tara. "You are not trying to set me up with Mrs. Di Angelo are you dear?"

"No, Dad! It's quite obvious that she is just waiting for her husband's return. And it's pretty obvious that you are more than fond of this 'Jenny' whose name leaves your lips about every other sentence."

"That obvious, huh?"

"Yup. Very much so."

Tara and her father met Laura outside her office at four o'clock. Laura had called Estelle to let her know about the dinner guests and had texted Luca telling him to spiff up because she was bringing Tara home.

Tara was a very young first-year student at Julliard, having graduated from high school after her junior year. After a year at Northern Arizona University, she had been accepted in the Piano Performance Program at Julliard and was eager to get on with her professional life as a musician. She had a delightful, happy personality and would hopefully coax Luca out of his doldrums. He was missing his last year of baseball, and the injury indicated he would also not be playing college baseball. Laura felt compelled to help her son find a new passion. At one time, he had loved music almost more than baseball. Maybe Tara could encourage him to re-engage with his keyboarding skills.

"Emma!" Luca was calling from his bed the moment Emma came in the door after school. "Help! You gotta help me. Quick!"

Both Estelle and Emma ran to the door of Luca's room. "What's wrong?" they both questioned at once. "Are you hurt?"

"No. Mom's bringing a girl home. I need to get out of this bed and get spiffed up."

"Ooh," Emma's long, drawn out "oh" and a smile teasing her eyes indicated her understanding of her brother's dilemma. He hadn't wanted to leave his bed, comb his hair, or wear anything but pajamas since he came home from the hospital.

"Help me get up. I need to take a shower."

"Indeed, you do, but I can't help you with that!" Emma shuddered at the thought.

"I'll keep my shorts on. You can roll me in, and I'll hang my leg out."

"I'll get a garbage bag and some duct tape. We'd better cover up that cast just in case," Estelle offered from where she had been standing in the doorway watching the humorous pleadings of her grandson, who was suddenly yanked out of his doldrums by the thought of a pretty girl seeing him in his sorry state. His mom had mentioned Tara often to the family, and said her student was not only an outstanding pianist, but a diligent musician who was kind, humble, and had very teachable qualities not always found in Laura's students over the years.

"Pick me some cool clothes, okay Emma? Something really dope!"

"Of course, but you will have to wear some workout pants with a zipper in the leg. No worries. I'll have you looking presentable. First, let's get you out of bed." She came to the side of the bed. "Arms up." She pulled his shirt over his head and threw it across the room into the clothes hamper. "Lay back. Let me get those week-old pajama pants off you. Hang on to your shorts. I don't want to see anything I haven't seen since we were toddlers in the bathtub!"

Luca willingly obliged, lifted his hips, and helped to slide the well-worn pajama pants over his cast. Emma held her nose with one hand and the waist of the pants with two fingers and dramatically tossed them into the hamper.

Emma brought Luca's wheelchair close to the bed and locked the wheels. "Okay, big boy, up and at 'em," she coaxed.

Luca's well-developed arms and core strength served him well when he was hampered by the thigh-high cast on his right leg. Estelle arrived with a thick black garbage bag used for leaves and some duct tape. They went about the ceremony of encasing Luca's cast with the hope it would remain waterproof. The expense of another cast and possible injury to his leg was just not a risk worth taking.

"All this, Luca, for a girl, and you don't even know her."

"But she is beautiful. I just know. Mom loves her. That must mean something." Luca disengaged the brakes and wheeled himself to the bathroom off his bedroom. He sat staring at the shower. "Now what?"

"Ugh," Emma responded. "Didn't think about getting the wheelchair in there. Just a minute," and she ran out the door, soon returning with a plastic patio chair which she placed in the shower. She grabbed Luca's crutches from the side of his bed, backed his wheelchair up a bit, and set the brakes again.

"Mmh," Luca looked up at her, relieved. "Good idea."

Emma sensed his vulnerability. He was used to being mobile and strong. These were new mountains he was climbing. She patted him on his back. "You got this. And I'm sure it will be worth it."

She started the water to warm it up and left it running from the faucet. She made certain Luca was settled in his chair and that soap and shampoo were within reach. Luca could turn on the shower when he was ready.

"I'll put a towel and some clean shorts here on the toilet seat. Dry the best you can and get those shorts on before you call me!" *Boys,* she thought with exasperation. Little to no modesty, perhaps because they ran around the locker rooms in front of each other, which is something most girls shied away from.

Emma and Estelle set about tidying Luca's room. "Might as well change the sheets while His Sweatiness is absent," Estelle remarked. Emma looked at the sheets in Luca's closet, passing over the ones with baseballs, which would surely make him sad at what he was missing. She picked some dark blue plaid flannel sheets which would not be a reminder of anything.

Luca seemed to be taking his longest shower ever and they hoped he wasn't soaking his cast. "You okay in there?" Emma called out, to which Luca finally turned off the shower.

"Yup. Kept my leg out the door, so the floor may be a bit wet."

"Don't slip."

"I won't," and then he screamed.

"Luca?" The panic was evident in Emma's voice and Estelle jumped from where she was sitting on the bed.

"Just kidding!"

"You brat. When you are better, I will get you for this. You scared me!"

Within a few minutes Luca called for Emma. He was out of breath from just drying and preserving his modesty with the shorts Emma had left for him. The floor was more than a little wet from the discarded garbage bag and Luca's attempts to get dry. Emma dried his back before mopping the floor up with his towel.

"I'm exhausted," he said, as he twisted on his crutches to drop into the wheelchair.

"I'll bet you are." Emma wanted to make a comment about his lolling about in bed so much but decided to err on sympathy. She wheeled him to his bed, set the brake, and waited as he hoisted his body onto the bed and lay back on his pillow. She tugged some black workout pants with zippers in each leg over his cast and he raised his hips and pulled them in place. She had chosen a navy-blue golf shirt and then put some thick socks on his feet.

"Best sister ever," he said ruffling her hair.

"Speaking of hair," she said, as she smoothed her hair back in place, "I'll get a mirror and your comb, and you can do something with that mop of yours."

"Bring some aftershave, too?"

"Wanting to impress someone?"

Luca turned his head away from her and toward the window.

"Aw, come on. Don't worry. Even with a broken leg you're still a total stud."

"Ya think so? Do these sleeves accentuate my muscles?" He flexed and grinned sheepishly.

"I know so. And yes, that is why I picked that shirt."

"Thanks, Emma. For a sister, you are the best, you know."

Emma wrinkled her nose and flipped a finger on the side of his head.

In fifteen minutes, Luca called from his room. He asked Emma to wheel him to one of the wingback chairs in the living room and then "disappear" the wheelchair. He sat upright in the sitting chair, his injured right leg resting on the heel of his cast.

"You're not supposed to sit with your leg down," Emma chided.

"I don't want to look like I'm weak," Luca hung his head.

"Come on, with those biceps bulging out of your sleeves and those pecs stretching the front of your shirt, that's all she'll see."

"You sure?"

"Double-sure. Besides, you've got Dad's good looks. What more can a girl want?"

Luca slugged Emma playfully in the arm. "Thanks, sis."

Watching the whole scene play out, Estelle couldn't help but smile. As much as these kids had suffered with their dad missing—and now Luca's accident—they still were kind and patient with each other. Anthony and Laura had raised them well. She went to her room and retrieved a small stool with a cross-stitched cushion that she called her prayer stool so she wouldn't have to kneel all the way to the floor. She placed the stool in front of Luca, and gently raised his injured leg to rest on the stool. Patting him on the knee, she mentally poured all her love in the boy who was so worried about how he would appear to the young woman his mother was bringing home.

Shortly thereafter, Izzie burst through the door, dropped her backpack, and sent her shoes flying. She spotted Luca in the armchair and let out a whistle. "Whoa. Who is this new man in our house? Lookin' good, big bro."

"Pick up your stuff, Izzie," Emma reminded. "Mom is bringing some guests home for dinner."

"Aw. That's why the invalid is all gussied up," Izzie teased, and grabbed her discarded bag and shoes and headed for the room she shared with Estelle.

"How do you manage, Grandma," Emma asked, "to share a room with that little disaster?"

"We do just fine. If she keeps her room picked up, I have cookies and milk ready when she gets home." Estelle's hand swept to the plate of cookies and chocolate milk on the counter.

"You are a good sport, Grandma," Emma replied as the door opened to Laura and her guests entering.

A distinguished looking man of about her father's age and a pretty blond girl followed her mother into the room. Laura first introduced them to Estelle and Emma, and then crossed the room to Luca. The man, who Laura introduced as Clay Holden and a professor of Sociology, put out his hand to Luca, who tried to raise from his seat on one leg.

"Sit, sit," he said as Luca tried to stand, while Tara also drew near and extended her hand.

Luca responded with a "nice to meet you" to both, although he couldn't take his eyes off Tara—who smiled warmly and didn't seem at all taken aback by his inability to move from the chair. "Guess that cast is keeping you out of any trouble," Clay said.

Luca nodded and laughed. The ice was broken, and the worry wrinkles disappeared from his brow.

Tara and Emma sat on the fireplace hearth near Luca's chair and began chatting amicably, with Tara mentioning that it looked like Luca had been working out. This brought a broad smile to his face as Emma regaled his baseball prowess.

Awaiting Sam's arrival, Laura and Clay joined Estelle in the kitchen while the youngsters bonded over shared stories about the lack of LDS youth either in the Di Angelo's area or at Julliard.

It wasn't long before the doorbell announced Sam's arrival and Izzie rushed to greet him. Sam's presence seemed to fill a void left by Anthony's absence and Izzie reveled in his attention.

"Izzie girl!" His outstretched arms enfolded her to his chest. "How was school? How are the guys?"

Izzie blushed and said his name emphatically. "You know I am not that into boys just yet."

"Won't be long," he responded. "Won't be long."

Laura introduced Sam as Estelle's fiancé as he entered the kitchen and pressed a kiss to Estelle's forehead while she moved in for a welcome hug.

Estelle signaled that dinner was ready and invited the family and guests to the table. Luca gave Emma a "what shall I do now" look, which Tara easily caught. Tara had always been in tune with the feelings of others and asked Luca if he would mind if she helped him out of the chair. Izzie ran for the crutches and with Tara's help, he moved slowly to the table. He had only used the crutches for a few steps before and sank relieved into a chair at the table. Tara took the crutches and leaned them against the wall and took a seat by Luca asking Estelle, "Okay if I sit here?"

"Of course, dear," Estelle responded.

Estelle had fixed a lovely dinner of baked croissants with a chicken and cream cheese filling, fresh green beans, a fruit salad, and lemon pie for dessert. This was one of the Di Angelo's favorite meals since their grandmother had come to care for the lonesome and struggling family.

Clay leaned back in his chair and patted his stomach. "Estelle, you are an excellent cook. That was absolutely delicious."

"Agreed," Sam said. "Isn't she amazing?"

Estelle blushed and squeezed Sam's hand. "Thank you. I do love having people to cook for."

"Kids," Laura said, "would you like to play some games here at the table while the rest of us retire to the study for a visit?"

"Yes," Izzie said. "Us young ones would be happy to stay here while you oldies go talk about boring things."

"Thank you, dear, for your permission to leave the table." Laura put a loving arm around her youngest daughter. "Mom? Clay? Sam? Shall we make ourselves scarce?"

"We'll clear the table, Mom," Emma said.

"I'll get some games that our gimpy brother can play," Izzie offered.

"I'm sure he will easily beat us all," Tara said, smiling in Luca's direction.

Once the door to the study was closed and the adults were comfortably seated in the leather chairs in what had been Anthony's office and study, Laura cleared her throat.

"Dr. Holden, I know in my heart, with my whole soul, that Anthony is alive. If he were gone, I am sure that somehow, I would feel his presence here with us, letting us know we could move on. I know that if he was alive and could get home to us, he would. There is something stopping him. Maybe he is injured. Could he have amnesia? Does he not remember us? And so, I am asking, based on your experience in sociology, is this possible?"

Sam entered the conversation. "May I interject before we continue? I haven't mentioned this before and I'd like you to keep this between us, but I think there is a very real possibility that Anthony is indeed alive. After interrogating Marty, we found that Salazar had hired some of his goons to rough Anthony up and dissuade him from investigating the fire. When they went back to the area where they had dumped him, his body wasn't there. Salazar shot them when the goons couldn't confirm with certainty that Anthony was dead. Marty continues to play innocent in the whole affair, but I think he is involved up to his neck and is scrambling to get free of Salazar and cover up anything that would lead us to uncovering his crimes.

Sam continued, "Salazar must have eliminated his guys because he thought there was a chance Anthony was alive and could identify them. But I don't want to create false hope. We have a team in Mexico investigating Salazar right now, but we have to tread carefully. The Federales and our counterparts in the FBI in Mexico get really upset if they think we are horning in on their territory."

Dr. Holden spoke next. "If he was injured, particularly a head injury, he could have what is called retrograde amnesia, meaning that he can't remember anything before the trauma. It is possible he has no idea who he is or where he came from. Retrograde amnesia usually involves memory loss of facts but a retention of skills and abilities. Anthony may be hiding from Salazar, perfectly able to take care of his needs, hold a job, and that sort of thing. He just won't remember his past or how he got where he is, but he may continue to make memories forward." Clay paused and then began again. "Did Anthony have any inklings about Salazar and why he may have wanted Anthony out of the picture?"

Sam and Laura both shared that Anthony had left notes indicating his suspicions that Marty had been involved in something illegal.

"What is the possibility his memory could return?" Laura asked.

"It depends on the severity of his injury. Hopefully if he was able to move from the site where they left him, he is recovering and gradually regaining his past. At any rate, when you are finally able to bring him home, there may be challenges. He will need a lot of love, and perhaps some in depth therapy."

The adults continued their discussion until Sam looked at his watch. "Goodness, Estelle. You are keeping me out late," he joked and put a loving arm around her shoulders.

"We should be going as well," Clay responded.

"Are you staying near Juilliard?" Sam asked. "I am going your way."

Clay stood and shook Sam's hand and then Estelle's. "Yes, I am. That would be great. Laura was going to take us to the train station, but I would rather not navigate that system with my beautiful daughter this late at night. It was such a pleasure to meet all of you."

Then taking Laura's hand in both of his he said, "We'll keep in touch. I want to help in any way I can when Anthony returns."

They found the young people laughing as they tried to get their teammate to guess a word on a card without saying any of the "taboo" words listed. Tara and Luca had teamed up against Emma and Izzie and their camaraderie was obvious.

"Mom," Izzie coaxed. "We want you to bring Tara home with you one weekend. She thinks it's a good idea, too. Don't you, Tara?"

"I'd love it, if it is not too much trouble," Tara looked first at Laura and then at Luca.

"Not at all dear. Not at all."

Goodbyes were repeated and Sam left with Clay and Tara.

Emma turned to Luca, balancing on his crutches, still watching the door. "I don't think she even noticed you are a gimp after you captured her with those beautiful, baby blue eyes of yours." She batted her eyes rapidly.

"She's gorgeous, isn't she?" he said, "but fun and nice, too."

"That she is," Emma replied.

Chapter 22

The days following Adelita's passing were interminable, a never-ending cycle of waking, moving through the day in a haze, and then lying on his cot in the dark, chest heaving, struggling against the sorrow that threatened to explode into the wracking sobs he'd experienced that night after her burial.

He had watched out for Adelita, tried to help with his meager attempts at gardening, and proudly shared his wages with her at the end of each week. He bought a few things here and there to brighten her home or make her life easier. What reason did he have to work now, to tend the garden, even to live? At the very least, Adelita had given him a sense of being, even though he had no idea who he was or the history of his past if he even had one.

Though of course he did have a past. He didn't just beam down from some foreign planet. There was a reason he was here in Mexico, though for the life of him he couldn't figure it out. There was a thick wall in his mind between the day he came to Adelita's and anything that happened in his life before.

Lane came by in the evening and sat by Anthony on his cot in the shed. "You know, you can move into the house. You don't have to stay out here in the shed."

"I am fine here," Anthony replied.

"I guess I hoped you would. Those boys of hers will surely destroy it if they come back to stay."

"I can watch them a bit," Anthony replied.

"Hah! You don't know what you are choosing. Those rascals are incorrigible. At any rate, I think they enjoy life in town."

"Maybe I was incorrigible before I came here. Surely, I must have caused some sort of trouble to get myself in this situation.

"I seriously doubt it," Lane replied. "Honestly, I think you are one of us 'dreadful Mormons,' as Adelita would have said."

"I don't know what I am anymore. I feel without purpose. Lost, not knowing what to do from day to day. Not knowing my past or future."

Lane put his arm around Anthony's shoulders. Lane was a tall man, lanky, fair. His arm hung loosely on Anthony's muscular frame. "May I make a suggestion? Focus on your feelings about God. Ask Him to help you remember who you were, to remember how you felt about Him. Ask Him to help you remember who this woman is that you painted on the side of the shed. Ask Him to help you remember why it is that you buried Adelita with the 'authority of the Holy Melchizedek Priesthood.' This is your purpose. To find who you are so that you can better serve Him. I know that is what Adelita would have wanted for you."

Anthony felt a tinge of relief pass through his tense frame. Perhaps he did have a future and a greater purpose for his presence. "Thanks, Lane. Thanks, brother."

"See, there you go, using the LDS vernacular again. I challenge you, Ramirez, to get to know your Savior. He will be by your side during this journey."

Lane rose to leave. He pulled the day's farming receipts from his briefcase and placed them beside Anthony on the cot. "Thank you, Ramirez. You can't imagine how this has helped the farmers to know where they stand weekly, instead of once a year. They are happier. Much less worried and stressed. Mmh. I think you were an accountant. Definitely, great with numbers."

With a slight wave of his hand, Lane ducked to clear the shed's wooden doorframe. Anthony never thought twice about easily entering or exiting his home. Yes, his home. He would stay in the shed. He had made it his with watercolor paintings made from colors created from the hues of plants and soil in his surroundings. With the notes tacked to the walls, he captured tiny clues about his past life.

Anthony painstakingly looked over the notes on the wall one by one. Clues to his past.

Top left, his first note: "A dark-haired woman, her back to me, looking over a lake."

Moving left to right: "Songs that seemed familiar the time I attended church with Lane and Graciela. The whole meeting seemed familiar."

Next: "I speak both Spanish and English fluently."

Next: "I read and write in Spanish and English."

Second row. "It was natural for me to use the ledger paper. Calculations are easy for me. I knew how to organize the information into a report for Lane."

Next: "Adelita's church seemed unfamiliar to me."

Anthony clutched his pencil, freshly-sharpened with a butcher knife Adelita had loaned him. He tore a sheet from the notebook Lane had given him to report his findings. He carefully creased the paper into fourths and then tore the paper along the creases.

He tacked another note on the second row: "I may have been an artist. My paintings are quite good."

Moving right: "I proclaimed that I held the Holy Melchizedek Priesthood. I must find out what that is."

Third row: I called Lane "Brother."

Next: "At Lane and Graciela's church, the people called each other Hermano and Hermana, Brother and Sister."

Next: "Am I already a Mormon?"

This would be his purpose. To make God and Christ his partners in finding out just who Ramirez was before he forgot his name and everything about himself. To serve God whether he cracked the mystery of his life or not. Anthony felt this must be the only way to heal this debilitating pain of losing Adelita, of losing his own life as it must have once been in times before Adelita rescued him.

Anthony stacked the farm receipts neatly on a homemade desk created from a discarded plank balanced on two tree stumps made even in height by Anthony's skill with a handsaw. Another note for the wall: "I have some carpentry skills."

The shed was growing dark as the sun dipped below the horizon. Anthony struck a match and lit a small candle. As he had mused over the notes representing his life, the light had grown too dim for him to start his calculations. He picked up a white cloth hanging on a nail by the door and went outside to a bucket of water he had brought up to the shed from the cistern that morning. He dipped the cloth into the cool water and wiped his face and neck, arms, and hands. He moistened his finger and poked it into the small pewter dish of ash and then rubbed it on his teeth to clean them. Last, he took a tin cup from a nail hanging above the bucket, scooped out a portion from the bucket and pressed the cup to his lips. Water from a tin cup was so refreshing.

A momentary flash of young boys around a campfire sipping hot chocolate from their blue tin cups broke into his memory and escaped just as quickly.

Anthony swished the water in his mouth to remove the ash, turned and spat away from the bucket of fresh water. He had to make note of that memory: "He was once camping with young boys his age, maybe twelve or so years old."

Anthony slept peacefully for the first night since Adelita's passing. There were no nightmares of finding her barely alive and no frustrating dreams of the woman gazing over the lake who wouldn't turn to look at him. In the morning, he rose and freshened himself with the water in the bucket again. He carried the bucket to the garden and, with his cup, poured water on the tiny plants struggling to grow without the loving attendance of their mistress. He talked to the plants as Adelita always did, encouraging them, expressing sympathy for their loss, for the unrelenting sun, and infrequent sharing of moisture from the skies.

He grabbed the hoe from where it leaned against the house and bothered the earth around each plant, allowing air and moisture to nourish them into adulthood. He was pleased when he finished with what he considered a good attempt at gardening. After all, not one plant was uprooted.

With great trepidation, Anthony opened the worn wooden door to Adelita's tiny home. Windowsills served as bookshelves, and he found Adelita's "Santa Biblia." Immediately the words "Holy Bible" flashed into his mind. He turned the Bible over and over in his hands, sensing the worn cover indicated much use. Gently he turned the delicate pages one by one until he came to a picture of Mary holding the baby Jesus with a white halo surrounding his tiny head. A love for this baby rose from his chest and Anthony knew that this tiny child held great importance in his life and had in his life before. Another book had stayed upright when Anthony removed the Bible and now landed with a soft slap on the wood shelf, catching his attention.

Adelita only had two books. This one must have had importance to her, too. "El Libro de Mormon" he read on the spine. He reached for the book. Mormon. This was the church Adelita was so opposed to since she felt it took her Graciela away from the church she had always attended with her mother since she was a child. Anthony turned the book over and read the cover "El Libro de Mormon." And below the title, "Otro Testamento de Jesucristo."

"The Book of Mormon. Another Testament of Christ," he immediately translated. Those words were so familiar. Lately he had thought as much in English as in Spanish. As he stood in Adelita's home, he read the testimony of Joseph Smith and other witnesses to The Book of Mormon. His heart thumped within his chest. It was as if his captive memory was being awakened to something he had known before. Something was very important to him. Clutching both the Bible and the smaller, softcover blue book in his hand, he left the humble dwelling and came to rest on the makeshift bench outside his shed. He set the Bible on the bench beside him and opened the cover of the "El Libro de Mormon" and began reading, only stopping when the sun set in the evening and light became too dim to make out the words.

With the first light of the day, Anthony was once again outside the shed with the blue book in hand. He read of courage, faith, and struggles that made him feel ashamed of worrying about his own trials. There were periods of great wars and periods of great repentance and peace. Often, he would find himself starting to read a scripture and finishing it in his mind without actually looking at the words.

"If ye are prepared . . . " he read, ye *shall not fear,* his mind finished.

In a section titled "The Book of Enos" he read, "Whatsoever thing ye shall ask in faith, believing that ye shall receive in the name of Christ . . . " *ye shall receive it.* It seemed Enos prayed day and night. Anthony determined that one night he would do that, asking and believing that someday his memory would return.

Anthony read as King Benjamin instructed his people to help others in need, to live the commandments of God, to return anything one borrowed. All of these instructions sounded so familiar, or maybe it was because he had been rescued and cared for by Adelita who was such a perfect example of everything King Benjamin asked his people to do.

Perhaps Lane was right. He had been or he still was a member of this church. This church, these people, loved and worshipped Christ—even if Adelita perceived that the Mormons didn't believe in Christ and were therefore sinners of the worst kind. This book remained on her shelf, unread like her Bible, but nevertheless on the shelf.

Anthony read again until late afternoon and stopped in a section written by the prophet Moroni and read, "And when ye shall receive these things, I would exhort you that ye would ask God, the Eternal Father, in the name of Christ, if these things are not true; and if ye shall ask with a sincere heart, with real intent having faith in Christ, he will manifest the truth of it unto you, by the power of the Holy Ghost."

That name Moroni sounded so familiar. And Christ was mentioned over and over in this book. He leaned his head back against the shed. *Is this true, God? It seems right. It seems like words I already know. It seems like the way I have lived my life in the past. Is it true?*

Anthony felt the pent-up tension of knowing so little about himself leave his body. He was completely at peace for the first time since he came to live with Adelita. He loved God and knew God loved him. He knew that if it was God's will, his mind would be healed, and his memory would return. He knew that however his life played out, as long as he was obedient and faithful, he could trust that it was the life God meant for him.

Anthony could hardly wait for Lane to arrive with the receipts for the day. Perhaps Lane was right. Perhaps in his past life he had been a member of Lane's church.

Chapter 23

Estelle busied herself picking up Luca's room, straightening, folding, observing her grandson continually smiling at his phone. "Someone on that phone is making you happy. A girl perhaps?"

"Yup," he responded, his thumbs flying over the phone screen.

"Any girl in particular?"

"Yup"

"Does she have a name?"

"Yup."

"Would that name be Tara?"

"Grandma!" He blushed.

"Shouldn't she be in class, and shouldn't you be catching up on your homework?" She took the books from his nightstand and placed them beside him on the bed. "Get to work, young man."

"She's waiting for a practice room and I'm . . . I'm . . . I'm waiting for my energy to kick in."

"Oh, I see. Well, the return of that elusive energy is now on a timer. When you hear the microwave timer go off, the studying goes on. And don't tell me you didn't hear it."

Luca tapped his pointer finger on the headphones he wore for continually listening to his favorite music.

"I'll help you with that." Estelle removed the headphones and planted a kiss on Luca's forehead. "Love you, grandson."

"Love you, too, Grandma," he replied, and he went back to texting and smiling.

Out on the road, the school bus crunched to a stop and Izzie jumped out of her seat, fought her way up the aisle, and swung out the door and down the steps. She had an idea that had been churning in her mind all day and couldn't wait to carry out her plan. The plan was superb in her mind. A way to get Luca interested in life again and maybe a way to find their daddy.

She speed-walked home and would have run had her backpack not been so full of books. Why they couldn't have lockers to leave behind the things she didn't need that night, she'd never understand. The excuse was that kids hid behind the open doors and sold drugs, and for that, they yanked out all of the lockers. Ridiculous. Why couldn't kids just follow rules? It made life so much easier for everyone.

"Grandma!" She burst through the door. "I need your help with something?"

Estelle turned from where she was putting the promised after school milk and cookies on the counter.

"Don't you want to have your cookies first?"

"No. Too important. Follow me." She dropped her backpack at the top of the stairs and headed for the basement, leaping over a few steps to the floor.

Estelle followed more carefully, two-footing the stairs as the kids called her method of descending. Izzie pushed open the door to a storage room and waved her hand at what looked to be a recording studio. The walls and ceiling were lined with royal blue foam squares. Izzie flipped a switch on the wall and tiny light strings shone from the perimeter of the ceiling. Izzie's guitar sat on a stand next to a chair in the corner. There was a music stand and chair to the right, and a keyboard and chair to the left. Microphones were placed in front of each instrumental set up, with speakers in the back corners of the room. A computer and monitor sat on a table between the keyboard and guitar.

"Izzie. Where did you get all of this?"

"Uncle Mark. He stored his stuff here when he was deployed to Africa. And then he decided to stay there so I texted him and asked him if I could use them. He said I could have them!"

Laura's brother Mark had been traveling the world as a photographer with the military since he got out of basic training. He had never settled down long enough to marry, or to give Estelle more grandkids as she at one time bemoaned. Now she had given up on his ever settling down. Mark had been as musical as Laura, but in his own rock 'n roll way, often tormenting their neighbors with his noisy garage bands. She looked around the room.

"No drums?" Mark had banged away on those drums late into the night, even exacting a few visits from police officers reminding him of the noise ordinance. But Mark would have been so involved in his rhythms he would have usually lost track of time.

"There are only three of us. The keyboard will have to play percussion. Here's where you come in."

"Oh," Estelle raised her eyebrows.

"I need you to get Luca and Emma down here when Emma gets home and help me convince them this is a good idea."

"A good idea?"

"Yes! We will make a YouTube video talking about how our dad is missing, show a picture of him and play some music that will be so awesome that we will go viral and someone, somewhere will recognize Dad."

"Definitely worth a try," Estelle responded. "I'm in."

Izzie went into her grandmother's arms for a warm, encouraging hug. "I love you, Grandma."

Estelle had never felt so loved and appreciated in her life since she had come to stay with the Di Angelos. There was something about these sweet grandchildren that just filled her heart to overflowing.

Emma entered the home much quieter than Izzie and took her backpack to her room before going to the kitchen to greet her grandmother.

"Hi Grandma. How was your day?"

"I've had a wonderful day. How about you?"

"It was okay. Just worrying about Luca and Dad. Wondering how I can help fix things. Everything seems so uncertain."

"I am glad you brought that up. Come with me to Luca's room. I have something to talk with you about."

Emma sat on the end of her brother's bed and Estelle on a chair beside the bed. Luca raised his eyes from his homework, giving them a quizzical stare.

"Waz up?"

"Izzie has come up with something she would like you to participate in."

"Oh boy," Luca breathed.

"Keep an open mind. She has worked hard. I think it is her way of trying to help both you, Luca, and your father. And it seems like a very good idea."

"What is it?" Luca was suspicious of anything quirky little Izzie might hatch up.

"Let's go downstairs and you will see."

Luca expressed great concern about how he would get down the stairs. Encouraged by Estelle, he hobbled over to the stairs on his crutches. Estelle sat down on the top stair and to the giggles of her grandchildren she demonstrated sliding from stair to stair on her bottom. She looked up at them. "Learned this when I broke my ankle right about when Izzie was born. I came to take care of you two, which meant chasing you up and down the stairs quite often in my clumsy cast."

Luca followed suit, and soon they were admiring the recording studio Izzie had set up in an empty room in the basement. Izzie grinned from ear to ear as her older siblings complimented her on the ambitious project.

"So, what's your big idea?" Luca asked.

"I want us to make a YouTube video with our music about Dad. Maybe someone will recognize him and let us know they've seen him. Emma will play her cello, I'll play the guitar, and Luca, you will play the keyboard."

"I haven't played the keyboard in a long while," Luca objected.

"Come on," Emma said. "I'll get my cello and we'll give it a try."

Estelle unfolded a spare chair and sat with arms folded admiring her resourceful and talented grandchildren. Luca turned on the keyboard and punched a few buttons and soon had percussion, chords, and melody blending into a delightful tune he'd made up on the fly. Luca had always balked at reading music but was adept at playing by ear and rendering clever improvisations.

Izzie had chosen songs from the public domain so that they wouldn't have to pay any royalties, especially since she planned for their efforts to go viral and maybe a few sponsors would get on board. She hoped they could earn some money to help find their dad.

Izzie grabbed her phone and pulled up YouTube and played a Billy Holiday version of "Back in Your Own Backyard." Luca and Emma loved the tune and the words but were concerned about using it publicly.

"Yup. Anything 1928 and before is in the public domain. I looked it up and it was written in 1927. Here are the words." She pulled a piece of poster board from behind her chair.

With that, Luca began playing chords and riffs on the keyboard, adding a snare drum for color. Izzie lifted her guitar and leaned into the microphone,

"We leave home expecting to find a blue bird,
Hoping ev'ry cloud will be silver lined,
But we all return, as we live, we learn
That we left our happiness behind."

"Wha what!!" Emma said and Luca's music came to a halt. "You are barely a teenager, and your voice is so, so . . . you could win American Idol."

"You do sound lovely dear," her grandmother encouraged. "Keep on, kids. This will be wonderful!"

Emma joined in with a nice harmony on her cello and they paused midway through the song for Luca's fancy piano riff.

Izzie set up a tablet on the computer table and said, "Let's record!"

Luca and Emma nodded their agreement and Izzie pushed the record button. The song ended with:

"Oh, you can go to the East, go to the West,
But someday you'll come weary at heart back where you started from,
You'll find your happiness lies, right under your eyes,
Back in Your Own Backyard."

Izzie pushed the button to stop the recording. "I'll add pictures of Dad later that will flow in and out of us playing. Hopefully I can find a picture of all of us in the backyard."

"One more. This will have pictures of Mom from when they were young until now. I've changed the words a bit to fit. The recording from the '20s sounds terrible with the fuzzy, scratching vinyl sound. It's a full orchestra, and, well, the singer is kind of awful. He warbles like a bird. But I guess that is how they sang back in the day."

Izzie began strumming on her guitar. Emma followed with a deep cello introduction and Luca put a light snare on the keyboard. And then Izzie began to sing the words she had written to resemble her mother singing to her dad.

"I am lonesome tonight,
I miss you tonight

It's so sad we've been torn apart.
Does your memory stray to a bright summer day,
When you kissed me and called me sweetheart?"
It was a simple, yet beautiful rendition, with a cello keyboard improvised interlude at Izzie's cue that made the words even more sorrowful when Izzie began again.
"The chairs in our parlor seem empty and bare,
We gaze at our doorstep and wish you were there.
My heart's filled with pain, please come back again,
My dear, I'm so lonesome tonight."
"Oh my." Estelle wiped tears from her eyes. "That was wonderful, truly wonderful." "Pretty dope," Luca said, choosing a word that was of the highest compliment in his world. "Totally lit."
"Awesome," Emma chimed in, realizing that when it came to music and lyrics her sister was a protégé. She imagined great things ahead for the teen.
"Yeah," Luca said. "We're pretty good. We need to do more of this. It may be even better than baseball."
Estelle winked at Izzie and mouthed "Mission accomplished."
Izzie worked tirelessly until she had produced a very touching video which she played for her siblings and grandmother before uploading to YouTube. To get the "thumbs up" started on YouTube each of them, including their grandmother with instructions from Emma, shared a link to Instagram and Facebook.
They were awakened at midnight with a squeal coming from Izzie's room. "We are blowing it up on YouTube. Someone for sure will see it and recognize Dad."
Laura woke with a start and ran to Izzie's room. "What's blowing up?" By this time Estelle was awake as well.
"Show her, Isabella. Play the video and show her what her amazing children have done."

Chapter 24

Anthony was sitting on a stump in front of Adelita's home waiting for Lane's arrival with the day's receipts and enthusiastically reading the Book of Mormon. The second Lane's car braked to a dusty stop, Anthony was on his feet running to the car before Lane could exit.

"What's up, man?"

"This book! I have found myself in it."

"Most people do," Lane replied recognizing the dark blue book in Anthony's hand as he unfolded his long frame from the vehicle. "Tell me what you have found. Let's go around back to your shed, I mean home."

Anthony could hardly contain his excitement. "Test me," he demanded.

"Test you?"

"Yes. Read the first part of a verse and I'll finish it."

"All right."

Lane turned the book to a page that read "Mosiah 5:13." This was one of his favorite scriptures, and a mantra to never be a stranger to the Lord. " 'For how knoweth a man the master whom he has not served, and who is a stranger unto him . . . ' "

Anthony answered, " ' . . . and is far from the thoughts and intents of his heart?' See! I am one of those Mormons. I must be. I feel in my heart that God is not a stranger to me. That I know Him. That I have served Him in my past.”

“You have been a valiant servant of the Lord in your kindness to others ever since I’ve known you. Okay. Try this one in Nephi, Chapter Three: ‘ . . . I will go and do the things which the Lord hath commanded . . . ’ ”

Anthony interrupted, “ ‘ . . . for I know that the Lord giveth no commandments unto the children of men, save he shall prepare a way for them that they may accomplish the thing which he commandeth them.’ Yes!!”

“Well brother,” Lane clapped Anthony on the back and shook his hand, “looks like you may just belong to the Church of Jesus Christ of Latter-day Saints.”

“Huh?” Anthony questioned. “The Mormons?”

“How about if I pick you up for church on Sunday? Are you ready to embrace your old and new religion.”

“Of course,” Anthony replied, “but I know how busy you are with your meetings, I will get myself there.”

“That’s over four miles, and church starts at 8:00 a.m. Let me come get you or send Graciela.”

“I don’t want her coming out here alone. It was bad enough she had to walk all that way to work before you came along and made her life so much better. Adelita walked that far each week to take her vegetables to the Mercado. I’m fine. I will see you before 8:00 on Sunday.”

“What will you do for a clock? As I remember it, you don’t have a watch or a clock. Neither did Adelita.”

“She taught me to calculate time by the location of the sun and by how I feel. Don’t worry. I will be there.”

The conversation turned to the success of the farmers with their crops with the agricultural advice of Lane and accounting system of Anthony. The pile of sales receipts grew bulkier each day, and the men were grateful for the service they were able to render these poor farmers who had struggled so long on their own. Water from streams had been utilized more effectively, and Lane had arranged with some of the many

Cabo San Lucas resort restaurants to buy local produce from the farmers. It was an undertaking Lane had embarked on as a graduate student after he had served his mission in the area, and a pursuit he intended to continue for his working life. While his salary, paid by a charitable organization, was much less than he would make in private industry, it was adequate and comfortable. He and Graciela were satisfied and happy with their life together and the home they had created.

Anthony rose just as the sun was peeking over the horizon. He had a sudden remembrance of being somewhere with the sun bursting into the sky all at once. While he wanted to grasp onto and dissect the memory, he instead chased it away. The fleeting thoughts, or maybe even memories, only served to antagonize him when they went no further than a flash across his mind.

Slipping into his sandals, he climbed the hill for fresh water to wash up for church. He checked out his dark hair that flowed nearly to his shoulders in a piece of tin he had hung on the wall. Lane's hair was cropped short. He wore slacks and a button shirt with a tie each time he visited Anthony on his church days. For a moment, Anthony contemplated staying home. Would he be out of place with his long hair and white linen pants and shirt that hung loosely on his frame? Usually, he felt comfortable in the clothes Adelita had provided that had belonged to her husband, though he was obviously a man of larger statue than Anthony.

Now Anthony pulled at the loose-fitting clothing, lifted up the shirt, and tied a piece of rope around his waist to guarantee the trousers would stay in place. He wiped the dust off his sandals, which were just some leather straps attached to a rubber sole that had seen better days and experienced another moment of angst. By the time he walked the dusty four miles to the church, his feet would be dirty again.

A story came to mind that he had heard when he went to a Catholic parish with Adelita of Jesus washing the feet of his friends during a large meal that Anthony thought they called the Last Supper. It had seemed to Anthony to be the ultimate kindness someone could do for another. Alas, today, he would have to figure that out for himself when he passed from the dirt to the paved road just before the church.

He slipped a piece of cloth into his rope belt for that purpose. He left early just in case his time instincts were at all skewed with the upcoming change of seasons. It may take him a while to adjust, although he typically had no reason to be anywhere at a certain time. He just always made certain to be home as the sun edged toward the western horizon, signaling Lane's impending arrival.

Anthony climbed the small rise leading up to where Adelita and her husband were buried. He stopped for a moment by her grave and in his mind offered an apology for going to this new church, Lane's church. The church she called a silly church. "Adelita," he whispered, "I think this church is the key to who I am. I know you would want that. But I will never forget you. Never."

Anthony headed through the brush to the dirt road. Dust quickly oozed between his toes and into his sandals. When he finally reached the pavement, each step was met with both a slap and puff of dust poofing out from each side of the sandals. He looked around for a home with a hose bib and found a small, painted plywood home that seemed of not much substance, but it appeared by the wires running overhead that it had electricity. Maybe it had running water, too. Hidden in a bush by the door he saw the red handle of a pump. He walked through the clumps of grass struggling to be a lawn, stepped onto the concrete landing, and rapped on the door. An older woman answered, probably close to the age of Adelita. Maybe they had known each other at the Mercado.

"You are Adelita's gringo. I remember you from the Mercado." She greeted him. "We miss her. She was so kind and had such nice vegetables."

The women gathered at the open-air market once a week to sell their produce or their embroideries, handmade jewelry, or pottery.

"I am Carmen." As she talked, she extended her hand. "Come in, come in. Ramirez? I believe that is what Adelita called you. Ramirez with no last name." She chuckled but held his hand with both of hers. "Poor lost soul, you are."

"Gracias, gracias. But my feet, they are so dirty," Anthony responded. "I am on my way to church and wondered if I could use some water from your pump to wash them."

"To church? You had better not go to that silly church of Graciela's. Adelita will look down and curse you."

"It is a church about Christ. I am sure if she knew more about it, she would approve."

"Humph," Carmen hissed. "We'll see." She stepped out and lifted the handle on the pump. Pulling a towel from the waist of her apron, she bent and lifted Anthony's sandals from his feet."

He protested. "No, No. I can't let you do that."

She dusted the sandals with her cloth and then instructed Anthony to dip his feet in the small tub that collected the water from the pump. "You will get those white trousers all dirty if you try to do this yourself," she said. Anthony lifted his trousers and reluctantly immersed one foot at a time into the tub. She wiped each foot dry quite tenderly as he lifted them from the tub. Tears came to Anthony's eyes. Carmen's kindness overwhelmed his emotions, and a small sob escaped his lips.

"Now, now," Carmen stroked his arm, "One day you will remember your life before. I will pray for you."

Anthony thanked her and leaned forward to gift her a light hug.

"Now is that the best you can do?" she asked.

Anthony gathered her slight figure into his arms and enveloped her in a warm and grateful embrace.

"Much better, now be off with you to your silly church." She waved him along with a flip of her hand.

Spider cracks etched their way along the pavement to the church, but at last there was no dust. The face of the one-story building of various shades of brown brick was lined with windows on either side of double, multi-paned doors. It provided a spot of welcoming beauty in a rundown neighborhood. Blue agave cactus nestled in neatly trimmed lawns. A long parking lot, complete with yellow striping for parking stalls stretched along the front of the building. The neighborhood was run down but spoke of hard-working people as a parked truck loaded with five-gallon water containers and another with landscaping equipment evidenced an industrious culture.

The strains of a hymn playing on a piano seemed familiar. Yes. It was sung at Adelita's little funeral on the hilltop. "O mi Padre." "O My Father." But somewhere, somewhere back in the recesses of his mind he had heard that hymn many times before.

A gentleman at the door dressed in a suit, white shirt, and tie clasped Anthony's hand in his and welcomed him to church. He introduced himself and asked Anthony if he was new to the area, to which Anthony responded that he was just meeting some friends. He breathed a sigh of relief as Graciela rushed up to greet him and guide him to where she was sitting. Lane waved to him from some seats on a platform above the other rows of pews. The men sitting on the platform were smartly dressed in suits, crisp white shirts, and ties, but others in the congregation were dressed similarly to Anthony. Otherwise, he would have felt woefully out of place.

Graciela introduced Anthony to the people on either side of her and to those in front and back, and then leaned back onto the upholstered bench. Anthony sat to her right. She placed her hand on her stomach and touched Anthony lightly on the arm. "We are expecting, Ramirez," she said with delight and excitement in her voice. "We are so happy."

Anthony squeezed her hand. He was so happy, too. So happy for this sweet couple who had clung to each other despite the odds and disapproval from family both for their marriage and for their religion.

The Catholic service he had attended with Adelita was nice but had seemed entirely foreign to him. As this service progressed, it seemed like his mind anticipated each coming event correctly. A hymn was sung before what became a very sacred sacramental offering, not just an act of following rudimentary requirements. "There is a Green Hill Far Away." He knew that tune, those words, but more so in the English that ran through his mind than the Spanish on the page in the hymn book.

His lips followed along with the sacramental prayers, hesitating when the words seemed wrong, and listening again as the young man repeated the words, this time agreeing with those in Anthony's mind. As the young boys walked up and down the aisles with the trays of bread and water, Anthony turned to "Oh mi Padre" in the hymn book. As he read the second verse, he fought back tears and swallowed the lump in his throat.

"For a wise and glorious purpose,
Thou hast placed me here on earth,
And withheld the recollection,
Of my former friends and birth.
Yet oft times a secret something,
Whispered, 'You're a stranger here,'
And I felt that I had wandered,
From a more exalted sphere."

He could relate to those words. He had been placed in a world where he was a stranger with no memory of where he was before or of the people he knew. He couldn't imagine, however, a people more exalted or Christlike than those he had met here. Adelita, Lane and Graciela, Carmen. Was there a better place? Did he want to find that place, those people? Was someone remembering him, missing him.

He couldn't shove that thought aside because clearly, he had been to this church before, sung these hymns, listened, or maybe even recited these sacramental prayers. What purpose did he have before? What was his purpose here? Why wouldn't God let him remember? All these thoughts were making his head feel thick and achy. As the sacrament ended, he shook all his worries aside and listened intently to the speakers.

After the meeting, Lane came down from the platform and shook Anthony's hand. There was so much handshaking and hugging taking place at this church. Graciela explained that the next meeting would be Sunday School, and they would be studying the New Testament. Lane stepped over Anthony and Graciela, squeezed between her and another couple and sat with his arm around her shoulders, pulling her close. Anthony noticed the adoring looks shared between the newlyweds and wondered if the Laura from his ring looked at him like that. Did he love her like Lane loved Graciela?

Nothing taught in the lesson was new to Anthony. It was all familiar, including the feelings: the warm, encompassing emotions that permeated his soul. He belonged to this church. Yes, at last he knew he was where he belonged. He may not remember why or how, but he knew this was the church God wanted him to embrace.

After the meetings, Lane and Anthony met Graciela in the cultural hall which was the big room behind the chapel. Long tables were set up and chairs in a big circle. Women bustled back and forth from the kitchen bringing out steaming casserole dishes of enchiladas, both beef and chicken, with salsa roja, which was a rich brick red sauce, and chile verde for toppings. Plates of soft, warm corn tortillas and an abundance of meats, cheeses, and peppers to make tacos covered the end of the table. A prayer was given on the food and adults tried to hold back their hungry children as they rushed for the tables. Words of gratitude and appreciation for the food tumbled in and out of conversations. After the main courses had dwindled, the teenage girls brought out plates of polvorónes, which appeared to be several colors of sugar cookies, as well as plates with round balls of baked sweet dough laced with crushed almonds and dipped in powdered sugar. Graciela explained that these delicacies were Mexican wedding cookies.

The men visited and the children played in the cultural hall, giggling, chasing, and receiving chastisement for not keeping the Lord's Day holy, all while the women and teenage girls cleaned up the lunch. The men, of course, didn't chastise the women for doing all the work on the Sabbath. The women put the tables away and finally the men reluctantly folded up the chairs and stacked them against the wall.

Anthony thanked Lane and Graciela and began his trek home while the sun was midway from overhead to the western horizon. As he left the pavement and stepped onto the dirt road, he saw Carmen rocking in a chair on her porch. At her beckoning, he left the road and stepped into her yard.

"And how was your silly church today, Ramirez," she called out. "Did they fill you with any foolish ideas?"

Anthony decided not to correct Carmen for calling his church, yes, his church silly. "The service was quite wonderful. All about Jesus. It made me feel really good to be there."

"Humpf," she replied, obviously hoping for a different answer.

"Maybe you would like to come with me sometime, see for yourself."

"Humpf. Well maybe I just might do that. Have a good night." She rose from her chair and went into the house, banging the wooden screen door behind her.

Anthony smiled. This amazing sensation of right, of being loved by God, of knowing that his church represented something really good was something he wanted to share. He'd find a way to coax Carmen to church one Sunday to find out for herself.

Chapter 25

Estelle wiped her hands on a clean kitchen towel and surveyed the spotless kitchen. It felt good to be of service to her family, to prepare meals, run errands, and take Luca to and from physical therapy. She smiled and reached for the ring she had placed in a candy dish for safekeeping. Settling on a bar stool, she held her left hand out before her and admired how her hand, naked for so many years, looked with the sparkling ruby and tiny diamonds. Dropping her hand to the counter she contemplated this wonderful turn of events signifying the end to her loneliness.

For over twenty years she had dreamed of this kind of love and had almost given up. She was married to Rex for the first twenty years of her adult life. At about the twenty-year mark, he had suddenly stopped speaking to her, wouldn't even look her way. Finally, she asked him if he couldn't bring himself to talk to her, would he please write a letter explaining what was wrong. And he did write a scathing letter, outlining every one of her faults, relating how he hadn't loved her for years, stating that she was no longer the cheerleader and beauty queen he married, just a tired old lady. Apparently, he felt like his life was over because he was trapped with her. He wanted to be rich and successful, but she—with no real education to help his cause, or even a desire to be wealthy—was holding him back.

Somehow, she realized when she read the letter, she already knew this, and while the revelations in print made her sad, it was also a relief, a possible end to years of belittling behavior, and the fear of his hot temper raining down on her and the children. Mark was nearly eighteen and planning to join the Peace Corps. Estelle understood his choice after high school was to get as far away from his father's wrath as he could. Laura was the quiet one, often secreted away in her own world of music, involved in preparing for her college piano performance audition. Estelle was confident that Laura did not even notice her father's silent rebuff of her mother. They had all learned to walk lightly, to keep from igniting Rex's outbursts over sometimes the slightest thing. The peace, however false, was the calm before a coming storm.

Estelle still loved Rex when she first read his words, but she realized it was only as a caretaker, looking out for his needs, his comfort, and what she thought was his happiness. Still, she knew that no matter how hard she tried, she couldn't please him. The fear of rejection was continually a partner in their relationship. At least the letter somehow released her. She was done trying, and even hoped he would leave of his own accord. But he didn't.

The isolation throughout all that time had been debilitating. She'd had a part-time job at a school library, which provided some relief during the day, but nights and weekends were difficult. Church had not been a part of Rex's life since the early years of their marriage. Originally, Estelle had taken the children to church faithfully, but her faith had dwindled as each Sunday was met with an anti-religion discussion that Rex brought to the dinner table after church. Eventually Mark struggled to attend church, though Laura never wavered. Estelle put up a good front, but she rarely attended the Temple. She began to find fault with the church leaders. How could they, with their stellar families and wonderful marriages, possibly understand her situation? She began doing almost nothing to boost her own spirit. The struggles in her marriage and Rex's cruel comments had brought her low.

Instead of turning to the Lord, she turned to the only person that wasn't an expensive, long-distance call, who knew her back when she was pretty and alive, not a fat old lady as Rex had labeled her at just forty-one years of age. When she and Rex had moved out of state, getting the family settled in a new area had taken top priority. That was before cell phones and free long distance were even a possibility, and all of her connections and her friendships went by the wayside. From the class reunion contact list, Estelle remembered Stephen lived somewhere near Mesa where they had settled.

Estelle and Stephen had been a dynamic musical duo in high school. Never romantic, just good friends. She found his number in the phone directory and called him. He was so happy to hear from her and talked to her for over an hour. She felt alive for the first time in many months.

While she was hesitant to do more than have one conversation, Stephen pursued her and reached out often. Finally, he confided that his marriage was on the rocks and hoped that if he were one day single, they could be together. Estelle fell in love with being loved and with being told she was beautiful and smart. She clung to every conversation, replaying Stephen's words over and over in her mind. She was certain that God had sent Stephen to rescue her. But so dull was her ability to recognize the spirit due to the lack of nourishment, that she felt the burning in her chest was the spirit telling her their relationship was right. Months later, once she turned back to the Lord, she recognized that the burning in her bosom was no more than anxiety and indigestion.

Confident that she and Stephen would be together, she didn't hesitate to agree when Rex eventually asked for a divorce. She was doing him a favor after all, saving his life, since he had become suicidal after feeling he was stuck in their marriage. When the divorce was final, she put her love and hope into the possibility of a life with Stephen. But when he realized she was now free, he quit calling or answering if she called. That was what the grandchildren now referred to as being "ghosted."

During those early days after the divorce and Stephen's disappearance, Estelle spent her summer mornings huddled in her bedroom closet, crying, sobbing. Not because she missed Rex. It was a relief to have the angst of pleasing him eliminated. It was because Stephen had broken her heart and taken away that wonderful feeling of being adored and loved. She was completely empty and doubted Laura even noticed her own sadness as she prepared for college.

Eventually, Estelle remembered the one place where she could be comforted and relieved of this burden of grief. She spent hours on her knees begging the Lord for Stephen's return. The scriptures became her lifeline for encouragement, and sometimes for more clarity than perhaps she wanted. She never felt any encouragement from the Lord that it was right for her that Stephen would return. She felt so much angst about the unknown but when she decided to move on with a life without Stephen, one scripture in the Doctrine & Covenants particularly helped her realize that this was the correct path.

"Verily, verily, I say unto you, if you desire a further witness, cast your mind upon the night that you cried unto me in your heart, that you might know concerning the truth of these things. Did I not speak peace to your mind concerning the matter? What greater witness can you have than from God?"

Estelle clearly remembered one particular night, when the tears and wrenching sobs would not cease. She dropped to her knees and begged the Lord for relief and was prompted to turn to this scripture. She knew that turning her life over to her Heavenly Father was the right choice, but it was hard. It was hard to give up on the love she felt for Stephen. It was hard not to call him, to beg him to reconsider. But she kept strong. Stephen's remembrance of her as a beautiful person of worth had been twisted into something that cankered. His words of love had been like an addiction, and she was struggling with the recovery process.

Little by little, as she clung to the scriptures and to her Heavenly Father, peace returned to her soul. Estelle laughed inside as her remuniations on the "Saga of Stephen" as she called it ended. She realized that as she turned back to the Lord, she could now tell the difference between the spirit speaking to her and indigestion.

It was over nine years before she considered dating again, and it wasn't her choice when it happened. Laura signed her mom up for an online dating app. The internet was in full swing, and there were many choices other than AOL for service and even more choices of dating apps. Laura chose an LDS dating site and told Estelle, who was appalled, after the fact.

However, when a white-haired man, and obviously a few years her senior, showed interest, Estelle began to enjoy conversations with those other than her coworkers. Based on their shared interest in bike riding, the gentleman asked to meet for a ride and lunch. He was a delightful conversationalist. Looking back though, he was a psychiatrist and more adept at asking questions than conversing.

Estelle quickly fell in love with what she thought was being loved based on the man's desire to kiss and hug her. She'd only dated Rex before she was married, so her knowledge of dating world habits was sorely limited. She and this new man dated often for nearly three months, when he confided that he was also dating another woman online. Estelle's heart sank. She had trusted this man. After all, he had been a Bishop and a High Councilman.

But there were signs she should have recognized. She had begun going to LDS Single's dances, but he had never invited her to go with him to a dance. Once there, he danced with Estelle only a couple of times and alternated between several other ladies who he held a bit closer than what Estelle considered appropriate for a church dance. Eventually the single's rumor mill made its way to Estelle where she found he had not just one other woman he was dating, but several.

A kiss was something special to Estelle. A commitment, not something to try on for size with many others. What she had learned was that she was more adept at falling in love than finding a lasting relationship. And she was skillfully adept at blaming herself for the reason the relationship ended.

Her heart was once again smashed, and the recovery wasn't any easier. Her insurance provided for a visit to a therapist who was incredibly helpful, bringing her back to reality and on the road to healing. When she explained the situation to him, he responded with "And what is it that you could possibly have done wrong?" His words had awakened her confidence in herself as a person of worth.

Estelle found things that brought her happiness, but she often wondered if she would have chosen those hobbies if it weren't a hobby of someone she was dating. While dating one gentleman, she took golf lessons, and while she enjoyed the peace of the golf course, the lessons were stressful. Still, the driving range near work became her lunchtime routine. Finally, being able to hit the ball 100 yards became a milestone once she was able to relax and not worry so much about the perfect stance and swing.

The mirrors showing off her less-than-slim frame were the main drawback to her time of ballroom dance lessons and the subsequent dance nights at various church dances and private dance studios. The experiences were ofttimes both entertaining and hilarious. Trying to look sexy doing the tango with a partner a foot taller—and the only rapturous eye contact being that of his chest—proved interesting. As one man told her his life stories of wicked wives and children in prison, she looked up to pay attention only to be sprayed with spit as he spat out the story of his life. Another short, thin man of Hawaiian descent smashed every woman he danced with to his chest. But he was an excellent dancer, so all the women in the dance circuit put up with "the smasher " anyway. Another moved his leading hand like he was wielding a potato masher. Thus, he was nicknamed "the masher."

Perhaps it was cruel to have mental names for these men, but it helped her cope with the sorry state of her single life. She did love to dance the swing, and perhaps the best swing dancer turned out to be a man who invited her out for New Year's Eve. Before the night was over, he had told her about seven ex-wives, one of whom he had married twice. She ended things when he threw a chair through her glass curio cabinet. Somehow it was her fault. Estelle suggested that maybe he should take a break from marriage for a while. But by March, he approached Estelle at a single's fireside, sat by her on the piano bench, and confided that he had already been married and divorced again. Estelle quickly conjured up a boyfriend for herself that excused her from spending time with this fellow.

After two more heartbreaks and rehabilitations of her self-esteem, she had finally given up on finding someone with whom to spend her life. But she had found her Heavenly Father. She had found Christ. Her testimony was unshakeable, and the Temple had become her sanctuary, her place of refuge. She had served as a Relief Society President, and with her experience, she guided and helped other single woman to avoid the pitfalls of making choices without the spirit as a guide.

Rex paid child support until the moment each child turned eighteen, right when they became the most expensive, particularly with Laura's educational goals. Laura enrolled at Arizona State in the music program to prepare for her Juilliard audition. With Estelle's job as a high school registrar and a side job teaching piano lessons, she was able to keep Laura afloat that first year of college, since Laura was able to live at home and also teach a few piano lessons of her own. They were blessed and cared for abundantly by the Lord. Estelle moved pennies around in her budget, but never missed paying tithing or any of her bills.

The following spring, after becoming a semi-finalist in the International Gina Bachauer Piano Competition, Laura was granted a generous scholarship to Julliard. It was a tender mercy, a kind blessing. Laura had put her best efforts to work and Heavenly Father had provided a way for her to achieve her goal.

Estelle's thoughts turned to Sam, an honest man. Those other men pretended to be religious, churchgoing men, but they didn't treat others in a Christlike manner. She remembered anxiety and uncertainty when dating them. She felt at peace with Sam. He was a good man. He loved God. They had that in common. And she felt a deep, genuine love for him that grew over months of association, not like the almost-instant, rapturous infatuation in times past.

*****

Emma came around the counter and surprised Estelle where she was still in deep thought. "Hi, Grandma. I'm home! I love you!"

"You are as quiet as a mouse. I never hear you come home. I love you, too."

The door to Luca's room opened and he swung out on his crutches. He would be back in school the following week. With his therapy complete, he was anxious to regain his former life.

"I'm starving!" It was his typical greeting.

"Of course, you are," Estelle replied as Emma pulled the milk from the fridge and a glass from the cupboard. A plate of fresh chocolate chip cookies was pushed in Luca's direction, and one was devoured before he was totally balanced on his crutches at the counter.

Izzie burst through the door shouting, "Have you seen all the views on our video? And all the thumbs up!" She dropped her backpack, kicked off her shoes at the door, and headed for her room, turning quickly to come back and grab a cookie. "I'm going to put it on Facebook and Instagram next. Someone is going to recognize Dad!"

"Alright but pick up your backpack and shoes on the way," Emma instructed. It was hard for her to let go of mothering Izzie now that her grandmother was there, or even when their mom was home.

"K." One syllable. And then a "Thanks, Grams," and she was off.

Emma hung her head. She agreed their performance was outstanding, but what if no one recognized their dad. Izzie would be so disappointed.

As if she anticipated her sister's hesitance, Izzie came back to the kitchen. "Look, even if no one recognizes him, we can make some money to help find him."

"And how will we do that," Luca said, "We can't afford to pay royalties so we can get paid to perform."

"Cinch," Izzie replied. "I'll be back."

She returned with her phone and pulled up her e-mail, the one she had listed as a contact on their video. "That really big Senior Citizens Center in White Plains wants us to put together a program. They will pay us and they have a license that allows us to perform for a fee at their facility."

"Sam probably has some attorney friends. Let's ask him to find out. We don't want to do anything we shouldn't do and end up paying for it."

"There's a whole list of songs in the public domain. They are oldies, but maybe goodies?" She raised her eyebrows and widened her eyes. "I'll send you a link. Pick out some and we'll start rehearsing."

"I'm in," Luca said.

Emma realized how much she really enjoyed jamming with her siblings and nodded her agreement. At least they felt like they were doing something for their dad rather than just waiting for others to make his return happen.

Chapter 26

When Anthony arrived at Carmen's house on Sunday, he bore a gift, a watercolor of the front of her home, complete with water pump, tub, weathered wooden chair, and the trumpet bush with its bright yellow, horn-shaped flowers.

After Adelita's services and seeing his handiwork on her coffin, Lane and Graciela had given him a real set of watercolors and several brushes to substitute for the plant-based colors and homemade brushes he had been using. The natural hues were subtly beautiful, and he used them for the base color on the piece of thick bark he had used for his canvas and sanded until it was smooth. He still returned to the natural colors from time to time.

Discarded bottles half filled with water lined the floor on one side of his home. Various plants were soaking in the water producing a plethora of earth tones. He had painted more than one rendition of the dark-haired woman looking over the water. Was she the Laura of his incoherent mumblings to Graciela when he was first injured, the Laura of the inscription on his ring?

Carmen was waiting on her porch chair in a crisp, brightly colored dress, a small hat on her head and a bag on her arm.

"You look lovely today," he remarked.

"Lovely enough to accompany you to your church? I need to make sure you are not being taught any lies about God.

Adelita would not be happy with me if I let that happen to you."

"I will be very proud to take such a beautiful woman to church with me where I learn nothing but the truth about God and his Son."

"We will see about that."

With a bow, Anthony handed her his gift, wrapped in a piece of white cloth. She seemed surprised and tears formed in her eyes before she even removed the cloth. She turned it over and over in her hands as if she was not accustomed to receiving a gift.

"Open it. Open it!" Anthony encouraged.

Tears poured down her cheeks as she lightly touched the painting. "So beautiful. So beautiful. For me?"

"Of course. Thank you for your kindness to me."

Holding the painting to her bosom, she struggled to her feet. "Let's get the dust off those feet before we go to church."

Anthony reached out and touched her on the arm. "This time I will do it. A lady as lovely as you should not be washing my dirty feet."

"Roll up your pants," she chided. "I can't go to church with a man whose trousers are muddy to the knees."

Anthony carefully rinsed the dust off each foot, holding up his pant leg and dipping his feet one at a time into the water Carmen had already drawn in the bucket. He pulled a rag from his belt, dusted his sandals, and dried his feet before slipping them into the sandals. "May I leave my rag here until on the way back from church."

Carmen nodded, opened the wooden screen door, and set the painting inside. She returned and the door slapped shut behind her. She took Anthony's arm without a word, but the signal was clear that she was ready to leave for church.

They walked in unusual silence to the church. Unusual since Carmen usually kept up a steady stream of conversation. As they went up the few steps to the main entrance, she hesitated for a moment before Anthony opened the door. "Are you okay?" he asked.

"I will be," came the reply.

Once in the building, several women welcomed her. They had met Carmen at the Mercado where she sold handmade jewelry and blankets. Carmen chatted amicably with the women, and the apprehensive look on her face was replaced with a smile.

They slipped into a pew by Graciela. The young woman stood and embraced Carmen, telling her how much she had missed seeing her at the market. Graciela had accompanied Adelita to the market until she had married Lane and moved to another area of the city. She and Carmen exchanged whispered memories of their times at the venue until the Branch President stood to begin the meeting.

Once again, the words to the hymn came to Anthony's mind as the prelude began. Prickles went from his spine up into his hair, the feeling that somehow, he had once been an active member of this church would not leave him throughout the whole meeting. But how to figure out anything more evaded him with his limited memory of the past.

When the Sacrament meeting ended, Graciela took Carmen and took her by the hand, and they strolled down the hall to the women's Relief Society room. Lane accompanied Anthony to the men's Priesthood Meeting, which was held in the gym, or cultural hall as they called it. Anthony followed the lines on the floor with his eyes and looked up to the ceiling where baskets had been cranked up parallel to the floor. This all looked familiar and for a moment he could hear the *"Thump. Whump. Ping."* sounds deep in the recesses of his memory of a basketball bouncing on a wooden floor that looked just like this one. He grabbed onto that memory and held it tight to transfer to a note on his wall of things he was remembering. It was like discovering a puzzle piece that fit but millions of pieces were still missing.

The lesson was on Joseph Smith's First Vision which Anthony realized he knew well. He could have given that lesson. In fact, he was quite certain that at some time in his forgotten past he had taught that lesson. Perhaps he had been a Spanish-speaking missionary. How else would this gringo speak and understand both English and Spanish so well? Another note for the wall. He was not sure, since he was not a Bona Fide member of this church—at least he couldn't prove it— if he would be allowed to participate. But there was so much he wanted to say. He knew that Joseph Smith saw what he saw. The swelling of his heart in his chest told him so.

When the men's meeting came to a close, they met Graciela and Carmen walking arm in arm down the hall, Carmen's smile expressing her approval of the message she had heard.

"So . . . " Anthony was anxious to assess the outcome of Carmen's visit to his church.

"So far, so good," she replied, giving Graciela's arm a squeeze. "I think Adelita would approve. Your Joseph Smith was a very nice young man. Did you know he actually saw an angel, and Jesus, and God?"

"Whew," Anthony feigned relief and wiped his brow. "Yes, I did. That is wonderful to know, isn't it?"

Carmen just smiled and squeezed his forearm. Lane led the way to the cultural hall where the women were setting out the food for the after-church mingle. Anthony excused himself and went into the hallway to a shelf by the entry door to retrieve a bowl of strawberries he had brought to share. He hoped this was something others would enjoy with their enchiladas and tacos. With no way to keep meat fresh, his typical meals consisted of beans, rice, and corn tortillas which he prepared on an outdoor oven. He used the beans, rice, and corn from Adelita's stored food with fresh vegetables on the side. Although Lane and Graciela had offered time after time for him to move into Adelita's home and be able to use her cast iron stove and box for storing ice, he couldn't bring himself to make the move. His memories of the sweet woman permeated every corner and crack of the small home and filled him with incredible gratitude for her care and sadness at her passing.

Lane, Graciela, and Carmen had found chairs in the circle placed in the center of the cultural hall as the chairs were gathered up from Priesthood Meeting. Hesitantly, he placed his bowl of strawberries among the offerings on the table and was met with oohs and aahs from the women arranging the dishes so that they were all accessible. "Fresh strawberries. Such a delicacy," were some of the comments. Anthony blushed with happiness at being able to contribute and please.

Carmen patted the chair beside her. "What do you think I should bring next week? What would you like Anthony?"

"I am just happy you are coming next week. Anything would be great, but I don't think you have to do that."

"I think I will make my special sweet empanadas."

"Oh, yes," Graciela voiced her approval.

"Sounds very tasty," Anthony replied.

"Make sure you have an extra hand to carry them for me," Carmen winked and elbowed him in the side.

With full stomachs and sleep pushing its way into their minds, they went about cleaning up with the other ward members and then began their walk toward home.

"Are you sure you won't let us give you a ride?" Lane asked.

"Oh no, it's not far. We'll be fine," Anthony replied.

"Speak for yourself," Carmen interjected, and they accepted a ride, but only as far as Carmen's house where Anthony insisted on walking home. He had a lot to mull over, and it was best done in silence although most of each day was filled with silence.

Chapter 27

The Di Angelo home buzzed with the happy noise of visitors and music. Sam joined the family several evenings a week for dinner and Tara visited most weekends, the strains of her piano practice filling the great room on Saturday mornings while the "3 D's," as they called themselves, rehearsed in the soundproof room Izzie had created.

The assisted living center residents were so pleased with their choice of songs and performance that they were invited to perform monthly. One spry gentleman found a carafe, which he carefully cleaned and dried and put on a chair by the group. To the group's surprise, as residents reluctantly left the room, they dropped spare change and paper bills into the carafe. The children had only expected the fifty dollars the center had offered them and were delighted as they regularly counted nearly fifty more dollars in tips. Tara usually sat back from the band, her sparkling blue eyes trained on Luca, but occasionally could be coaxed into playing a fancy ditty on the keyboard, to the enchantment of the audience with her flying fingers.

Overcoming the temptation to stop at Cold Stone Creamery for ice cream took exemplary fortitude to save the money earned for their dad's cause. Emma always reminded them there was ice cream at home and they returned to doll up the plain vanilla and chocolate ice creams with chunks of brownies or chocolate chip cookies, nuts, and chocolate syrup.

Usually, they found Estelle at home with Sam's arm encircling her, talking on the couch in front of the fireplace with its typical dying embers without Laura there to stoke the blaze. One night, Luca hobbled over to the bookshelf and grabbed a Bible. Limping back to the couch, he made sure the Bible would fit satisfactorily between Sam and Estelle and then said, "Carry on, youngsters."

Despite their losses, their worries and concerns, the significant change in lifestyle with their dad's absence and their mother more and more often away for concerts, there was much happiness in the Di Angelo household.

"While I have the Bible here making sure Grandma and Sam are keeping it honest," Luca winked that same night, we should do "Come Follow Me" scripture study, since mom will be late. Mmh. Where are we Emma?" He knew his sister would always be on top of this. She was a practiced and proficient scheduling and notetaking addict.

"Matthew 6 and Luke 24."

"Consider the Lilies," Estelle interjected.

"Yes," Luca replied, firmly in charge of the meeting. He had taken his responsibility as the priesthood leader in the family in his dad's absence seriously, and always made certain they had their scripture study and family prayer even when he could barely sit up in bed. "Can you tell us about that, Grandma?"

Estelle quoted the scripture from memory. It had been her mantra for many years as a single woman trying to survive in a complicated world. "'Consider the lilies how they grow: they toil not, they spin not; and yet I say unto you, that Solomon in all his glory was not arrayed like one of these.' "

"It says here to read Matthew, chapter six, verses twenty-five through thirty-four. Will you do that Emma?"

Emma opened her scriptures and in her quiet voice began reading. " 'Therefore, I say unto you, Take

no thought for your life, what ye shall eat, or what ye shall
drink; nor yet for your body, what ye shall put on. Is not the
life more than meat, and the body than raiment?

Behold the fowls of the air: for they sow not, neither do
they reap, nor gather into barns; yet your heavenly Father
feedeth them. Are ye not much better than they?

Which of you by taking thought can add one cubit unto
his stature? And why take ye thought for raiment? Consider the
lilies of the field, how they grow; they toil not, neither do they
spin: And yet I say unto you, That even Solomon in all his
glory was not arrayed like one of these.

Wherefore, if God so clothe the grass of the field,
which today is, and tomorrow is cast into the oven, shall he not
much more clothe you, O ye of little faith? Therefore, take no
thought, saying, what shall we eat? or, What shall we drink? or,
Wherewithal shall we be clothed? For your heavenly
Father knoweth that ye have need of all these things.

But seek ye first the kingdom of God, and
his righteousness; and all these things shall be added unto you.
Take therefore no thought for the morrow: for the morrow shall
take thought for the things of itself. Sufficient unto the day is
the evil thereof.'"

"What does this mean to you?" Luca asked the group.
Estelle remained silent, anxious to hear her grandchildren's
responses.

"Don't worry," Izzie said. "But we need to do our
best."

"Yes, I agree," Emma said. "The lilies don't just sit
there and do nothing. They open their petals to the sun and sink
their roots into the ground for nourishment."

Estelle smiled and squeezed Sam's hand and looking
into his eyes said, "Aren't they wonderful," she said. He
nodded in the affirmative, too choked up to speak.

Tara mentioned her father who had been in the Di
Angelo home previously. She told them of his new wife, Jenny,
who had "Follow the Lilies" on a plaque on their living room

wall, reminding Dr. Holden and their little daughters to follow the example of the lilies and not be anxious or encumbered with worry, to just do their best and know that Heavenly Father would help with the rest. She related some of her father's wife's story sharing that Jenny's husband was killed in a plane crash as he was escaping from debts he had accrued in the United States and also with a woman with whom he had begun a relationship. Having to start over as a young mother with little children, one who was crippled and needing surgery, Jenny tried diligently not to worry, to do her very best and rely on her Heavenly Father. Their family motto had been to "Follow the Lilies." She lost everything, furniture, vehicles, and their home to collectors.

Jenny was hired to come back to Brigham Young University in the office where she had previously worked. She met Tara's dad who worked in the same department. They had fallen in love, only to be told she had to leave the department or end their relationship because inter-office dating was not allowed. Since Tara's dad was a respected and tenured professor, it wasn't reasonable for him to be the one to leave. And Jenny desperately needed the job and the insurance for her daughter's surgery.

Tara stopped and sighed. "And then my dad totally botched proposing marriage to Jenny. They broke up and my dad left the university for a sabbatical, and even though Jenny's heart was broken, she kept working there to care for her family."

Tara stopped. Took a big breath. "Am I going on and on?"

"No!" Izzie cried out. "Finish the story."

Tara continued explaining that to make ends meet, Jenny moonlighted as a singer with a university student band whose soloist was out on a maternity leave. Then Tara's voice turned dramatic. "One snowy night near Christmas, my dad had returned from the sabbatical and was coaxed to a dinner on campus by another professor in the department who knew

Jenny would be singing for the program. Of course, the rest of the story is that he was seated so he couldn't help but see Jenny. They were reunited after the dinner, and the rest is history," Tara said as she patted her heart. She related how Jenny would often say, "He feeds those who love Him and guides them, just like your dad and I were guided back together."

"Wait." She pulled her phone from her back pocket. "Let me play this for you, I mean if it is okay with you, Luca. I think it goes along with your lesson."

Luca nodded and smiled. Tara slid closer to him, swiped her phone to YouTube, and then typed in "Consider the Lilies." She motioned the others to gather round her. The first song that came up was by The Choir at Temple Square. A male clarinetist began, then the beautiful flutist, followed by a single, plucked-violin with soft strings accompanying in the background. The men in the choir began, "Consider the lilies of the field . . . " The song built and built, with a story woven around the words from Matthew. The women of the choir joined in, and more and more instruments until there was an emotional climax.

"Oh my," Estelle wiped tears from her eyes as Sam pulled her close. "That solo oboe. It made me feel like Heavenly Father was speaking just to the one. Just to me. Just to you."

Luca slung an arm around Tara. "Thank you, Tara." He sniffed and his sisters joined them in a group hug with Estelle melting into Sam's arms as they looked on.

It was nearing midnight when Laura arrived home. Her face was etched with exhaustion and Emma jumped to take her mother's coat and portfolio. While she performed without music, she always had it nearby to review in her dressing room.

"Thank you, dear. Where is Grandma?"

"All that cuddling with Sam wore her out," Izzie teased. "She just went to bed. We have been sitting here discussing the world's problems."

"And solving them," Luca added. "Want some ice cream. I'm ready for a second round."

"Sounds wonderful." Laura sunk onto the couch, lifted her legs to the ottoman, and rested her head back on the cushions.

"Hurry," he motioned to Emma and Izzie. "She's going to fall asleep." They all knew that once their mother sat down, she would fall asleep almost instantly.

"Of course, sir. We'd be glad you serve you." Izzie bowed and headed for the kitchen where Tara scooped dishes of vanilla and chocolate ice cream, Emma mashed in bits of Oreos and nuts, and Izzie swirled Hershey's chocolate syrup on top. It was an efficient assembly line, with Luca promising he would put the dishes in the dishwasher for his part in the effort.

Laura's eyes were just beginning to droop when Izzie handed her the delectable treat as skillfully created as in any commercial ice cream parlor. She snuggled up close to her mother as they each took tiny spoonfuls of their treats to make them last as long as possible.

Each placed their bowl on the coffee table and nodded at Luca to remind him that cleaning up was his job. He had become adept at carrying a bowl while on crutches, and while it would take his five trips to the dishwasher, they weren't about to let him off the hook.

Tara stood and put out her hand to Luca. "Come on, Crip. I'll help you just a little." Her smile was engaging, and Luca responded without hesitation and put his hand in hers. He held it a little longer than necessary as he stood before she disengaged to hand him a bowl. "I'll bring the spoons just so you don't dump them," she mocked him.

"Just you wait until I am off these crutches," he threatened jokingly.

"Wait for what," she said.

"You'll see," he replied.

"Hey," Izzie spoke up. "We are still here. Getting sick from your flirting."

Luca just smiled and reached for Tara's hand again, slipping it through his arm. "You'd better keeping holding on to my arm so I don't fall and break a dish."

Five trips later, the dishes were loaded, the previously melting ice cream was secured in the freezer, and the condiments were put away. Tara wiped the counter and, winking at Luca said, "You owe me."

"I will be glad to pay up. Soon I hope."

A rhythmic breath of sleep came from Laura's corner of the couch. "Come on, Izzie," Emma said. "Help me get Mom up or she will sleep here tonight and have a crick in her neck in the morning."

The girls shook their mom lightly and, each taking a hand, pulled her to her feet. With a parting warning, Laura said, "Luca, to your room now, and Tara, you to Emma's room. No one comes out until morning. Understood?"

"Yes, Ma'am," they both responded and relinquished entwined fingers with a parting wave and a good night.

Chapter 28

Attending church provided Anthony with more
purpose. The financial calculations for the farmers and caring
for the garden and himself took up the major portion of his
time, but he found himself anxious for Sunday.

He even bought a clock when he was in town. It was an
exceptional day for Anthony to venture into a shop. It was not
that he was poor. Lane deposited his salary directly into an
account at CIBanco Los Cabos and brought him cash as
needed. Without an ID Anthony couldn't open his own bank
account and his heart told him that he could trust Lane. Not
that money mattered to Anthony. He could live without money,
as long as God provided rain and sun.

His errand was to find something to contribute for the
gathering after church, and he walked both sides of each aisle
at the Mercado looking for something that didn't have to be
kept cold or be cooked. He settled on the cheeses first, looking
at the Oaxaca cheese—which was long streamers of creamy
cheese wound into a ball. He couldn't see how he could
prepare that cheese to be shared, although it did look delicious.
He settled on a white, aged Cotija cheese that he could cut into
squares and serve on a plate with some fresh corn tortilla chips.
With tomatoes, onions, fresh herbs, and jalapeno peppers in the
garden, as well as spices from Adelita's kitchen, he could make
a spicy salsa picante before he left for church. A sigh of

satisfaction and relief escaped him as he handed some pesos to the proveedora, telling her to keep the extra. The vendor smiled and placed her hands together under her chin in a sign of gratitude.

With the cheese wrapped in paper, he continued on, looking for sandals. He would wear his old sandals, the ones that had belonged to Adelita's husband, as he walked to church. Then he would change into his new ones at Carmen's. He hoped she would continue going to church with him, but if not he would always stop, perhaps pick some desert flowers on the way, or take her some fresh herbs from his garden.

In a stall close to the end of the Mercado hung crisp linen trousers and shirts. Anthony searched through the racks, holding up the loose-fitting clothing to ascertain the proper size. He felt honored to have worn Adelita's husband's clothing, but it was worn and somewhat discolored from work in the sun and soil. And he had to admit, it was difficult to keep the oversized garments from dragging in the dirt from his heels. Adelita was tiny, but her husband must have been a large man. A set of fresh clothing for church would show respect for God's house and His Son.

A colorful sarape caught his eye. It would come in handy for cooler winter nights. He purchased a large bag woven of brightly colored yarns from Carmen's booth, marveling over her handiwork as she smiled broadly and reached to tuck his other purchases inside.

"I will see you Sunday," she said, clasping his hand in both of hers. "You will look handsome in your new clothes."

Anthony's heart soared within his chest. Carmen was planning to see him on Sunday. Hopefully this meant she would also accompany him to church.

Anthony rose early to pick fresh tomatoes, peppers, and herbs, and set about making the picante salsa. He cut the tomatoes into small cubes, chopped the peppers and herbs, including cilantro and parsley, and added a few cloves of garlic. The only items he had purchased for his salsa recipe were a lemon and a mango. Somehow the taste of the fresh mango balanced out the spicy just right. A few squeezes of lemon juice, salt, and pepper completed the dish. He tasted it with a clean spoon and pronounced to no one but him and the chickens pecking for insects that it was just right.

"Delicioso."

He wondered at the odd pronunciation that fell from his lips, as well as the thumb and little finger pressed together that he first held to his lips and then swooped outward, middle fingers extended.

That was an odd gesture. I wonder where that came from, he asked himself as he duplicated the movement.

It bothered him to go inside Adelita's home. "Raiding her kitchen" was how he thought of his occasional forays into what he considered almost a sanctuary. He needed a nice bowl. His bowls were ones he had clumsily crafted from the clay soil and baked in the sun. He found a brightly painted earthen bowl that would be the right size. Pieces of aluminum foil were folded neatly for re-use and stored in a small carboard box on the shelf. He took a piece to cover the salsa picante.

The sun was barely over the horizon when Anthony stoked the fire in his makeshift oven. In a pot he had also borrowed from Adelita's kitchen, he heated water and then poured it over the masa and sea salt he had combined in a bowl. Once the dough was thoroughly mixed, he placed a round ball in a tortilla press he had purchased at the Mercado when he began cooking outside by the shed in which he felt very much at home. He put a little lard on the cast iron skillet he had resurrected from a junk pile he had found while hiking in the area. It was dirty and well-rusted, but he restored it with much scrubbing and treatment with melted lard. Once the tortillas were fried to a golden crisp, he let them cool.

Anthony took his bucket and hiked up the small rise to the well and drew enough water for the day. He portioned half the water into his washing and bathing tub and washed himself before putting on the new linens. He combed through his beard and slicked back his hair, which brushed against the neckline of his shirt. He analyzed his reflection in the tin mirror. Perhaps some scissors and a razor should be his next purchases?

Even though he had purchased a clock, he still based his tasks on the location of the sun, as compared to the horizon, and it was nearing time for him to leave for church. He broke the tortillas into dipping size pieces and wrapped them in a clean cloth.

He wrapped the bowl of salsa in several layers of Adelita's used, but clean, tin foil and placed it in the bottom of the bag with the chips on top. He placed the now well-read Book of Mormon beside the salsa. He cut some fresh herbs and tomatoes and placed them in the bag atop the salsa and then the chips. The new shoes were tucked on each side, holding the salsa bowl secure. The produce was a gift for Carmen. The desert was just beginning to bloom. Next week, if there was a next week, but of course there would be, because he would always stop at Carmen's. Next week he would pick a bouquet on the way to church.

The anticipation of seeing Carmen, Lane and Graciela, and the friendly people at church, as well as learning more about Christ and about this church to which he was certain he already belonged made his steps light as he trod the dusty path toward town.

Not only was Carmen waiting with a bucket of water and a cloth to wash and dry his feet, but three other ladies were waiting in lawn chairs on the porch, neatly dressed, complete with hats and handbags. They eyed him with curiosity. "Is this Adelita's gringo with no last name?" The woman at the far end of the porch looked expectantly at Carmen.

"Si. This is Ramirez. He is a good man. Good friend. Ramirez," she turned to Anthony, "These are my dearest friends, Guadalupe, Yesenia, and Eugenia. They are coming with us today. I have told them that your church is not silly at all and that your people love God and Christ just as we do."

Carmen turned to her friends. "They talk about Christ in the most wonderful way. They believe Christ and God are two separate people."

The gasp from the three onlookers was audible.

"Si," Carmen replied, "and so do I." Another gasp.

Holding up first one pantleg and then the other, Anthony dipped each foot in the bucket of water, rubbed the dust away with his hand, and then dried his feet. He reached into the bag and brought out his new woven leather huaraches with closed toes.

"Aw." Three voices expressed their approval, and the outspoken Guadalupe said, "He is a handsome one." She lifted her eyebrows, and a small smile raised her cheeks.

Carmen opened the screen door and lifted her handbag from a chair. It surprised Anthony to see her tuck a navy blue Book of Mormon inside.

"What?" she goaded him. "You think you are the only one with this book? It is a good book. Good story. Some good people. Some bad people. Lots of wars. But lots of good words from God, too."

"Yes, yes. I agree," Anthony responded.

"And you are wondering where I got it, aren't you?"

Anthony opened his mouth in denial although he really was wondering how her possession of a Book of Mormon came about.

"Two young men stopped by and asked if I wanted to learn more about Christ. One couldn't understand a word I said. The other was pretty good, although, like you, he had a gringo accent. They gave me the book and asked me to read it. So I am, because I said I would." She rushed into the house and brought out a platter with sweet empanadas. "Make yourself useful," she chided, as she covered the platter with a clean cloth and handed it to Anthony.

The aroma of the still warm empanadas instantly tickled Anthony's taste buds. Mmh. He hoped his food would look as delicious to the others as Carmen's offering smelled to him. He had caught a glimpse of the crispy treat sprinkled with sugar before she covered it with a crisp white linen cloth.

Step by step, they trod the paved road toward the church. Anthony insisted that he bring up the rear and he smiled as they walked, listening to Carmen tell the other women every thing she knew about this wonderful church she had found. They feigned distrust and disappointment in Carmen as a traitor to their religion, but he could tell they were intrigued with a church where members participated, and sang, and worshipped joyfully together.

Anthony had to admit that the few times he attended church with Adelita, he found it unusual that the Priest stood and read from a large book and the congregation repeated whatever he said. The music was sad, too, in a minor key, he supposed. *Now how did he know anything about music or minor keys for that matter?* Their gathering after church, however, was very friendly and delightful, with the Priest interacting warmly with the parishioners who were loyal followers of their religion.

Once they'd arrived, Anthony's group was greeted warmly as they entered the chapel. Much handshaking and many hugs and kisses on the cheek as ward members recognized the ladies from frequent visits to the Mercado. Some members even had stalls adjacent to these cautious visitors.

Anthony could tell that the mood of the women changed from one of mistrust to one of interest. Graciela slid down the pew to create a space for the five of them. Carmen made her way quickly to Graciela's side. Anthony sat on the outside end of the row, next to Guadalupe—who eyed him like he was a little boy about to cause trouble in church.

Once again, Anthony repeated the sacramental prayers word for word in his mind. How he wished that he could fully participate in the sacrament, commit himself to Christ in gratitude for His life He had given for everyone there. Everyone everywhere could live with their Father in Heaven again. One day when he figured out who he was, he could be baptized, if he wasn't baptized already, and then participate in these ordinances he seemed to already know so well. But then he would have to leave, to return to those he knew before. He wasn't certain that was what he wanted. He felt comfortable and at peace here.

Graciela explained that both the men and women would stay in the chapel for a lesson from the New Testament. The women nodded eagerly. The New Testament was familiar. The Book of Mormon was not, and they were leery of what was contained in a book so new to them.

The teacher talked about all the names for Christ, not just the more familiar names like Jesus, Lord, and Jehovah, but others such as Healer, Emmanuel, First Born, and The Gift. She told the story of the woman who had wanted to be healed and had so much faith that by just touching the hem of Jesus's robe, she was healed.

Carmen and her friends listened intently. Based on his experience in Adelita's church meetings, Anthony thought this more tender way of speaking about Christ must be touching them.

"Welcome, Señoras. Welcome." Anthony heard those greetings over and over followed by warm hugs as the women in the Branch recognized their acquaintances from the Mercado. Carmen, Yesenia, Guadalupe, and Eugenia glowed with pleasure. As the women chatted, Lane came to sit by Anthony and pulled a photo from his pocket. He held it in front of Anthony.

"A sonogram? How exciting?" Anthony turned to Lane. Broad smiles stretched across their faces.

"Yes! Yes! In September. Mmh? So, you know what a sonogram is? Interesting."

Anthony looked more closely at the picture. "Aw. It's a little girl. Congratulations."

"How can you tell that?" Lane asked.

Anthony pointed to the baby. "See there. No third leg."

"That's what the doctors said. We're pretty excited. Do you wonder at all how you could so easily recognize a sonogram or even tell the baby is a girl. Do you understand what this means?"

Anthony's brow creased. He took a deep breath and sighed. "I must have children," he replied.

"You should be happy, man." Lane slung an arm over his shoulder and gave him a rough man hug.

"I know. I know. But I don't remember them. If I ever get back, will they still want me? I mean, who knows? Maybe I wasn't a good father. Maybe that is why I am here, lost. Was I running away from them?"

"I am sure you were a great father. You didn't just happen to wake up with a kind heart and a good spirit. Those things were naturally in you."

"I am not sure I want to leave. I feel safe, at peace here. Loved. I feel so close to God. You, Graciela, and Carmen are my friends. Leaving what I have here behind to go to people I don't even remember is daunting, to say the least."

"I can't even imagine," Lane replied, "but we will cross that bridge when, and if, we come to it. You may be stuck with us forever." He punched Anthony lightly on the shoulder as he removed his arm.

The group was offered a ride home again and this time Carmen declined, which puzzled Anthony. She wasn't the type to seek out a walk for her health. Anthony brought up the rear of the little troop. With the exception of Carmen, the ladies chatted amicably, but she seemed deep in thought and dropped back to talk with Anthony.

"Your church," she paused, "teaches that Jesus and God are loving. My priest teaches us to be afraid of Deity for how strong and angry they are with us sinners, and how they will punish us if we sin. Your church teaches that God and His Son love us and will comfort us when we have troubles. I like your God, your Jesus. I want to know them. I want them to be proud of me. I don't want to be afraid of them or hide from them."

"I know that God loves me. I know Jesus died for my sins so that I could live with God again. I also know that he suffered in Gethsemane not just for our sins but that he felt our sorrows, too. So, when we are sad or afraid, we know that someone, Jesus, knows exactly how we feel. And we don't need to keep feeling that way. We can move on and be happy. I know that he protected me when I was hurt and found a way to get me to Adelita to be healed. And even if I can't remember anything about my life before, I do remember Him. I am glad that you love my God, my Jesus, too, and I know they love you."

They walked in silence until they reached Carmen's porch. As they said their goodbyes, Carmen called out, "The missionaries are coming tomorrow afternoon if you want to join us. You, too, Ramirez," and she winked as Anthony handed her the sweets platter and reached for his sandals for the walk home.

"I'll be here," he said knowing that afternoon was a relative term, meaning after siesta. Monday was the only day Carmen wouldn't be at the Mercado.

With his sandals back on for the dusty walk, Anthony put his Book of Mormon in the bottom of the bag, Adelita's dish on top of it, and a shoe on either side to hold it secure. He mulled over the happenings of the morning, particularly the sonogram Lane had shown him of his child. Anthony had recognized the black and white picture instantly as a baby in the making. He opened the door to the shed, freed his hands from their burdens, and grabbed a pencil and a small piece of paper. "I most likely have children," he wrote and tacked the note, along with the other clues to his life, on the shed wall.

Chapter 29

"Mom. We need to talk." Luca crutched out of his room the moment Laura came in the door.

"This sounds serious."

"Very," Luca replied, and reached for her bag and set it on the coffee table. He had waited until he was certain his inquisitive sisters, one in particular, would be out of the house for a while. A church activity had taken them away for a service project, so the timing was perfect.

He led his mother to the kitchen counter where he pulled out a stool and went around the counter. He poured water that was heating on the stove in a small copper-bottomed pan into a mug. The pan was one item Laura had requested when her grandmother passed away. He dropped in two bags of Laura's favorite Bengal Spice herbal tea bags. Sliding it toward her, he placed a few Oreo mint cookies on a plate for her.

"Do you expect me to eat those like that?" she joked, pointing to the Oreos. The kids continually teased her about her habit of holding the Oreos under running water before eating them.

"How could I forget?" Luca turned on the faucet and swung it closer to Laura but still over the sink. She took the cookies, one at a time, held them under the water, and skillfully dumped them into her mouth before they crumbled.

"Mmh. So good. So good. Now what did you want to talk about?

Luca was never one to dance around a concern and went straight to the point. "I want to serve a mission."

Laura opened her mouth to reply, and he raised his hand at the wrist from the counter. "Hang on. I know I can't go on a foreign mission. It will be a miracle if I can even go stateside. But I want to try. I've beat the odds for recovery so far. I need to do this, Mom. For Dad. For me. For the family. For God. I could have been killed. I am alive for a reason and the only thing I know to do is to give back to Him. To serve."

"Okay, then." Laura had been sitting straight-backed on the stool and relaxed. "We will do our best to make it happen. If you are committed, I am committed."

Luca hobbled around the counter without the help of his crutches and hugged his mom, lingering longer than a typical teenage boy hug. "Thanks, Mom. It is only May, and I won't be eighteen until August. I will be sprinting by then . . . er maybe at least walking without pain and a noticeable limp."

Just as they released their embrace, Izzie burst through the door and slid to a halt at the counter. "What's going on?"

"Nothing, squirt," Luca replied.

"Aw, come on. I know something is up."

"Izzie . . . " Her mom's look brought her curiosity to a standstill.

"What's for dinner?" Izzie's interest in Luca and her mother's conversation dissolved as quickly as an M&M in a child's hand. Her mom pulled her close and ruffled her black curls. The child was as exasperating as she was lovable. She was the spark that kept the fires of hope alive in the more pensive family members. She gave each of them, in her own energetic way, a reason to believe that something good was just around the corner.

* * * * *

"Vzzt." Luca's cell phone vibrated simultaneously with the lunch bell. He pulled open the flap on the pocket in the leg of his cargo pants. It *would* be his mother. She was always careful to call at a class break, although more likely at lunch.

"Mom?" He put the phone to his ear as he unfolded himself from the desk with his usual awkward exit. The desk was more of a trap with his gimpy leg. At least he didn't get caught and completely fall over his desk anymore.

"Hi, Son. How is your day?" She kept going without a pause for an answer. "Could you call a family meeting for tonight after dinner? Do you have time to let the girls and Grandma know, and could you conduct the meeting."

"Sure, Mom. What's up?"

"Thanks, Luca. I've got to run. See you at dinner."

Luca half-smiled at the phone and looked at the blank phone face. They all knew who Izzie inherited her energy and rapid-fire conversations from, and it wasn't their dad. Luca leaned against the wall in the classroom. If he tried to text and stand up at the same time in the jam-packed hallway, with everyone pushing toward the cafeteria like it was their last-ever meal, it wouldn't end well.

He sent a group text to his grandmother, Emma, and Izzie, who currently wanted to be called Isabella—although no one could remember to do so. He changed her name in his phone from Izzie to Isabella. That was the best he could do.

The answers were predictable. "Certainly," from his grandmother, thumbs up emoji from Isabella, and a heart from Emma. Both girls knew better than to ask the subject of the meeting, which was never disclosed until their dad, and now their mom, began speaking.

Back at the house, Estelle whipped up a batch of cream cheese chicken rolls, a family favorite comprised of shredded chicken, green onions, and celery mixed with cream cheese, plenty of seasonings, and melted butter. It was a gooey mess as she dropped a large spoonful of the mixture on rolled out triangular crescent roll sections, folded the edges into a nice pocket, and dipped the roll into melted butter and seasoned breadcrumbs. She would bake them to a golden brown and serve them with a cream of chicken soup gravy and a salad. If Laura was calling a meeting, the talk would be serious. Better that the children were filled with a favorite meal first. She only hoped it wasn't bad news about Anthony. No news was less threatening, less alarming, than knowing something bad had happened.

Later that day, Laura came through the door and signaled to the family gathering at the kitchen table a "be right with you" gesture, a pointer finger held up, signaling "just a moment." She went to her room, stood in front of Anthony's picture for a moment, and then knelt by her bed. This family needed a miracle, more than one miracle, and their God was a god of miracles.

She kicked off her shoes by her bedside and padded down the hall to the kitchen. She bent over each child, kissing them on the forehead, and then wrapped her arms around her mother.

"Luca, from now on, you will preside at meals and meetings, whatever the occasion with, of course, motherly guidance if needed." She winked at her son. "Would you call on someone to pray?"

Luca cleared his throat. "Emma, will you please bless the food?"

Emma bowed her head. She had a soft voice. One sometimes had to strain to hear her prayers, but they were tender, and she asked for the Lord's help in any decisions they may make. She asked for her father's safety and return, asked for Luca's leg to be healed in a manner that his injuries wouldn't be lasting. She expressed gratitude for the food and asked a blessing upon it.

Estelle marveled at how her grandchildren had been taught to pray as though they were speaking directly to someone they knew well. And they were, she knew that.

Talking while eating was allowed, since everyone was always in a hurry. It was Laura's philosophy that waiting for every bite to be chewed only wasted valuable time and the kids could be out the door and on to their next commitment without sharing the events of their day. They just had to try hard not to load their mouths to overflowing and were prohibited from spewing food when they talked. Conversely, elbows on the table and licking fingers versus using a napkin were strictly banned.

Estelle received many thanks and compliments on the meal and, following Laura's request, the children cleaned up the kitchen and stored away the leftovers in faux Tupperware while Estelle and Laura relaxed and visited.

Once the cleanup crew finished, Luca called everyone to the counter explaining that their mom had called a meeting. "Izzie, I mean Isabella, will offer a prayer to begin the meeting."

"Don't worry about it, Luca. Just call me Izzie. I've given up." She sighed and then smiled.

Surprisingly, since the teen's exuberance usually burst from every pore, her prayers were very articulate, prayers of someone with an outstanding command of language, someone with a soul that was filled with a grand spirit as big as her heart.

Luca conducted the meeting, formally stating the meeting now belonged to their mother.

"Children," Laura wasn't about to beat around the bush. She and Luca were alike in that regard. "Luca has expressed a desire to go on a mission."

"Yippee," Isabella shouted and raised both hands high in the air.

Emma looked perplexed, worried. "How can he do that? Won't he have to walk a lot, ride a bike?"

Laura leaned over the counter and took one hand of each daughter in hers. "Do you believe in miracles?"

"Like Jesus's miracles," Izzie asked.

"Yes. To go on a mission, Luca will need to be able to walk without pain. He will need to be strong and healthy. So yes, the kind of miracle Jesus can perform for us.

"But after all we can do," Luca interjected. "I will get out of study hall and into the weight room beginning tomorrow. The trainer can help me devise a program to strengthen my leg, or should I say my whole body, since I have been such a slug since the accident. I will do my best and hope that Christ can make up the rest."

"Those are wise and faithful words," Laura responded. "The other miracle we need is to be able to pay for the mission."

"I've got that covered, too," Luca said, but I will need a bit of help. "There are three sophomores who are struggling in math. I've made arrangements to tutor them. I am hoping you can help me with this Emma, until I am cleared to drive. Could you do your homework or cello practice at the school while I tutor and then drive us home?"

"Of course. I am happy to do that," Emma was looking less worried and more positive.

"Izzie," Luca turned to his youngest sister, "I want to ask if our band could contribute their earnings to the mission fund. I know that you are saving for a private investigator to find Dad, so it is a lot to ask."

Big tears came to Izzie's eyes. She swiped at one that overflowed its bounds. Her greatest desire was to find her father, but in her heart, she knew they could never earn enough money from gigs at senior centers, even on big tipper nights, to bring him home.

"Sure," came her one-word answer.

Luca rarely showed affection to Izzie. He just didn't know how to handle her larger-than-life approach to most situations, and while there was no animosity between them, he felt bad that he didn't often seek out conversation with her. But her musical abilities astounded him, and the band had brought them closer. He left his seat at the head of the table and went to her side and simply said "hugs," and held out his arms. She wrapped her arms around his middle, and he murmured "Thank you, Izzie," into her curls, somewhat on the wild side after a day at school.

"A lady at church asked me to give her daughter cello lessons," Emma added. "That will help some."

"But you should save that for your mission," Luca protested.

"First things first, big bro. Let's get you out there to save the world and then we will figure out my mission."

"Maybe I will just bring you home my favorite companion." He raised his eyebrows up and down, a mischievous look crossing his face.

That comment received a slug to his arm, to which he responded with a yowl and a pretense of immense pain.

"I will make up some flyers, too, and hopefully get us some more gigs," Emma said.

"You go, Emma. Thanks!" Luca reached over and gave his sister their special handshake, fist bump right, fist bump left, and a big circle of jazzy fingers.

"So, what we are saying is that we need to do our part and expect miracles," Laura summarized.

"Yes!" was the resounding reply.

"Family motto," Luca said. "Expect Miracles. Emma, could you make a sign for the fridge." She nodded and made a note in her ever-present journal.

Laura turned to Luca. "Okay if I talk about this for a moment."

Luca looked surprised to be asked and then remembered how his dad conducted meetings. Permission was asked to speak if more than just a quick comment. It kept order to their family meetings and prevented everyone from talking at once. "Sure, Mom."

"First of all, thank you for being such generous sisters. I know your dad would be pleased with your willingness to help. And Izzie, Sam is making some great progress on your dad's case, particularly with the information he was able to squeeze out of Marty. With all of the FBI agents in New York, Heavenly Father has sent us the one who would truly care about us as a family."

"And especially Grandma," Emma interjected, and sent a smile her grandmother's way.

Laura then spoke about how she felt the family had been trying to do too much alone without relying as much as they should on Heavenly Father and Jesus Christ to help. Of course, they prayed for their father to be found and come home, they tried to save money for an investigator, they had contacted police and everyone they could think of to find him, but did they expect a miracle in his and their behalf after they had done all they could do?

Laura mentioned how they were often sad, afraid, and worried, and related how Christ had already felt exactly how they were feeling now when he was at Gethsemane. He understood their fears. She reminded them that if they focused on Christ, He could heal them from this sadness and fear.

Laura said that perhaps their focus should turn to trying to be happy, helping others in difficult circumstances to be comforted, and to doing everything they could to show Heavenly Father that the Di Angelo's would do their part, trust Him, and know that things would work out according to His will. She suggested they turn their focus to Christ. Let Him be the source of their hope, their comfort, and even joy.

"I know it has been a long time since we have felt much joy. We've been consumed by your father's disappearance and then Luca's accident." She didn't mention the burden of trying to survive financially without Anthony's salary. "We need to focus on Christ in everything we do, trust Him to help us carry these burdens, and then expect a miracle for your father to be found and for Luca to be able to serve the Lord by sharing the gospel with others."

She reminded them that there were people out there hungering and thirsting for a knowledge of Christ. There were people who needed to be loved and nurtured.

"We can do that! And then we can trust our Heavenly Father, our Jesus, to put people in your father's life who will care for him."

It was a lot to grasp for the children, to let go of their fears, their worries, and to turn their lives over to God, to even feel joy again. It was a lot for Laura herself to fathom. She had always been a woman of action, managing any situation that came her way. But Anthony's disappearance had left her feeling helpless and alone. She needed to partner with Christ, who had never left her alone. She knew that. It was time to fully accept His help, to listen for His guidance, and to stop trying to manage everything herself.

"Remember, our best is good enough," Laura reminded her children, especially since Emma tended to go overboard in helping and achieving. And now Luca might push himself too hard. "Don't be running faster than you have strength. Jesus loves us, and His grace makes up the difference between what we can do and what He can do with us and for us. I know that if we keep all of God's commandments as best we can, we will be at peace with whatever happens."

"Emma, can you make a cool chart for the fridge that is titled 'Expect Miracles,' and then below it 'Focus on Christ,' and what else?" Luca swiveled to look at each member of the family.

Emma flipped through the pages of her journal. "How about 'I can do hard things with Christ.'"

"Yes. Good one, Emma" he confirmed.

"Isabella?" He turned to his youngest sister. She wanted to be called Isabella. He could give her that respect. She responded, beaming at the consideration her brother demonstrated for her opinion, "My best is good enough."

"Could you write, 'My best is good enough?'"

"Definitely," Emma replied.

"Grandma?" Luca turned to his grandmother, who beamed with joy at being included.

"How about 'Christ,' then the equal sign, then 'Hope, Comfort, Joy.' "

"I like it! Thanks, Grandma. Emma, I am assuming you took notes, I mean minutes of our meeting." Luca was trying his best to mimic his dad's method of conducting a family meeting.

"You know it," she responded, holding up her journal with a smile.

"I know it doesn't feel like that now, but I am hoping if we each focus on Jesus, peace will soon fill our hearts and minds. I love you kids and you too, Mom," Laura turned to Estelle, "so very much."

"More than crinkle potato chips?" Izzie asked.

"Even more than crinkle potato chips."

Estelle wiped tears from her eyes. These children and her daughter were so precious, so loving, giving, and faithful. She, too, would expect miracles for this family.

Chapter 30

It had become a tradition for Anthony to leave early on Sunday morning for church. He picked fresh fruits and vegetables, and Carmen combined his offering with her ingredients to team up on a tasty dish to share with the members after church. Guadalupe, Yesenia, and Eugenia still attended occasionally, but only on weeks that the women and men met together. Those three had an eye for the men.

Anthony washed his feet, dried them with the rag he left hanging on a limb by Carmen's pump, and put on his good shoes. Carmen met him at the door as soon as she heard the pump screech open. Her open-armed greetings to "my Ramirez," were the highlight of Anthony's week. She took the bag from his arm. "What have we here?"

Anthony had brought broccoli and cauliflower crowns, along with small carrots He would boil the stems for himself another day. The carrots were tiny still, but sweet.

"Oh, these will roast up nicely, Ramirez. Could you get a roasting pan and drizzle some oil in it? And turn on the oven." She left the kitchen to pick some rosemary from a terra-cotta pot on her patio at the back of the house. Chopped onions sauteed in butter, green peppers, zucchini squash, a small jalapeno, and a touch of garlic from Carmen's trip to the Mercado rounded out the savory potpourri.

Anthony had to admit that the roasting vegetables made his mouth water, and he hoped the church members would enjoy their simple offering. Carmen brought out a heavy dish with a tight lid and instructed Anthony to scoop the vegetables from the hot oven into the dish and put the lid on securely to keep the heat in. If they arrived at the church early enough, they might be able to find a space in the warming oven.

Carmen put a light shawl over her shoulders and picked up her handbag from the table by the door. It was a given that Anthony would carry the potluck dish. Carmen seemed excited about going to church and kept a brisk pace up the road to the church building.

They slipped through a side door to the kitchen and claimed a spot for their dish in the pre-heated warming oven. Anthony wondered if some of the members anticipated the lunch after church as much as the actual spiritual meetings.

The female missionaries, Hermana Wells and Hermana Vincent met Carmen as they came out of the kitchen, each looping an arm through one of hers. They ambled down the hallway, chatting amicably. He wondered at this new association. As far as he knew, she had only briefly spoken to them the last week at church.

As they entered the chapel, a member of the branch presidency greeted Carmen by name, accompanied by a hearty welcome and handshake. Carmen turned to Anthony, "I would like to sit with the Hermanas. You'll be okay?"

"Of course. You ladies enjoy yourself," he replied and looking up the aisle for Graciela. Graciela's light-tan face, with her slightly rosy cheeks, absolutely glowed. Pregnancy gave her a beautifully healthy look. Anthony wished Adelita were here to see her beautiful daughter. Graciela's sons wiggled in the seat next to her and pushed past their mother's knees to sit by Anthony. "Will you draw us some pictures?" they asked in unison.

Anthony drew his finger to his lips. "If you promise to be reverent."

"Reverent? What's that."

"Reverence is when you show respect for Heavenly Father by thinking of Him and being quiet when you are in the chapel."

"Okay. We can do that. Can you draw cowboys and a covered wagon."

"Sure. But after the sacrament, okay?"

"Yup," they replied, as the organ prelude ended, and the Branch President stood to begin the meeting.

The music for the opening song began and Anthony retrieved the dark green Himnos with gold lettering and a thin gold border from the book rack on the back of the pew in front of him. As usual, he sang in Spanish while the English words tried to fit themselves into his thoughts. He longed to fully participate in the meeting, to offer a prayer, to bless the sacrament. Admittedly, he felt at peace with his life, if he could just find the information he needed to confirm he truly belonged to this church.

It had been at least a few years, he assumed, since he had been wherever he was from, with a family who by now had forgotten him. The Laura of the inscription in his ring, who might possibly be the beautiful woman overlooking the lake, had surely moved on with someone else. A yearning to have a companion rose within him, forcing a deep breath and a sigh. But he was certainly a married man. Or was he?

Anthony absorbed the words of the sacrament hymn. He reflected on the Prophet of the Church, President Nelson's words that "the answer is Jesus." He felt a love for Christ deep within his soul, a trust that this man knew him, knew who he was, and who he could be. He committed, as the sacrament tray passed him by, that he would focus on Jesus, everything He taught, everything He asked that his followers do. He would succor the weak, lift up the hands which hang down, and strengthen the feeble knees. Wait!! Where did those words come from? He had the New Testament and Book of Mormon practically memorized, and he did not remember those words.

He jotted the words on the program he had picked up from the table at the entrance to the chapel. It was all he could do to wait through Sacrament Meeting so he could ask Graciela or Lane. As always, Graciela gave her complete attention to the speakers, and he didn't want to interrupt to ask if she knew the source of those words. But he knew with his whole heart that those words were his mission here in Mexico for always, and not just until he was found.

Before Sunday School began, Anthony handed his program with the words to Lane. Lane removed his arm from where it rested around Graciela's shoulders and opened his Book of Mormon, which was a nice brown leather-bound copy quite a bit thicker than Anthony's blue copy. He flipped past Moroni, the last chapter in the Book of Mormon to another section called "The Doctrine & Covenants."

Yes! The affirmation shouted in his mind. He knew this book. Excitedly, he tapped his fingers on the words he was looking for when Lane had thumbed to Doctrine & Covenants 81:5. "Yes! That's it. Where could I get a copy of these scriptures. I know this book."

"What comes after the Doctrine & Covenants?" Lane quizzed him.

"The Articles of Faith and the Pearl of Great Price?"

"Yes, my brother. I will get you a copy of all of these. I'll be right back."

Lane jumped from his seat. He caught the Branch President in the hallway and told him of his discovery, that Ramirez No Last Name was almost for certain already a member of the Church of Jesus Christ of Latter-day Saints. He asked if he could borrow a triple combination from the library for Ramirez.

"I'll do you one better," the Branch President replied. "I have a gently used copy in the Branch President's office he can have. Oh dear, I just remembered it is in English. A visitor left it some time ago."

"Shouldn't be a problem," Lane smiled. "He speaks English like an American, which he probably is."

Lane slid into the seat by Anthony, handing him the black, faux-leather bound book with the words BOOK OF MORMON, then a thin gold line, DOCTRINE AND COVENANTS, another thin gold line, and PEARL OF GREAT PRICE.

Anthony turned the book over and over in hands and thumbed the thin, gold-edged pages. Tears formed in his eyes. It was the closest he'd come to feeling like himself, or maybe less like a stranger to himself, for some time. He couldn't speak, and managed to mouth a thank you to Lane, who patted him on the knee and then put his arm around Graciela, who wiped a tear from her cheek. Lane pulled her close, turning slightly away from Anthony, allowing him his privacy in this most recent discovery.

Carmen mingled with the members easily. She had taken a seat between the two Hermanas and chatted graciously with each member who came by to greet her and express their happiness to have her with them. She beamed with pleasure and very obviously enjoyed the rest of their day at the meeting and luncheon.

Someone had already kindly washed Carmen's dish when they went to pick it up from the kitchen afterward. She handed it to Anthony to carry and slipped her arm through his as they left the building. "I have something to ask of you, Ramirez," she said.

"Anything for you, Carmen," he responded.

"The Hermanas came to my home on Wednesday, and I have invited them back this week on Wednesday, too. Will you come?"

"Of course I will, but wouldn't you rather it be just you and the Hermanas?"

"It will do us good. You are a gringo. Of that, I am sure. You try to cover up that American accent, mixed with your Spanish." She shrugged and pursed her lips in a teasing manner. "It will do you good to talk to some Americans about your church."

"How do you know they are Americans?"

"Hermana Wells is a cowgirl from Idaho. Hermana Vincent is from Texas. Even I know that is in America."

Anthony smiled. Those places sounded familiar. Why? How? He didn't know, but his church was bringing such joy to Carmen. Even though her friends didn't join her, she was making her way in this new religion. He vowed to protect and watch over her to the best of his abilities.

And there was the question of his abilities. Lane pointed out that Anthony must have been an accountant due to his capability with numbers and his natural accounting instincts. Yet, he felt most at peace, most connected to his soul when he was painting or working with wood. Had he been an accountant by trade and were painting and woodworking his hobbies? He also seemed to be adept at fixing things, which gave him an instant idea how to serve Carmen.

"I will come, but are there any things you need repaired around your home that I could do before or after?"

"I am sure I can find something." She winked.

They parted when the sun was nearing late afternoon with Anthony back in his sandals and what Carmen called his church shoes in a bag. As soon as he entered the shed he called home, he began writing on slips of paper and tacking them to the wall.

"Hymns—Spanish and English at the same time."

"Doctrine & Covenants."

"Articles of Faith."

"Pearl of Great Price."

"I know that Idaho and Texas are in America."

"I sound like a Gringo."

"I can paint."

"I am a woodworker."

"I can fix things."

Chapter 31

Luca rolled over on his back and held his phone to his heart. He had just asked Tara out on their first real date, a date where he would pick her up at Julliard and she would not just come home with his mom on the weekend. A date where he would be making a dinner reservation, where he would hold the car door open and then walk around to the driver's side instead of her handing him his crutches so he could walk her to the door.

For weeks now, he had been driving Emma and himself to and from school. Now that he could bend his leg and put pressure on his foot, he was almost back to normal, although now he drove more carefully. In fact, he did everything more carefully. He was not anxious to take any risks and experience that kind of horrendous pain again.

Their date was on Friday night and the plan, which he had Emma review and approve, was that he would pick Tara up at the Meredith Residence Hall, which was Julliard's campus student housing and park in his mother's parking space in the Lincoln Center Parking Garage. It was cheating, he knew, but there was no way he could walk the one and half miles to the sushi restaurant where he had made reservations, and finding a parking space would be an impossibility. They would Uber to the restaurant, and he could still open her door like a real gentleman.

Tara, who was from Utah, had never experienced sushi until she came to New York for school, and she delighted in telling him the different types she had tried. She had only been to a sushi bar, where the sushi rolled by on a conveyor belt and one snatched whatever looked good before it got away. Luca had experienced such a place as well and never found the sushi to be of the quality of the actual sushi restaurant on Times Square, where his dad had taken him. And he wanted the ambiance to be just right, too, not a brightly lit room with a noisy conveyor belt and a waitress adding up the color of your dishes to calculate your final bill.

One of the restaurants had a $$$ notation and the other $$. Cognizant of how much his mission would cost and how much he had saved, he had scrolled through dozens of pictures on the $$ restaurant website with the golden glow atmosphere and cleverly presented sushi. One review said the sushi was delicious and like the whole ocean exploding in your mouth. Emma approved and said it was almost like he was going to pop the question to which he explained it would not be the big question but a hope she would be around for them to continue their friendship when he got back.

"Friendship?" Emma asked.

Luca only smiled.

The week dragged on like a month-long reading of "Macbeth" in Honors English class. The only break was a chance to get out of school early on Wednesday to play at the White Plains Senior Citizens Center luncheon. They had performed there several times for a small fee, but the seniors were kind, appreciative, and generous tippers.

Emma had needed her cello for orchestra class and lugged it to the car where Luca waited. Emma and Luca picked Isabella up from the White Plains Middle School just before lunch. Their mom had previously arranged for them to miss afternoon classes, and they had packed the trunk of the car and part of the back seat with their instruments the night before.

A new parking garage swirled layer by layer into the sky across the street from the distinctive yellow brick building with a sculpted statuesque eagle topping a large brick marquee in front. After their first gig, they had read the inscription stating that it was the site of the county courthouse where in July 1776, the Provincial Congress proclaimed the passing of the dependent colony and the birth of the independent State of New York.

"Pretty impressive," Emma had remarked.

"Terrible acoustics," Luca had responded, accompanied by a giggle from Isabella who said, "Let's go count the tips!"

Luca daydreamed his way through two more days of school and skipped his workout to get home as soon as possible to prepare for his date with Tara. He had been on many dates in the nearly two years since he turned sixteen, but none were met with such great anticipation. He headed straight for his room and flung open his closet door.

"Emma!" he called frantically.

"What's the emergency, are you hurt?" Isabella appeared at the door.

"Can you get Emma?" he asked.

"Nuh uh. She's texting with a boy."

"Ugh!" Luca slapped his forehead. "How do you know it is a boy?"

"By the way she smiles."

"Maybe you can help, squirt. What should I wear?"

"I'll get Emma."

Moments later Emma appeared at his door, crossed the room to his closet, and pulled out a pair of navy-blue Dockers and a long sleeve, blue pinpoint, button-down shirt. She examined the shirt for wrinkles. "Still crisp. Want a tie?"

"Would that be too much?"

"Nope, not if you want to impress."

She picked a matching solid color tie, told him he could pick his own socks and underwear, and grabbed his brown dress shoes saying she would polish the left one since the right one hadn't been worn since the last polishing before the accident.

"Good thing he has his own bathroom," Isabella said after Luca's date preparations continued for over an hour.

Luca pushed his wallet into his front pocket. No way would he get pickpocketed and not be able to pay for their meal. Clutching the car keys in his hand, he yelled "see ya" to his sisters just as his mom came out of her room.

"Do I not even get a good-bye?" she asked. "My, you look handsome. Be careful and home by eleven."

"Eleven!"

"Are you eighteen?"

"No ma'am. But almost. Love ya, Mom." And he was out of the door.

The traffic was leaving New York and in the opposite direction of his route. He was about a half hour early for his date with Tara. Not wanting to seem too anxious, he parked the car and wandered around the Lincoln Center courtyard and was just about to make his way to the Julliard residence hall. He felt a light touch on his elbow.

"You're early, Luca."

For a moment he was embarrassed but realized she, too, was early and had anticipated his route from the parking garage to the residence hall which passed by the fountain. "You, too," he replied and grasped her hand. The sparks shot through him. This wasn't good, these feelings. How could he leave this behind for two years?

Luca tapped the Uber icon on his phone and entered the information for pickup and drop-off. He was amazed how easy it was to talk to Tara about school, about her classes, and about news from her dad in Utah. Within ten minutes "Martin in a black Toyota" arrived with the correct license plate number indicated in the Uber app. Luca opened the door, and Tara scooted to the middle of the seat, and he noticed that was just to the middle, not all the way to the other side. Luca prayed he could get in the car without his usual gimpy struggle, and his prayers were answered.

They were soon dropped off at the sushi restaurant. Luca found the area to not be as nice as the pictures and decided right away that they would go back to Julliard to talk afterward. Tara was enthralled with the different sushi possibilities and had a hard time choosing, so Luca told her to go ahead and order for both of them. That way, he thought, if she was having trouble choosing between two or three, she would get all of the ones that interested her.

"Really?" she asked.

"Of course. I want to see what you like."

She chose a sushi for two that had two spicy tuna rolls, two yellowtail, three salmon, two eel, and two albacore tuna rolls. "That should be enough," she said.

"You'd better get a couple more. I'm a growing boy!"

She chose a tuna, avocado, and mango roll wrapped with crunchy spicy salmon and topped with black caviar.

"Have you had a crunchy roll before?" Luca asked.

"No. But I wanted to try it."

"You will love it. My favorite. One more."

She chose a Crazy Roll with smoked salmon, mango, and cream cheese, rolled and topped with avocado, red tempura bits, and sautéed cashews, then drizzled with mango and sweet eel sauces. Luca added seaweed salad, which she had never tried, and some tempura vegetables for appetizers.

This was going to cost him, but to him, Tara was worth everything he owned. He wasn't quite eighteen. People found and married their forever companions at his age. It wasn't like she was the first girl to whom he had ever been attracted. But this was more than a mere attraction. He was almost smothered in a good way by her nearness. They had sat together in the booth rather than across from each other. He was at peace in her presence, the kind of serenity and harmony he imagined heaven would hold.

They were lost in "yums" and "mmhs" as they poked mouthfuls of seaweed salad into their mouths with chopsticks and dipped the tempura vegetables into the eel sauce and the spicy mayo that Luca had asked the waitress to bring. Tara had an odd way of holding her chopsticks. But she was able to bring as much food to her mouth as Luca did with the chopstick training his mom had given them in their early years when she prepared "around the world" meals.

Fortunately, the sushi rolls came out one at a time and they made inroads into each serving until they both proclaimed they were going to burst.

"Do your roommates like sushi?" Luca asked.

"No. They are all on diets, a new one each month."

"We can split the leftovers then, and we can call tonight and have a midnight snack together."

She giggled. "Cool beans!"

"Cool beans?"

"Yup. Utah expression. My dad uses it all the time."

Luca felt proud to whip out his credit card to pay for the meal. As his mother taught him, he would pay it off immediately when he got home to avoid creating a mountain of unpayable debt. He left a generous tip. The waitress brought two containers, and they divvied up the leftovers, laughing again over their midnight plan, Luca saying he hoped he could get past his sisters without too much sharing. Emma wouldn't eat the sushi, but she liked the tempura vegetables. Isabella loved any kind of sushi. He pushed some of each to one side of the container to share. His mom never ate after eight o'clock, unless it was ice cream, so she wouldn't want any.

It would have been fantastic to walk back to Julliard hand in hand if he could have walked that far and if the area wasn't questionable. Luca scheduled an Uber pickup. The driver arrived within moments, and once again they sat close together. Luca exited the car in front of the Lincoln Center and reached his hand for Tara's. She smiled, grasped his hand, slid to the edge of the seat, and then twisted gracefully to put her feet on the ground. When she stood, she was so close that his breath caught in his chest. Luca didn't remember if he thanked the driver or not but put his arm around Tara's waist and guided her to the lighted fountain in the center of the plaza. He had been fascinated with the golden-night lights of Lincoln Center and the huge, rounded orb of the lighted fountain.

It had been light when Tara had met him at the plaza, but tonight, he would not let her walk a step alone. They sat side by side on the masonry wall around the fountain, and Luca took her hand. As usual, he didn't circle around the potential conversation and stepped right into the weight on his mind.

"I am going to go on a mission." He looked for her reaction.

"I hoped you would," she replied. "What can I help you do to get ready?"

This was not the reaction he expected. Did she want to get rid of him?

She continued, maybe aware of his concern. "Luca, I will miss you terribly, but you will be an amazing missionary, and I know this is important to you."

"So, you aren't anxious to have me be sent halfway across the world?"

"Of course not, but what kind of a girlfriend would I be if I was not supportive of such a worthy goal."

She'd said girlfriend!

"I know it is not fair to ask. You are beautiful. There will be and probably are so many guys who will want to date you."

"I don't want to date musicians or dancers."

"What about lawyers?" He nodded toward the law school on the edge of the Lincoln Center property.

"I want to be with you, Luca. Don't you want to ask me to be here when you get back?"

"Yes, yes, very much." For once he had not stated his mind and held back for fear of rejection. "Yes, I want to pick up right where we leave off, but I know what happens when a guy leaves a beautiful girl alone and unattached for two years."

"Then attach me," she said.

Luca could barely speak as he drew her closer and touched his lips first to her forehead, then her cheek, and then finally her lips. The kiss was tender, not a teenage, sloppy kiss. He slid his hand along her silky blond hair catching the glow from the center's lights.

"Tara Holden, I don't have a ring, even a promise ring, but will you be my girl when I get back? Will you think about eternity with me? I love you with all my heart. I have since we first met. You are someone absolutely very special to me."

"I love you, too, Luca, and will support you on your mission and prepare for your return. But remember, you are to devote two years to the Lord, not to me. I will be here when you get back, and then you can devote your whole life to me."

They sat with arms around each other and heads together until concertgoers began exiting the concert hall. Luca stood and pulled Tara into his arms and pressed a soft kiss on her upturned mouth. He led her to 65th Street where he walked her to the residence hall and held her close, and they shared a kiss he knew he'd remember forever.

Chapter 32

Anthony typically kept track of the days of the week based on Lane's visits to bring receipts each Friday. Then he knew it was one more sunset until Sunday. He liked the freedom and peace of not being aware of the particular day of the week. His days, however, had a routine. Wake up. Freshen up. Cook breakfast. Clean up. Tend the garden before the sun arched to the blazing stage. In the afternoons, he would inevitably get lost in his work for Lane. Numbers fascinated him in the story they could tell.

This day followed the same pattern and when he had finished his work for the day he tucked his scriptures in the cloth belt holding up his trousers and climbed the hill to the well holding two earthenware vessels by their rope handles. An old tree stump served as a bench under the shade of a scraggly mesquite tree.

With scriptures in hand, he settled onto the stump and began reading until the sun became serious about leaving the day. As the sky began to relinquish its hold on the day, he stood, stretched his legs and back, and slipped his precious book back into his belt. He lowered the bucket hanging from a rope over the well and filled it with clear, cool water and then filled each vessel. He bent his head to sip from the refreshing liquid.

Twilight fell over the desert as Anthony placed the jugs inside his shed and poured a small amount into a terra-cotta bowl. Undressing, he hung his trousers and shirt from a nail pounded into the wall of the area he had declared as his bedroom. He washed his tanned and toned body, the coolness a relief from the heat of the day. Kneeling by his straw mat, he began to pray, asking the Lord to help him know if he should pursue a return to his former life and asking him to protect and care for those he left behind. Once he had finished his conversation with his Father in Heaven, he took time to be at peace, to quiet his mind, and to just listen.

He stepped to the doorway and gazed at the millions of stars turning the dark sky into a speckled glow. Somewhere there was a family he had left behind underneath this same moon, these same stars. Somewhere. But did he want to leave this life he knew for a life he didn't remember at all.

Anthony awakened as the light was sneaking through the cracks in the wall of his shed. It was the gray light of early morn before the sun lifted itself from its night's rest below the horizon. Soon the sky would be streaked with the gentle pinks and whites of the early morning.

He counted the sunrises since Sunday and realized it was Wednesday, the day Carmen had invited him to meet with her and the Hermanas from church. He really should buy a calendar and the thought surprised him. He found it odd that he could remember things like calendars, calculators, personal hygiene, carpentry, and painting, but he had no recall of what was most important. His name.

Did he really want a calendar? He clung to the peace of only knowing the time by the location of the sun or moon, or by how he felt. Hungry, tired, energetic. He decided to forgo the calendar and keep any pressure to rush past any day at bay. He would enjoy each minute, each hour. Time would be something to treasure and enjoy, not to calculate. He would only use the clock if it was imperative that he be somewhere on time or perhaps for cloudy days when it wasn't as easy to determine an exact time of day when he couldn't see the sun as clearly.

Anthony eyeballed the distance between the horizon and the sun and estimated that by the time he walked to the Mercado, it would be open. He had seen a booth displaying tools and another with backpacks. He would get a backpack first and then all the tools he thought might be needed for handyman projects.

He knew Carmen wouldn't be at the Mercado since she was meeting with the Hermanas, but he anticipated her friends would be there and give him his fair share of ribbing. "Ramirez No Last Name. Handsome gringo. Carmen's shadow."

It didn't bother him terribly, except for the "No Last Name." This lack of a name prevented him from fully participating in the religion he knew to be true. His desire was to serve God with his whole heart and with all his strength, but his obscured past held him back.

A light breeze whispered through the bushes as Anthony trod the dirt road. He passed Carmen's home and headed for the Mercado a short distance down the now paved street. His stomach growled, guiding him to the burritos in one of the first stalls. He nibbled on a scrambled egg and chorizo burrito stuffed with cheese and fried potatoes and wrapped in a flour tortilla. He admitted that he didn't have the typical Mexican appetite for hot sauces, the chorizo was spicy enough and additional hot sauce would just dribble down his chin and on to his white shirt. But this burrito was just right.

He tossed the empty wrapper in a trash can just outside the display of purses, backpacks, and luggage. A heavy-duty black canvas backpack with metal zippers versus the plastic zippers on the designer bags caught his eye. He looked it over carefully, examining two large sections with multiple zipped pockets on the outside. Perfect. He didn't feel like bantering over the price and handed over the amount requested. He could afford what was asked, and these people surely needed every last peso they could get.

Slinging the backpack over his shoulder, he crossed the street to the side-by-side booths offering a plethora of tools. The proprietor warned him to leave his backpack at the door. That was a mistake to buy it first, and he just hoped it would still be there when he had selected all of his tools. He tucked it behind an over-sized toolbox and made quick work of selecting a hammer, screw drivers, a wrench, and a socket set. Thank goodness he only had to worry about metric. And then he asked himself how he knew that sockets in his last life were also measured in inches.

Anthony chose a box of multiple sizes of screws and then one of nails. He picked out a measuring tape and a level. Pliers were a necessity, and he also chose a container of multi-colored, multi-sized zip ties, which he had nicknamed the new duct tape. For a long time, simple repairs were done with duct tape until zip ties became popular. He reminded himself that this knowledge was another tip from his past.

He bought oil for hinges, a small saw, and then electrical and plumbing tape rounded out his purchases. He would surely have a painting project at some point, but he could get brushes when he purchased paint at a regular hardware store further into town. With his items paid for and bagged, he breathed a sigh of relief as he pulled his backpack from behind the toolbox. He felt a sense of pride at having these supplies to help others and walked with his head held high to Carmen's.

By the time he arrived, the missionaries and Carmen were engaged in a lively discussion that carried through the screen door to the street. He knocked lightly and Carmen looked up and beckoned him inside. Dropping his backpack just outside the door, he brushed off his sandals on the mat, pulled the door open, and stepped up one step over the threshold.

"Senor Ramirez," the missionaries greeted him excitedly. "We are so glad you are here."

"Come sit, Ramirez," Carmen patted the seat beside her. The weathered and worn sofa was evidence of a loving family raised in this very home by poor parents. Most of the sofa was hidden by brightly colored crocheted afghans. He observed the room, love on every wall. Memories in every corner of grown children, grandchildren, and Carmen's long since passed husband.

Anthony wasn't certain how many times Carmen had met with the missionaries, but they seemed to know her well and she them, asking after their families. A soft-spoken Hermana from Idaho had brought her guitar. She sang a song about families being together forever. The words flowed into Anthony's thoughts slightly before they were vocalized. The lesson the missionaries taught about the sealing power and of families having the opportunity to be together not just in this life but for eternity brought tears to Carmen's eyes and questions to Anthony's mind. Was he sealed to someone, to this Laura, to children for eternity? The thought was both comforting and provoking. If his memory ever returned, or if he was somehow discovered here in Mexico, he would have to go back. Leaving this peaceful land, the love and acceptance he felt, and the joy of being needed would be difficult.

The missionaries stayed for lunch, but Anthony insisted on setting to work on Carmen's projects. He rearranged and hung pictures, oiled hinges, leveled cupboard doors that were drooping, and took measurements to buy a screen to replace the ripped screen in the front door that would soon give flies easy access to the home. As he carefully placed his tools back in the bag, Carmen patted him on the arm and thanked him profusely, insisting that he take a few tacos for the road that she had wrapped in paper.

It was a remarkable day in many ways. He was tired, but incredibly filled with the joy of serving. So much more to do here. He would win Guadalupe, Yesenia, and Eugenia over yet. Full-fledged member of his church or not, there was still

much good he could do. He would pray for ways to serve these
people and the Lord.

Chapter 33

Handing her burden to Christ had infused Laura's music with renewed energy and fluidity. With her mind continually immersed in thoughts of Anthony and her life crashing into a series of brick walls as hope piled upon hope was dashed, it had been as if she grasped wildly to complete each passage, with the notes struggling out versus just pouring forth. No one seemed to have noticed, but she did. She'd felt tense and unmoved by even the most emotional performance and never understood the thunderous applause or standing ovations that followed. Her audience deserved better.

Emma had designed a note for her dressing room mirror from Philippians 4:13, giving her renewed ability to perform not just for the audience but for God, to show appreciation for his help in her endeavors as a concert pianist.

"I can do all things in Christ who strengtheneth me."

Laura parked in a reserved spot for performers in the Lincoln Center parking garage. She checked her appearance in the mirror, even though Dorothy would soon work her magic for the stage. She reached for her bag lying on the passenger side floor and lifted it toward her. Upside down! Why, oh, why did she do this kind of thing all the time? She seemed to have the curse of clumsiness, as in seemingly slow motion, the contents spilled onto the floor.

Laura slipped her cell phone under the left front shoulder of her bra strap. Her mother taught her at an early age where a woman with decent cleavage could deposit items for safe keeping, although Laura couldn't count how many times she had searched for her phone and couldn't find it until it rang in its hiding place.

She leaned over and gathered up the scattered contents of her purse. Closing the clasp tightly, she opened the door and swung her legs to the pavement. Her heels echoed between the walls of the parking structure.

The security guard at the entrance to the backstage area was new. He didn't call her by name as the others would normally do. "Good evening," and a nod was all she received, although she was used to a vote of confidence for her upcoming performance, or a "break a leg, Ms. Di Angelo."

Dorothy was waiting with a black cape to cover Laura's street clothes. She had a method of applying Laura's makeup from which she never diverted and tsk, tsked when the hairdresser was a few minutes late. Laura always wore a button-up blouse to avoid damaging her makeup or hair. While some performers stripped to their underclothes for makeup and hair, Laura preferred to remain modest.

Since Dorothy provided make-up service several nights a week, Laura asked her about the new security guard. It seemed odd a new person would be placed in the one area that needed the most oversight.

"New to me tonight. He looks reasonably bright. We may just survive," she joked and squeezed Laura's shoulders. "You look lovely, my dear." She motioned from where Laura's hair swept up on the sides and to where it caressed her shoulders. "Let me help you with your dress."

Laura hung the robe that had been over her street clothes on a polished hook on the back of the dressing room door. She stepped behind a screen and slipped out of street clothes, with the exception of her hose. With care, she unzipped the dress bag, revealing a full-length, concert black gown. She unzipped the dress and slipped the gown up over her waist and her arms into the sleeves.

Laura had been wearing concert black for many years and felt almost as comfortable in that attire as in a pair of jeans and a T-shirt, maybe even more so. Anthony had helped her choose this dress, the most exquisite of her career. Sequins bedazzled the scoop neck and three-quarter length sleeves. A wide satin band separated the bodice from a full tulle skirt lined with satin. Laura always chose a gown with a back zipper. Otherwise, she had to wait for hair and makeup until after she was dressed. The gowns were expensive and particularly now, Laura worried about even the slightest damage, which would be prominent under the glare of the stage and spotlights.

Laura stepped outside the screen, Dorothy pulled the zipper to the top and handed Laura some dangly rhinestone earrings. Dorothy noted how some performers insisted on renting diamonds and appreciated Laura's conservative approach to life. Even though on Dorothy's birthday, holidays, and special occasions, Laura was very generous with her appreciation.

Simple black patent-leather heels finished the look just as a light knock on the door signaled the moments left until Laura would be seated at the grand piano and the curtain would rise. Journalists often mentioned Laura's outstanding stage presence. Just before the conductor stepped to the podium and raised his baton, she would always turn to the audience with a slight smile, an acknowledgement that the performance would be for them.

On stage, and as the baton was raised, she met the eyes of the conductor, letting him know that she respected his every move. Orchestras in many cities across the United States had accompanied Laura's performances. The musicians adored the humble pianist who always nodded in their direction and acknowledged their applause after a particularly difficult or beautifully played passage. This was unusual, given the egos and temperaments of many instrumental soloists. She always sent a handwritten thank you note to the conductor expressing appreciation for their expertise and professionalism.

This performance of Schumann's Piano Concerto in A Minor marked the first in a long time when Laura felt like she wasn't fighting for every note. The music flowed from her fingers flawlessly even when a slight vibration on her upper left breast reminded her that she had forgotten to remove her cell phone. She played on, confident that the phone ringer was off, with the exception of a light vibration for texts. She hoped that no more messages would come in until after the performance.

Along with one of New York City's favorite solo instrumentalists, the conductor and orchestra delivered a stellar performance. The musical conversations between the instrumentalists and the pianist not only highlighted the virtuosity of the performers, but the true connectivity of their relationship. After a long-standing ovation, the conductor, concert master, and Laura left the stage and returned during the curtain call to acknowledge the performance of key members of the orchestra.

Laura's dressing room was empty when she returned to change for the drive home. Dorothy usually left long before intermission. She sat down on a stool in front of the mirror, removed her earrings, and released her hair from the combs holding it in place. The black combs were practically invisible in her dark hair. The hairdresser had wanted to use some rhinestone-studded combs, but Laura insisted that her earrings would be enough bling.

She bowed her head to offer a prayer of thanks for a successful performance, one during which she felt she was able to give her best offering to the audience. As she raised her head and opened her eyes, an arm went tightly around her neck and something cold was pressed into her temple.

"Don't scream. Don't move, or I will start shooting through these walls and some of your precious musician friends won't live to play another note."

"Marty?" She recognized his voice immediately. "What are you doing? You are supposed to be in jail. How did you get in here?"

"Told the new guy at security I was your husband. And what am I doing out of jail, free as a bird, you ask? Get out of jail free card perhaps. Ha ha. There just happens to be a police officer, who along with his fireman buddy, benefited from one of my most exceptional appraisals of a fire. Release on bail was easily arranged."

"What do you want, Marty?"

"You. I want you. You were always mine, and Anthony stole you from me. The only dishonest thing that man ever did. He was such a prude."

"I was never yours, and Anthony doesn't have a dishonest bone in his body."

Marty grabbed her by the chin and jerked her head toward him. He hauled her roughly to her feet. "I think you mean 'didn't.' Anthony is no more, and now we are going to leave here, and you will act like you are happy about it, or I will shoot whoever looks your way. Got that?"

Laura nodded, disgusted at Marty's intimation that Anthony was dead, and reached for her purse.

"No purse. No phone."

Laura wished a goodnight to each person she passed and felt her heart sink as the stage door to the alley closed behind her and the panic burned through her chest. A red Porsche convertible waited with the engine running. It appeared that Marty had paid off the valet parking crew, too. And weren't his assets frozen? Where did he get this car?

Laura's mind was running at high speed. Getting into a car with Marty set alarm bells off throughout her body, but as he swung open the door and pushed her inside, she realized she had no choice but to acquiesce if not only to save her life, but the lives of anyone else who got in their way.

Laura felt like she was having an out-of-body experience as Marty made his way into the country outside the city. By this time her family would wonder where she was and hopefully call Sam.

Marty put his hand possessively on her thigh.

"Stop it, Marty." She pushed his hand away.

He drove recklessly, with the gun in his left hand and only his pinky and ring fingers grasping the steering wheel. In the confines of the vehicle, the stench of alcohol made her stomach churn.

"You're drunk, Marty. Pull over and let's talk about the trouble you are getting yourself into."

He snickered. "Like I am not already in trouble. But that will all end tonight. If I can't have you, no one man will ever touch you again." Once again, his hand clutched her thigh.

Her phone buzzed at her shoulder, and Marty jerked his head in her direction. He was driving hastily along a road with hairpin turns and jerked toward her when the phone vibrated. He let go of the steering wheel and pointed the gun at her. He grabbed her dress at the shoulder, ripping the sleeve from the bodice, and assailed her with a string of profanity as the car veered to the right. "I told you no phone," he shouted, as he grabbed for the steering wheel and jerked the car back to the left.

Laura's phone flew to the floor, and Marty reached down to beat her to the retrieval, yanking the steering wheel as he leaned. Laura watched—in what seemed like slow motion— as Marty's side of the car swayed up in the air and the ground met her window.

She felt weightless, floating, and then . . . nothing.

*****

According to witnesses, the vehicle swerved, skidded, spun, rolled over once, then flipped end-over-end and again side-to-side. It rocked up on the passenger side, slammed down to the ground, and remained there.

Inside the car, Laura blinked, trying to bring the night into focus. She shook her head and crumbles of glass dropped onto her lap. Someone reached into the window and put their fingers on her neck. She turned to the person in a fireman uniform. "What happened?" she said.

The fireman said, "You've been in an accident. You are one lucky lady. We'll get you out of here."

She looked to her left. The top of the car was smashed all the way down to the seat. A leg and one arm were all that was visible. "Marty? Marty, are you okay?"

The fireman covered her with a heavy blanket and a loud roar assaulted her as metal was ripped from metal. The side of the car was pulled away and the fireman lifted her from her seat.

"Is Marty okay?"

"I'm sorry, ma'am. Your companion didn't make it."

"So, he's dead.

"Yes ma'am."

"I didn't want him dead. I just wanted him to leave us alone."

The fireman and police officer exchanged quizzical looks.

A female police officer walked with Laura and the fireman to the ambulance. Laura sat on the bumper and an EMT shone a light into her eyes.

"You are one lucky lady."

Why did people keep telling her she was lucky?

"Can you tell me what happened?" A detective had joined the female officer and started questioning her.

"I just remember that Marty got mad because my phone rang. He pointed his gun at me and grabbed for my phone. That is all I remember."

The detective jerked his head toward another officer. "Find the gun."

Sirens assailed the quiet night, and a black sedan skidded to a stop by the ambulance. Sam rolled out, leaving the driver's door open. He was at her side within seconds, flashing his badge simultaneously. "Give us a moment, please."

The EMT attending Laura stepped back.

Sam put an arm around Laura's quivering body and pulled her to his chest. "He's gone, dear. He can't hurt you ever again."

She turned her face up to Sam. "Yes, I am free, but he ruined my dress. I can't perform without a dress." She smoothed the fabric over her lap. "I can't play without a dress."

And then the tears fell, and the EMT stepped back in to complete her checkup. She spoke to Sam, clearly respectful of his authority on the scene. "We'll need to transport her. She seems okay. But I mean, look at that car. There's almost a protective bubble where she was sitting. But we've got to rule out internal injuries."

Sam noted that Laura was unusually fixated on her ravaged performance gown. He hoped that was how she was coping with the rollover, which would surely affect her for a long time to come.

He consulted with the police detective and then called his office to send an agent to the police station to figure out how Marty was released, hoping Laura would be able to shed some light on the situation once she recovered from the shock of the accident. The detective gave Sam the location of the hospital where Laura would be taken, and Sam called Estelle and filled her in on the accident, asking her to let the children know their mother was fine and was being transported to a hospital for observation.

He wiped his brow and looked up into the sky for answers. Anthony's disappearance was fraught with some even deeper chasms of crime than he had originally imagined. Was the Di Angelo family safe, or were there more of Marty's cohorts out there wanting to cover up any trace of their misconduct?

Chapter 34

Sam settled into the still-running vehicle. He slammed his hand on the steering wheel. Feeling like he had let Laura down after he had assured her that Marty was locked up for good and that she was safe, he slid his fingers through his hair and shifted the car into gear. He'd get to the bottom of it before the night was over. There would be no sleep until whatever slip-up that released that monster Marty was resolved. A gun. Marty had a police revolver in his possession! How did that happen?

Sam's phone dinged, and he punched the electronic display on his dash to listen to the text. Great news. His lead agent was on the case. He pushed the microphone icon and said, "Call Agent Ream."

Johnny Ream answered immediately. "It's a mess down here, boss."

"Fill me in." Sam's voice had a calming influence. He never gave in to panic or stress and shouted, as the other senior agents were pre-disposed.

"The officer that released Marty has taken a hostage and is threatening to shoot himself."

Sam could hear shouting and screaming in the background. "See if you can get control of the situation. Put a damper on all that yelling. I'll be there within a half hour. Marty had taken Laura way out of town."

Sam once again slammed his hand on the steering wheel. He almost cursed as he would have in the past, but Estelle had warned him that she would put up with absolutely no foul language. It was an intense workout to break the habit. This case had some deep tendrils. Just how deep was the question.

Sam pulled into the precinct garage and took the elevator to the main floor. He was met by a scene of officers, all with drawn guns pointing at an officer with one arm around the neck of a female clerk and the other raising a gun to his own head.

"Okay, men. Let's take it easy. Lower your weapons."

He nodded at Agent Ream who kept his gun pointed at the errant officer. Weapons were reluctantly lowered, but not holstered. Sam squinted to see the name on the officer's badge. He knew even the clerks had been trained in self-defense. The woman looked fairly calm and seemed to have her wits about her, while the officer was threatening his own death through sobs.

Sam nodded again at Agent Ream and winked at the clerk. "Officer Trent here is not winning any congeniality contests tonight, is he?"

The clerk blinked and then recognition burst on her face as she recognized the reference to a popular movie where an FBI agent turned beauty contestant lays another agent out on his back.

Within seconds, an elbow slammed into Officer Trent's gut and the clerk ducked as he jerked away in surprise. While she didn't finish the series of moves, it was enough for Agent Ream to shoot the gun from the embattled officer's hand and for other officers to apprehend him. Officer Trent collapsed into a moaning and crying pile on the floor until he was hauled to his feet and whisked away to an interrogation room, followed by the Chief of Police, Sam, and Agent Ream.

The brave clerk was surrounded by her team and both comforted and congratulated. Sam pointed at her with a "you did it" motion and said "catch you later" as he strode down the hall to the last room.

The officer rolled on his cohort, the fireman, who had burned down his own home to keep it from going to his soon-to-be ex-wife. When Marty had met the officer who had been on the scene and the fireman, he had offered to write up the fire as accidental for a share of the insurance payout. Greed overtook common sense, and the two men became Marty's cohorts in other fraudulent schemes.

Marty had threatened to expose the police officer, who then wrote up the release papers and provided Marty with the weapon and ammunition.

Sam left the police chief to deal with the subdued officer and to coordinate the arrest of the fireman with the fire chief. How Marty got into Lincoln Center with the tight security would be another mystery to solve in the morning. Lincoln Center would have long since locked its doors tight against the night.

Sam checked his watch. The time was inching toward four in the morning. He hesitated to call Estelle, but she was an early riser, usually by five a.m. He selected her name from his recent calls.

"Sam!" Estelle answered immediately, obviously fully awake.

"How are the kids?"

"Finally asleep. They surprised me. This family has truly turned their lives and thoughts over to Christ. There were no tears, no worrying or fretting. Just confidence that their Father in Heaven would protect their mother. But they did stay close to me, wide awake until the wee hours of the morning."

"Sweet kids. Wish I could be more trusting like them. I am going to catch a few zzz's and then head over to the hospital. Laura seemed quite unscathed physically. Mentally she seemed a bit in shock. Marty having been killed in the accident didn't appear to have sunk in yet. She just kept worrying about her torn concert gown."

"I can't imagine how she ended up in a car with Marty, but I can understand her worries about the dress. She loved that dress because Anthony chose it for her. Now money has been so tight without Anthony's income it will be difficult for her to get another performance gown."

Sam headed for the police lounge with the phone at his ear. If he didn't lay down right away, he would fall down. He didn't have the "stay up for days" strength he had as a young agent.

"Keep in touch, Estelle. I'll call you once I see Laura. She couldn't remember much last night, but I'll talk with her this morning. I am sure she wasn't there willingly. I love you, Estelle. So glad you are my girl."

"Love you, too, Sam. Very much. Take care of my little girl."

"I will do my best, Estelle. Didn't expect a crooked cop in the mix. But it won't happen again."

Sam leaned back on the couch in the breakroom. He had just drifted off to sleep when his phone vibrated, and he shot upright. The screen identified the caller as the North Shore University Hospital, which was quite a distance from Manhattan. Marty had driven almost out to Manhasset Bay. Who knows what he had planned?

"Agent Sam Brady here," he answered.

"Sam?" Laura's voice came through strong, anxious.

"Yes, dear. How are you doing?"

Laura completely ignored his question and launched into a discussion of the security guards at the Lincoln Center. "There was a new security guard last night, backstage." She explained that she had asked Marty how he was able to get backstage, and he said he told security he was her husband. "Do you think Marty planted a new guard there and in that case . . ."

Sam interrupted. "There could very well be one of the regular security guards in danger. I'll call you right back." He quickly tapped on Agent Ream's number and asked him to send agents to Lincoln Center and contact the head of security about the possibility of one of his team being missing.

Selecting recent calls, he dialed the hospital and asked for Laura's room. The operator was reluctant to transfer the call until he identified himself and stated that Laura had just called him.

Laura answered immediately after the call was put through to her room. "Oh, Sam, I had always hoped we could get Marty to lead us to Anthony. Is it hopeless now?"

"Never give up hope, my dear. When you least expect it, a lead will come your way, and everything falls into place. You know, it is a miracle you survived the accident. Doesn't your family have an "Expect Miracles" motto on the fridge? This applies to finding Anthony. Expect miracles." He sighed, because a miracle was what it would take for Anthony to be found after such a long time.

"I will expect a miracle, Sam. But it is hard, especially when there is nothing I can do to help."

"I think your mom always says to rely on God and quit stirring the pot."

Laura chuckled. Her mom and her strong testimony were surely rubbing off on Sam.

"Let me get an hour or two of sleep and I will come spring you."

"Thanks, Sam. You are indeed a miracle in our lives."

Chapter 35

Accounting for Lane and gardening for Adelita—as
Anthony liked to think—only took up a small portion of
Anthony's day. Once his work was done, he would climb the
hill to read and study the scriptures. At church, it was always
recommended to begin the day with scripture study, but
Anthony found that his mind kept wandering to work or
gardening if he didn't accomplish those tasks first. When his
work was done, he could fully immerse himself in his
scriptures studies without distraction. Although lately he was
finding hours toward the end of the day when he was at a loss
to fill his time.

He was beginning to look forward to Wednesdays when
he could go to the Mercado and bring home a little meat in a
small cooler he had purchased along with a wheelbarrow to
haul materials for his projects. The ice block usually lasted two
days if he kept the chest in the shade, so tonight he would grill
some chicken thighs spiced with fresh herbs from Adelita's
garden.

One evening, he randomly started carving on a piece of
wood and before he knew it, a small wooden truck lay in his
hand. He found another scrap and created a tiny doll. This
became a regular evening pattern and each week when he went
to town, he shared the toys with little children playing along
the way. Many were quite poor but used their imaginations

effectively to create small towns out of sticks and rocks. Now as he walked by, they ran eagerly to greet him and receive his offering of another wooden creation. He branched out into small animals, tiny tractors, and even a miniature wagon or two. The children were excited and pleased with each unique toy. He determined that he would start painting the toys and somehow get some wheels to fit his creations.

Anthony finished his last carving for the night and leaned back against the shed. The fire in the oven went from small flames to embers as the full moon rose higher in the sky. Out in the bushes, Anthony saw two bright eyes staring at him. For a moment, he thought it might be a coyote until the moon rose higher and he could see it was a mestizo, just a common street dog. Some were friendly. Some not. He beckoned to the dog. Surely it must be hungry or thirsty if it was way out here in the desert. The dog raised up on its forepaws and whined, then settled back down low to the ground.

"Here, buddy," Anthony called out, holding a morsel of meat that had been stuck to the grill on the oven.

The dog whimpered again, limped a couple of steps toward Anthony, and then lay low again. Up, down, up, down, the dog inched toward him, finally tentatively stretching out its nose to sniff the offering before eventually gently pulling it into its mouth. Anthony poured water into an earthen bowl he had fashioned from the clay soil and baked in his oven. The dog lapped it up and looked up appreciatively at Anthony with water dripping from his scraggly jowls.

Even in the dim light, Anthony could see that the pup was matted with burs and put little pressure on its right forepaw. He let the stray sniff his hand and then slid it up between its ears. Tail wagging, the dog inched closer. Anthony slid his hand down the dog's leg and picked up its paw.

"Aw, got a big sticker in there, don't you, buddy," Anthony soothed as he removed the cause of the dog's pain. He left for a moment, hoping the pup wouldn't retreat, and retrieved a piece of cooked chicken from his ice chest, which he kept under a bush at the side of the shed. The lost animal, looking mangy and forlorn, sunk to its belly beside the bench where Anthony had been sitting. Anthony broke the chicken into small bites, and the dog gobbled them hungrily, licking its chops after each bite.

"Wanna be my dog?" Anthony asked the pup, as if he could answer.

A wagging tail and pricked ears spelled the animal's desire to be with Anthony. It was late when Anthony took the pup inside and settled him on a mat in the corner. "Bath for you tomorrow and a trimming. We'll get those burrs out."

After more scratching behind the ears and petting in the few areas that weren't knotted with burrs, appreciative tail wagging and joyful panting signaled that Anthony indeed had a new friend. "You're going to need a name, boy. Let's see, how about Tobias? It is a good strong name. Goodnight, Tobias."

Anthony scratched Tobias behind the ears, went to the pewter basin, and washed his face and hands, brushed his teeth, and relaxed on his mat. He wasn't alone anymore. He didn't think he minded his solitary existence except when Lane came by or on Wednesdays and Sundays in town. But he must have been lonely because just having this poor street dog wander into his life was immensely comforting.

The sun peaked through the cracks in the shed and eventually ended up right in Anthony's eye, pulling him from the deepest sleep he had experienced in a very long time. His internal alarm clock usually awakened him before the sun could peak over the horizon. He rolled over and looked to where he had settled Tobias the night before and found his new friend staring back at him.

"Want some breakfast?" It was odd to hear his own voice. He only spoke aloud when he went to town. This lost street creature had wandered into a home where company was direly needed. Tobias was indeed a blessing.

The pup would have to eat what Anthony ate. There was not a full menu of food choices at Anthony's home in the desert. He fixed a corn meal mush with butter and tiny bits of dried bacon and picked a few peas from the garden. Some silly food pyramid always popped in his mind every time he made a meal, so sometimes he accommodated this aberration and ate something from each level. Today fit the bill. Corn meal for his carbohydrate. Butter for his dairy. Bacon bits for the protein. Garden peas for the vegetable group.

Anthony's next project would be to make some more bowls now that he had company. He could buy them at the Mercado, but molding his own creations and baking them was so satisfying.

Tobias slurped up the mush and peas within seconds, licked his chops, and laid down for a morning rest, giving Anthony a chance to work on the pore disheveled mutt. For several hours, Anthony snipped the mats out of Tobias's fur. A good brushing would have to wait until he went to town and bought a brush, but a bath would be in order. The dog looked awfully ragged with chunks cut out of his fur here and there where it was particularly matted or thick with burrs. Perhaps a trip to town would need to come sooner than next week.

After clearing breakfast and washing the bowls, Anthony carried two buckets up the hill to the well and hauled them back down. He put the dog into the washtub, surprised at how compliant he was with a bucket of water being sloshed over him. Using just the minimum amount of his own soap, he coaxed suds into the black and gray fur and scrubbed the pup thoroughly. Carefully, so as not to frighten Tobias, he slowly poured a portion of the second bucket over the pup and used a cup to dip water over his head. He watched as the shock of fur running from the dog's belly to just under its chin turned from gray to snowy white. Other random gray spots were transfigured as well.

The water in the tub became a muddy swirl of water and discarded soap. Anthony used the remainder of the water to rinse the pup, careful to get all of the soap out so Tobias wouldn't itch like he personally did when he didn't rinse his hair thoroughly. Just as he finished, Tobias shook furiously, with water flying every which way, and especially all over Anthony. But Anthony laughed aloud and then wondered how long it had been since he had ever found a reason for a hearty laugh.

Tobias lay on the wooden porch Anthony had built in front of the door with the sun drying his shaggy fur while Anthony tended the garden and looked over his tasks for the farmers, deciding the accounting could wait for later in the day. He would make an extra trip to town to get some battery-operated clippers and a brush to finish the restoration of the dog's piebald coat. He hesitated at the thought of his purchases. How did he know about battery operated anything let alone dog clippers.

A length of rope lying in a discard pile was fashioned into a leash. They started out walking, but Tobias was still limping a little from the damage the thorn had done to the pad on his foot. Anthony put him in the wheelbarrow for an easy ride to town next to the cooler he had brought along as well. With his new guest, who he hoped would take up permanent residence with him, he would need to have more meat on hand.

A cool breeze accompanied their morning walk to town. He stopped at Carmen's booth in the Mercado, somewhat regretting his decision as Guadalupe called out, "Hola, Ramirez with no last name." It was just salt in a wound he couldn't heal, though quite honestly, he didn't know if he even wanted to know who he really was.

"Hola, Carmen's handsome gringo." Yesenia flirted shamelessly, batting her eyelashes heavily coated with mascara. Eugenia, the ever quiet and shy one of the three, smiled a sweet smile and Anthony winked and smiled in her direction.

"Hola, Mijo," Carmen came out of the booth to throw her arms around Anthony. "What brings you to town on a Friday? And what do we have here?"

"This is Tobias." He patted the pooch on the head affectionately. "He wandered out of the desert to visit me last night and stayed."

Before he could ask Carmen if there was a booth with pet supplies, Guadalupe resumed her chiding. "Tobias No Last Name?"

"Si," was Anthony's only reply and he headed in the direction of the booth that Carmen indicated carried pet supplies. The Mercado booths had everything one could possibly need and a hundred more attractive but useless items. He saw tourists often leave the mercado area with newly purchased, brightly colored luggage just to hold the treasures they had discovered.

The operator of the pet supply booth beckoned Anthony with a leather leash in one hand and a ball attached to a braided rope in the other. "Something for the doggy. Something for the doggy," he called out.

Anthony chose a thin nylon leash. He wouldn't need heavy duty leather to keep Tobias by his side. A blue tennis ball attached to a short blue and white braided rope looked just right for both fetch and tugging. He was looking forward to playing with his pup and perhaps teaching him a few tricks. He noticed Tobias eyeing some bone-shaped dog treats and bought a few for special occasions. He selected a brush that looked sturdy enough for Tobias's thick coat and in the absence of battery-operated clippers, he found a set of rechargeable clippers with several attachments. Although he had no means of recharging the clippers, he could bring them to town when he went into Lane's office and recharge them while he worked.

With Tobias in the wheelbarrow happily munching on a treat, Anthony sauntered in the direction of the meat market. Specific directions were not required as one only had to follow one's nose to the delectable aromas wafting from the outdoor grill in front of the Carne Mart. In addition to the fresh meats inside, as well as some seafood, the store offered burritos, carne asada plates, tacos, and hamburgers smothered in cheese.

He spotted the Hermanas from church, along with two elders he didn't recognize who must have just been assigned to their area. They appeared to be worriedly counting their money, with one typing into his phone, scrolling with his finger, and shaking his head with a frown.

"Elders, Hermanas," Anthony approached the group and the new elder immediately gravitated to Tobias. "How are you today?" He spoke in Spanish although all of them were as American as could be.

Elder Crane, who had been in Cabo for a few months, responded in Spanish. The Hermanas rushed forward and shook his hand, excitedly asking him if he had talked to Carmen.

"Just at the Mercado. Is everything okay?"

"More than okay. You will have to ask her to tell you her news when you see her next."

"You can't tell me?"

"She will want to," they said in unison.

Elder Crane spoke next, gesturing toward his companion who was still petting Tobias. "Hermano Ramirez, this is Elder Davis. Fresh from New Yawk." He laughed and put his arm around the elder. "Good guy. But he can't speak much Spanish and most definitely has trouble with the English." Elder Crane went on to explain that Anthony spoke both Spanish and English if Elder Davis preferred to stick with his butchered English instead of Spanish.

Elder Davis put out his hand. "Pleased to meet you, Hermano Ramirez." The boy couldn't have been more than eighteen, stocky with a shock of dark hair. But his handshake was firm and there was maturity about him. It was obvious he had enough confidence in himself that the teasing of the other elder didn't affect his confidence at all. Anthony thought it wouldn't be long before he was so fluent in Spanish that he wouldn't need his New Yorker English. But still, the way the new elder spoke seemed so familiar. Somehow comforting. His vowels were all drawn out and his r's were missing, but it reminded him of something, someone.

"Have you found anything good to eat here?" Anthony asked, making conversation, but was met with confused, silent looks thrown between the four of them.

"Naw," said Elder Crane. "We'd better run. See you at church?" And the four turned in unison to leave.

"Hold on. Hold on." Anthony said, beckoning them back. "What's going on?"

Clearly the spokesperson of the group, Elder Crane confessed, "Just a little short of funds until tomorrow. We get money in our accounts tomorrow."

Anthony shoved his hand in his pocket. He had plenty of money and much more than he needed for a couple of days' worth of meat. "I'm kind of hungry and could use some companionship. Let's go in and choose some things to share."

"You sure?"

"Of course, let's go." The missionaries eyed the food inside the booth with anticipation. Anthony wondered how long it had been since they'd had enough to eat. He was sure the Church wasn't shortchanging them on funds. Perhaps they just had a bit of struggle with budgeting?

The missionaries were hesitant to choose, so Anthony chose a monstrous, thick carne asada burrito, two large carne asada plates with generous portions of meat, rice and refried beans, and a big salad with various greens, tomatoes, and carrots. The butcher smiled and handed Anthony five paper plates with some plastic forks and knives and nodded toward a canister of water, a bowl of lemons, and some plastic cups.

Talking was sparse as they ate with Tobias eyeing them from under the table.

"May I give him a piece?" one of the Hermanas asked.

"Probably should before he decides to take one himself," Anthony joked.

"So, tell me about yourself," the new Elder Davis asked.

"Not much to tell," Anthony sighed. "I guess they've told you I'm really Ramirez No Last Name because I have amnesia from what I hear was an accident of some sort, and I don't even know who I am."

"Oh gosh. Sorry. Sorry I asked," Elder Davis said with honest concern.

"But I have found that in my previous life, I probably liked to draw and paint, I'm good with numbers, and some think I was probably a member of your church. That is about my only sadness. I can't fully participate because I don't know enough about myself to either continue as a member or be baptized as a new member. I love God. I want to serve Him, and I can't in the way I would like."

One of the Hermanas who had been quiet touched him lightly on his arm. "You are serving Him. 'If ye have done it unto the least of these, ye have done it unto me,'" she quoted from the New Testament. Tears gathered in her eyes and began to spill. The other Hermana put her arm around her. "We were really hungry. You have been so kind, and we are so grateful. He is grateful," she looked skyward.

"Thank you, Hermana." Anthony said, and pondered on her words. Maybe this is how he would serve the Lord, by caring for those in need. Maybe he didn't need to be a formal member of the Church of Jesus Christ of Latter-day Saints. But he did want the privilege of taking the sacrament, repenting weekly, and making promises to God. For now, he would remember Christ in his heart as others physically partook of the sacrament. He would commit in his heart to try to live as He did.

Chapter 36

With the half-sheet cake placed on the back seat of the car, and her purse in place to keep it from sliding to the floor, Laura slid into the driver's seat, grateful for the cloud cover that would keep the sun away and prevent the frosting from slithering to the base of the cake.

Opening a mission call was a special occasion in their church, and several of Luca's friends from the baseball team and, of course, Tara who was coming by train after her classes for dinner and the "grand opening." Estelle and Sam had just returned from their honeymoon, with Estelle already diving in to prepare for the event.

Laura had ordered Luca's favorite lemon cake with white frosting from Lulu's Cake Boutique only a few miles from White Plains. She had ordered small plastic decals from Amazon depicting Luca's hobbies and a small Italian flag for good measure. She knew Luca was resigned to serving stateside, and while his dream would have been to serve his ancestors in Italy, he hardly dared to hope. But Laura's mother's intuition all along led her to feel Luca would serve a foreign mission. As part of his interview with the Stake President he had to demonstrate is ability to walk without pain if he wanted to serve even a traditional mission. And he had done it after weeks of grueling physical therapy.

The little flag was a symbol of her hope and faith that the Lord would reward her son for his hard work and diligence to achieve the miracle of walking as he once had before the accident.

Emma ran down the steps and met her, anxious to see the cake. She had asked her mom to get a plain cake so she could do the decorating. Laura was all thumbs at artsy things like cake decorating, and Estelle had taken over teaching Emma how to adorn a cake with fancy writing and flowers.

"Perfect," Emma responded when she saw the blank cake top. "Don't worry. I'll make it fun and masculine. No flowers!"

Sam manned the barbeque on the deck with an assortment of hot dogs and hamburgers ready to be grilled. Izzie was arranging strawberries, blueberries, and melons on a platter, with sodas and chips rounding out the menu. Laura had learned from experience that a nice vegetable assortment would be underappreciated by the teens and surely go to waste, except for a few pieces consumed by the adults in attendance.

Promptly at 7:00 p.m., Luca burst through the door, tossing his baseball glove into the coat closet, a significant improvement since the days of cleats, bats, and gloves cluttered around the entry way. While he couldn't play ball as he had in the past, he had learned to become satisfied with coaching a Little League Team and umpiring to earn money for his mission.

"I'm home," he shouted, as if they didn't notice his obvious entry.

"Hi, son," Laura called back and went to give him a hug. Then, thinking better of it, turned him toward his room. "Quick shower before everyone gets here?"

"Of course, Mom," though he threw his sweaty arms around her and hugged her, nonetheless. "Tara's coming!"

Emotion choked Laura's throat as she hugged him back and sent him on his way. She would miss this ball of love and energy, her firstborn who had overcome so much adversity in the last year, but always with a smile, always positive. She sincerely hoped he would be delighted with wherever he was called to serve. And she could only hope that when he returned, Tara would be waiting.

Later, with friends and family all gathered in the living room, Luca stood before them in front of the fireplace and drew his phone from his pocket. A picture of the family all together before Anthony's disappearance hung above the mantle. It was as though Anthony was still looking over his family gathered together for this exciting moment.

Luca opened his e-mail with the mission call. "Luca Anthony Di Angelo, you have been called . . . " Luca paused and started to cry. Deep sobs stopped him from speaking for what seemed like minutes.

"Son?"

"It's okay, Mom," he replied. "You have been called to serve in the Rome, Italy Mission, speaking the Italian language and will report to the Missionary Training Center in Provo, Utah, on Thursday, September 22, 2023."

The cheers that erupted were deafening and the hugs were rib-crushing tight. But the joy and elation on Luca's face was something Laura would hold close to her heart forever. He would be serving in the land of his ancestors. Anthony was a first generation American, although he never really managed to speak fluent Italian like his parents. When they would launch into their Italian dialogue, complete with various hand gestures punctuating their communication, he would zone out and wait for them to return to the language of the Americans they so desired to be.

As newlyweds Anthony's parents had joined the Church of Jesus Christ of Latter-day Saints in Pescara in the Abruzzo region of Italy, where Anthony's father worked as a carpenter. With excellent skills as a finish carpenter, he was able to find work in the United States. The only English he spoke was taught to him by American missionaries, but both he and Anthony's mother took community classes to learn English once they reached New York City.

Now Luca would be able serve and love the Italian people and learn about their culture, since his grandparents had passed away before they were able to share much about their experiences in their native country.

Laura shook her head to wake herself from her thoughts, scurried to the kitchen, and reached to the top of the refrigerator where she had hidden the flag. The green, white, and red colors caught Luca's eye as she walked toward the cake.

He rushed to her side. "Mom, how did you know?"

"I hoped in my heart and bought this little flag of faith. But I still held my breath a little as you opened your e-mail."

"I love you, Mom. You're the best." Taking the flag from her hand, he placed it in the center of the cake. "Come get some cake, guys. You, too, ladies," he motioned to his sisters, grandmother, and Tara.

When all of the friends had gone home, Laura leaned over the deck railing, remembering the last morning before Anthony left for Mexico. It would have been wonderful to have him here for this astonishing moment in their son's life, when he was called to serve a mission in the land of Anthony's ancestors. She turned as Luca and Tara approached her hand in hand.

Extending both arms, she pulled them into an embrace. "I love you both so much and am so happy with the good choices you make. You are indeed amazing young people, and I can't wait to see where your lives take you."

"Hopefully together," Luca said and squeezed Tara's hand. She smiled up at him.

Hope was a wonderful thing. A balm on a lonely heart, a remedy to lessen the pangs of waiting, a comfort to fortify faith. They hoped. They expected, and they'd received a miracle, and maybe there would be many more in their lifetimes.

Chapter 37

A yoke he had carved out of wood from a sturdy branch sat across Anthony's shoulders as he made his way down the hill with two buckets of water and his scriptures tucked tightly in his belt. He noticed two men plodding along the dusty trail in his direction. He knew Tobias would be on alert and was not in the least worried about their proximity to his home. As they drew closer in their white shirts, ties, and dark pants, he recognized them as the missionaries from church.

"Hola, Elders," he called out. They rushed toward him.

"Can we help?" they asked.

"Let's just go down by my house. It is easier to set the water buckets down and untie them than hand them off. Gracias!"

The missionaries headed for the main house, Adelita's home, and Anthony redirected them with a nod of his head in the direction of the shed, his home. He set the buckets on the ground, untied them, and relocated them just inside the open door to the shed.

"Welcome to my home," he motioned toward the shed, oven, and smattering of benches and homemade stools in front of his beloved home.

"This is where you live?" Elder Crane asked, incredulous at the humble circumstances in which this obviously intelligent man resided. He had served in areas other than Cabo where members lived in corrugated steel and plywood shacks but didn't expect these circumstances for someone as well-educated as Ramirez seemed to be.

The response of his companion was the complete opposite. But that was Elder Davis, excited and curious about everything that came his way. "This is awesome. Do you think we could see inside?" Elder Crane put an elbow to his ribs and gave him a sideways glance.

"Of course, you can," Anthony responded.

Elder Davis's eyes adjusted from the bright sun to the darker room. "Wow. You've made it very comfortable," he motioned to the thick straw mattress on the floor, homemade table, and stool.

Anthony felt proud of his home. He loved it. He loved the peace and tranquility of the desert, the beauty of the sunrise, and the calming of the sunset. Although people were bent on finding out who he was, he loved it here. He may have, and probably did have a family, but it had been a long time since they'd seen him. They would have moved on and given up on him by now. Maybe they were angry at him for disappearing.

Elder Davis noticed the handwritten notes on the wall and studied each one carefully.
"Mmh," was all he said.

"Could I fix you boys some breakfast?" Anthony asked.

"Oh, we wouldn't want to bother you, really," Elder Crane replied. Surely Ramirez couldn't afford to feed them from his meager supplies. He looked around. No fridge. He couldn't have much.

"I insist," Anthony replied, heading for the ice chest. He brought out five eggs, realizing he would have to replenish sooner than later. He had tried to have a chicken coop for a while, but the coyotes made quick work of the eggs and the chickens. The butcher had cut the meat into tiny chunks for him and bundled the meat in small packages and froze them for Anthony to pick up after his meeting at Carmen's.

"No, really," Elder Crane insisted again. "We can't."

"Why?"

Elder Crane stuttered out a barely intelligible answer. "Uh . . . uh . . . "

"Elders," Anthony said, "I choose to live this way. I have a job, plenty of money. I could live in an apartment in Cabo, but I love it here. So, grab a stool and make yourselves comfortable, and tell me what brings you all the way out here."

Anthony busied himself frying the meat and scrambling the eggs with some chilis from the garden he had dried and then reconstituted. Usually, he made his own homemade tortillas, but on the spur of the moment, he had bought a package of thin flour tortillas at the Mercado. He wrapped the meat and eggs in tortillas and handed one to each of the missionaries, who devoured them with oohs and aahs of appreciation.

"Well, the reason we came out to see you . . . " Elder Crane paused. "This is so good!"

"Gracias," Anthony replied. He had begun speaking in English in deference to Elder Davis, who looked lost in most conversations, but insisted that Anthony speak Spanish so he could learn.

"We want to invite you to Carmen's baptism on Saturday morning."

A rushing warmth of happiness filled Anthony's soul. He could have only been happier if Adelita had accepted the truth of what he was certain was his religion. Tears came to his eyes and emotion choked him as he nodded his acceptance of the invitation, with a barely muttered, "I'll be there." The missionaries stood and he shook each of their hands and they hugged him.

"One day it will be you," Elder Davis said confidently as they waved goodbye. "We'll figure this out."

As they walked toward the city, dust puffing up about around their leather shoes, Elder Crane cautioned his younger companion. "We shouldn't promise anything we can't deliver, you know."

"I agree. But all my life I have hung around my grandpa. He is an FBI agent. They have facial recognition software now. It maps points of a person's face from a photograph and then compares it to photos in a database. If Ramirez is missing, he should be in a police database wherever he is from."

"Pretty cool, but we had better talk to the Branch President before we do something like that. Do we send it to your grandpa or what?"

"Yes. But I need a picture of Ramirez first, and then can you make an appointment with the Branch President?"

Elder Crane agreed, although with trepidation. Unmatched enthusiasm drove his new, young companion. This constantly worried Elder Crane, an overly cautious trainer.

Saturday dawned a beautiful day for a baptism, although storm clouds were gathering to the east as Anthony made his way to Carmen's, changed shoes, and headed for the church. He assumed she would go early for this important occasion. He had seen a few member baptisms since his association with the Church of Jesus Christ of Latter-day Saints began several months ago.

The baptism took place in a font adjacent to the women's meeting room called the Relief Society Room. Anthony recognized the apt name for the room as the women of this church surely provided much needed relief to those in need.

Carmen sat in the front row next to Elder Davis. She was lovely in a white dress with her long hair braided and then secured in a swirl on top of her head. She turned as Anthony entered and winked at him, motioning him to her side. He crouched down before her. Placing her hand on his shoulder she leaned to whisper in his ear. "I am joining your church, Ramirez."

Anthony kissed her on the cheek. She was his mother, his grandmother, his friend. "I am so happy for you, Carmen. You will be a wonderful member of this church."

"I hope so. Really, I do." Being a fully participating member of the Church of Jesus Christ of Latter-day Saints was the only reason Anthony would ever want to know who he really was. What if finding out his identity took him away from this place, his home? He could hardly bear to think of leaving, even briefly. Could he even navigate the world he left behind?

At a signal from the Branch President, Elder Davis entered the baptismal font and crossed to take Carmen's hand and lead her down the steps into the water. He showed her how to hold his wrist and to pinch her nose shut. After saying a short prayer, which sounded quite familiar to Anthony, he dipped her down into the water, fully submersing her and her dress, which threatened to float for just a moment. She rose from the water and threw her arms around the young man who had just baptized her a member of the Church of Jesus Christ of Latter-day Saints.

While Carmen dressed in dry clothes, one of the women from the Branch played soft music on the piano. Carmen practically glided from the changing room wearing a black dress with colorful embroidery around the neckline and sleeves. She winked at Anthony as she was guided to a chair at the front of the room. Elder Crane confirmed her a member of the Church of Jesus Christ of Latter-day Saints and pronounced upon her the gift of the Holy Ghost. The Branch President spoke, explaining the baptismal ordinance, and the gift of the Holy Ghost and what an incredible comfort and guide it would be in Carmen's life.

All in attendance were invited into the cultural hall for refreshments. Anthony was surprised to see Guadalupe, Yesenia, and Eugenia rise from the back of the room. He knew he should acknowledge their presence but was reluctant to hear whatever Guadalupe had to say about Carmen's decision.

"Hello, Ramirez," she said, not even joking with her typical, 'Ramirez No Last Name.' "It looks like our girl has gone and joined your church. Got herself soaking wet. You

only need a sprinkle in my church. But if it makes her happy . .
."

"It does make her happy, Guadalupe. I am so glad her three best friends came for this special day. May I accompany you to get some refreshments." He held out an arm for Guadalupe and smiled at the other two.

The cultural hall was buzzing with people exclaiming over the beautiful display of food. "This looks like the handiwork of you three. Did you make all this food?"

Eugenia smiled shyly. Anthony couldn't believe it. As much as they railed against Carmen's involvement in her new religion, they still supported her with hours of time spent making a bountiful supply of tasty treats for the attendees at the baptism.

"You three are wonderful friends, true fairy godmothers. I will call you Flora, Fauna, and Merriweather."

"Who?" they asked in unison.

Who? Yes who? And where did he come up with those names?

Sometimes his strange, forgetful mind just spat out something totally random. It was something he couldn't even put in context with anything in his life now, or the little he remembered from before.

Elder Davis asked if he could take Anthony's picture with Carmen. Anthony slid his arm around her back and gave his best smile, not that it was all that easy to see his smile with his bushy mustache and beard.

Anthony began the walk home as raindrops lightly fell, making tiny indents in the dust. The rain continued until it was quite the downpour, and a song ran through his head about wanting one's life to be like earth right after rain. It was a baptism song, he was sure of it, but he thought so hard trying to figure out where he had heard it, his head started feeling heavy with so many thoughts clamoring to solve the mystery.

Chapter 38

The weeks after Luca's mission call were an entanglement of doctor and dentist appointments, budgeting, shopping for mission clothes, more budgeting and worry, worry, worry about how Laura could support her son on his mission. She prayed continually for inspiration and usually the best advice from the Lord came while she was playing the piano. *Worry does nothing, just like worrying about a performance will not improve the performance. Practice improves performance. Put your shoulder to the wheel!* The words came to her so clearly. She had always been a worrier, and it just sapped her strength. She made up her mind that however difficult, she would do her best and trust in the Lord to send a miracle her way.

And the miracles rolled in, one after another like waves on a beach. As much as she disliked being an accompanist rather than a soloist, she easily engaged several opportunities to accompany vocalists performing at Lincoln Center and Carnegie Hall through the current and next year, weaving them among her solo performances with the New York Philharmonic.

Luca had found a summer job not just umpiring but managing Little League games. At first Laura fell into worrying about his leg if he was umpiring, as he usually did in the summer. Just as she pushed the worry back into the dark hole from which it escaped, she found that Luca would be working in the Parks and Recreation Office scheduling the umpires and fields. No more a target for an errant ball behind the plate. What a blessing!

Emma received a call from the owner of several assisted living facilities in White Plains and nearby asking her and Izzie to organize sing-a-longs once a week for the residents. Emma enjoyed teaching cello lessons to junior high students and helping out with summer orchestra classes while Izzie put together the music for the sing-a-longs. The evening concerts at various venues continued with the three siblings and Tara occasionally joining in as their guest artist.

They grew even closer as a family with everyone focused on the same cause: to support Luca as he spread the gospel to their ancestors in Italy. And then they were still reveling in the joy of Estelle and Sam's beautiful marriage ceremony on the deck overlooking the lake. While Estelle's friends were all still in Arizona, she said the only people she needed at the wedding were Laura and her grandchildren. Sam, on the other hand, had numerous friends and colleagues who joined them for the happy day. Sam's daughter, her husband, and their daughter were warm and accepting of Laura's family. Their son, Sam's grandson, who was on an LDS church mission in Mexico, had been able to join by Facebook Messenger for a short time. The tender comradery between him and his grandfather was evident in their sweet exchanges.

Shortly before Luca was to leave for the Missionary Training Center in Provo, Utah, Tara's father, Clay, his wife, Jenny, and their newborn baby came to see Tara in a solo recital at Julliard. Laura invited the family to stay in the Di Angelo home, which was more amenable to a newborn who might awaken and cry during the night rather than in a hotel atmosphere.

Emma doted on the baby and offered to stay home with the baby while the others attended the concert. The joy on her face as she cuddled the little one was something that had been missing from her countenance since her father's disappearance. While Emma still had her senior year of high school to complete, she hoped to attend Brigham Young University after graduation. Jenny had plans to pursue her degree as well and offered Emma a job as a nanny for the little one, along with her two older sisters who were staying with Clay's parents during this trip. Emma eagerly accepted and they made plans to coordinate their class schedules once Emma was at BYU.

Luca graciously offered to send his very best companion to meet Emma so that soon she would be nanny for her own children. His sister gave him a good-natured slug in the shoulder, but secretly she wished that sooner than later she could be a mother. Her mom had encouraged her to attend Julliard as an instrumental major, but her plans were to get a degree in music education and hopefully teach from home. It took some convincing, but her mom finally acquiesced, realizing how hard it had been, especially when the children were young, to be on the concert tours.

Laura appreciated Clay's presence and influence in the home. He had been especially helpful when Tara had brought him to talk with her shortly after Anthony's disappearance. She missed Anthony, his solid guidance, encouragement, and support. As she watched Clay and Jenny, she hoped beyond hope that it wouldn't be long before Anthony returned to his family.

Chapter 39

Elder Crane made an appointment with the Branch President the very next Sunday afternoon. The Branch President understood more English than he spoke, and Elder Davis spoke slightly more Spanish than he understood as words and syllables flew by him before he had a chance to comprehend. But he studied hard with some flashcards he had made, and Elder Crane continually buoyed him up, giving him confidence in his progress.

Haltingly, Elder Davis explained his thoughts regarding Ramirez No Last Name. The Branch President suggested they meet with Lane and Graciela Peterson, who had known Ramirez since he was first found badly injured in the desert by Graciela's young sons. He related how Graciela's mother had nursed Ramirez back to health and how he had cared for her until her death. The Branch President agreed that it did seem that Ramirez was most likely a member of their church.

On their next preparation day, or P-day for short, the missionaries met with the Petersons, who agreed with their theories. Lane felt Ramirez was happy where he was, but truly desired full membership in the Church. Without his true name, his records couldn't be found, nor could he be baptized anew.

Typically, Elder Davis called his whole family on Facebook Messenger, and his parents and sister and his grandparents on both sides would join in from wherever they were. That evening his grandfather was in an office setting that was not his own with his new grandmother, Estelle, who seemed like a warm, loving grandmother, something he had not experienced from his maternal grandmother before her death. There was a large picture of a family on the wall behind where they were sitting that Elder Davis could see on his phone. He jotted a quick note to Elder Crane to take a picture of the framed portrait. Elder Crane gave him a look like he'd lost his mind. Not unusual so far in their relationship.

After the call ended, Elder Davis explained that his grandfather had married into a family whose father had disappeared on a trip to Mexico at about the same time Ramirez was found in the desert.

They rushed to Lane Peterson's home and asked to use his computer. They showed him the picture on Elder Crane's phone and explained they wanted to add some facial hair and alter the skin color. The church computer didn't have the program to do that, and they wondered if he had a photo editor, which he did. Lane motioned to Elder Davis to sit in his chair and said, "You drive." Elder Davis added a beard and mustache, lengthened the hair considerably, and changed the skin color from a light olive to a deep tan. The resemblance was uncanny.

"So, you know this guy's name, where he lives?" asked Lane.

"He disappeared a couple of years ago on a business trip to Mexico. He had a corrupt business partner that may have been involved in his disappearance, but the partner was killed in an accident leaving the family with no means to figure out what happened."

"Honestly, I hesitate to bring this to Ramirez in case it is just a coincidence. Is there any way we can be sure?"

"I can send the picture taken of Ramirez at Carmen's baptism to my grandpa and he can have his technician run it through the facial recognition program they use to find criminals. If Ramirez is in the database, and he probably is if he was reported missing, then the software will find him based on common facial feature points, if there are any. And I am pretty sure there are."

"Think we'd better tell President what we're up to?" Elder Davis glanced at the missionary responsible for training him to do the right things on his mission. Somehow it didn't seem wise to keep the Mission President in the dark about trying to determine Ramirez's identity.

"Yup. I'll call him," the older missionary responded.

An assistant answered in the mission home, headquarters for the Mission President and his wife and the office staff that kept the mission running smoothly. He hesitated and then became more amicable as he recognized Elder Crane as one of his former mission companions in the early days of their two-year missions. When the Mission President came on the phone, Elder Crane briefly introduced the situation about a possible member who had been robbed of his identity due to an accident and amnesia. He then handed the phone to Elder Davis who explained his theory and the possibility of his grandfather's help through FBI software.

A long drawn out "mmmh" was surely being accompanied by a hand rubbing his chin as the Mission President was known to do when deep in thought. "I think you should go ahead with approaching your grandfather, Elder Davis, but with the utmost confidentiality. And I don't want either of you to discuss this with Ramirez. If there is anything of worth to impart to him, we will do that through the Branch President and Brother Peterson. Do you understand?"

"Of course, of course," they both replied. While it would be exciting to uncover someone's lost identity, they would prefer to be observers in the matter.

Elder Davis received permission to contact his grandfather that evening rather than wait for the next P-day, and the young men hurried from Brother Peterson's home to their apartment and prepared for the call to Sam Brady, FBI.

"Hi, Pops," Elder Davis called into his phone when his grandfather answered. "Yeah, yeah. We need your help to solve a mystery, actually to save a life."

"Sounds serious. Lay it out for me."

Elder Davis put his phone on speaker and both he and Elder Crane related the story of Ramirez No Last Name and the possible discovery that they may know his identity. They texted the picture of Ramirez at Carmen's baptism to Sam and the photoshopped picture with Ramirez' long head of hair, facial hair, and tanned complexion, as well as the family photo Elder Crane had taken with his phone.

"What do ya think, Pops?"

Sam was adept at keeping a straight face and giving no impressions of his own, whether in person and on the phone. "I'll check into it," was all he said.

They hung up and Elder Johson said, "That's it. He's not going to corroborate our theory?"

"That's Pops. Poker face. You never know what he's thinking until he's ready to let you know. We'll just wait and pray. As exciting as this is to uncover such a mystery, I feel more anticipation to watch Ramirez take the sacrament for the first time. That will be an awesome day."

Chapter 40

Sam shared the photos from his phone to his e-mails both at home and work. He printed the pictures and scrutinized them side by side and was still processing the uncanny likeness when Estelle came into the study.

She gasped. "Darling . . . oh my . . . is that? Can it be?"

"I don't want to say, dear, until I have run it through the facial recognition software in the lab tomorrow. But I think, I think it just may be." He went on to relate the story of the man the missionaries called "Ramirez No Last Name."

Sam tossed and turned all night, as did Estelle. As she rubbed Sam's back and shoulders to try to bring on relaxation, she realized how hard it was going to be to keep the possibility of Anthony's existence from Laura. Her daughter had been adamant that Anthony was still alive. Estelle felt some relief that amnesia may have played a role in Anthony's disappearance. There was always the tiny feeling trying to worm its way into her thoughts that he had disappeared on purpose, even though she knew the love he had for his family was undeniable.

With the first morning light, Sam was out of bed and in the kitchen fixing a cup of coffee. Estelle abstained from hot drinks like coffee and tea, something to do with "Words of Wisdom" from her church. His daughter, Shawn's mother and now a member of Estelle's church, abstained as well and often bugged him about his addiction. Estelle on the other hand did not. She seemed to understand that a morning coffee was a lifelong ritual in which he partook. But maybe someday. Maybe. That dark blue book in his desk drawer beckoned him to read more and more often. It was an intriguing story. Completely plausible, even to his scientific mind. He had promised he would read it while Shawn was on his mission. He just didn't expect a book supposedly translated by a young man from gold plates with ancient writings to feel so true. He had always believed in God but never understood the importance of His Son, Jesus Christ. But every week Shawn wrote his grandfather a personal letter testifying of the truthfulness of the Book of Mormon and the love Jesus had for everyone, especially his grandfather, and how all things were possible with Christ. So, Sam read, but fought against the warm feelings that told him the story was true.

Sam called ahead to the lab and the technician was waiting for him when he came through the sliding glass door that opened at the recognition of his badge touched on the sensor. The door slid shut quickly behind him.

It would have been easier to just hand the technician the photo of Ramirez and ask her to see if it compared to the missing Anthony Di Angelo. But he just gave her the picture with no name and allowed the facial recognition software to run the gamut of people in the database. He knew Anthony would be in the database, having been reported missing and initially thought to have committed insurance fraud.

The screen blinked contour lines of faces with tiny bright triangular marks flashing on and off. It seemed like hours, and probably was, as Sam glanced at the round, black-rimmed clock on the wall above the computer equipment. 11:00 a.m. Three hours since the program had begun its search. A piercing beep brought the technician running to the console. A match. Sam hardly dared look. The name, Anthony Di Angelo, flashed on and off in bold at the top of the screen. It was Anthony. Now what? He didn't want the law involved. He still wasn't sure how many in the system had been cohorts in Marty's schemes. He would go to Mexico himself and approach this man, this Ramirez No Last Name.

Sam thanked the technician for her time, and she winked at him. "Just between you and me, Sam, as always," she assured.

Involving his missionary grandson further in Anthony Di Angelo's disappearance seemed unwise. Sam called Estelle. She knew everything there was about being Mormon, or being a Church of Jesus Christ of Latter-day Saints member as she reminded him when he slipped up with the name of her church. She would know the person who was responsible for Shawn and the other missionaries in Mexico.

"Hello, darling." Sam could never get enough of Estelle's loving greetings whenever he called.

"Hello, dear. I need your help."

"Everything okay?"

"Yes, yes," he responded, and went on to tell her his predicament. She suggested that he call his daughter and get the contact information for Shawn's mission president. Sam worried about divulging too much information. He was so used to keeping any information he had close to himself, but he knew his daughter would follow his lead. She had grown up in an FBI home. She knew the drill. *Don't pester Dad for more information than he is willing to give you.*

By evening, he had spoken to the Mission President, who had received some knowledge of the situation from Shawn, or Elder Davis, as his mission leader called him. The kind man offered to put Sam in contact with Lane Peterson and that connection was made the following day, with Mr. Peterson promising to talk with Ramirez No Last Name as he called him and then get back with Sam. *Soon* couldn't come too soon for Sam. He wanted Anthony safely back home before either the New York police or the Cabo police got involved. After the incident with Laura's kidnapping, it would be a long time before he trusted anyone.

Sam wanted to provide Mr. Peterson with as much information about Anthony as he could gather without alerting Laura or the children. Estelle already had been apprised of the turn of events and provided a valuable resource into Anthony's past life, at least as far back as his mission as a nineteen-year-old boy to Mexico.

* * * * *

Lane pressed the red button to disconnect the call from Sam. Such mixed feelings flowed through him. While he wanted Ramirez to find his true home, he would miss not only his help with the farming projects, but he would miss his friendship and gentle spirit.

Graciela came to the door of the den and crossed to where he sat, his head in his hands. She put her free arm around his shoulder, and he leaned back against her. Adelita Diane was warm against his cheek, and he reached for the tiny bundle to be named for both of her grandmothers the following Sunday in Sacrament Meeting.

Surely Ramirez would come to what would be an enormous offering of food and socializing after church at their home. Perhaps he could have a moment with his dear friend then. But what would he say? How would he break the news? Ramirez had said so often how much he loved his home here, his friends, his dog, his little shack, his sanctuary when his lack of memories got the best of him.

Baby Adelita cooed and looked up at her dad with the windows to the soul of a little one who had come to earth so wanted and loved, forever protected in the arms of her parents. It tore through Lane's heart when he saw the bedraggled and neglected children as he went from area to area, counseling with the farmers. Even Graciela's children, as poor as she was in their early years, were always clean and tidy, happy children who knew that no matter what, their mother would care for them.

The next day, when Lane pronounced Baby Adelita's name upon her to be used for the rest of her life, the words of the prayer seemed very familiar to Anthony. The circle the priesthood holders formed around the baby, hands on each other's shoulders, felt familiar to Anthony. Although he was not able to be in the circle, he was asked to hold the microphone in front of Lane so the congregation could hear the beautiful blessing he gave his tiny Adelita Diane. After the blessing, he held her aloft so the congregation could see the babe in the lovely white gown with colorful embroidered flowers her mother had hand stitched for her.

The baby slept through most of the sacrament meeting. She fussed a bit during the women's meeting, but Graciela was able to take her to the mother's room and nurse her back to slumber. Lane and Graciela's home was within walking distance from the meeting house, so the usual after-church lunch would take place in their home. Nearly every member of the Branch made their way to the Peterson's with a tasty dish they had stored in the kitchen during the meetings.

Baby Adelita's patience turned into an incessant mournful wail as her normally quiet surroundings became crowded and noisy. First her mother and then her father packed her around in one arm while they attended to their guests. Seeing the predicament of the parents, Anthony stepped forward and offered to tend to the child.

"You sure?" Lane asked.

"Yes. I will just take her in the nursery and rock her if that is okay."

"She's all yours!" Lane handed the squirming, now screaming baby to Anthony.

Anthony slipped quietly from the room so as not to attract the women who each wanted to peek at or hold the new little one. He placed the baby, and the gauze blanket hanging loosely around her, on the changing table and rewrapped the blanket, swaddling the child just as Mary swaddled the baby Jesus.

He gazed in wonderment at how his deft folding, wrapping, and tucking technique eventually formed a smooth swaddle that immediately settled the child. *How did he know how to do this?* Another note for the wall. He must have had tiny baby experiences.

With the babe snuggled to his chest, the pitiful sobs relented. Her eyelids started to droop, so he carefully lowered himself into the rocker by Baby Adelita's crib. He didn't notice Lane watching him from the doorway. Without thinking, he sang a tune that came to his mind as he stroked the baby's soft dark hair.

> "Sleep little Izzie, sleep baby dear,
> Daddy is with you, no need to fear.
> Sleep baby Izzie, sleep baby sleep,
> My love for you, forever you'll keep,
> Close to your heart, where 'ere I am ,
> Sleep little Izzie, sleep baby sleep."

As he sang, a vision of another tiny baby girl with dark curly hair, unlike Adelita's straight, dark hair, was captured behind his closed eyes. He was momentarily startled as he started the tune again and noticed he was singing to a Baby Izzie. But then nothing that stole into his mind surprised him too much these days. In the last hour alone, it had become apparent that he had been the father of a young child, an infant in fact, and her name was most likely Izzie. Where was this Izzie now? How old? Did she remember him? Even miss him after all this time. Would he ever know her and love her again?

Lane backed away from the doorway, not wanting to be seen witnessing this tender scene, which surely confirmed that the man rocking Lane's precious baby girl was indeed Anthony Di Angelo.

All the puzzle pieces were beginning to fall in place. According to Sam, Anthony had served an LDS mission to Mexico. That explained his command of the Spanish language.

His college roommate and best friend had been the now-deceased, crooked business partner. His wife was Laura, the same name engraved inside Anthony's wedding ring, the one Graciela's mother tried to hide so she could save this handsome man for Graciela. Lane only knew this from the notes on Ramirez' wall and the story Adelita eventually related when she finally decided not to fight Graciela's marriage to the gringo from the strange religion.

Anthony had three children, Luca, Emma, and Isabella whom they called Izzie. Anthony had a bachelor's degree in accounting and a Master of Business Administration. He and Marty had begun the insurance adjustment business shortly after college, with Anthony managing the business side and stateside investigations and Marty managing marketing and out of country investigations.

It seemed that Anthony had gone to Cabo to investigate a hotel fire when Marty had been in the hospital for emergency gallbladder surgery. Marty's insistence that Anthony wait for him to get out of the hospital to do the investigation was ignored. It was an odd request on Marty's part because the best chance of determining the cause was immediately after the fire. Anthony never returned from the trip. When a charge for insurance fraud arose due to the amount of these suspicious fires associated with hotels in Mexico, all owned by Salazar, Inc., Marty immediately placed the blame on Anthony. But after Emma and Izzie broke into his insurance office, new evidence came to light that placed Marty as the instigator of the fraudulent claims.

Lane knew that Ramirez No Last Name, or Anthony Di Angelo now, had been found beaten and left for dead in the desert by Graciela's youngsters. With the help of Graciela's brothers, Ramirez was brought to Graciela's mother's home where Adelita nursed him back to health. There Lane met him when he was dating Graciela and the two formed a fast friendship and compatible and productive working relationship.

Lane determined that he would drive out to Ramirez' home the following day when they would be alone. The house was still full of ward members enjoying time together and celebrating the baby's blessing or he would have shared the new findings with Anthony that night. Somehow he would gently impart the news of the fact-finding mission Elders Crane and Davis had conducted to discover Ramirez's real name so that he could be a full-fledged member of the Church tomorrow when they were alone, and Ramirez could absorb this new information.

Chapter 41

The dust cloud with the black speck bouncing in front of it alerted Anthony to a possible visitor early Monday morning, which was odd since his only visitor was usually Lane on Thursday or Friday mornings. But from the well on the hill, it became certain Lane was making an earlier trip that week. Anthony hurried down the hill with the yoke over his shoulders carrying the water buckets.

"Hola," he called out, as Lane parked by Adelita's home. "What brings you out so early this fine morning?"

"Um, news," Lane replied. "I have news."

"Well then, come sit down and I'll make you some breakfast. You haven't eaten yet, have you?"

"No, I haven't but I need to get back pretty soon." Lane was finding that he just wanted to get the revelation over with. This could go really well or really bad.

"It's all ready." Anthony lifted the lid of the cast iron pot on the homemade stove to a delicious aroma. "It's eggs and chilis day. You sure you won't have some?"

Lane couldn't resist. "Okay, okay. You got me. Thanks, Ramirez."

They ate quickly in silence and Anthony stood to take Lane's tin plate and dip it into a small tub Anthony used to wash dishes.

"Well, Ramirez," Lane rubbed his chin. "I have some news. News about your identity."

Anthony looked up, his eyes wide.

"Seems our Elder Davis's grandfather is in the FBI. After seeing the notes on your wall, which he calls the wall of evidence, Elder Davis was certain you were a member of the Church and wanted you to be able to fully participate. He gave a picture taken of you at Carmen's baptism to his grandfather who ran it through a facial recognition program, and you matched completely to a gentleman from New York who went missing in Mexico about the same time as you were found in the desert."

"Mmmh. Mmmh." Anthony groaned. Did he want to be found? This was his home. "I guess you should tell me more. Who am I?"

"It seems your name is Anthony Di Angelo." He drew a picture from his pocket and handed it to Anthony. "This is you with your family taken shortly before your trip to Mexico to investigate a fire at a Salazar Resort in Cabo."

Anthony ran his finger over the picture, touching each person. It was surreal. Such a shock that he joked. "Handsome fellow this guy is." And then more seriously. "Do they even want me back? It has been so long. I would have thought they would have given up."

"They haven't been told yet that you are found. Sam, Elder Davis's grandfather, would like to come down here to talk to you before he talks to the family. Your family has been searching in earnest for you all this time, and Sam became very close with the family, even recently married their grandmother."

"That so," Anthony replied. *What did this mean?* He gazed at the picture. This beautiful woman must be the Laura engraved in his wedding band. Maybe the woman by the lake he tried to paint. The curly headed teenager must be the little baby in his dreams, in the lullaby he sang to Baby Adelita. The other two looked like nice kids.

Lane went on to relate the story of Marty and Anthony's insurance business and how Anthony came to be in Mexico to investigate a fire, not intending to end up beaten and left for dead in the desert.

"Will it be okay if I ask Sam to visit and tell you more of the details and see where you want to go from here?"

"Do I have a choice? Looks like I have a family I need to take care of . . . " His voice trailed off. But he had people here, too. People he knew and loved. Not like this family that he didn't even remember. This woman and children, strangers really.

The men stood, shook hands, and embraced. "A lot to digest, isn't it," Lane commented. "I will leave you to your thoughts. Sam said he could be here by the weekend. Will that work for you?"

"Yes, of course. I have no plans or places to go. Well, at least I didn't used to."

Lane turned and headed for his dusty black jeep. He hated to leave Ramirez there, slumped on his handmade furniture with this new revelation about his identity, particularly since he could see it didn't thrill him to know that he was Anthony Di Angelo from New York with a wife and children.

Anthony could only tell he'd been right there on the bench for hours by the sun now being directly overhead and sweat pouring from his forehead into his eyes. Tobias had stayed faithfully at his feet and was surely overheated and in need of some water. He rose rather stiffly, his body having formed into the curved wood of his log-and-rock supported seat.

He poured water from the bucket into the clay bowl he had crafted for his beloved dog, who lapped anxiously until the bowl was empty. Anthony set the buckets inside the shed to keep dust and twigs at bay. "What do ya think, Tobias? Am I really this guy from New York?" He asked the question but knew the answer. Now what was his future?

If he went to New York, he would be leaving this home he had so lovingly created for himself, and now Tobias. He would go nowhere without Tobais. That was certain and he bristled to think it might ever be suggested.

But he would also miss the sun slipping below the horizon and its shining tentacles reaching through the cracks in the shed to wake him in the morning. He would miss the desert breeze, the sprinkles and then torrents of rain, the tiny vegetables peeking through the warm earth and growing into maturity. He would miss the beautiful black eyes of Carmen and even her three pesky friends. He would miss Lane and Graciela and never see Baby Adelita learn to walk and talk. He would miss the wonderful colors and aromas of the Mercado.

And what about the farmers? Who would keep their books and find ways for them to be more profitable? His life was here. What did life in New York really hold for him?

The whole debacle gave him a headache and he left the bench for his mat in the shed and slept away the afternoon trying to forget that his life was going to change drastically. He should be happy, ecstatic even. But he was not. Not yet anyway. Maybe someday.

Chapter 42

The eight-hour Jet Blue flight from JFK Airport in New York City to Cabo San Lucas landed at the Los Cabos International Airport at 3:00 p.m. on Thursday afternoon. Sam took a shuttle to the Hilton Hotel, where his administrative assistant had reserved a room. It was definitely pricier than a typical hotel he would choose, but he was advised to stay in a high-quality hotel unless he wanted to end up like this man he was going to meet.

The view of the ocean and the softly rolling waves slapping against the sand did little to calm his nerves. How would this guy react to everything Sam was going to tell him about his past, about the interim between his disappearance and now? What would he decide? Would Sam be carrying back good news, or more difficulties in Laura's future if Anthony chose to stay in Mexico? Lane had told him some of the man's concerns and that worried Sam. He had hoped Anthony would be overjoyed at being found.

Sam slept fitfully and rose early to meet Lane in the lobby of the hotel. They shook hands and he threw his bag in the back seat of the jeep waiting at the entrance. Lane had previously told Sam everything he could think of about Anthony, so they rode in the thoughtful silence that accompanies men with much on their minds. Forty-five minutes passed until they slid to a stop by Adelita's home.

"This is it?" Sam remarked.

"This is my mother-in-law's home, where she nursed Anthony back to health. She passed away nearly a year ago, but Anthony wanted to continue living in a home he created out of a shed behind the home. He was very fond of her."

As they walked around the side of the small home, really not much more than a shack itself, Sam was astounded by the view of a lush garden, handcrafted furniture in a semi-circle in front of an also handcrafted stone and mortar oven, and a small shed, which must be Anthony's home. The aroma of spiced meat simmering in a cast iron skillet on the stovetop greeted them.

Anthony himself came striding down the hill, water buckets balanced on his shoulders with a beautiful black and white dog trotting beside him. The dog barked and was immediately silenced with a "Shhh. These are friends," from Anthony.

"Hola," Anthony called out, trying to be welcoming despite his uneasiness. He would make them breakfast. That would delay the conversation that had to be for at least a little while.

"I didn't expect you to make it out here this early, Lane," he said, teasing his friend about not being an early riser. "Have a seat. I will whip up some breakfast."

He lifted the yoke from his shoulders and set the buckets on the porch he had built in front of the shed. Lane introduced Sam to Anthony and the two shook hands, looking directly into each other's eyes. Sam knew Anthony was sizing him up to determine if he was an honest man, someone he could trust, or not.

"I am pleased to meet you, Ramirez." Sam gave Anthony the respect of using the name that was most familiar to him.

Anthony nodded and Lane pulled him into an embrace, patting him on the back. "It's going to be okay my friend," he whispered.

The men protested about Anthony having to cook for them, but as he warmed some tortillas on the stovetop they conceded to their growling stomachs.

Anthony chopped some fresh onion and bell peppers from his garden and threw them in with the meat, tossing the mixture gently before spooning it into a tortilla and deftly folding the tortilla to keep the meat and vegetables from spilling out. He poured a bit of sauce kept warm in a small pan into individual bowls and offered the burritos on tin plates to Sam and Lane. Dashing into the shed, he brought them each a colorful cloth napkin. He plated a burrito for himself and put the excess meat into a bowl for Tobias who was sitting on his haunches warily eyeing Sam.

"Come, Tobias," Anthony called. "It's okay." He then took a seat on a bench to Sam's right.

"This was delicious, Ramirez," Sam remarked. "But how do you preserve your food? I don't see any electrical source out here."

"I go to town mid-week for a meeting at Lane's office and bring back enough meat in an ice chest to last a few days. Thursday, Friday, and Saturday are my 'meat' days, and the other days are my 'egg' days." He motioned to the chicken coop on the other side of the garden. A few weeks ago, I finally made the coop secure enough to ward off the coyotes, and I was able to get some laying hens in town. I have plenty of fresh vegetables. Quite often I make my own tortillas, but these are from the Mercado." He rose on these last words and took the men's empty plates and put them in his dishwashing pan by the stove. He poured a dash of water over them to keep them from crusting and being hard to scrub.

The soiled napkins were placed in a reusable grocery bag he used for his dirty clothes just inside the shed door. He returned to his seat by Sam.

"Well, Ramirez. May I have your permission to begin, to bring you the information I have about your life."

"Yes, sir. Go ahead," Anthony acquiesced.

"First of all, I would like to understand how you are feeling. Tell me about your memory, your amnesia, what is that even like?"

Taking a deep breath, Anthony related that for a long time he fought against this loss of memory. He spent every waking moment trying to remember his life before wondering if there were people he left behind. It was like pounding on a big black door to his past that would not open no matter how hard he tried. Gradually he decided to embrace his new life and be satisfied with the little inklings of his old life that were presented to him.

He rose and asked Sam to follow him to where he pointed out the notes tacked to the wall of his shed. He said perhaps he would one day remember, but for now he had decided to build a new life with new memories, and he loved his life, his home, the people he counted as dear friends. He had a job he loved and was not concerned about any career or bank account he had left behind. He had been fairly certain that his family would have moved on, forgotten him, if indeed he had had a family. And if so, why had they not found him.

Sam gulped. There were reasons, so many reasons, why Laura and her children had not been able to find Anthony. He began by explaining Laura's financial circumstances after Anthony's disappearance, trying not to impart guilt on Anthony's part for not being there for his family. "Let me show you this video I've downloaded to my phone." Sam had prepared beforehand, learning from Lane that not only did Anthony not have Wi-Fi, nor did he have electricity or running water.

Sam slid closer to Anthony and held his phone so that this father could see his children performing and begging the world to help find their dad. A single tear escaped under Anthony's eyelashes. He didn't remember these children, but he was touched by their sincerity in wanting to find their father.

"They were thwarted at every turn to find you. Marty had a corrupt contact in the police department, one who owed him a favor, and Laura's missing person police report was never filed. The FBI became involved when Marty deflected insurance fraud charges, blaming you for the lack of investigations into the rash of fires in the Salazar Hotel chains." He explained how Laura had provided Sam with documentation that exonerated Anthony.

Sam related the upstanding character of each of Anthony's family members and their love for each other. They had survived on Laura's salary as a teacher at Julliard. Until Estelle came to live with them, her performance schedule had been curtailed. The children had been very frugal and with their musical abilities found jobs performing at different senior living venues for a nominal fee, plus tips.

Sam outlined their struggles including Luca's accident, which was determined a hit and run by Marty, and the girls' run in with Marty when they broke into the insurance office to try to find documentation proving Marty was involved in the hotel fires and not Anthony. He told about Marty invading the family's home and how fortunate Sam felt to have been there at the time. Ultimately Marty had kidnapped Laura and while driving erratically was killed in a car accident. Miraculously, Laura had survived unscathed. Sam chuckled, "She was more worried about her ruined concert dress than anything."

Sam also divulged how hard Luca had worked to not only provide financially for his mission, but even to learn to walk without pain so he could serve a mission. His sisters had also found jobs to help save for this mission to serve the Lord.

Anthony took all of this information in, but as an outsider. He felt compassion for this family, but he still didn't feel like it was his own. Inwardly he chastised himself for having a heart that cared, but not as deeply as he would have if he really knew these people.

He sighed. "They've gone through a lot. I am sorry this happened to them."

Sam drew back. It was obvious Anthony had disconnected from his family and saw them as strangers, just people he had never cared for or known. Now what? What would he tell Laura? He had found her husband and father of her children, but he seemed not interested in coming home to them.

After what seemed like many minutes, Anthony looked over at Sam. "I should go. I should at least go meet them. If they are indeed my family, I have a responsibility to them to end their suffering both financially and in worrying about a missing family member."

Sam breathed a sigh of relief. Surely once he met his family, he would learn to love them as Sam had in a very short amount of time. They were such lovely, sincere, warm, and welcoming people.

"You are probably without proper documentation to get you across the border, or even to fly home. I will arrange for an FBI plane to transport you and I will be with you the whole way."

"What about my dog. I can't leave without Tobias."

Sam reached to pat the pooch on his silky head. "Tobias will be no problem at all." He bit his tongue for a second. If he remembered right, Laura did not like dogs at all. This would take some talking to change her mind about the "no pets" rule in her home. He had been on hand several times when Izzie in particular had begged for a puppy. Her siblings were moving on to a mission and eventually to college. Izzie needed something to cling to as family members embarked on new adventures.

Chapter 43

With just a week to prepare, Anthony made sure his shed was secure for the upcoming winter. Although he didn't plan to stay long enough in New York, he had a feeling he should be prepared for a possibly lengthy stay, just in case. He repaired the cracks in the shed and prepared the garden for next year's plantings. He went to town and had a tender visit with Carmen, telling her how much he had grown to love her and how he would miss her and her friendship. He thanked her for filling the void of not having a family, then he showed her the picture of himself with his family.

"You are a good-looking man. Your family is beautiful."

Anthony mentioned that he was considering cutting his hair before going to New York and also becoming clean shaven.

"Keep the beard and mustache, dear," she said. "It makes you even more handsome and without such a baby face." She touched his cheek, and they both laughed. Carmen didn't hold back her opinions.

"But you could cut your hair. When my husband learned he had cancer and the treatment would cause him to lose his hair, the nurse told him about how he could donate his hair for Wigs for Kids with cancer. Go down to Alejandro's barber shop. That is where my sweetheart went, and Alejandro took care of the donation."

"Come." Carmen took Anthony's arm. "Let's go to the Mercado. I can't wait to see Guadalupe, Yesenia, and Eugenia's faces when they learn you have a last name."

They strolled arm in arm to the Mercado and stopped at the booth of the "pesky sisters," as Anthony referred to them endearingly. He explained the new findings about his identity and offered his last name, thinking it would stop them from teasing him about his lack of a last name. But did that even matter? He was leaving this beloved place. Could he come back?

The three pesky sisters giggled amongst themselves, with Carmen shushing them.
"Ramirez Di Angelo. Mexicano Italiano?"

Anthony rolled his eyes. They were incorrigible, but he loved them just the same.

He teased them back. "Let me know when you are getting baptized into my church."

More giggles and a humph. "Like that will ever happen."

"It will. It will, and I will be back to make it happen." And then it struck him. With his name and surely his baptismal certificate that this woman, Laura Di Angelo, could provide, he could be a real member of this religion he cherished.

Anthony picked up a few cans of dog food that looked somewhat appetizing. He held the can in front Tobias. "What do you think boy? Will this do until I can cook for you again?"

Tobias sniffed and pawed the can. "Guess that's a yes." He picked up five cans and a small can opener for the trip. He asked Lane to draw out several hundred dollars in cash from the bank since with no ID he still didn't have an account in his name. At home, he built a wooden box and wrapped his tools in a cloth and put them into the box. He placed the box carefully on a high shelf he had built along the length of the shed. He brought the pots and utensils inside and placed them on the shelf as well. He collected his and Adelita's gardening tools and leaned them upright in a corner and put the wheelbarrow on its front edge against the wall.

He touched each note tacked to the rough wood wall, read it, and understood how it now fit into his past life. He collected the notes and placed them carefully in the zipper pocket of his tool bag, along with the money Lane brought him from the bank. His precious Book of Mormon was placed in the bottom of the bag so it wouldn't get bent or wrinkled. He lined the edges of the bag in a balanced manner with canned dog food. In the morning, he would roll his mat and Tobias's smaller mat and put them on the shelf for safekeeping, and then pack his best extra shirt and undergarments, his hairbrush, and the few toiletries he used. He would be back. He had to come back.

Sobs burst from his chest. He had once fought the unknown and won. He could do it again.

Lane pulled up by Adelita's home just as the sun popped above the horizon. He would miss his weekly trips to his dear friend's home. Ramirez, or Anthony now, who listened well and only gave advice when asked. But his words were wise and always spot on with what Lane needed to hear.

Anthony was waiting with Tobias at Adelita's front door. Perhaps he had been inside to say goodbye to the first home in his life that he could remember. It was a home where he had been loved and tenderly nursed back to health. Lane chuckled to himself thinking of Adelita's schemes to match Anthony with Graciela. She had been adamantly against Graciela marrying a gringo from that strange religion. But with Ramirez' coaxing, she had eventually relented and welcomed Lane into the family.

Anthony nodded a hello from where he was waiting. Lane could see that he was choking back the emotion of leaving this place he loved. Lane came around the jeep, took Anthony's backpack, and placed it in the back seat. He wrapped his arms around his friend, who now cried openly. "It's going to be okay," he soothed.

"Sorry to be so emotional. It's just . . . it's just . . . I've loved it here. This is home."

"I know. Maybe you will have two homes now. You can come back whenever you want. I will come to New York in the next few weeks and see that you are settled in for however long you want to stay. You can do your job here, or you can do it there. Don't worry about that one bit."

Anthony opened the passenger door of the jeep and stepped up into the seat. He pulled Tobias, who had probably never been in a moving vehicle other than the wheelbarrow, onto the floor between his legs. He stroked the nervous creature, telling him, just like Lane had told Anthony, that it would be okay.

Everything would be okay.

Sam had flown back to New York after his visit with Anthony and talked first with Laura and Estelle and then the children. He explained how nervous Anthony was about leaving his home in Mexico. He told them in detail how the amnesia had affected their husband and father, who no longer remembered them. In fact, he remembered almost nothing from before he was beaten and left for dead in the Los Cabos desert. Luca had received permission to join them on Facebook Messenger as Sam related the details of Anthony's last few years. Sam made certain that while they were completely excited to have their father back, they understood he wouldn't be the same. Anthony had at first fought against his memory losses but eventually recognized the futility of his efforts and allowed himself to build a new life with a home and people he loved.

"He has a dog, Tobias. The two are inseparable."

The room and Luca's computer transmissions went silent. "Mom hates dogs," Izzie mouthed to Emma.

"If he loves the dog, we will love the dog," Laura replied to their surprise.

"He keeps the pup very clean, and it is well-behaved. Thank you, Laura. I know that isn't an easy capitulation for you," Sam replied. That one thing had been a big worry for him.

Sam gave Laura a copy of Anthony's flight schedule and said that he would be flying on an FBI turbojet non-stop from Cabo to White Plains Airport. Without the proper documentation, it was the only way to get him home. Sam would accompany him and bring him to the Di Angelo home late the next Friday afternoon. He asked Laura to let neighbors and church members know that Anthony would not remember them and to just introduce themselves as if they were meeting him for the first time. Since it was uncertain how long Anthony would stay, Sam asked if Luca could get permission for another Facebook Messenger chat on Friday evening.

*****

The sleek, white Gulf Stream turbojet with its blue and black stripes and light blue wing tips was adorned with an American flag on its tail. The engines were whirring as it waited on the tarmac for the long-lost American who would soon be returned to his home country.

Sam led the way up the stairs to the plane, hoping that Anthony would continue following and not turn and run to the home where he felt comfortable and at peace. But he followed, trudging up the stairs, looking like a man going to the gallows. Sam again questioned the soundness of his decision to bring Anthony back to his home. Anthony must have realized his companion's angst and said, "It is the right thing to do, Sam. Hard. But the right thing."

The plane could seat nineteen passengers comfortably. With just Sam, Anthony, and a few crew members aboard, there was plenty of room to spread out, but Anthony motioned for Sam to sit beside him.

"This is new for me. I'm a bit nervous."

Sam gratefully sat by Anthony, wanting to be closely available but not wanting to intrude. Of course he would be nervous. To him, this was the first ever flight in an airplane. As the jet roared down the runway, faster and faster, and as its nose lifted into the sky, Anthony gripped the edges of the seat. Sam leaned across him and opened the shuttered window, pointing out the glistening ocean below and the homes growing smaller and smaller as the plane climbed.

"Whew. I about lost my stomach." Anthony leaned back and closed his eyes, losing himself in the memories of the land and home he loved, reviewing conversations and moments at church when he was overcome by spiritual feelings undeniably testifying that Jesus loved him and that one day all that was lost would be made right. Maybe this flight to the unknown was a beginning, and he felt comforted that through it all, he would not be alone.

Chapter 44

The plane touched down at Westchester Airport in White Plains, New York, just after four p.m. Most private planes landed at this airport rather than run the gamut of traffic at New York City's larger airports. Not particularly grateful to land at White Plains and be required to take a train to his home in Manhattan, this time Sam was glad this was the destination, close to Anthony's home and without exposing Anthony to New York City right away on his journey back to his former life.

Sam's assistant had a car waiting for him at the airport and they pulled into the Di Angelo driveway within fifteen minutes. "So, this is home," Anthony remarked, surveying the two-story Cape Cod home.

With Tobias in hand, Anthony followed Sam up the steps to the front door. Sam reached for the doorbell. It gave a sickly buzz. Sam shrugged. "Laura tries to fix things. Sometimes she succeeds. Sometimes not." He pointed at the buzzer.

Heels clicked toward the door and once it opened Anthony recognized the stunning woman from the family picture he now carried in his backpack. Sam made the introductions and Laura extended her hand in greeting, tears glistening in her eyes. Sam had said she was a strong woman, and Anthony was grateful that he wasn't enveloped into an unwelcome embrace. He took her hand and the only emotion she showed was to place her hand over both of theirs as their hands clasped for the briefest moment.

"Daddy!" An exuberant curly headed teenager threw her arms around Anthony's waist. It was all he could do to avoid taking a step back, but he didn't want to hurt this child who had been through so much. "You must be Izzie," he said. "When she looked surprised, he responded, "Sam gave me a picture."

Another young woman stood quietly in the background and stepped forward at her mother's beckoning. "Welcome home, Dad. I'm Emma," she said also extending her hand.

"Hello, Emma." Anthony shrank back a bit, but Izzie moved forward, throwing her arms around Tobias's neck, who surprisingly rolled over on his back for a good belly rub.

"What's his name?" she asked.

"Tobias, and it looks like you've made a quick friend." The girl smiled and went back to loving the dog.

"Come in, come in," Laura urged.

They entered the home and the first thing Anthony noticed was the grand piano. "Sam tells me you are a concert pianist."

"Yes. Yes, I am." Disappointment surged through Laura. Anthony had attended so many concerts, always meeting her backstage with a rose and a kiss. She remembered the Rachmaninoff she was playing the night he disappeared. A heaviness had enveloped her, but as she played the passage that now belonged to a song titled "Full Moon and Empty Arms," she had imagined that although she and Anthony were not together that night, they were at least under the glow of the same moon. But even so, that night felt different, and it was the beginning of many, many lonely nights.

"Would you like to sit?" Laura led them to the circular couch in front of the fireplace. Anthony sat at one end, Tobias lying by his side. A huge family picture of the Di Angelos looked down at him. How could he possibly slide back into the role of husband and father to these people who he only knew by what Sam had shared with him?

They made uncomfortable small talk for about fifteen minutes when Estelle excused herself from Sam's side to prepare dinner. Laura asked Anthony if he would like to see his office, and he accepted. He was surprised that she said it had remained exactly as he left it, although Marty had given it a good toss one day when he was looking for something in Anthony's desk. There was not a speck of dust anywhere on the surfaces of his desk, shelves, pictures, or books. The emotion that kept welling up in his chest was back again at this simple gesture of respect in his absence.

"Marty," Anthony remarked. "I don't remember him at all. Maybe a good thing." He winked at her, and a warm, genuine smile replaced the tension that had played on her face since his arrival.

"Would you like to see my music room?" Izzie appeared at the doorway.

"Certainly. Come Tobias." But Tobias had sidled up to Laura and was gazing up at her as she patted his soft head. "Tobias?"

"He's okay," Laura replied. Tobias was the name of his boyhood dog, but she refrained from reminding him. Stroking the silken coat was oddly relaxing. Maybe she could like just this one dog.

After Izzie showed her father every aspect of her music room, and when he recalled the video Sam had shown him and complimented her on her talents, she beamed.

As they came upstairs, he noticed Emma sitting silently across the bar from her grandmother as she made dinner. "Tell me about you, Emma," Anthony asked.

"Mmh. Not much to tell. I just like to go to school and play my cello."

"Sam told me you have been a tremendous help to your mother. Thank you for that. I am sorry that you had a heavy burden. I understand you were instrumental in your brother's recovery."

"I like helping. It was no problem."

A girl of few words, Anthony thought. Like her mother, it seemed..

Anthony relaxed during the delicious dinner Estelle had prepared with roast beef, mashed potatoes, gravy, and cooked carrots. "This was one of your favorites," she said as he dove in hungrily. Tobias whined a little and Izzie immediately jumped up and found an old bowl.

"Can we give him some, Mom?"

"Of course, dear, if it is okay with your father."

Anthony nodded a yes, emotion choking him at the acceptance of this animal whom he loved with all his heart.

Just as they finished dinner and Emma and Izzie were clearing the plates from the table, Laura's phone chimed. She looked down to see Luca's face requesting she accept his call. She tapped the green button. "Hello, dear. Just a moment. We will go in Dad's office where it is a little quieter and you can talk to him."

She turned to Anthony sitting at the head of the table in the chair they had always left empty in his absence. Izzie had informed him of this tradition and Laura had noticed the surprise and tender emotion register on Anthony's face at this revelation. "Luca is on the phone. Would you mind coming in your office for a few minutes."

"Oh, yes. Certainly." He rose, excusing himself to the others who remained at the table.

Laura motioned for Anthony to sit in the chair at his desk and propped the phone up on a small stack of books. The young man wearing a white shirt and tie with a black missionary tag appeared in the screen. Anthony recognized the tags from spending time with the Elders and Hermanas in Cabo.

"Hello, Dad," the boy said confidently. "I am your son, Anziano Di Angelo, serving in the Rome, Italy mission, home of your ancestors. You knew me as Luca."

"Caio, Anziano," Anthony replied with the Italian slipping easily from his tongue.

"Sono cosi felice che ti abbiamo trovato."

"I am happy to have been found, too," Anthony replied. And then looked quizzically at Laura. "I must speak Italian."

Luca took over the conversation, giving Anthony a history of his Italian ancestry. "Ha ha, Dad. You understand Italian, but you speak molto poco and he pinched his thumb and forefinger together to demonstrate very little."

Luca continued the story of Anthony's parents coming to America as newlyweds. His grandfather was a builder in Italy and Anthony's father continued that trade in America. While his parents spoke Italian to each other, they spoke only English to Anthony. Hence his ability to understand but considerable inability to speak it. Luca joked as he explained Anthony's ineptness with Italian and all three laughed momentarily.

"Dad, I am sorry I can't visit long tonight. We have an appointment to teach a couple. Doesn't happen very often here. These people are pretty set in their religions. If I can though I would like to bear my testimony to you in Italian before I leave."

"Of course. Please," came Anthony's reply.

As Luca began earnestly speaking, Laura longed to slip her arms around Anthony's neck and press her cheek against his as in previous times when he sat at the desk, and she had stood behind looking over his shoulder at something he wanted her to see. She resisted the urge and listened to Luca, not understanding the words, but feeling the spirit fill her with gladness and warmth. Anthony nodded in agreement from time to time and tears flowed down his cheeks. He dug in his pocket and brought out a soft cloth to wipe his face. Gentle words came automatically from Anthony as Luca concluded his testimony. "Thank you, son."

"Love you, Dad."

"He's a wonderful boy. You have been a good mother to your children, our children, Laura."

"I didn't do it alone. You were there, guiding and teaching for most of their growing up years."

Anthony didn't reply. He couldn't remember and for the first time in a long time, he wished he could.

Sam had advised Laura to continue with life as usual once Anthony was home, so she rose early and dressed in a light pink, mid-length dress with black pumps for her day at Julliard. She thought she had made Anthony comfortable in Luca's room before she retired for the night. It didn't seem right that they should share a bed since they were not much more than strangers at this point. Anthony had seemed relieved when she offered the room and showed him where the linens and toiletries were kept. But when she got up for a few moments in the night to get a drink and a few crackers, the light had been on in Anthony's office, with Anthony curled up on the floor by Tobias.

Laura had retrieved a soft blanket from the couch in the living room and placed it over him. Love and compassion nearly overwhelmed her. Her confident and sometimes loud and rowdy husband had been replaced with a gentle and humble man. But a good spirit surrounded him and gave her the comfort and peace that had been long missing in her life. If only they could soon regain the friendship and romance that had been at the core of their relationship.

Chapter 45

Laura leaned against the deck railing overlooking the misty lake as she did every morning, breathing in the fresh air and collecting her thoughts to begin the day. She turned as she felt Anthony's presence, not knowing he had been watching her for some time.

As her dress flowed around her in the light breeze and long dark hair slid way past her shoulders, he was reminded of the earliest years he could remember when he tried over and over to paint "the lady at the lake" as Adelita called his efforts. The woman always had her back to him looking over a lake. Her clothing flowed from her body and dark hair swept midway down her back. He had been trying to capture a day such as this. He must have been here at this table and Laura must have been at the railing looking over the lake. So why couldn't he feel what he knew he must have felt for this lovely woman?

She turned. "Good morning, Anthony. Did you sleep well?"

He smiled. "Sorry about ending up on the floor. I am used to sleeping on a mat and when I got tired . . . " His words drifted off. How could he explain how his life had been? How could he explain how foreign this home with its furniture, carpets, kitchens, and bathrooms seemed, not to mention beds? How must he seem to her in his now-wrinkled linen pants?

She checked her watch. "The girls will be up shortly. I need to catch a train to the city, but they can show you where everything is in the kitchen. Pop Tarts, bagels. I got out of the habit of cooking while my mom lived with us. She and Sam were married recently, so we are on our own now. Emma has become a fine cook, and she and I tag team dinner depending on our schedules."

He could tell she was embarrassed. Perhaps she was not living the life she wanted to live either.

Emma was the first to come out of her room dressed for school. She rapped on her sister door. "Up, Izzie. I'll make you a Pop Tart. Bus will be here in twenty."

"Good morning, Dad," she said then, noticing him looking lost in the kitchen. "Can I fix you something?"

"Could you tell me how this thing works?" He pointed at the stove. Carmen had a stove. He just didn't know how to turn it on. There was no flame, but Emma twisted a nob and said the black swirly things that were gradually turning red were burners. She explained the various levels of heat, grabbed a box of "Pop-Tarts" from the cupboard and popped one in each slot of a silver rectangular box that was plugged into the wall. "Toaster," she said with a small smile and showed him how to push the lever down to begin the heating process.

Izzie hurried into the kitchen, her curly hair hastily secured in a bun on top of her head. He received another exuberant hug and a "Hi, Dad. Gotta run," as she grabbed the hot pastry and juggled it from hand to hand. "Ouch. Ooh."

"Don't forget your backpack," Emma reminded. It was obvious to Anthony that Emma either was expected to or just took responsibility for getting Izzie out the door in time to catch the bus.

Emma wiped the crumbs off the counter and asked her dad if he was okay to fix himself something to eat. She explained that she drove to school because she left school an hour early each day to assist the elementary music teacher with her beginning orchestra class. It was just a volunteer job, but it would look good on her college scholarship applications.

"You'll have to tell me more about your college plans when you get home."

"Of course, Dad. I'd be happy to." And the quiet, efficient one was out the door.

The door had thudded shut behind Izzie, but he only heard the tiniest of clicks when Emma left. Which reminded him about the sickly doorbell. He wished he had his tools. After searching in vain in his office and then through the kitchen drawers for a screwdriver, he opened the side door to the kitchen and found himself in the garage with a well-organized workbench and a myriad of tools hanging from pegs on the wall. He was in business!

He located the items he would need and headed for the front door. He unscrewed the button from the doorframe and examined the wires. Just as he expected, one of the wires was loose. He tightened it around the screw and pressed the button. A clear "ding-dong" rang out, so he reattached the doorbell to the frame.

He puttered around the kitchen, trying to find something other than pastry or bagels to eat. There were a few eggs in the refrigerator, and he fried a couple in butter in a pan he found in one of the cupboards. Anthony cut one of the bagels in half, buttered each side and put the fried egg in between. He graded it as not too bad. He marveled at the coolness of the fridge and the hot water running from the tap as he washed the pan.

Tobias whined at his side, so he got the small rope from his bag, attached it to the pup's collar and took him through the garage and out into the yard. He didn't dare turn his friend loose with all the ducks and geese on the lake. If he stayed long, he'd have to educate the dog on sticking close by and not running off after the geese as he was used to running free after the rabbits in the desert.

They came back in, and Anthony opened a can of dog food and put it in the bowl Izzie had offered at dinner the evening before. Tobias gobbled it hungrily. Anthony rinsed the bowl and filled it with fresh water. Now, what to do with his day? He didn't feel comfortable exploring this home that apparently was his, other than to examine the tools in the garage. Could he help while he was here? Fix anything else? He was busily pulling weeds in the back when Sam came around the side of the house.

"Doorbell about scared me to death. You fix it?"

"Yes. Trying to find something to do."

"Feeling a little lost?"

"A lot lost," Anthony replied. "But do you think you could take me to the grocery store? I want to fix the kids some breakfast in the morning."

Sam chuckled. "Estelle said Laura used to be an excellent cook before . . . well you know what I mean."

"Wish I could make up for all the hard times I caused."

"You caused? No way. That was all Marty."

"I still feel guilty."

"No need, my man. No need. Laura and the kids understand. They did what they had to do. But they were always waiting for your return. Did you see their motto on the fridge? 'Expect miracles.' "

"Yes. I wondered about that."

"Well, having you here is the miracle, as well as all the things that fell into place to find you."

Sam took Anthony to the grocery store and Anthony filled the cart with food he could store in the wonderful fridge. He planned a traditional Mexican dinner, not too spicy, per Sam, for that evening. While he was here in this home, he would be of some help.

Later, as he was putting the last of the weeds in the trash, a man from next door who introduced himself as George welcomed Anthony home. They shook hands and Anthony began to explain his memory loss but was stopped short.

"No worries about the past. We will go from here. But I do need to tell you one story about that feisty little wife of yours . . . " George related the happenings of the day Luca was hit by the car and the girls spotted his bike off a curve on the road that dropped steeply into the lake. Izzie had taken off in their boat. George had been tying up his small fishing boat when Laura came running out and demanded his keys. She jumped into the boat in her dress and high heels and zoomed off to rescue her children. "She's a good gal, Anthony. Feisty and strong, but the kindest person you will ever meet."

Even though George said all that was important now was the future, he dug up story after story from the past about living next door to the Di Angelo family. It was quite entertaining, but exhausting when Anthony knew he should remember, wanted to remember, but couldn't. Anthony mulled over what George said about Laura. He could see that she had done what she had to do to care for her family. His family. She had loved him so much she never stopped searching. She never gave up on him or her children. She was beautiful in every way possible. Suddenly he found himself wanting to explore what they could be together.

Anthony had chicken enchiladas baking in the oven when first Izzie and then Emma returned from school. The return was the same as the leaving, with Izzie bursting through the door, dropping her backpack loudly at the entrance, and then plopping onto a stool at the counter. Anthony set a bowl of cut fruits in front of her. "Hungry?" he asked.

"Mmh, yum. Thanks!" She launched into the happenings of her day, words tripping over fruit.

Anthony heard a slight click as the front door opened and Emma called out. "Backpack, Izzie!"

Izzie rolled her eyes. "She thinks she's the mom." She left the counter, took her backpack to her room, and was back in an instant.

"What smells so good?" Emma asked.

"Enchiladas. I'm trying out the oven. And the fridge. Love the fridge."

Emma giggled. "Guess you didn't have a fridge? Tell me about Mexico. Where did you live? What was it like?"

Emma and Izzie were still at the counter, enthralled in Anthony's stories when their mom arrived. "What smells so good?" she called out.

"Enchiladas!" Both girls shouted at once.

She rounded the corner to the kitchen and found Anthony with Tobias at his feet in the kitchen and the girls smiling and laughing at the counter. Emma hardly ever smiled anymore. It was good to see her happy face again.

"Dad has been telling us stories about his life while he was missing," Izzie explained. "He was roughin' it!"

"I see. Well, you will have to tell me all about it sometime, Anthony."

Anthony only smiled and began searching for dinner plates.

"I'll help, Dad," Izzie hopped over the counter.

"Walk around, dear," her mom reminded.

For over a week, the daily routine continued, with Laura going off to work, the girls attending school, and Anthony puttering around the house trying to find things to repair. There was plenty of work in the yard. Emma said they had kept it quite nice until Luca broke his leg and after that everything "went to rack and ruin."

He found the church members to be welcoming. He was certain that these were people he probably had known for quite some time, but he didn't remember any of them. They kindly introduced themselves as if he were a new member just having moved into their area. But the hymns were familiar, although in English. His hand shook and tears overflowed as he was handed the sacrament tray and was able to partake for the first time that he remembered. Izzie tucked her arm through his and put her head on his shoulder. He marveled at the love he was beginning to feel for this daughter of God and his daughter, too.

He was riding on high spirits after church but when he awoke on Monday morning the sorrow and sadness over leaving his home in Cabo were close to overwhelming. He felt dark and empty. He shook his head and rolled to his knees on the floor by his desk. After the first night, Laura had brought him a woven mat she had found at an outdoor market on the way home from work. Her kindness often left him at a loss for words. How could he want his old life when a full life awaited him here?

He poured his heart out to his Father in Heaven and realized that Satan was jabbing at him with these awful feelings, this misery. He remembered those feelings from when he first woke up at Adelita's. Hopeless. Lost. But her loving care, such as he received now at the hands of Laura and his daughters gave him courage to continue to build something wonderful of whatever he had.

He had begun rising long before Laura, showering and making himself presentable for the day. She was always in a rush, so he fixed her a healthy to-go breakfast with cold juice in a thermos. Her gratitude for his efforts delighted him, making him want to do more to ease her life. Emma had relinquished her hold as a substitute parent and seemed more at ease chatting about her days at work and school. Izzie turned more to Anthony for advice. He always managed to chide her with humor about picking up after herself and getting ready for school on time, and she responded well. A conversation would go something like this: "Izzie, do you like boys?"

"Yes, Dad. Well, some of them."

"Okay, then you need to get up early enough to do something with that crazy hair of yours so you don't scare them away." Her thick curls were difficult to manage, so each day she just wound them into a sloppy bun, not realizing how very attractive she was when she took a moment to create a style of some sort.

"Dad! Honestly!" she would respond. But the next day she would wear her hair long or partially pulled back and would prance in front of him doing three-quarter turns. "Cute enough for ya, Dad?"

"Lovely," he would respond. This child had so much personality it was just bursting out of her. Everything she did or said deserved an exclamation point. She spent evenings coaching her dad on the finer points of using a computer. She was a good teacher, and he could create and save a document, order from Amazon, and most importantly Google almost any question that came to mind.

But it was significant that this child who had dressed in nothing but black in the years since her father's disappearance had borrowed some colorful shirts from her sister, who promised to take her to the thrift store to find a new wardrobe. Her father's return had truly brightened her life.

Emma helped Anthony obtain a duplicate driver's license, listing his as lost since it had not expired. But she insisted he take several online driving test questions to make sure he could manage the rules of the road. He had not yet taken a turn at the wheel but looked forward to getting around on his own. With the new driver's license, he was able to open a bank account with some of the cash he had brought with him. Emma had kindly driven him to the bank after school one day and then Lane had wired a portion of his savings in the Cabo account to the new account in New York. But he had plans to coax George into taking him vehicle shopping in the near future so that he could be independent and not be a burden on his family.

The more he threw himself into his new life, the more at peace he became. Izzie helped him buy postage stamps online and he penned lengthy letters to Carmen. Cabo would be forever in his heart. He would go back, but more and more he knew it would not be to stay.

Chapter 46

Lane, Graciela, and Baby Adelita visited after Anthony's second weekend in New York. Apparently, Lane had talked to Laura beforehand, and she had invited them to stay in their home, with Emma bunking with Izzie for a few days.

Emma gravitated to the baby and spent every moment she could rocking and attending to the sweet child.

Lane and Anthony spent hours in the office on Saturday going over the new laptop Lane brought and software he had installed to release Anthony from the green ledger sheets and solar calculator he'd used before modern-day technology. Anthony grasped the ins and outs of the programs easily and Lane was pleased as he imparted some good news for both of them.

Lane had been promoted to manage the services to the farmers over the entirety of Central America. The non-profit organization he worked for believed that if he connected them with the correct resources and training, rural farmers and agricultural business could become more productive and engage in greater business opportunities. He needed Anthony to collect and analyze the data and recommend procedures for managing the financial side of the farmers' businesses. He pointed out the books on Anthony's bookcase about his desk.

"You have an accounting degree and an MBA. I need that help."

Anthony was uncertain. He didn't want to fail Lane. "Wouldn't it be better if you actually hired someone who still remembered what he had learned."

"You do, man. I just watched you do it. You've been doing it for several years for me. You just didn't know where all your good ideas came from. Now you do. Review your books. Take a refresher course, but I am not accepting this position without you. And one more thing, my parent company is based in New York City. You won't need to go into the office but a couple of times a year. You can travel to Cabo to meet with me and survey the farms whenever you want."

"Shake on it?" Lane extended his hand, which Anthony gratefully grasped. God was providing a way for him to have the best of both lives.

Laura had a concert on Saturday evening and invited Graciela to go with her. Graciela had brought a dress for church which would also be acceptable for a Lincoln Center performance. Hesitant at first due to her difficulty with the English language, and unsure about finding Laura after the performance, she was reluctant. But since Laura always had at least two complimentary seats, Izzie, who was not at all fond of classical music, offered to go along. Graciela came back raving about the wonderful music and the beauty of Lincoln Center. She was astounded with Laura's performance and the orchestra's as well. Izzie rolled her eyes. "She actually liked that long-haired stuff, Mom."

Anthony was excited to introduce Lane and Graciela to his new acquaintances at church. The Bishop asked to speak to Anthony a moment after church and invited him to be part of the ward missionary program. Anthony readily accepted. If Laura would allow it, if she could give him time to figure out how to be a real husband to her, the man she deserved, he would be staying and could fulfill this responsibility for the bishop and for the Lord.

Day by day, Laura and Anthony became more comfortable with each other. Every day he became more entranced with the amazing woman who was legally, and as far as God was concerned, eternally his wife. He couldn't get enough of drinking in her beauty or of absorbing the joy he felt in her presence. He wanted to be her husband, but how? How did one proceed to recapture something she could remember but he couldn't? What did he do in the past to make her happy?

Estelle and Sam invited them on a double date to a restaurant in New York that had become Estelle's favorite. It would be Anthony's first trip into the big city, and he had to admit he felt true to the saying "scared spitless."

Laura drove to the train station. He vowed that one day soon, he would be able to do the driving. The Metro-North train whipped through city after city, finally stopping an hour later at Grand Central Station. Anthony must have looked perplexed even though he was trying to appear completely at ease with the tumult and seeming bedlam of New York City, because Laura took his hand and headed for the subway station. If he wasn't already befuddled, he was now completely baffled by the shock waves running through his body at her touch.

The subway was crowded but she didn't relinquish his hand and reached with her other hand to grasp the bar above the isle. He followed her example and was soon hanging on for his life as the subway rocked and rolled its way to their destination.

"Whew!" he remarked as they stepped on the platform. "That was crazy."

"Always is," she smiled. "Usually, I drive if I am going to work. I have reserved parking there. Parking is unreal anywhere here in Manhattan. Sam and Estelle will meet us over there by the fountain. They live in a lovely rowhouse not too far from FBI headquarters, but I think they are considering moving closer to White Plains when Sam retires.

The Lincoln Ristorante boasted Italian cuisine, which Sam thought Anthony should try in light of his newly discovered heritage. It was just a one-minute walk from Lincoln Center. Laura was flooded with memories of romantic after-concert dinners at this restaurant with Anthony, but she held those thoughts silently in her heart.

They had finished a hearty and delicious meal and were waiting for the check when Anthony turned to Estelle. "Estelle," he reached for her hand. "I would like to ask your permission to date your daughter."

Estelle squeezed his hand and choked back tears. "I would be delighted to have you date my daughter, providing she approves as well."

Laura reached for Anthony's hand where he had placed it on his left leg near her. She entwined her fingers with his and left both their hands resting on his leg, shooting sparks and warmth through his body. "I would like nothing more." She looked him directly in the eye and smiled that tender, sweet smile he had come to adore.

They held hands as they walked, and he put his arm protectively around her on the subway. Sitting close together on the train, their hands clasped, her head slumped to his shoulder, she slept, only jolting awake as the train pulled into the White Plains Station.

"Oh my, Anthony. I'm sorry. I usually have such a hard time going to sleep."

Anthony only smiled. How could he put the feelings he had with her so close to him into words. He had wanted the moment to never end.

Chapter 47

In consideration of Laura's hectic schedule at Julliard and weekend concerts, Anthony tried to plan short dates for just the two of them like getting ice cream at Cold Stone. He was amazed at the odd flavor combinations she chose. Licorice and Butter Pecan together? But then he had noticed at home that she liked to hold her Oreos under running water from the sink faucet before popping them whole into her mouth. It wasn't just ice cream. When they went out for pizza, she ordered orange juice and dipped her pizza in the juice. The girl had a strange palette, and he loved watching whatever came next.

Eventually, he asked George for advice. What did Anthony and Laura used to do together? George told him they used to spend hours out on the lake hanging a pole over the side while the boat rocked back and forth. He didn't ever remember them bringing in any fish.

Anthony found a couple of fishing poles in the garage, scraped away the cobwebs, and was pleasantly surprised that he could still rig one up for fishing. He found a sparkly lure with a hook on the end to complete his handiwork.

One of the most entertaining aspects of dating Laura was their daughters' delight in each outing, occasionally making suggestions of how their father could best romance their mother. Anthony had easily acquired the habit of ordering groceries on-line for delivery. He had become the family cook, and he planned well ahead for each meal, including the picnic for the evening excursion on the lake. He set aside sandwiches and chips for the girls, as well as fresh strawberries and blueberries. He made a small potato salad and divided it into individual servings.

Laura now drove home each day from Julliard, an air of anticipation chasing away the fatigue of a long day of lecturing and teaching piano lessons to talented students who sometimes didn't practice diligently.

Each Friday since Anthony asked Estelle for permission to date her daughter, Anthony had prepared a short but enjoyable date. One week it had been bowling at a nearby lane. Beforehand, he kept apologizing because the girls had told him he was a lousy bowler, and he didn't want to frustrate Laura, who they said was an awesome bowler. Those girls. The truth was quite the opposite and she'd decided to let Anthony find out for himself. She explained the scoring system to him and after three strikes in a row, he quizzically asked, "Aren't strikes good? The kids said I was lousy."

"Muscle memory, dear," she laughed. "They got you!"

Laura managed to get quite a few pins knocked down each turn. "See, Anthony. I am adequate but not awesome. You are awesome."

She wondered what this Friday's surprise date would be and was immediately informed when she opened the door and Izzie ran to greet her. Throwing her arms around her mother, she whispered in her ear, "Dad has made a picnic."

"Hello, sweetheart." Anthony surprised her with a hello hug and a peck on the cheek. Rest a few minutes and then change into something comfortable for a boat ride.

"Hello." She stroked his bearded cheek. Why did she suddenly feel so shy?

Moments later she had changed into capris and a T-shirt, as anxious as a teenager dating her crush. Anthony put the picnic basket and fishing poles in the boat and held out his hand to help Laura, although according to George, Laura could nimbly hop into the boat dressed in heels and a skirt. He wasn't prepared for the electricity of her touch and almost jerked his hand away.

They floated lazily and nibbled on sandwiches as the sun lowered in the sky basking the lake in a golden glow. Their poles had hung over the side of the boat for hours, never bending with even the slightest nibble. George was probably right. They never brought in any fish. Suddenly Laura's pole bent at a sharp arc. "Your pole!" Anthony yelled.

"Huh?"

"You've got a fish on!"

"Oh, oh. What do I do? I've never caught one."

"Grab it and pull back a bit as you reel it in."

She followed instructions well and before long they had a shiny, footlong trout flopping in the bottom of the boat. Anthony removed the hook and held it up for Laura to see.

"Nice one! Shall we keep it?"

"Of course, and we need to show George. He said we couldn't catch a fish if we tried."

Like two giddy kids, they marched up to George's door, rang the bell, and held out their catch for him to see. Recognizing the absolute joy on their faces, not just because they had finally caught a fish but because of the love growing between them, he heartily congratulated them.

Anthony cleaned and filleted the fish, dusted it with flour, and fried it in butter, and they all sat around the table with many yums and much finger licking.

Laura had a concert the following Friday. Anthony had never travelled to the city by himself, only with Laura as his guide. He thought it was something he could manage. There was always a taxi if he totally messed up his public transportation plans. He wanted to be there after the performance. Now adept with on-line purchases, he bought a ticket to the concert even though he knew Laura probably had some guest tickets available, but that would ruin the surprise.

Emma had told him that he used to always meet her mother backstage with a red rose. He needed to reprise the past. It was time. Time for something special.

One afternoon, when Emma was home early, he borrowed the car after a short lecture on safe driving from his daughter. He had Googled the directions to the closest jeweler, intending to choose something that reflected the depth of his love for this woman he once thought he would be able to meet, forget, and leave behind to return to Mexico. He knew that while he would travel back to his Cabo home from time to time, every moment away from her would seem like eons of time.

He chose a solitaire diamond infinity heart necklace. It was beautiful and he hoped it would impart all the love swelling his heart. He consulted Emma about how to get a red rose unscathed into the city while riding on the train and subway, and she told him that on the night of a concert, street vendors were always stationed in front of the concert hall.

Laura left early with her gown in a clothing bag and drove to New York. When Anthony found out about her concert dress being ruined by Marty, he had left an envelope of more than enough cash on her bed asking her to please buy the dress of her dreams. She had done so and thanked him profusely but hadn't let him see the dress. Tonight, would be the night and she would have no idea he was in the audience. Emma again helped him with the arrangements to secure one of the seats reserved for Laura's guests.

He patted himself on the back for a successful, uneventful trip to the concert hall. Vendors were everywhere offering flowers, and Anthony found one with exquisite, deep red roses and selected the best one in the water-filled container. The vendor wrapped it in cellophane and tied it with a thin black ribbon. Anthony thanked the vendor, tipped him well, and headed for the concert hall, barely able to contain his excitement.

He was guided to his seat by an usher and before long the lights dimmed, and a hush came over the audience. The concert master tuned the orchestra from the conductor's podium and then stepped aside as the conductor strode onto the stage. He shook the hand of the concert master and then turned toward the wing to his left as Laura stepped from behind the curtain. She was breathtaking. The dress she had chosen was indeed lovely, but the woman in the dress was beautiful beyond compare.

Anthony listened to the concert with rapt attention, however at one point wishing it would soon end so he could meet Laura backstage. After the final curtain, he jumped from his seat and headed toward the hallway to the backstage door as Emma had instructed.

A guard met him at the entrance. Anthony identified himself as Laura's husband.

"ID," the guard grunted.

Grateful for the duplicate driver's license he had recently procured, he dug it from his wallet, and thrust it hurriedly toward the guard. The guard looked at the clean-shaven guy on the license, and then back at the now bearded Anthony. "No way."

"But . . . " Anthony had begun to protest when a burly man whose vest buttons struggled to hold the material together over his ample belly interceded. "Anthony, my man," he called out. "Laura said you were back."

While Anthony had no idea who this man was, he was grateful as the guard stepped aside and the man whose nametag identified him as the Stage Manager escorted him to Laura's dressing room.

He knocked lightly on the door and a woman he didn't recognize answered. "Oh, Mr. Di Angelo. Welcome back," she said. "I'll leave you two alone."

Laura turned from where she was removing earrings from her ears.

"Anthony. What a surprise! Did you watch the concert? I am so glad you came."

"You were wonderful." He handed her the rose, and she lifted it to her nose.

She buried her face in the rose and drew in the fragrance. "How did you know?"

"I only have to ask Emma. She knows everything. How you do you think I got here in one piece tonight?"

Anthony opened the box with the necklace, and she gasped. The diamond gleamed inside a heart twisted into an infinity loop. "Laura," Anthony cupped her face in his hand and then dropped to one knee. "I love you so very much, my dear." He traced the white gold heart on the necklace. His finger continued tracing over the infinity loops. "I am asking if you will consider letting me love and care for you now and forever."

"Oh Anthony, my darling Anthony. I love you, too. I never stopped. I was certain that someday a miracle would return you to me."

Sleep Little Izzie

Julie K. Matthews

References

The Book of Mormon. Trans. Joseph Smith, Jr. Salt Lake City, UT: The Church of Jesus Christ of Latter-day Saints, 1981.

The Doctrine and Covenants, Joseph Smith, Jr. Salt Lake City, UT: The Church of Jesus Christ of Latter-day Saints, 1921.

The Bible. (Santa Biblia). Print. King James Ver.

Text: Snow, Eliza R.; Music: McGranahan, James McGranahan. Hymns of The Church of Jesus Christ of Latter-day Saints, English #292, "O My Father," "O Mi Padre", Spanish, # 187.

Text: Cecil Frances Alexander; Music: John H. Gower. "There Is a Green Hill Far Away." Hymns of the Church of Jesus Christ of Latter-day Saints, #194.

Joson, Al; Rose, Billy; Dreyer, Dave. "Back in Your Own Backyard." Irving Berlin, Inc., 1972.

Lyrics: Buddy Kaye and Ted Mossman. "Full Moon and Empty Arms," based on Rachmaninoff Piano Concerto No. 2, 3rd Movement. 1945.

[You Tube]. (2023, April 6). Consider the Lilies [Video]. You Tube. https://www.youtube.com/watch?v=OevE4olt6_I

Rachmaninoff, Sergei. "Piano Concerto No. 2 in C Minor." Gutheil Publishing, Moscow, Russia, 1901.

Arensky, Anton. "Piano Trio No. 1, Op. 32." P. Jurgenson, Publisher. Moscow, Russia, 1894.

Schumann, Robert. "Piano Concerto in A Minor, Opus 52." Dresden, Germany. December 4, 1845.

Anna's MVP

Making the varsity basketball team and being cool enough at school were Jake Steed's only worries. All the guys talked about the draft, but the way he saw it, if the Vietnam war was still on when he turned 18, he would be in college on a basketball scholarship.

But that all changed the day his daredevil father worked without his safety equipment, plunged to the bottom of the mine and dropped out of their lives forever. His dad, his hero. Gone.

Jake's mom, suffering from the loss of her husband, and afraid that Jake, who looks and acts just like his dad, would meet the same fate avoids him and neglects the needs of her children leaving sixteen-year-old Jake responsible for his eight-year-old sister, Anna. When his Aunt Coraleen, Queen of

Mean, threatens to take Anna away, Jake realizes that he must make some changes to keep Anna from a stern and unloving environment. His childhood buddy, Jessie, steps in to help.

As his life becomes tougher from lack of food and too many worries, Jake remembers that if he does the best he can, God will help him with the rest. He recognizes God's hand in help from others. Food miraculously appears on their porch, and he has a good idea that the doer of these good deeds is Hatch Enumclaw, an awkward soul who has remained silent since the brutal murders of his parents over 20 years ago for which he was erroneously blamed.

While waiting for Jake at football practice in a park by the Purple Sage Mansion, Anna witnesses a horrifying murder and is told to keep silent, or the perpetrator will harm Jake. When Hatch rescues Anna from an arsonist set fire in their barn, the police chief and his deputy try to arrest Hatch. Both Anna and Hatch break their silence, and the arrest is foiled by the city attorney who listens to Anna's story about the Purple Sage murderer. Jake and Jessie are determined to solve the murders of Hatch's parents to absolve him from the stigma that has hung over his head.

While some hopes are denied, doors begin to open for Jake and, trusting in the Lord, he walks though those doors and sees his way to a life beyond basketball, a life that will be satisfying and successful as he does his best to follow the will of God.

Follow the Lilies

J. J. Lane is a pseudonym I created by combining my birth mother's first name (Jacquelyn) and my name (Julie) and her last name (Lane). She was a poet and tried many times to be published. You will read one of her poems in "Anna's MVP" and I will try to include her work in my next book, "Dear Jessie".

Intimidating phone calls and crippling threats invaded Jenny's life from the moment she learns of her husband's death. After repossessing her car and furniture, creditors give Jenny and her two little daughters thirty days to vacate their home. But her late husband's financial schemes aren't the end of her horrendous discoveries. Who was her husband? Who was Eric Trent? And would she ever be able to trust another man again.

A raw and primitive sadness engulfs Clay Holden as the plane descends into the Salt Lake Valley, returning him to Utah from a semester-long research project. Recently divorced and living alone, Clay considers himself a tough, self-sufficient guy, but the truth of it . . . he is lonely. Instead of being met by his friend and colleague at the airport, he is greeted by his colleague's new secretary, Jenny.

The warmth and kindness in her voice kindles a spring thaw on his frozen heart. While their affection for each other grows and quickly wraps them in a cocoon of joy, it is just as quickly unraveled by the secrets she is desperate to keep as well as their employer's unrelenting policies forbidding inter-office dating.

About the Author – Julie K. Matthews

I am so enraptured and joyful when playing keyboard
with my 70s rock band, playing the organ at church, or
performing as a lobby pianist on Temple Square. I recently fell
in love with kayaking. My children and grandchildren make me
so happy along with my sweet maltipoo puppy, Skipper, who is
my walking and biking partner.

My adventurous husband takes me flying in his plane,
boating on the ocean (as long as I can see land), and even scuba
diving. Wherever we visit, I find the setting for a story. After a
career in technical writing, I delight in creative writing and the
soaring of my heart when a character falls in love or outsmarts
a villain.

May you find hope in every nuance of life and trust
God to help you when you have put forth your best effort.
Expect miracles! You are not alone.